Published by Red Giant Entertainment
(www.RedGiantEntertainment.com)
an imprint of Active Media Publishing, LLC,
614 E Hwy 50 #235 Clermont, FL 34711 USA.
Benny R. Powell, President. David Campiti, Creative Director.

Library of Congress Cataloging-in-Publication Data

Fuqua, Jonathon Scott.
 Medusa's daughter / written by Jonathon Scott Fuqua ; illustrated by
Steven Parke.
    p. cm.
 Summary: Fifteen-year-old sideshow star Maia Vitikos is enslaved by
brutal huckster Rictus Finch, who claims he rescued her when her
Gorgon-mother left her to die, but as the carnival travels through
small, Eastern European towns, her friend Skelly teaches her to think
about her life and its possibilities.
 ISBN 978-0-9848808-2-9 (hbk. : lib. ed.) -- ISBN 978-0-9745645-8-6
(hbk. : standard ed.)
[1. Abnormalities, Human--Fiction. 2. Freak shows--Fiction. 3. Coming of
age--Fiction.
4. Gorgons (Greek mythology)--Fiction. 5. Europe, Eastern--Fiction.]
I. Parke, Steven, ill.
II. Title.
 PZ7.F96627Med 2012
 [Fic]--dc22

2007028519

ISBN 978-0-9745645-8-6
Printed in China.
First Printing
10 9 8 7 6 5 4 3 2 1

There's something vaguely depressing about Medusa's Daughter.

Not that I have issue with the story; you understand. In fact, I love it to pieces. It's a beautiful, haunting fairytale I would recommend to anyone—a creepy, moving slice of American gothic my wife read from start to finish in a single sitting. This is unusual, you see, and made me feel more than a little jealous. I don't think she's even actually STARTED one of my books, never mind FINISHED one. "What's so great about Jonathon Scott Fuqua?" I asked in a huff.

"Read it and you'll understand," she explained. And as always, she was right.

But this isn't the depressing part. Nor is the art. Because Steven Parke has long been on my professional dance-card and we came so close to working together just last year on a project for Marvel Comics. Unfortunately, it never happened, but I know and he knows and anyone with a head knows that we need to collaborate as soon as those stars align. Because this is just absolutely one of the most beautiful comics (not graphic novels, only poseurs say graphic novels) to ever grace a shelf. But you don't need me to tell you this, unless you're that oddest of person who would look at my clumsy words before flipping through those gorgeous pictures.

No, what makes this book slightly depressing is because it makes me feel how silent stars must have felt when they first saw The Jazz Singer. Like the heart of Orville Wright if he'd ever been given a Virgin Galactic brochure. What you hold in the hands is the future, my friends, a comic more rich and alive and bursting with colour than anything I've seen before. These people are at the very cutting edge of the medium and you're here with them as they plough new ground.

Lucky you.

Mark Millar
Glasgow
Scotland

Medusa's daughter

Written by
Jonathon Scott Fuqua

Illustrated and Directed by
Steven Parke

Typography by
Susan Mangan

Story by Steven Parke and Jonathon Scott Fuqua

For Calla… Your dazzling temperament and internal and external beauty—all combined with your incredible theatrical and artistic sensibilities—consistently belie the fact that you are my sweet daughter. I hope the world and those whom you care for always provide you with a great soft embrace. I will always love you.

—Jonathon Scott Fuqua

To my mom and dad who have relentlessly supported me through all kinds of crazy ideas, and to my son who inspired me to let my stories out.

—Steven Parke

My name is Maia.

If you ask me about
myself, and you won't,
all that I can say with
any certainty is that
I'm a monster.

Even my dreams tell me that I'm
capable of doing terrible things.

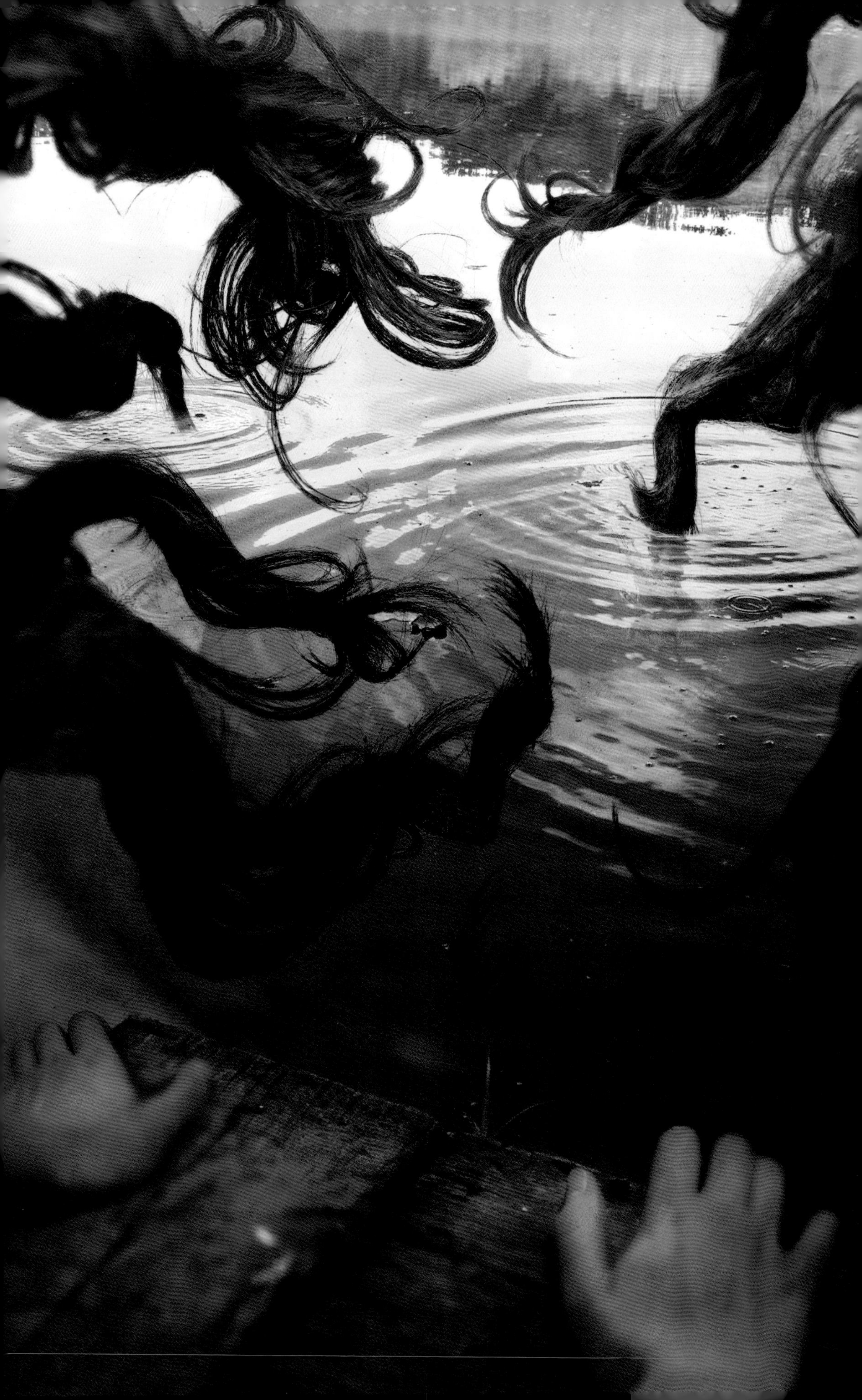

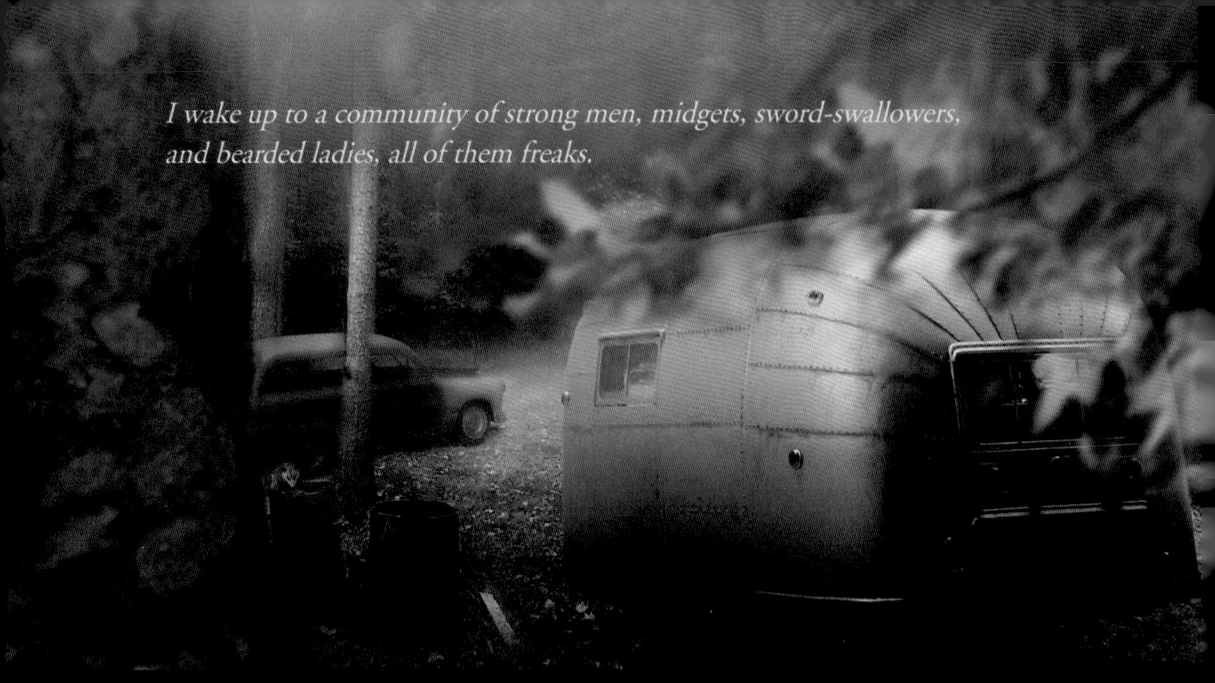
I wake up to a community of strong men, midgets, sword-swallowers, and bearded ladies, all of them freaks.

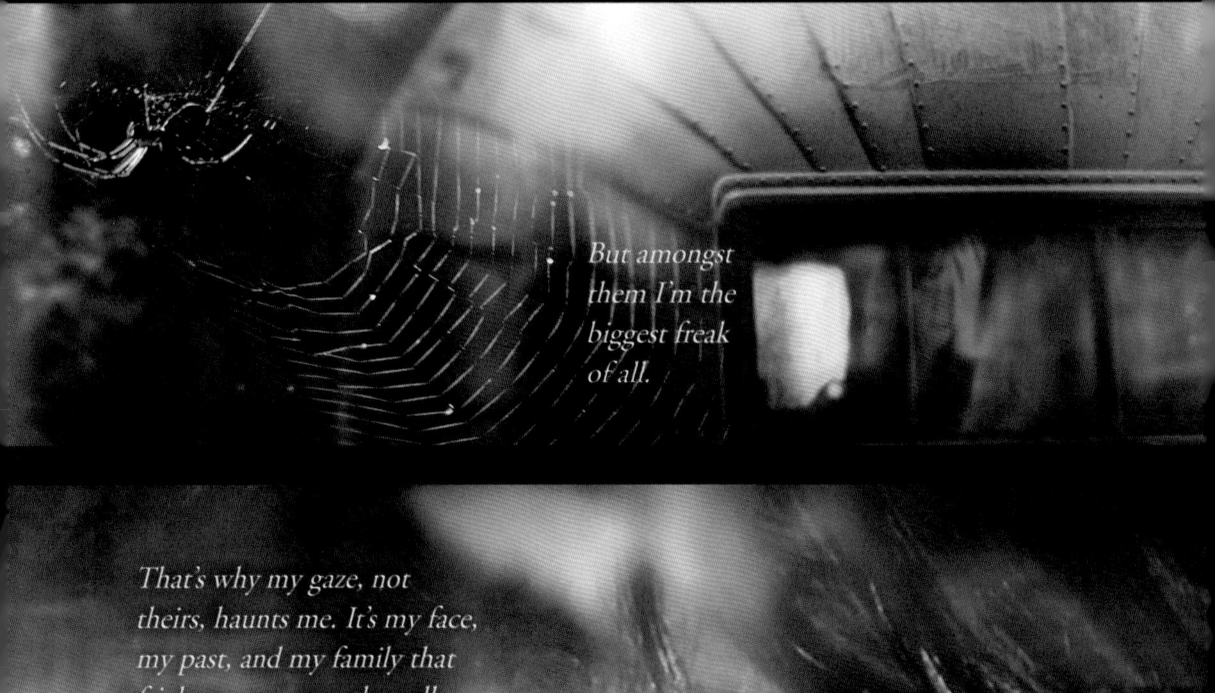
But amongst them I'm the biggest freak of all.

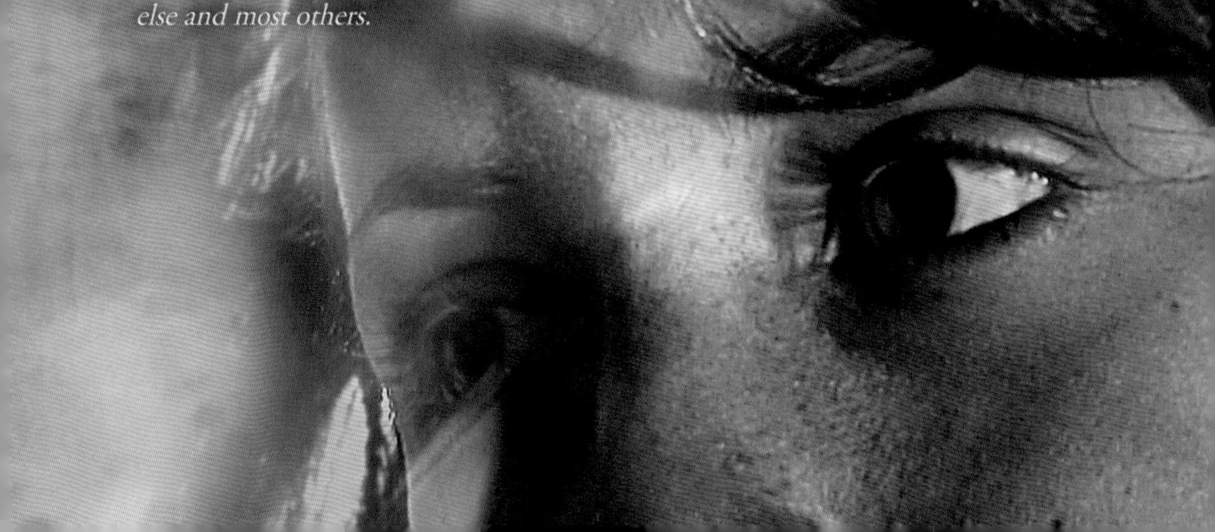
That's why my gaze, not theirs, haunts me. It's my face, my past, and my family that frightens me more than all else and most others.

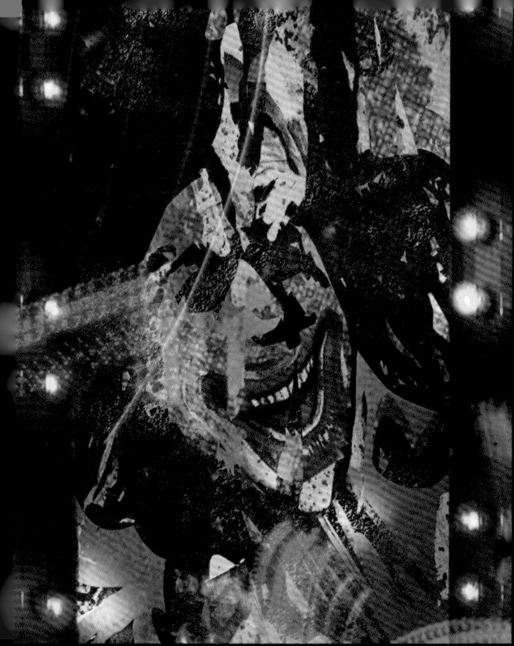

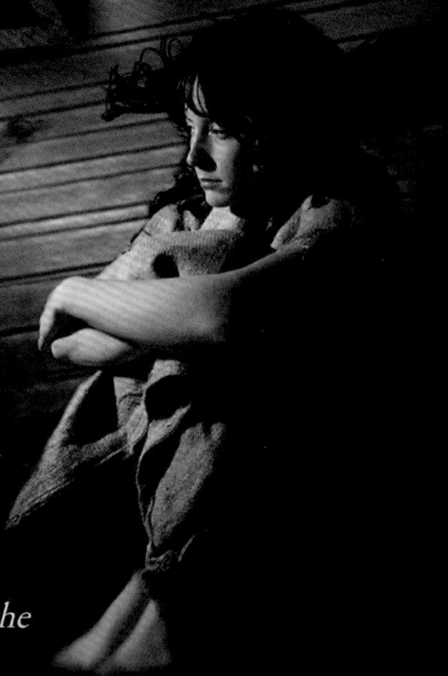

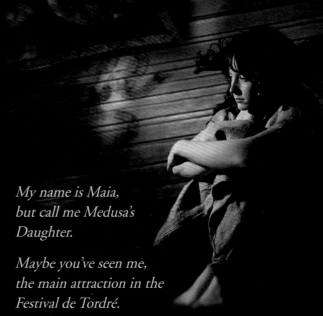

My name is Maia, but call me Medusa's Daughter.

Maybe you've seen me, the main attraction in the Festival de Tordré.

In Greek mythology, Medusa is one of the monstrous Gorgon daughters of the gods Phorcys and Cito. She had hair like viperous snakes and teeth sharper than daggers. She was a creature so dreadful that her gaze transformed everyone who returned it to stone.

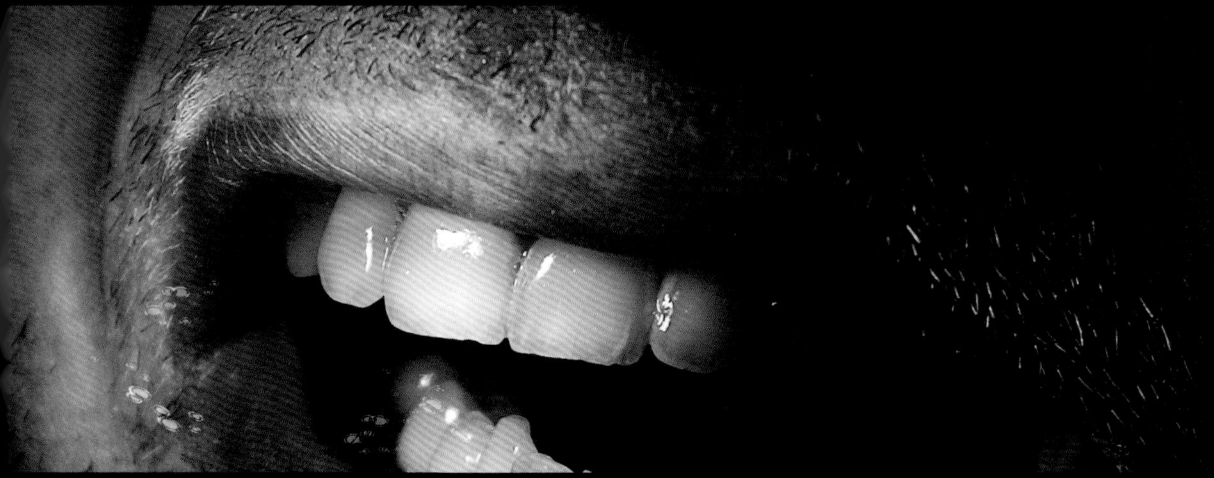

However, mythology, Rictus often says, **"is merely an attempt by the naïve, such as yourself, to explain what they don't understand. The stories of Medusa and her sisters are likely just a way to explain something that was hard to believe. Personally, I believe Gorgons were just failed freaks of evolution. Disgusting mutations, basically."**

"That makes you a mistake," *he has told me more than once.*

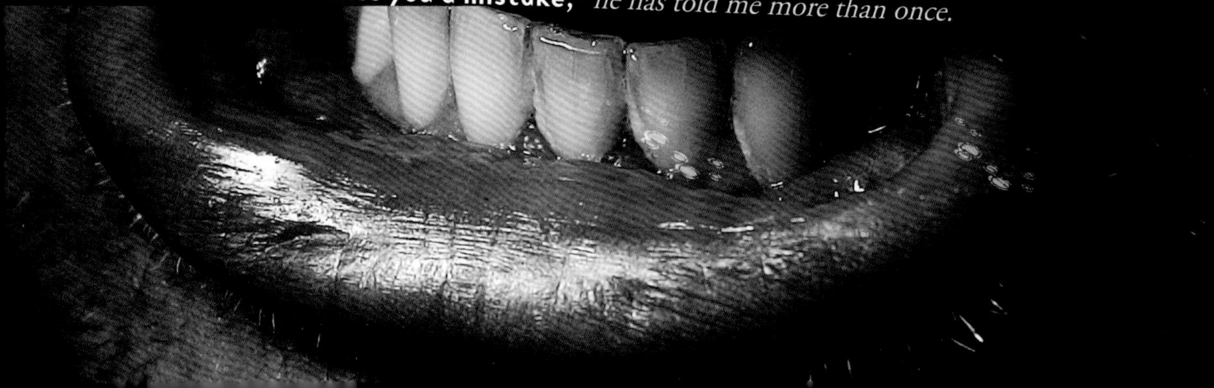

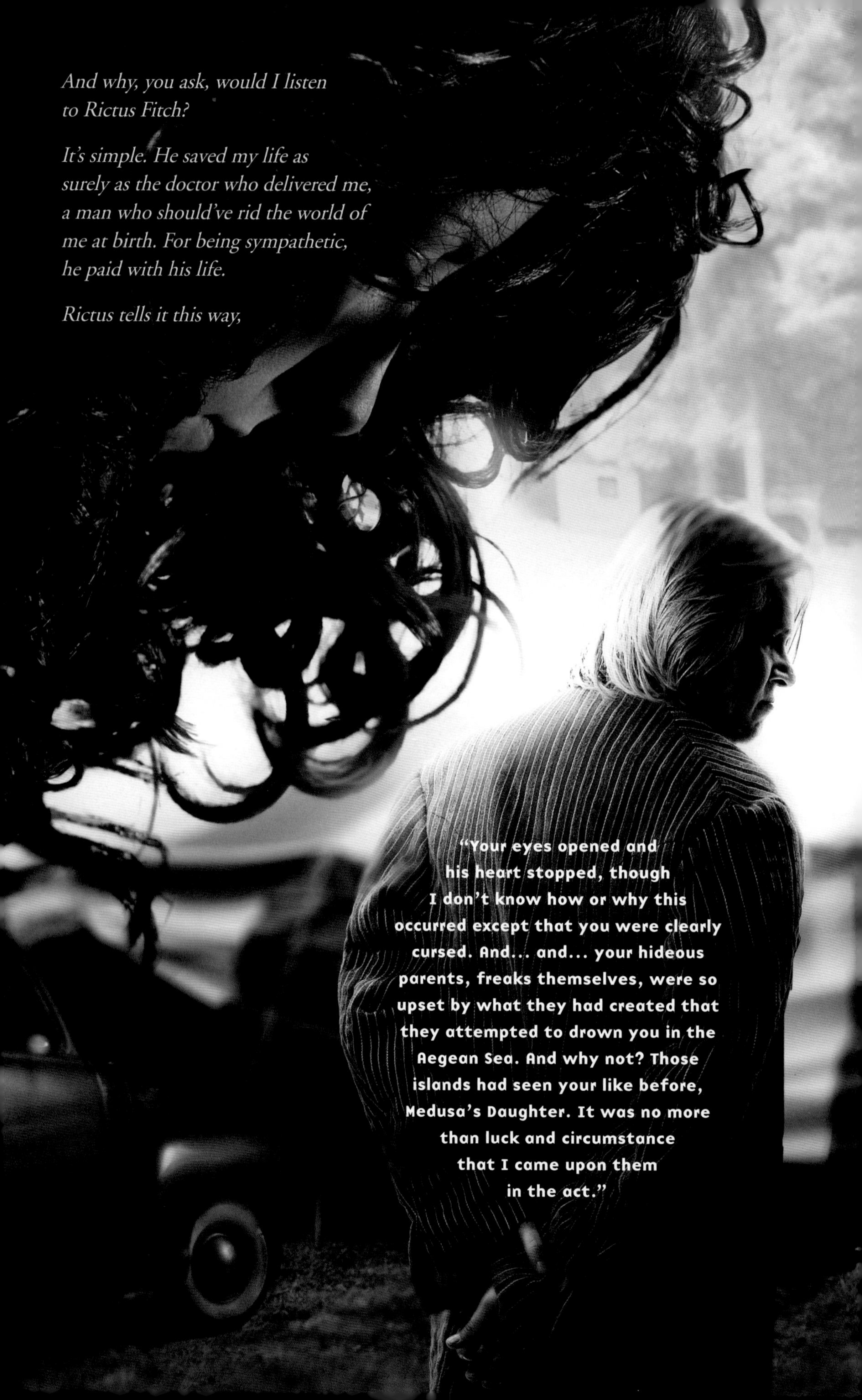

And why, you ask, would I listen to Rictus Fitch?

It's simple. He saved my life as surely as the doctor who delivered me, a man who should've rid the world of me at birth. For being sympathetic, he paid with his life.

Rictus tells it this way,

"Your eyes opened and his heart stopped, though I don't know how or why this occurred except that you were clearly cursed. And... and... your hideous parents, freaks themselves, were so upset by what they had created that they attempted to drown you in the Aegean Sea. And why not? Those islands had seen your like before, Medusa's Daughter. It was no more than luck and circumstance that I came upon them in the act."

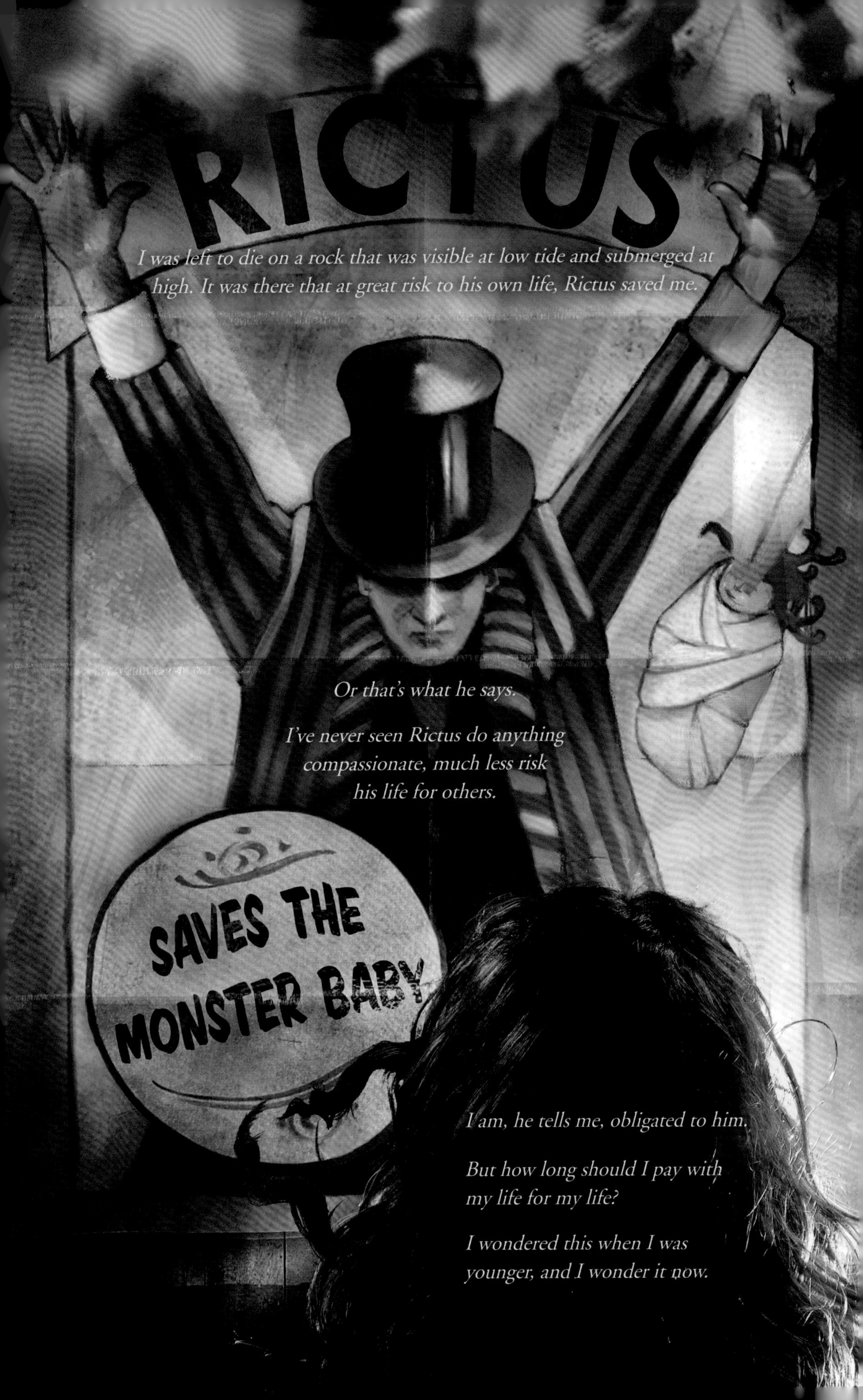
RICTUS
SAVES THE MONSTER BABY

I was left to die on a rock that was visible at low tide and submerged at high. It was there that at great risk to his own life, Rictus saved me.

Or that's what he says.

I've never seen Rictus do anything compassionate, much less risk his life for others.

I am, he tells me, obligated to him.

But how long should I pay with my life for my life?

I wondered this when I was younger, and I wonder it now.

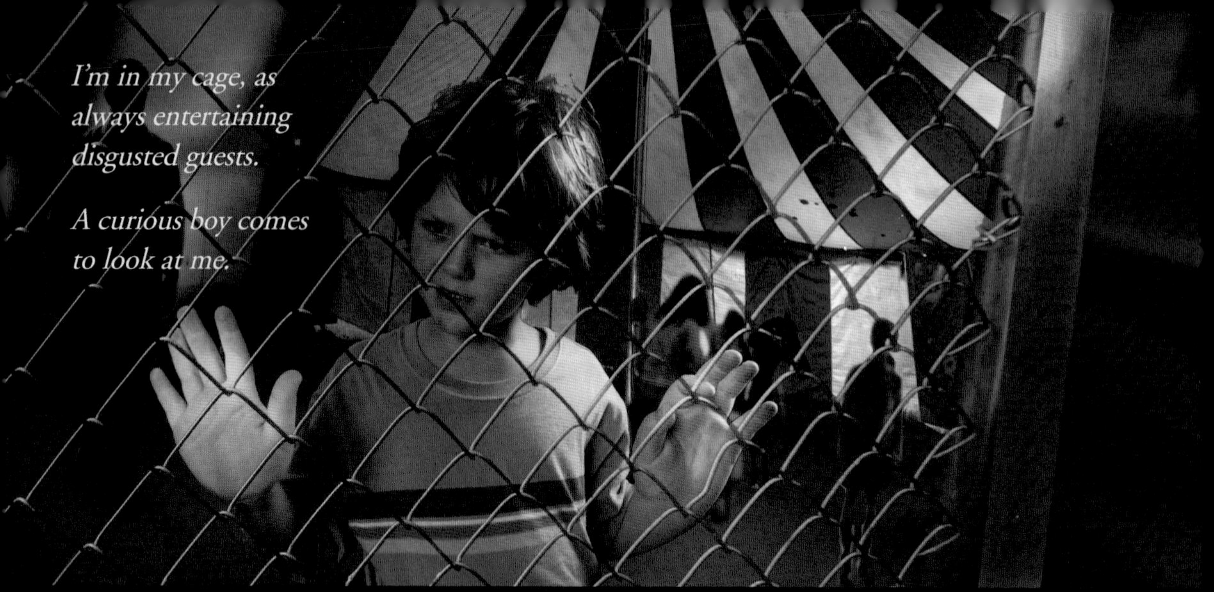
I'm in my cage, as always entertaining disgusted guests.
A curious boy comes to look at me.

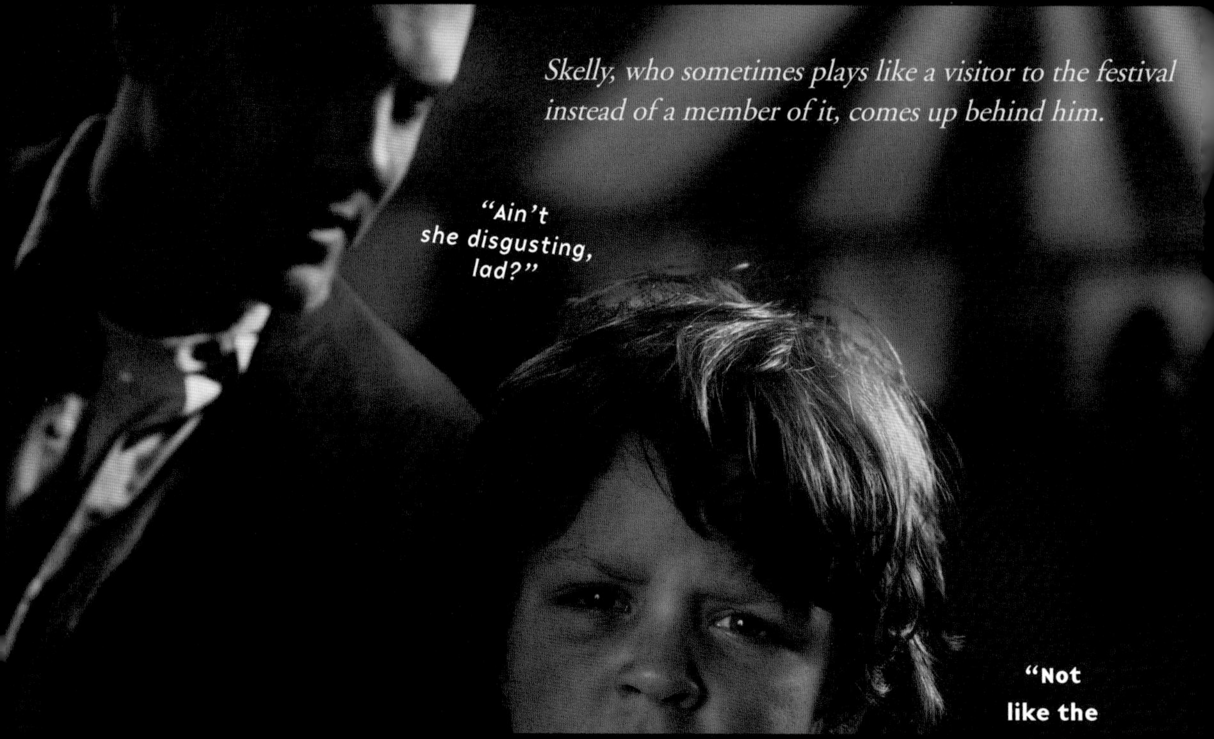
Skelly, who sometimes plays like a visitor to the festival instead of a member of it, comes up behind him.
"Ain't she disgusting, lad?"
"Not like the painting."

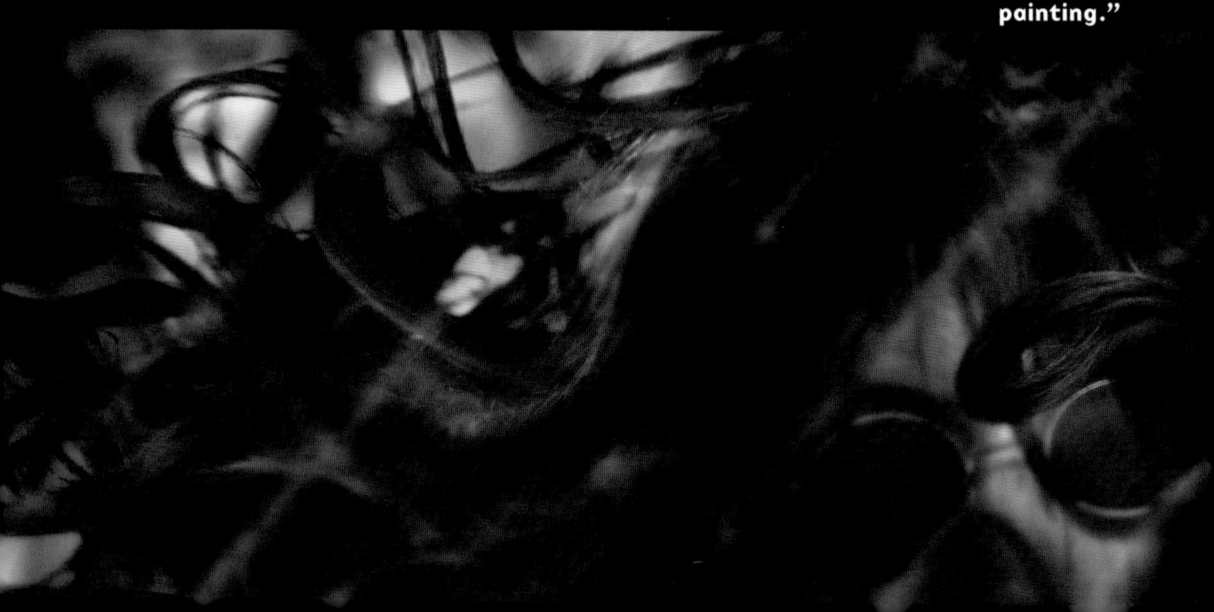

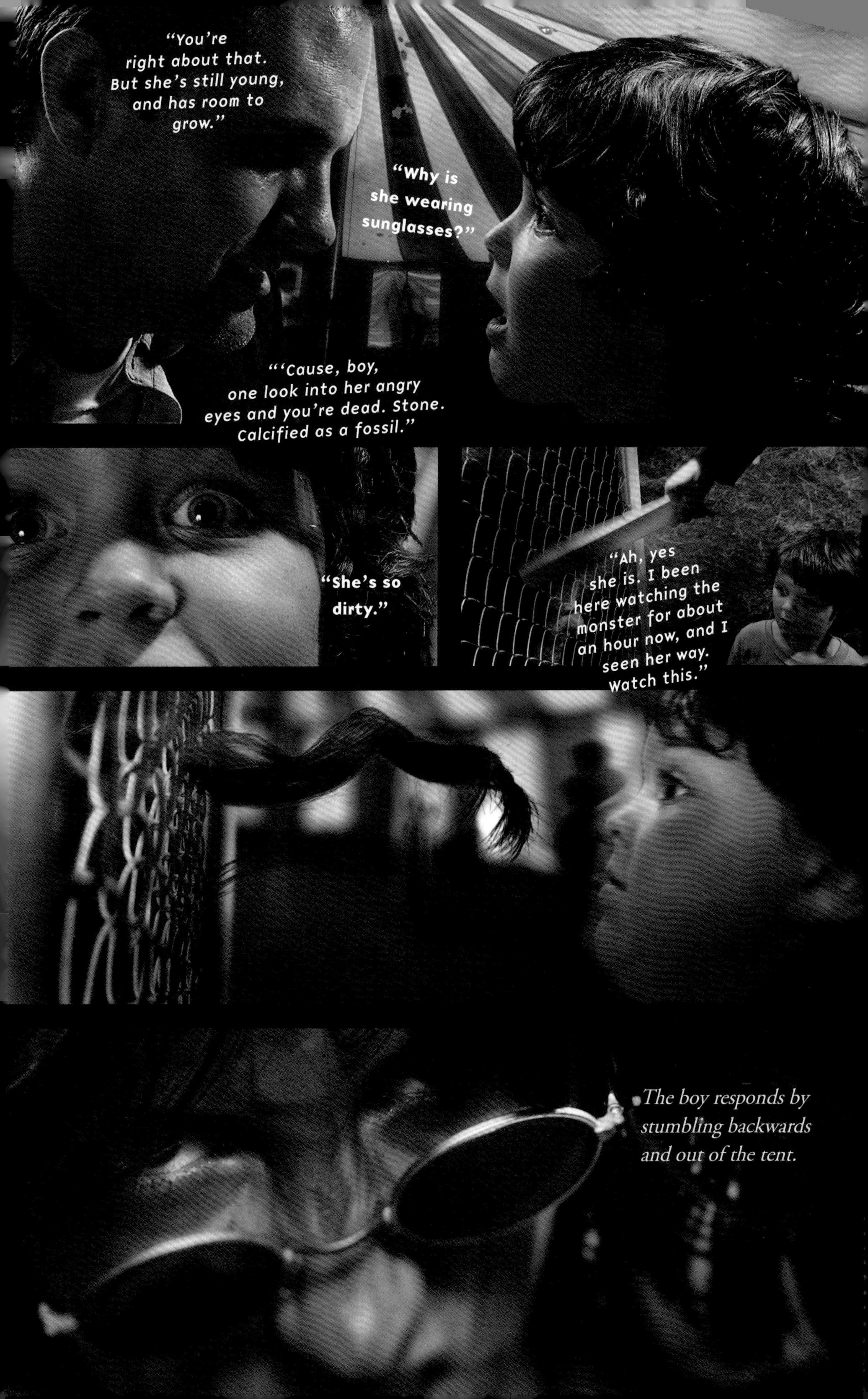
"You're right about that. But she's still young, and has room to grow."
"Why is she wearing sunglasses?"
"'Cause, boy, one look into her angry eyes and you're dead. Stone. Calcified as a fossil."
"She's so dirty."
"Ah, yes she is. I been here watching the monster for about an hour now, and I seen her way. Watch this."
The boy responds by stumbling backwards and out of the tent.

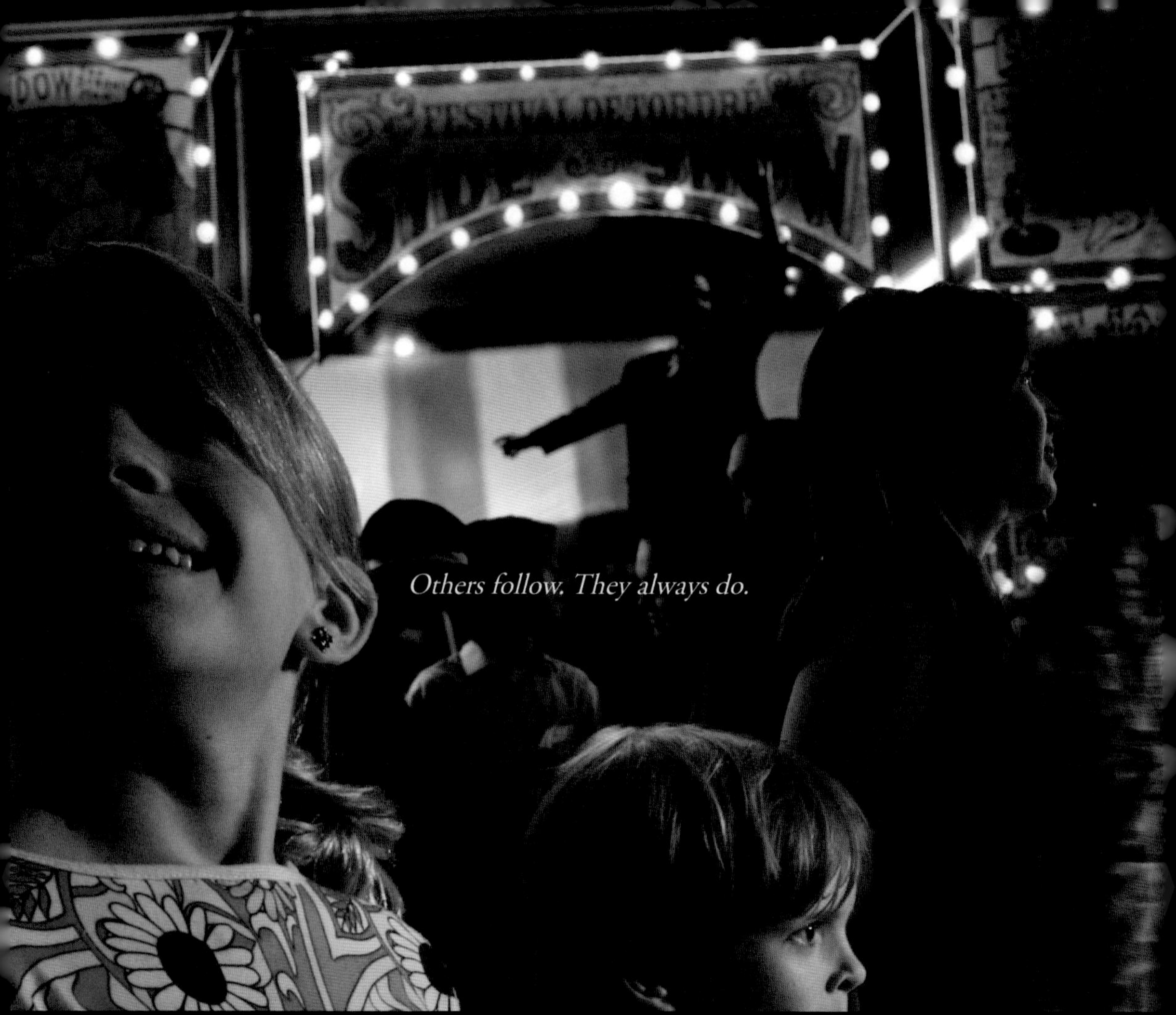

Others follow. They always do.

Hour after hour, I hiss and show my teeth. To Rictus, I'm a commodity, another freak to be kicked around, one more piece of the mad little community he lords over. And I hate that. It can crush me. But I do as I'm told. Rictus, more than anyone else, scares me.

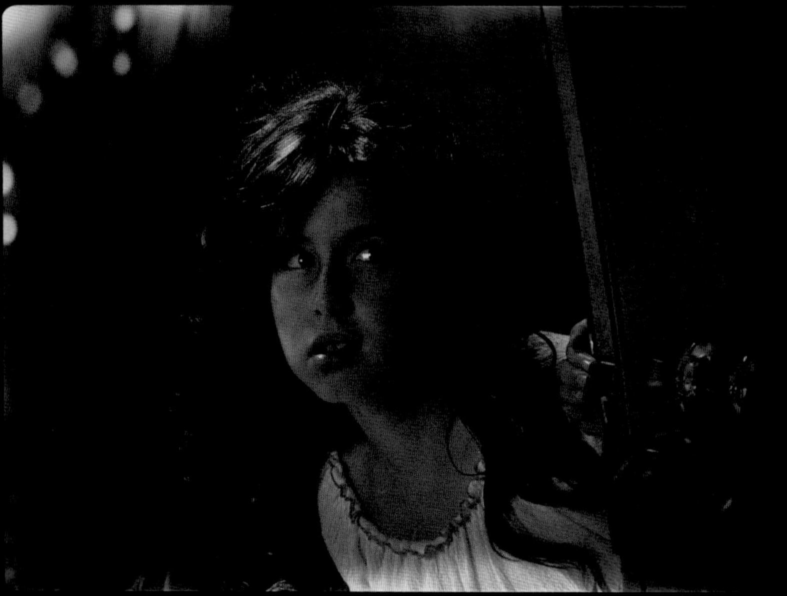

It's for that reason, at the age of eight, and despite the fact he'd saved my life, I ran from Festival de Tordré seeking the safety of my parents' arms. At the time, I'd been reading A Little Princess, *which is a beautiful story about the undying love between a father and his daughter.*

Because of it, I began to hope that maybe, in some small way, my parents would take me back

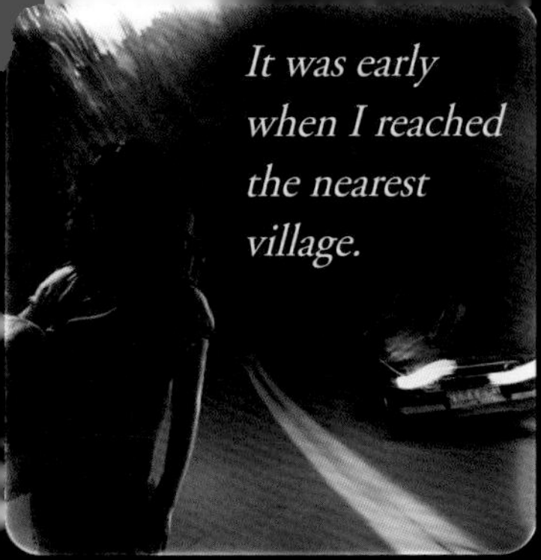
It was early
when I reached
the nearest
village.

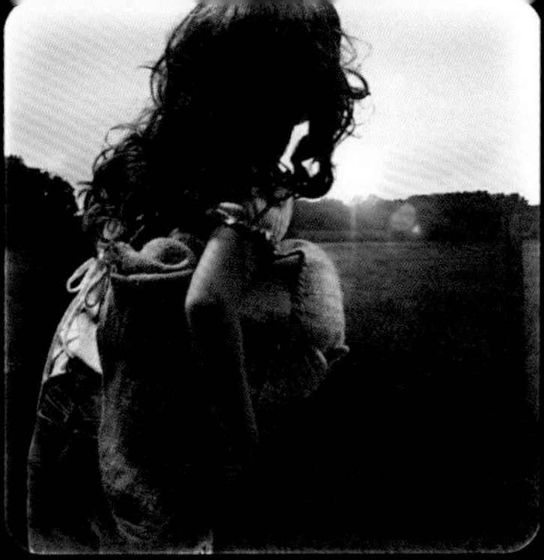

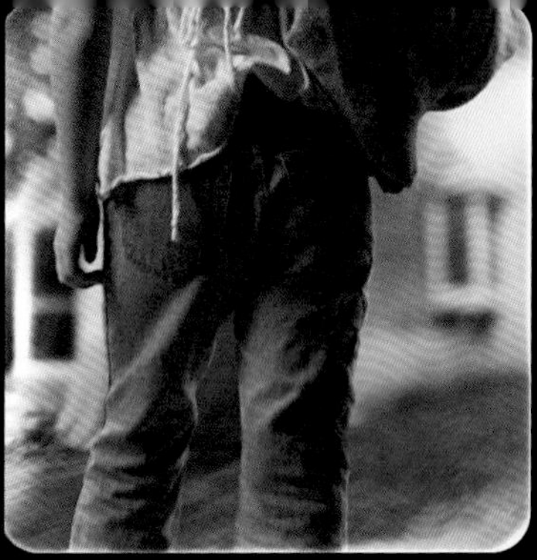

I went into the only building that was open, a bakery.

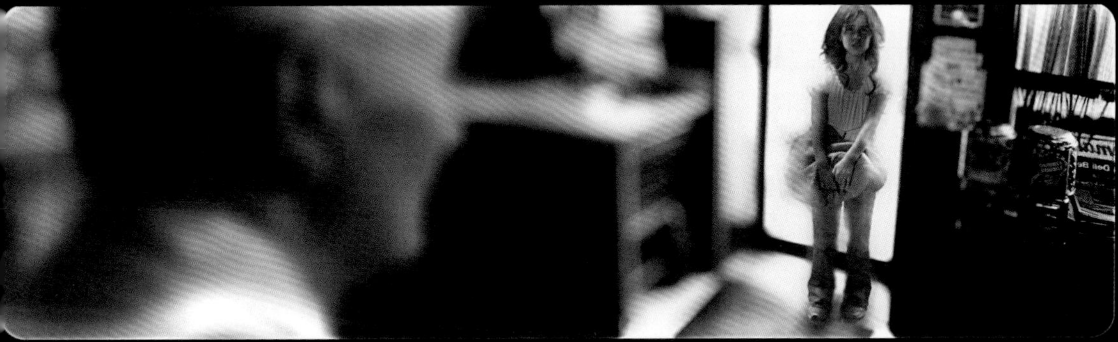

"Sir, do you know which direction I need to walk to get to Mikonos?"

"Never heard of it, child."

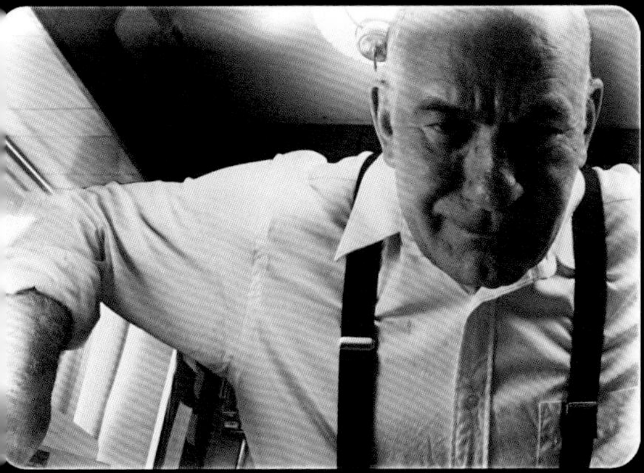

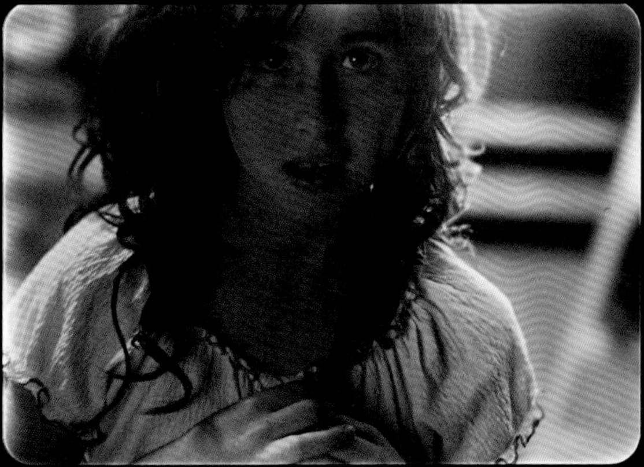

"I was told it's a small island off the coast of Greece in the Aegean Sea."

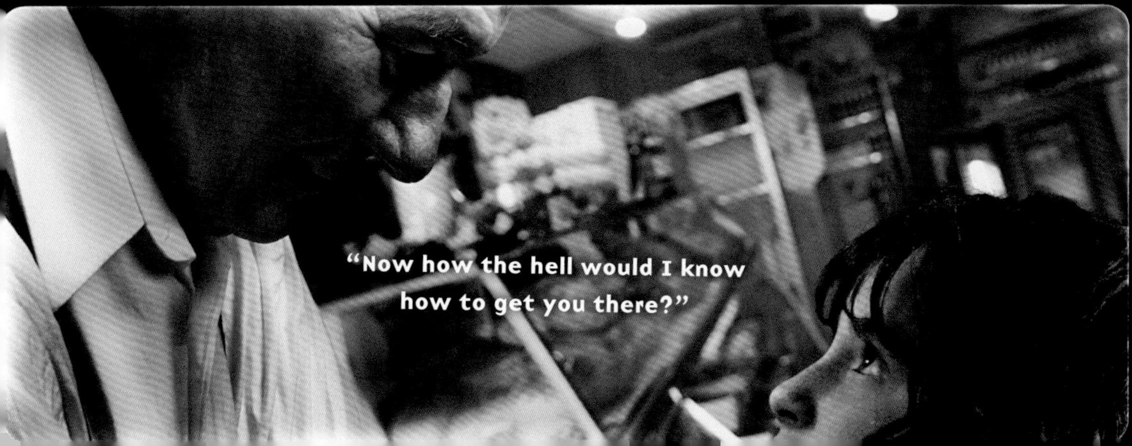
"Now how the hell would I know
how to get you there?"

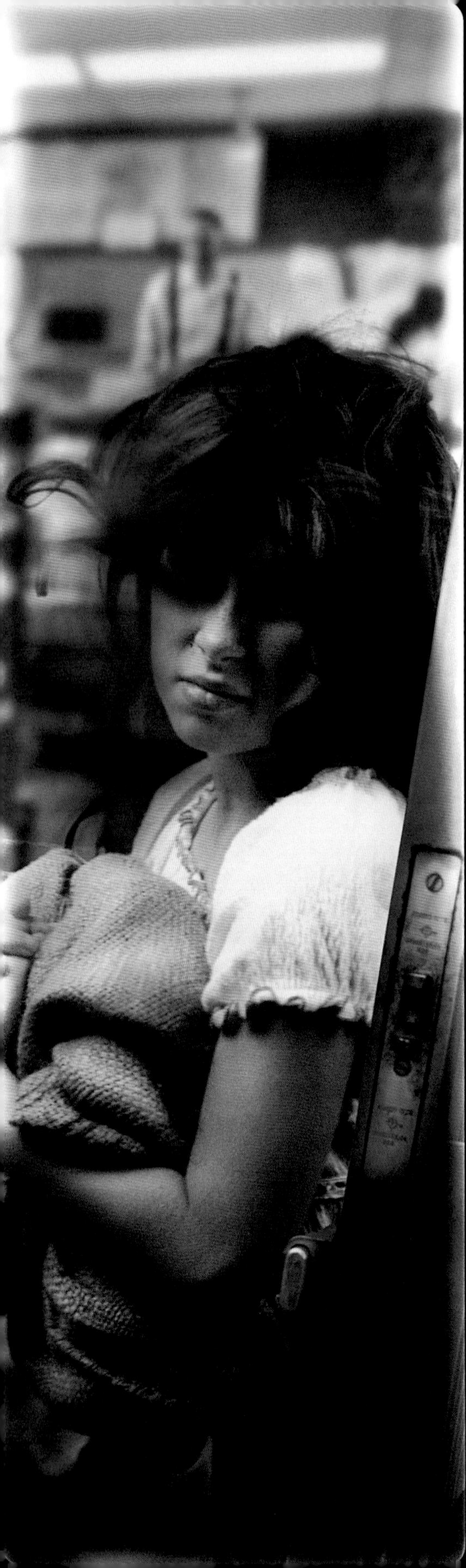

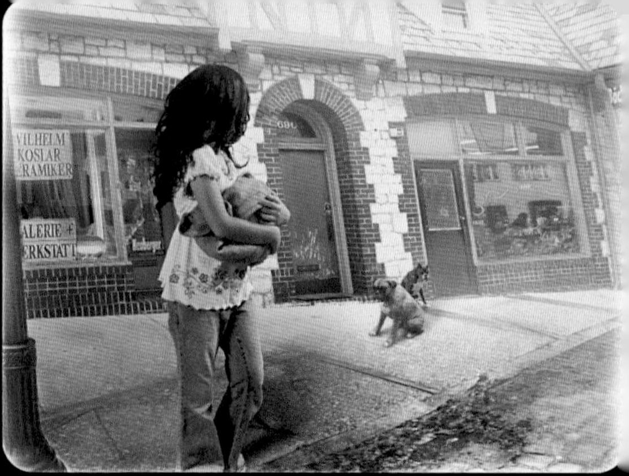
VILHELM
KOSLAR

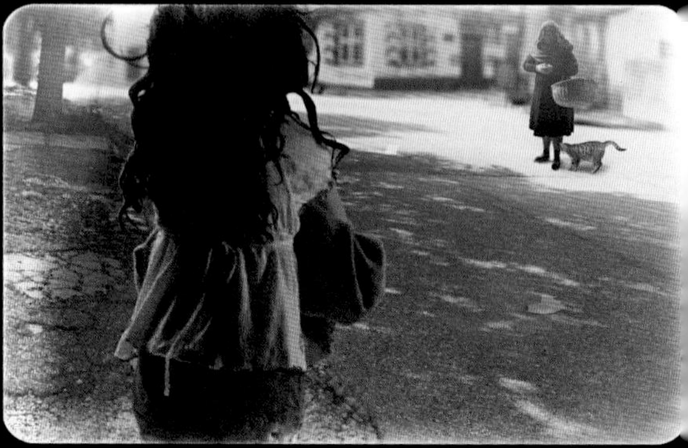

"Ma'am, I am searching for the
direction of Mikonos, an island."

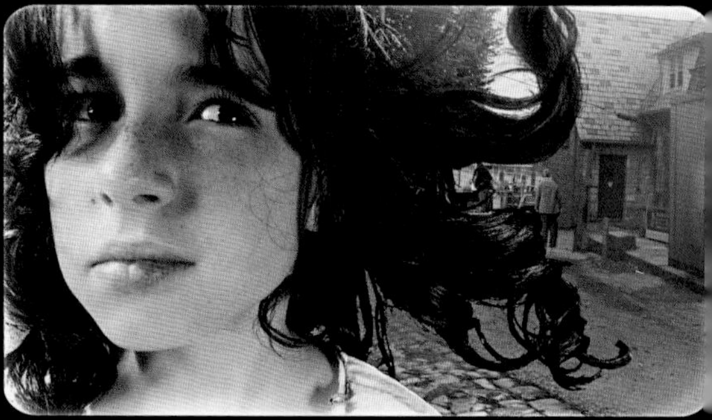

"Have you ever heard of it?"

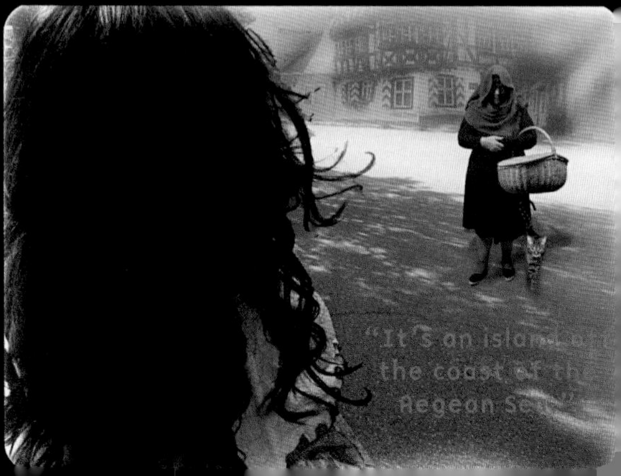

"It's an island off
the coast of the
Aegean Sea."

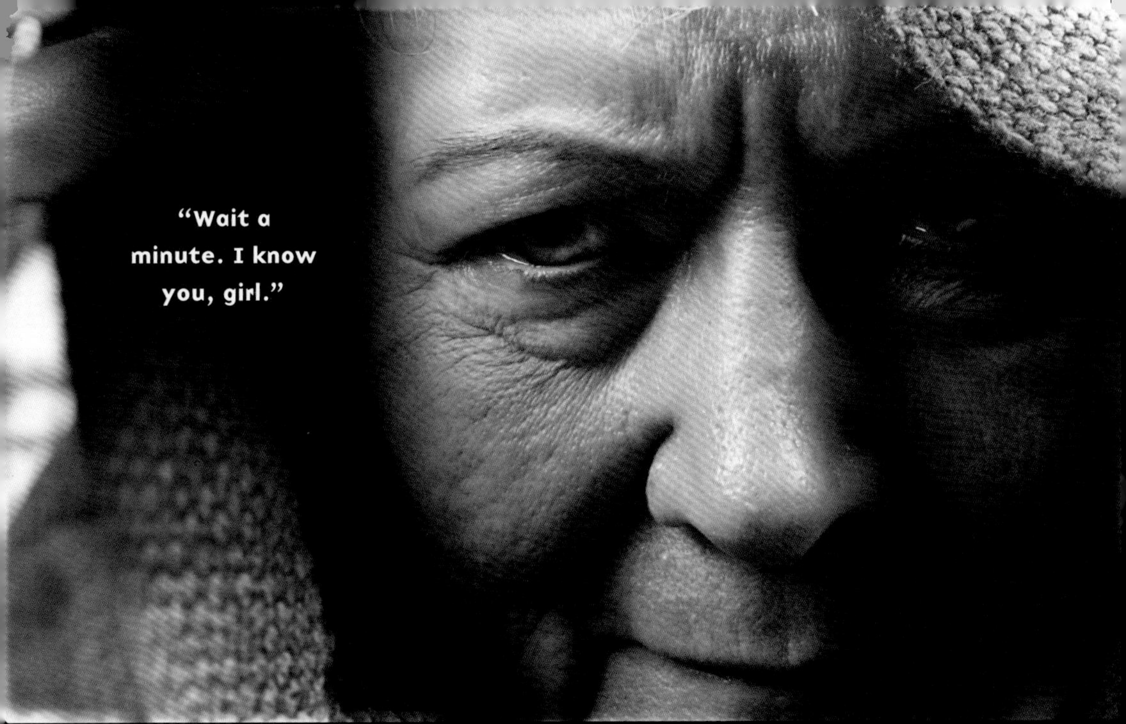
"Wait a minute. I know you, girl."

"You're the monster child from that traveling show."

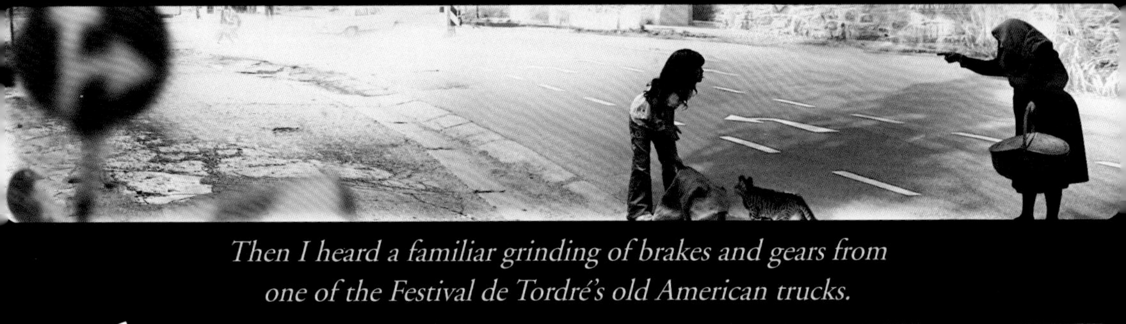

Then I heard a familiar grinding of brakes and gears from one of the Festival de Tordré's old American trucks.

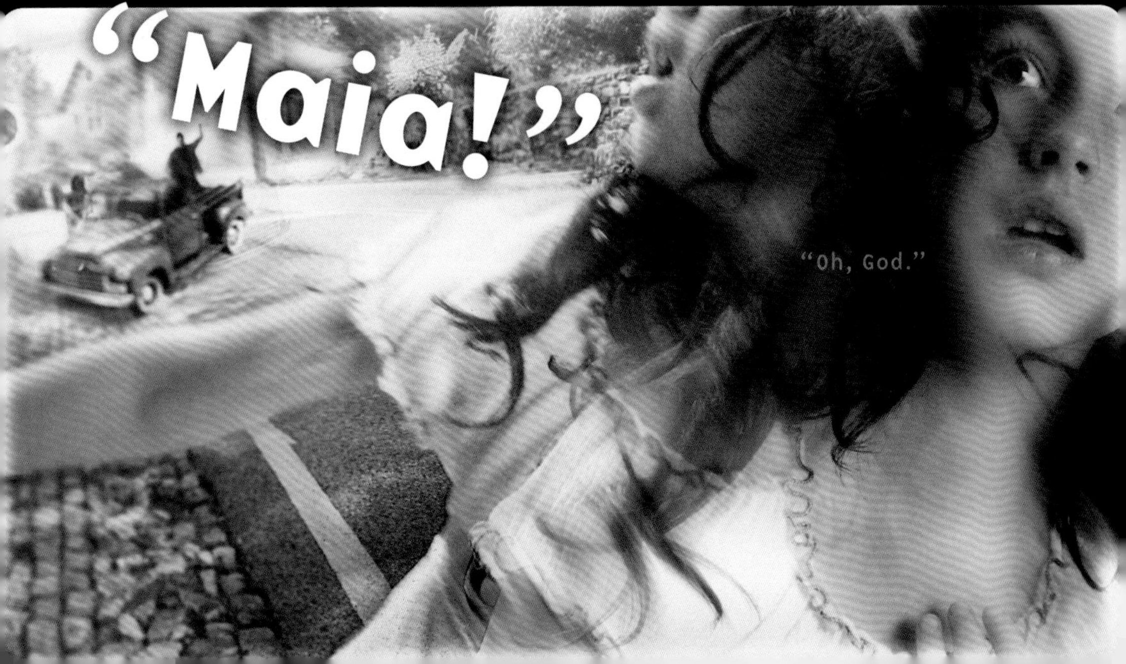
"Maia!"
"Oh, God."

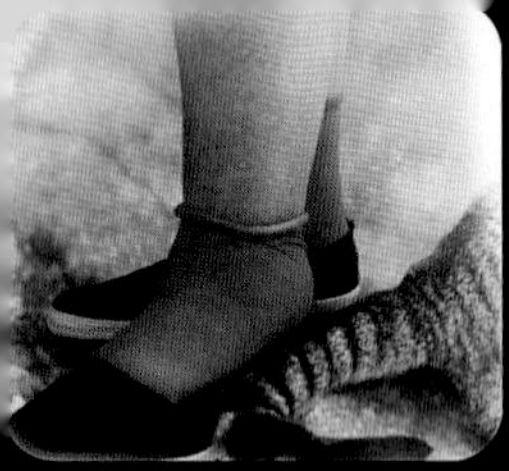

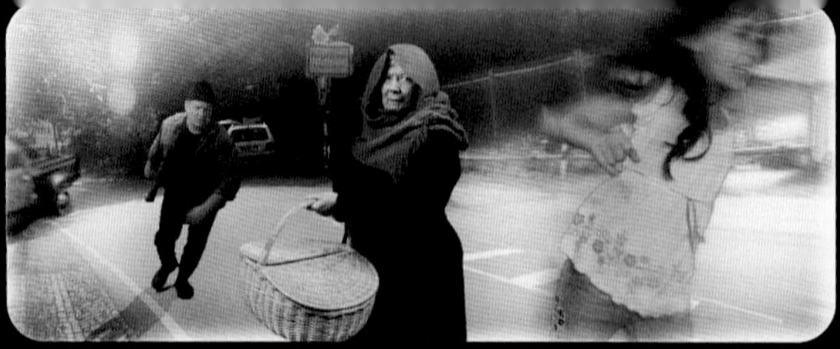

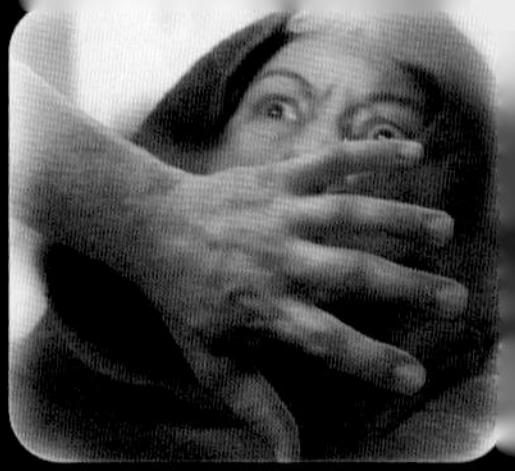

I was terrified. I knew how the festival strong man, Horst, battered people for disloyalty to Rictus and his freakish kingdom.

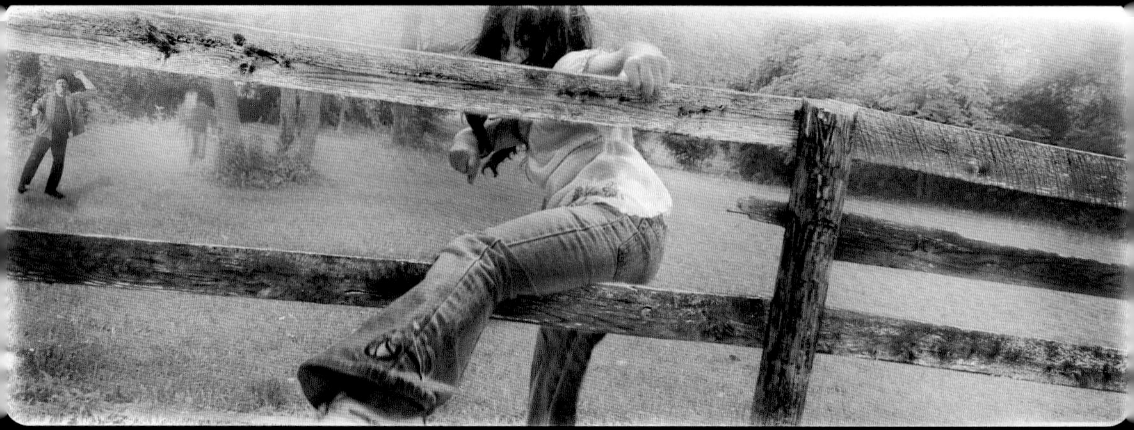

Years ago, he'd beaten my friend Skully up for simply cursing at Rictus.

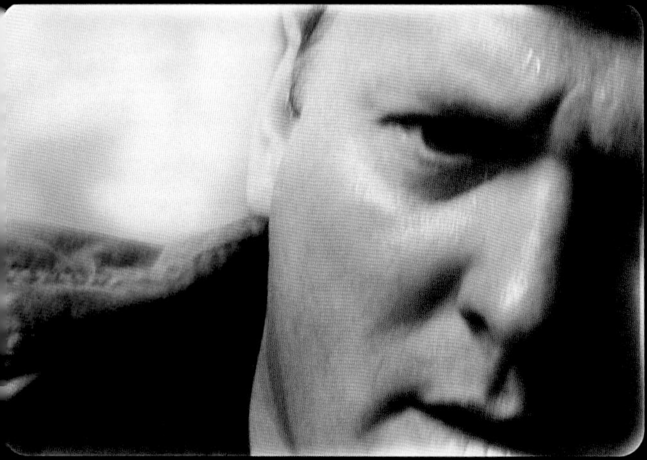

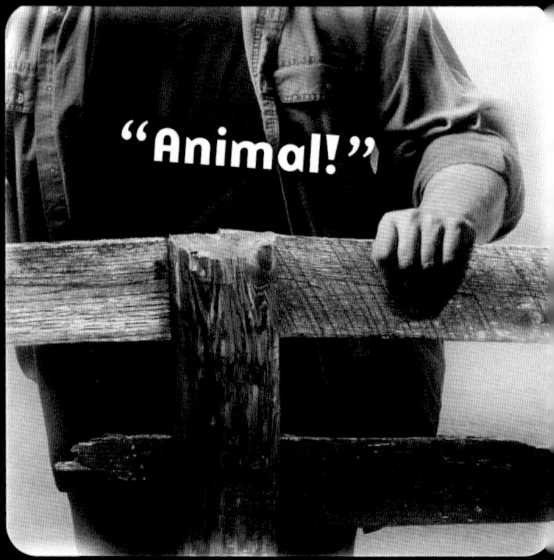
"Animal!"

So I ran, passing through a field and into a wooded area.

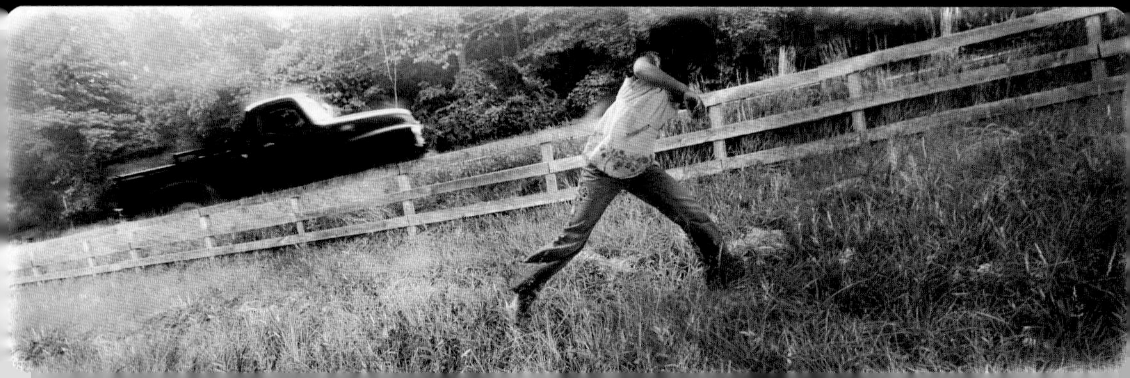

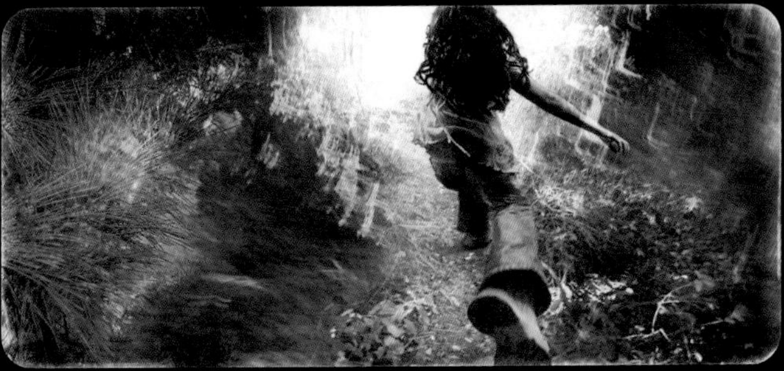

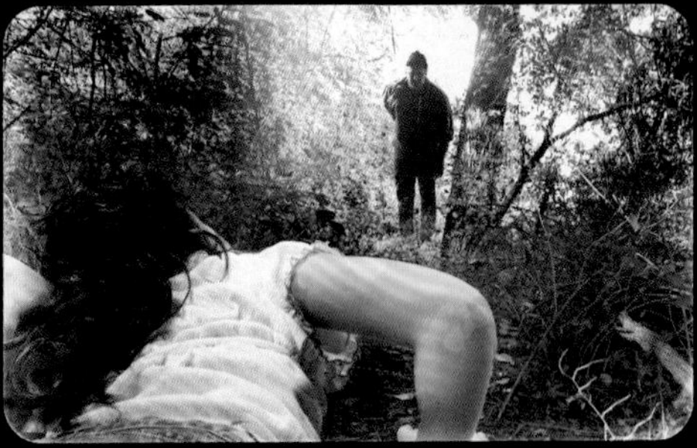

Scared, I scrambled wildly through underbrush 'til my head struck a tree limb. Confused, I stumbled up a small hill before collapsing.

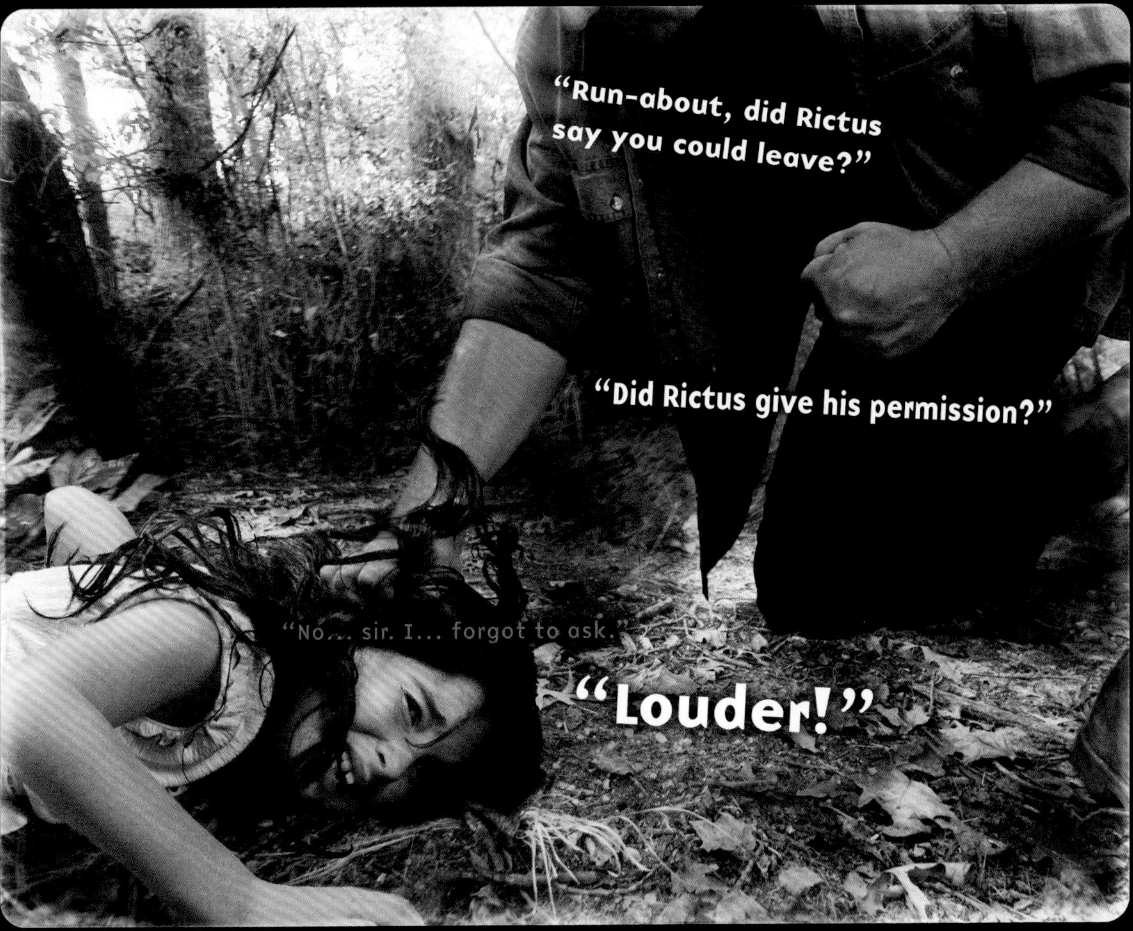
"Run-about, did Rictus say you could leave?"
"Did Rictus give his permission?"
"No... sir. I... forgot to ask."
"Louder!"

I was intimidated and terrified, but the anger driving my coils was not.

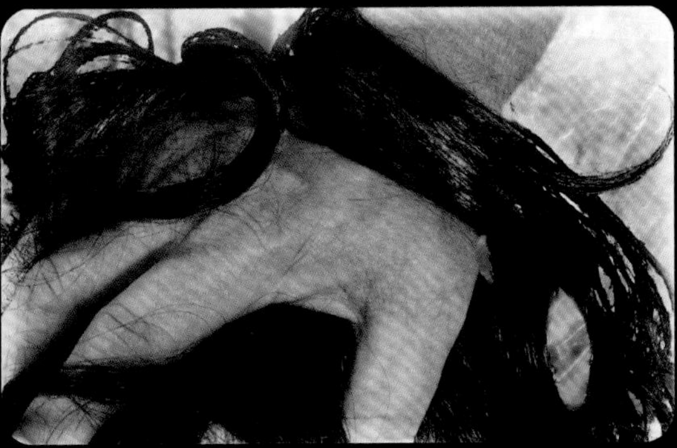

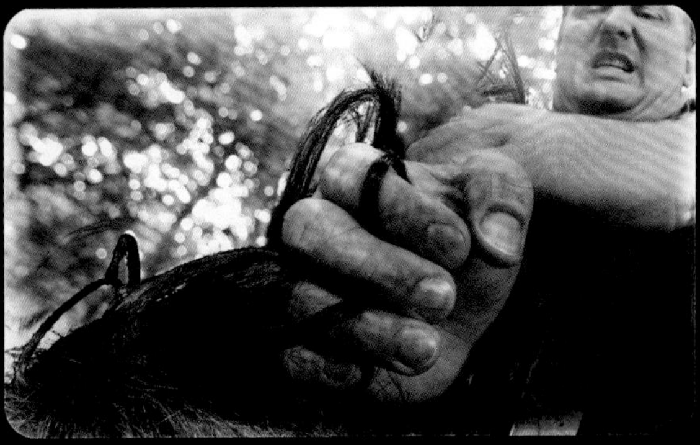

He tried to pull away as I slowly crunched his hand with my hair.

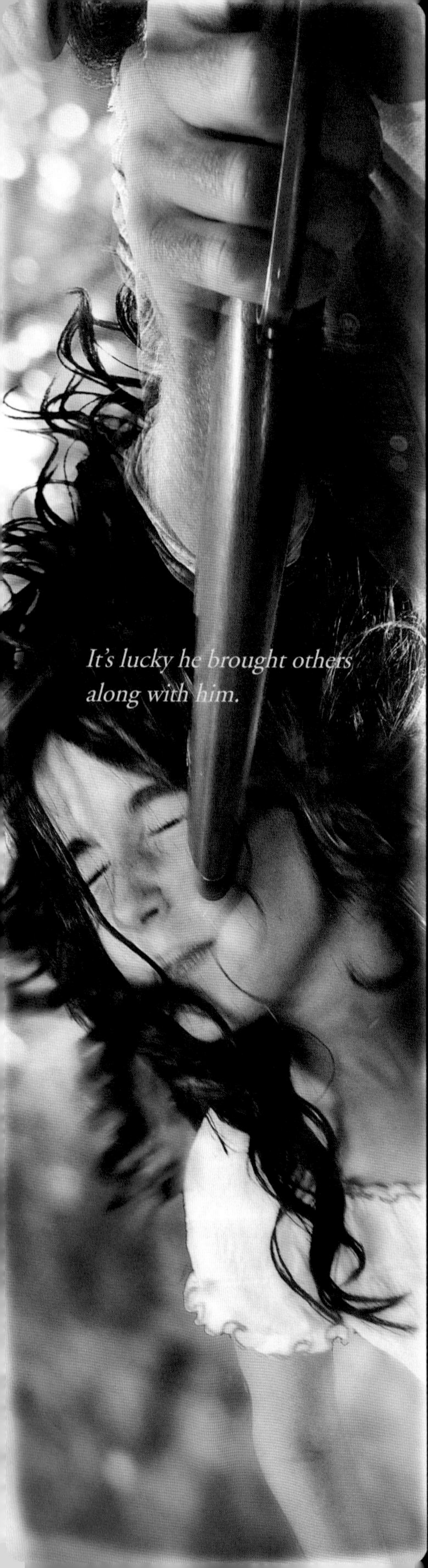
It's lucky he brought others along with him.

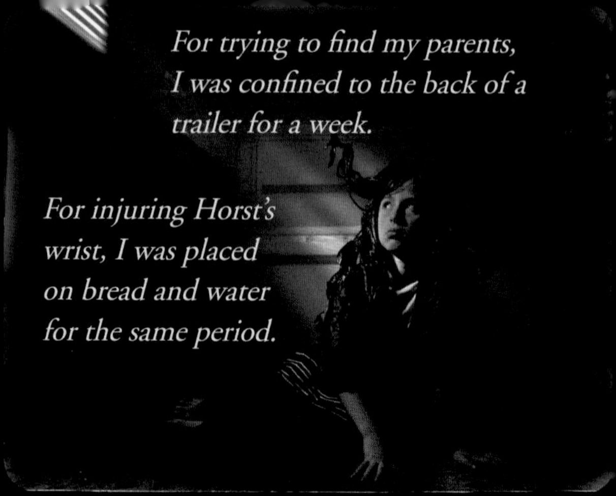
For trying to find my parents, I was confined to the back of a trailer for a week.
For injuring Horst's wrist, I was placed on bread and water for the same period.

But for insulting Rictus, I got worse.

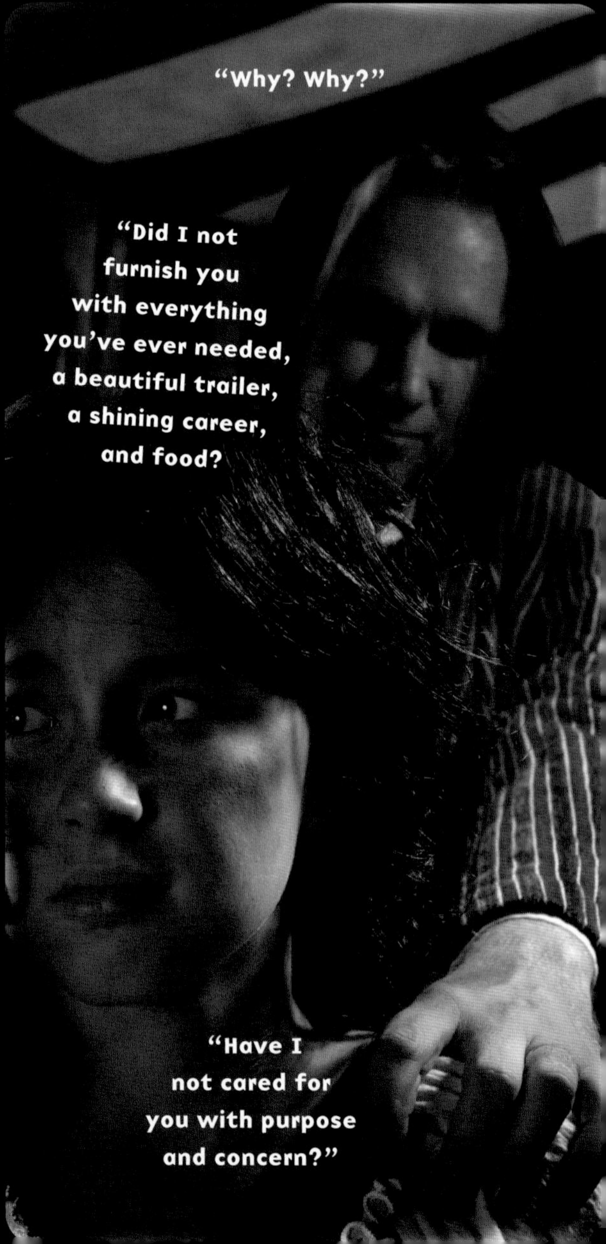
"Why? Why?"
"Did I not furnish you with everything you've ever needed, a beautiful trailer, a shining career, and food?
"Have I not cared for you with purpose and concern?"

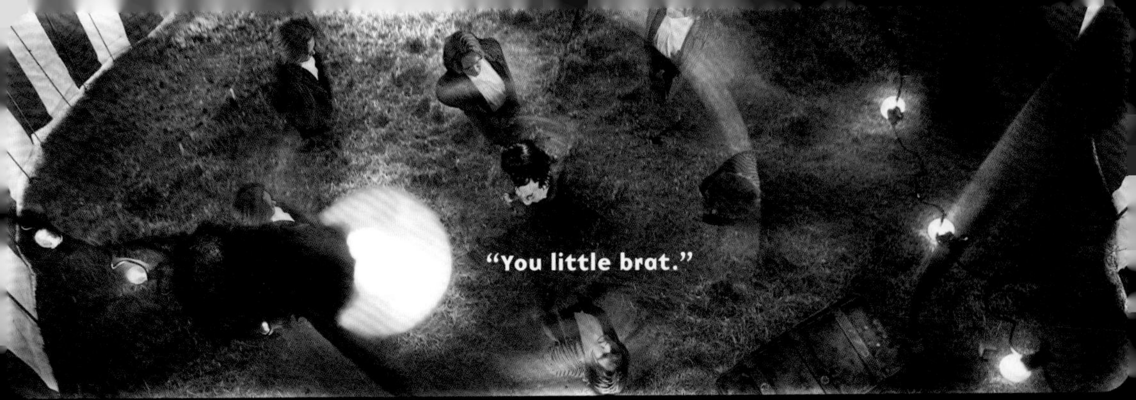
"You little brat."

Rictus is like something large and vicious pacing a cage.

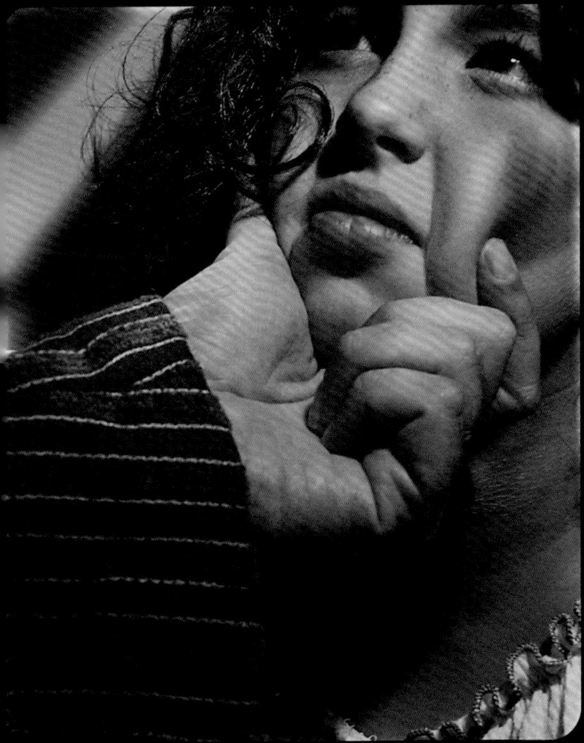

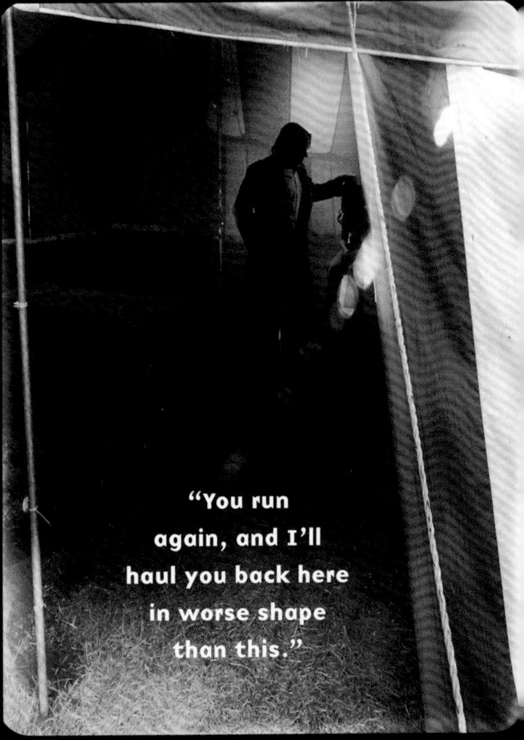
"You run again, and I'll haul you back here in worse shape than this."

"Yes... sir."

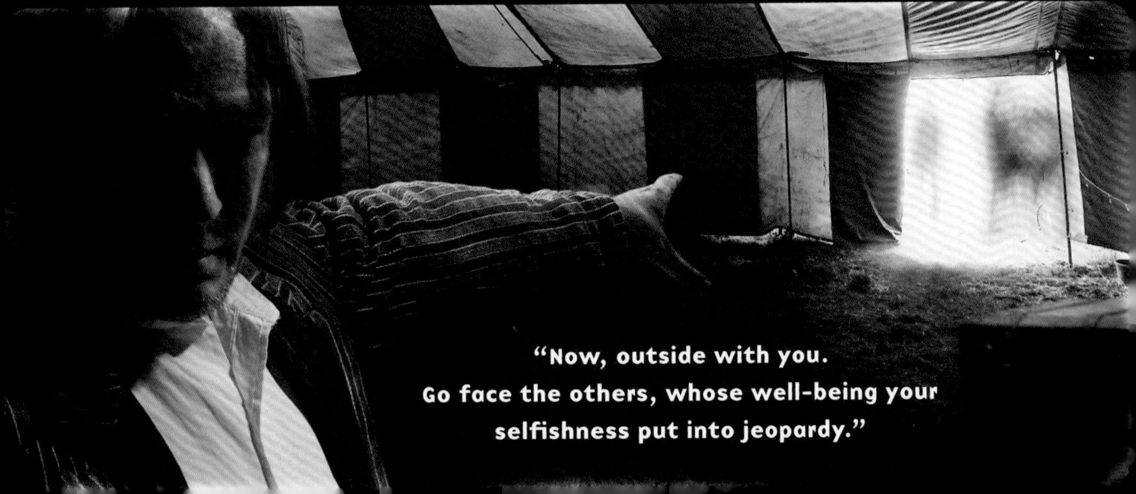
"Now, outside with you.
Go face the others, whose well-being your selfishness put into jeopardy."

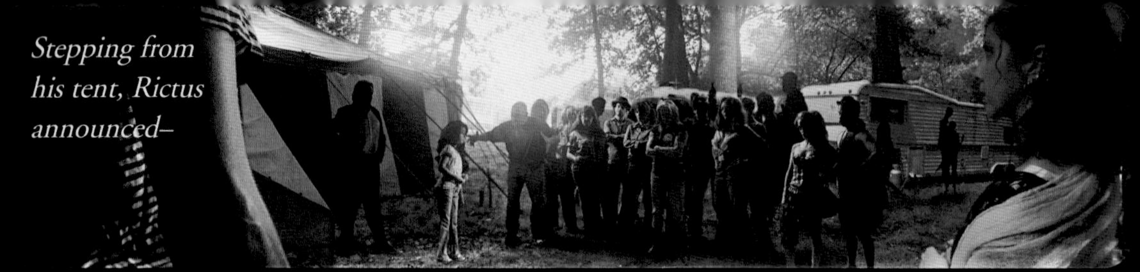

Stepping from his tent, Rictus announced–

"She thinks herself better than all of you. She thinks she would be properly suited to life with a higher class of losers. Show her what we think of her arrogance. Let her bathe in it!"

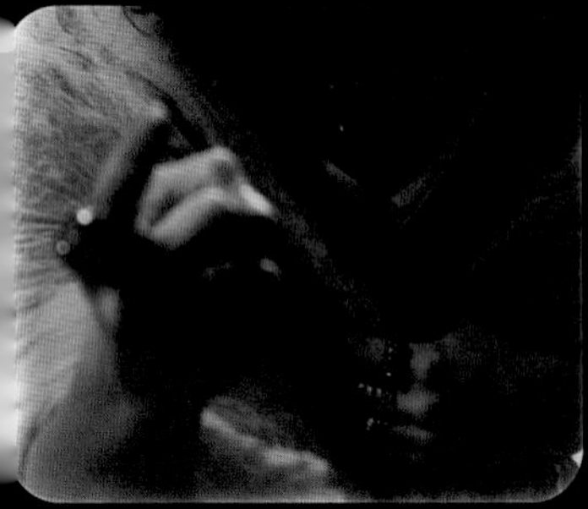

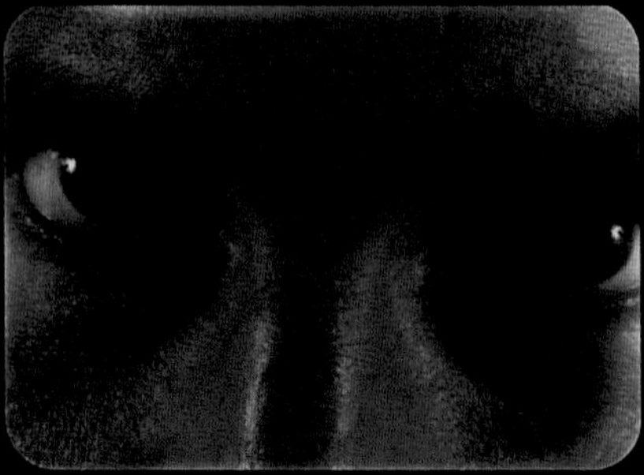

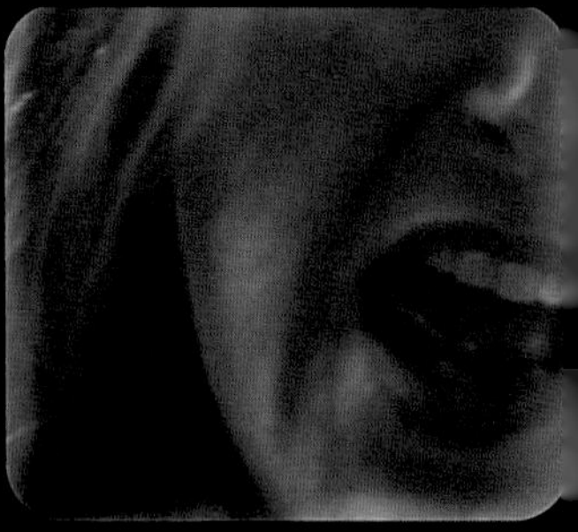

Some hollered at me, others spit, and my knees grew weak.

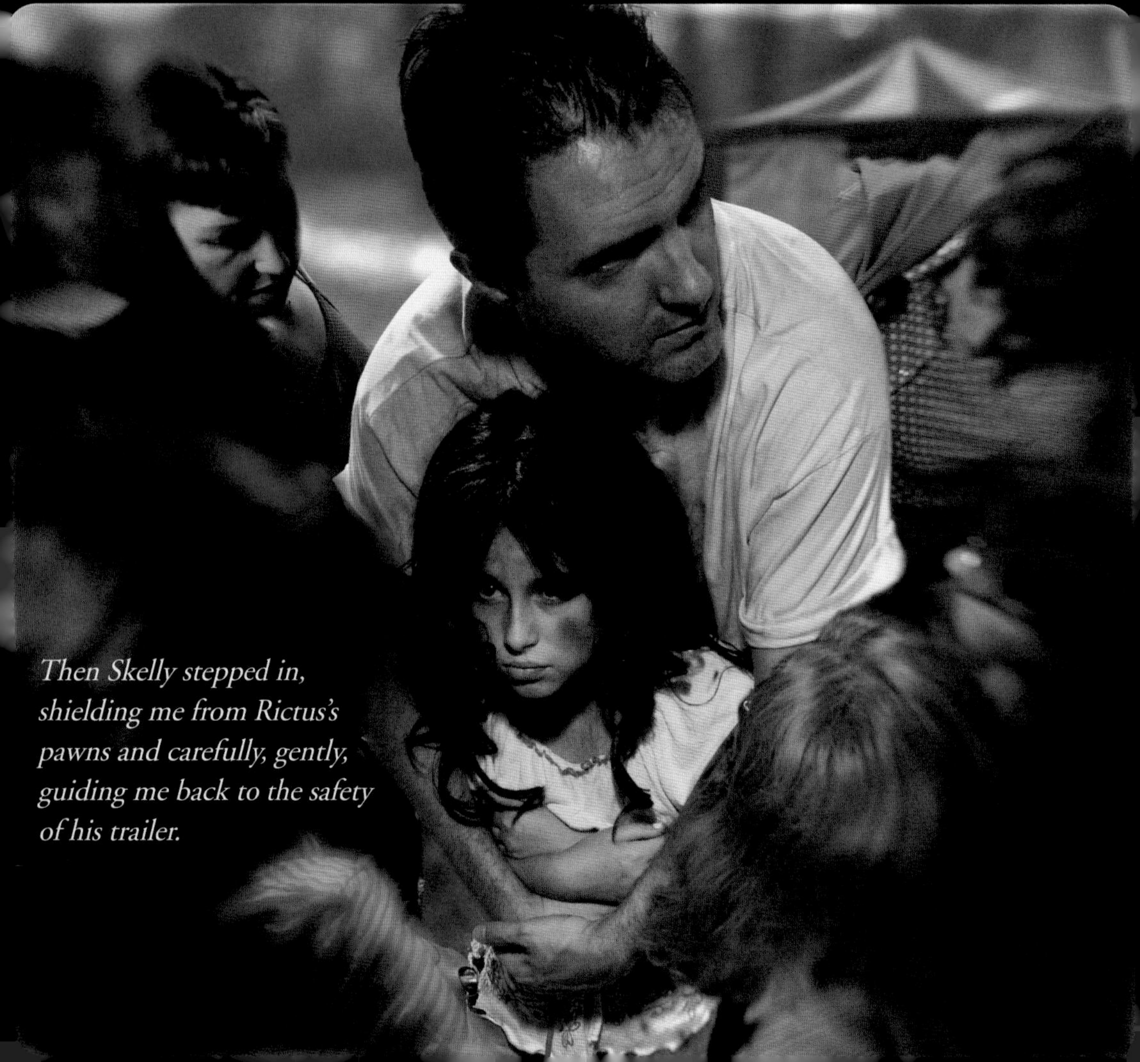

Then Skelly stepped in, shielding me from Rictus's pawns and carefully, gently, guiding me back to the safety of his trailer.

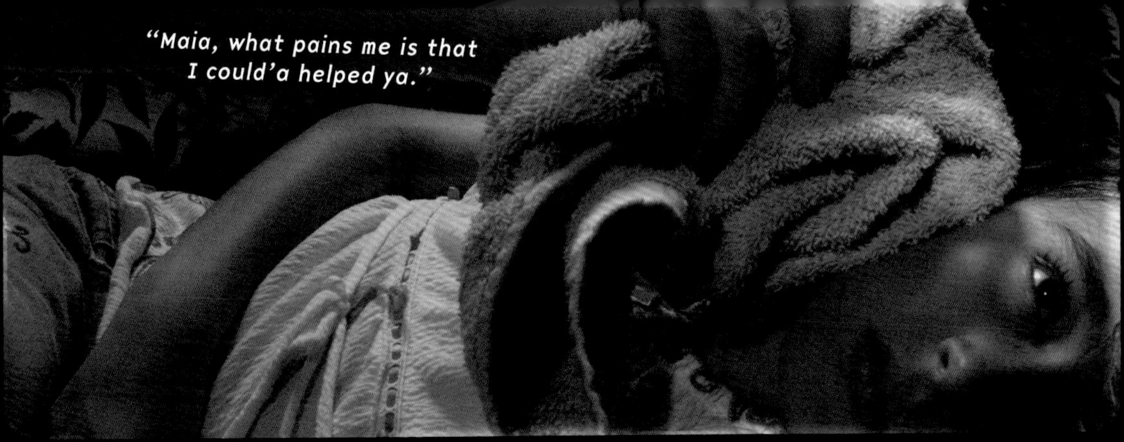
"Maia, what pains me is that I could'a helped ya."

"My god, ya should'a told me what ya was gonna do, and I would'a helped."

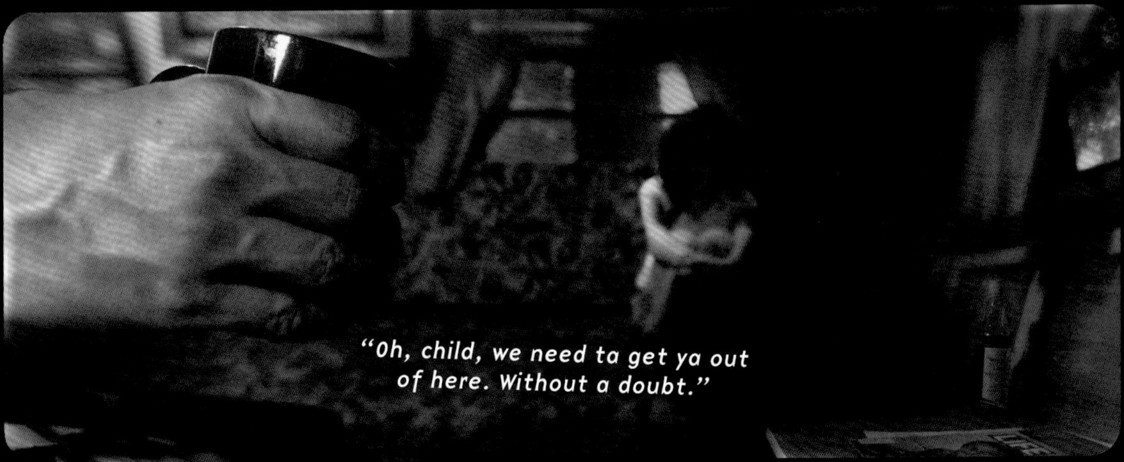
"Oh, child, we need ta get ya out of here. Without a doubt."

"But we need ta do so in such a way as ta prevent Rictus from finding ya ever again."

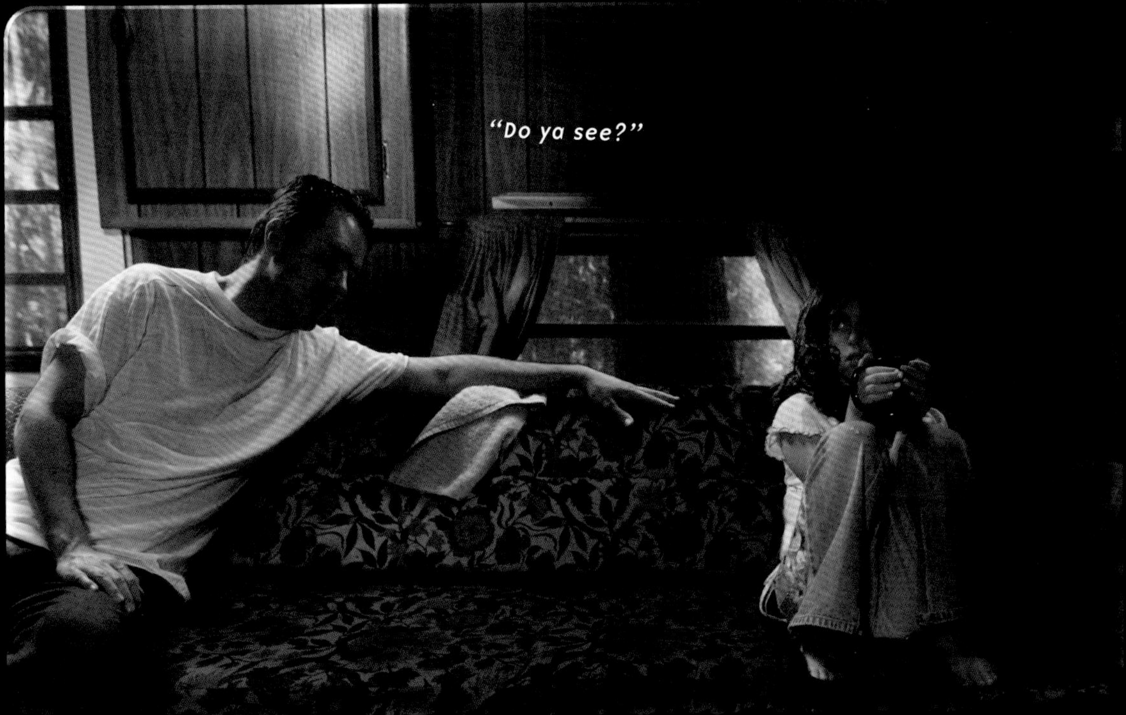
"Do ya see?"

"Maia, I fear... now.... ya've set course in dangerous waters."

"I... I only wanted to see my parents again."

"Because, I'm... I'm not as bad as they might think. Do you know?"

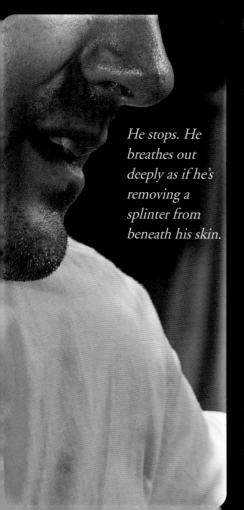

He stops. He breathes out deeply as if he's removing a splinter from beneath his skin.

"Yes, of course you're not. You're not awful at all. Not in the least... and ya should know ya never were. Now, it breaks me heart, but... but I got to take ya back to Rictus."

"Don't, Skelly. Please."

"My hands are tied, dear. My hands're tied."

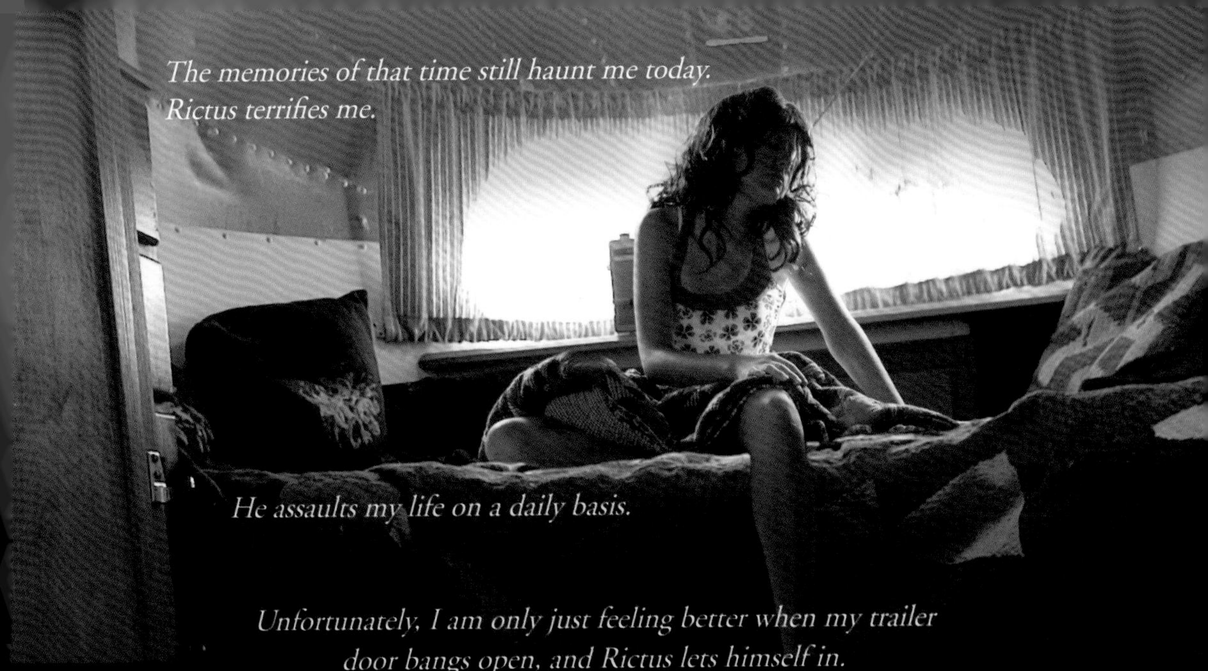
The memories of that time still haunt me today.
Rictus terrifies me.
He assaults my life on a daily basis.
Unfortunately, I am only just feeling better when my trailer door bangs open, and Rictus lets himself in.

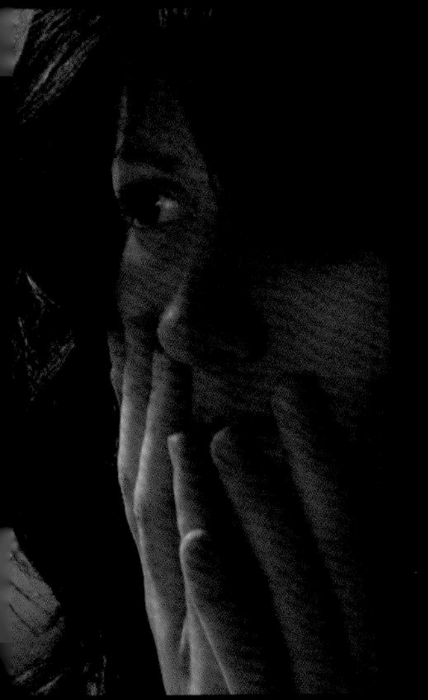

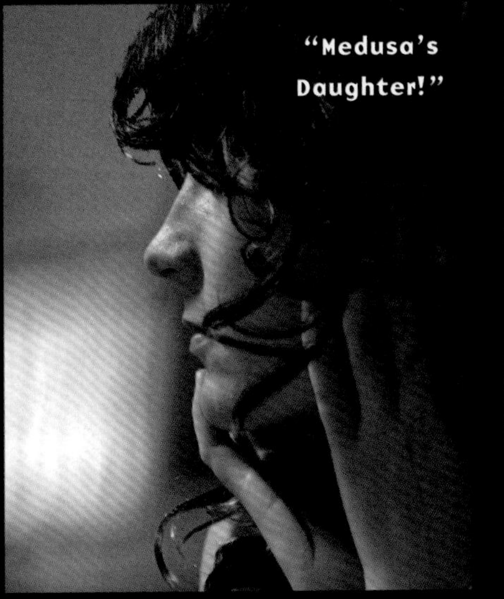
"Medusa's Daughter!"

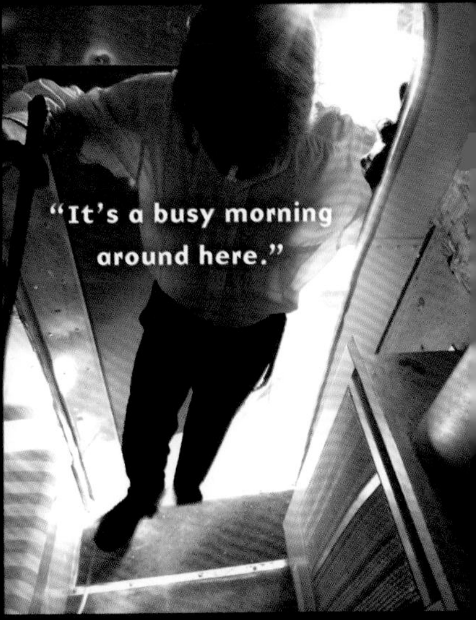
"It's a busy morning around here."

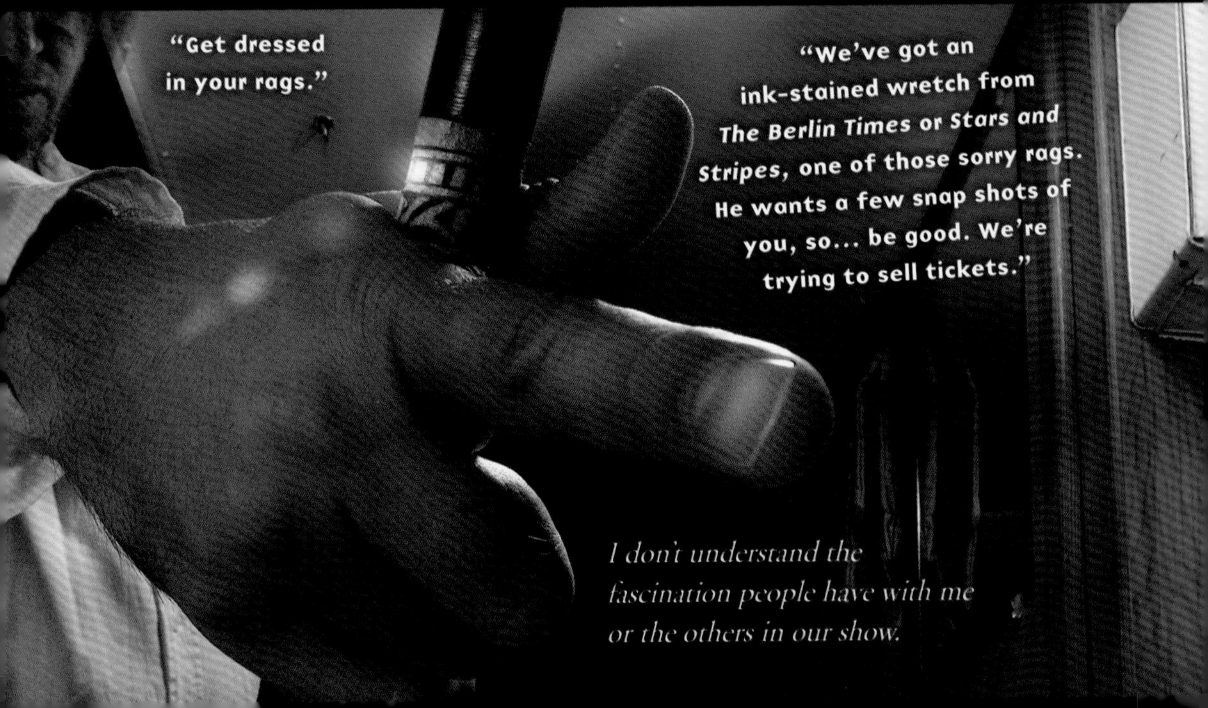
"Get dressed in your rags."
"We've got an ink-stained wretch from *The Berlin Times* or *Stars and Stripes*, one of those sorry rags. He wants a few snap shots of you, so... be good. We're trying to sell tickets."
I don't understand the fascination people have with me or the others in our show.

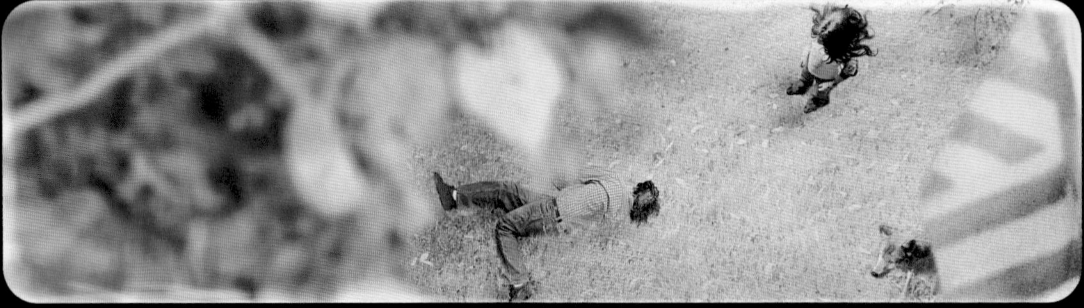

People are told I live like a jackal, that my tresses are so fearsome they can crush bone, bend steel fencing from its heavy moorings…

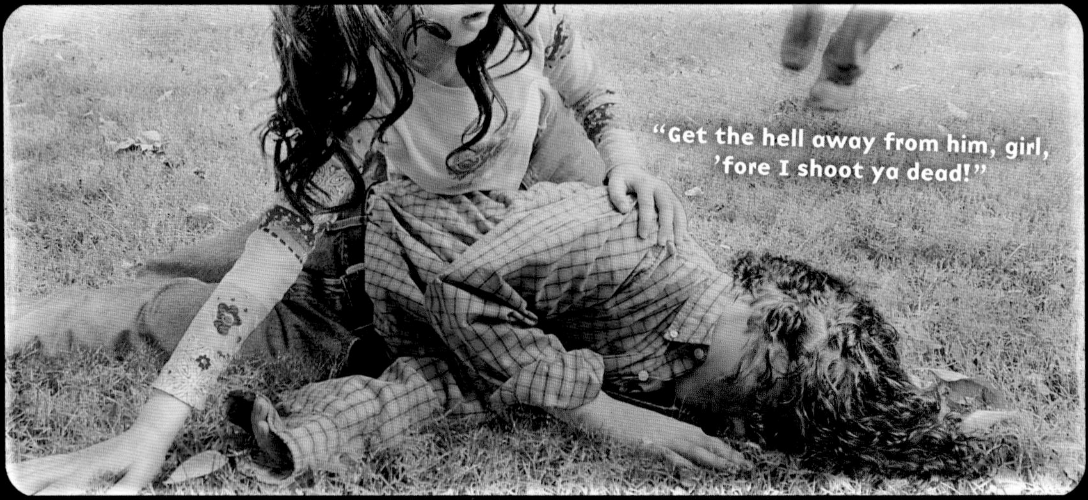
"Get the hell away from him, girl, 'fore I shoot ya dead!"

…and harm people around me, which I did once when I was young.

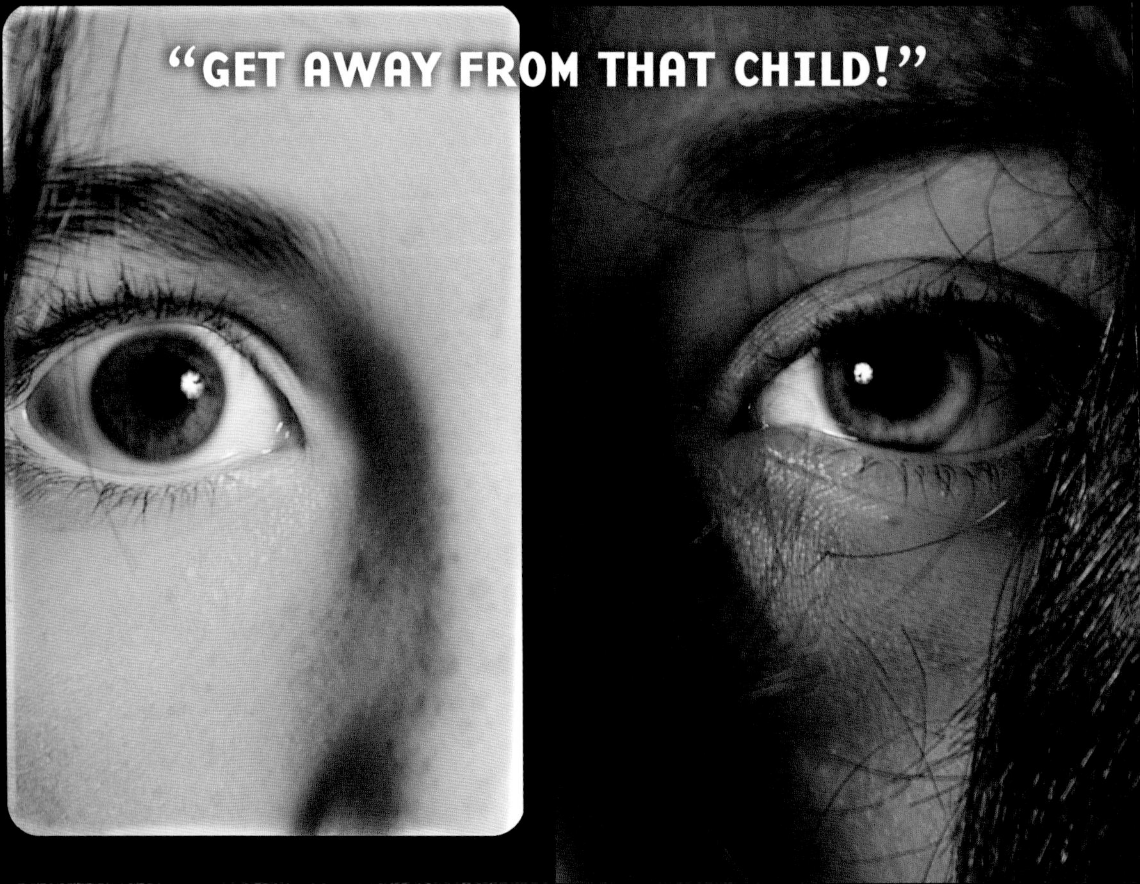
"GET AWAY FROM THAT CHILD!"

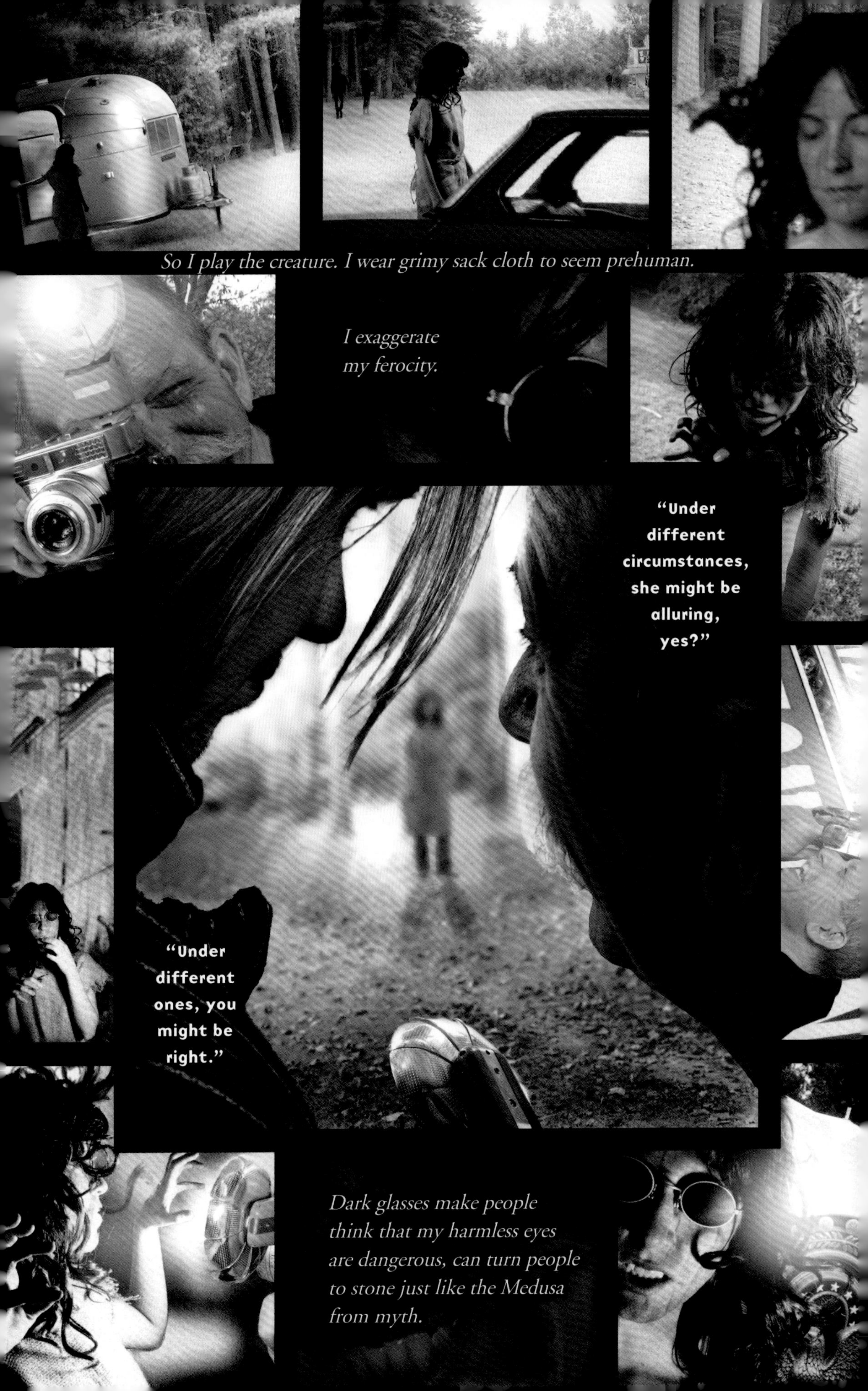
So I play the creature. I wear grimy sack cloth to seem prehuman.
I exaggerate my ferocity.
"Under different circumstances, she might be alluring, yes?"
"Under different ones, you might be right."
Dark glasses make people think that my harmless eyes are dangerous, can turn people to stone just like the Medusa from myth.

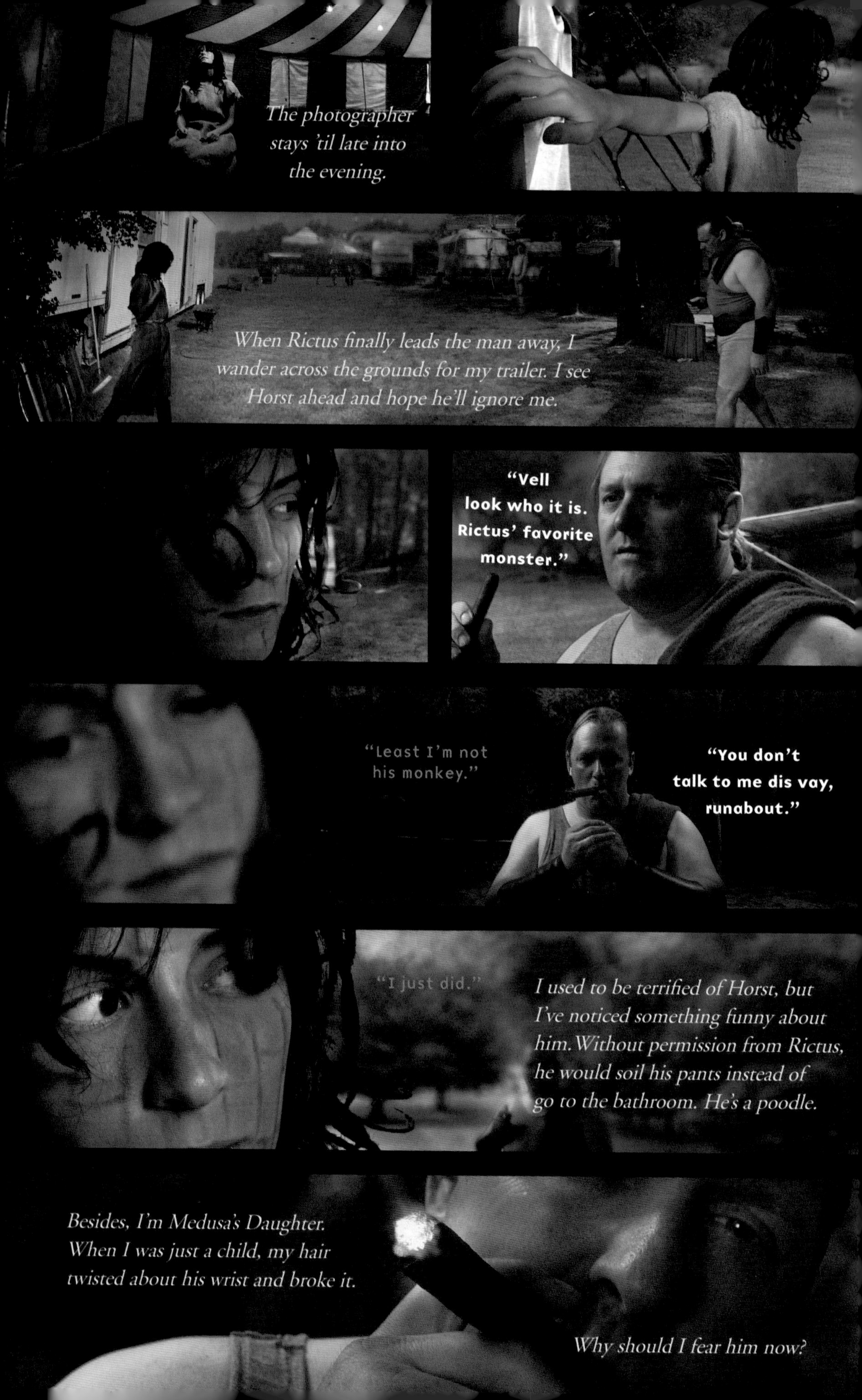

The photographer stays 'til late into the evening.
When Rictus finally leads the man away, I wander across the grounds for my trailer. I see Horst ahead and hope he'll ignore me.
"Vell look who it is. Rictus' favorite monster."
"Least I'm not his monkey."
"You don't talk to me dis vay, runabout."
"I just did."
I used to be terrified of Horst, but I've noticed something funny about him. Without permission from Rictus, he would soil his pants instead of go to the bathroom. He's a poodle.
Besides, I'm Medusa's Daughter. When I was just a child, my hair twisted about his wrist and broke it.
Why should I fear him now?

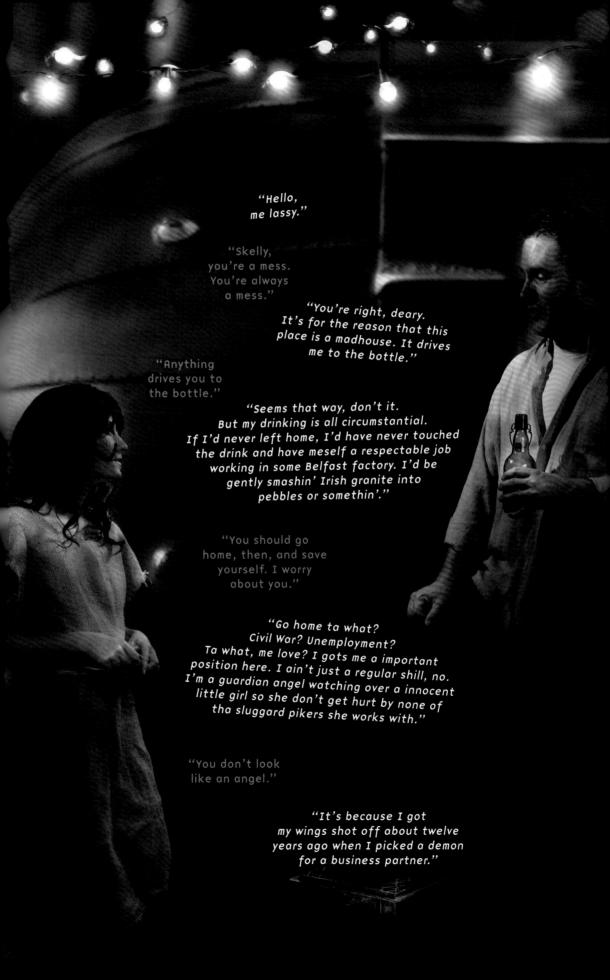

"Hello,
me lassy."

"Skelly,
you're a mess.
You're always
a mess."

"You're right, deary.
It's for the reason that this
place is a madhouse. It drives
me to the bottle."

"Anything
drives you to
the bottle."

"Seems that way, don't it.
But my drinking is all circumstantial.
If I'd never left home, I'd have never touched
the drink and have meself a respectable job
working in some Belfast factory. I'd be
gently smashin' Irish granite into
pebbles or somethin'."

"You should go
home, then, and save
yourself. I worry
about you."

"Go home ta what?
Civil War? Unemployment?
Ta what, me love? I gots me a important
position here. I ain't just a regular shill, no.
I'm a guardian angel watching over a innocent
little girl so she don't get hurt by none of
tha sluggard pikers she works with."

"You don't look
like an angel."

"It's because I got
my wings shot off about twelve
years ago when I picked a demon
for a business partner."

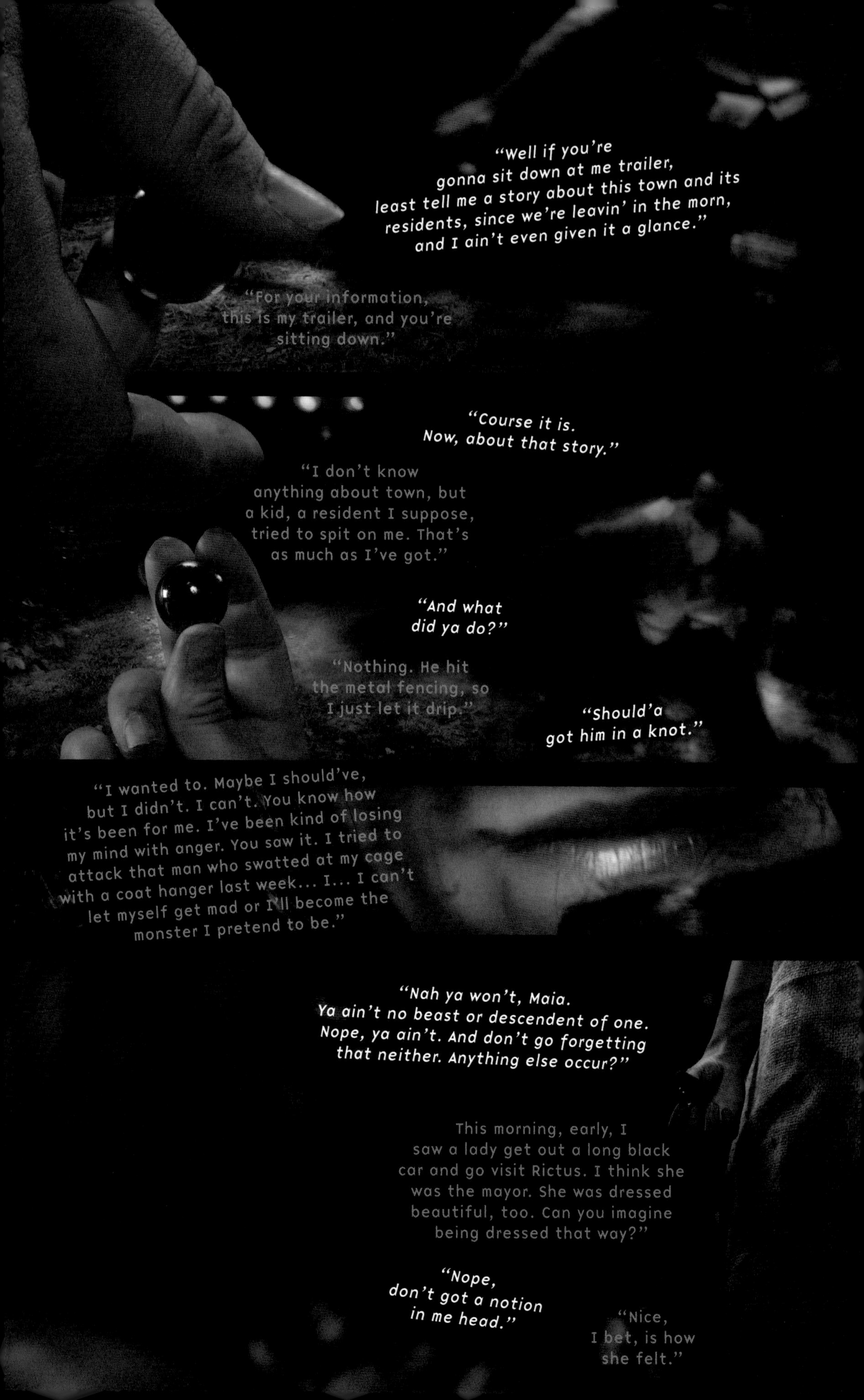
"Well if you're gonna sit down at me trailer, least tell me a story about this town and its residents, since we're leavin' in the morn, and I ain't even given it a glance."
"For your information, this is my trailer, and you're sitting down."
"Course it is. Now, about that story."
"I don't know anything about town, but a kid, a resident I suppose, tried to spit on me. That's as much as I've got."
"And what did ya do?"
"Nothing. He hit the metal fencing, so I just let it drip."
"Should'a got him in a knot."
"I wanted to. Maybe I should've, but I didn't. I can't. You know how it's been for me. I've been kind of losing my mind with anger. You saw it. I tried to attack that man who swatted at my cage with a coat hanger last week... I... I can't let myself get mad or I'll become the monster I pretend to be."
"Nah ya won't, Maia. Ya ain't no beast or descendent of one. Nope, ya ain't. And don't go forgetting that neither. Anything else occur?"
This morning, early, I saw a lady get out a long black car and go visit Rictus. I think she was the mayor. She was dressed beautiful, too. Can you imagine being dressed that way?"
"Nope, don't got a notion in me head."
"Nice, I bet, is how she felt."

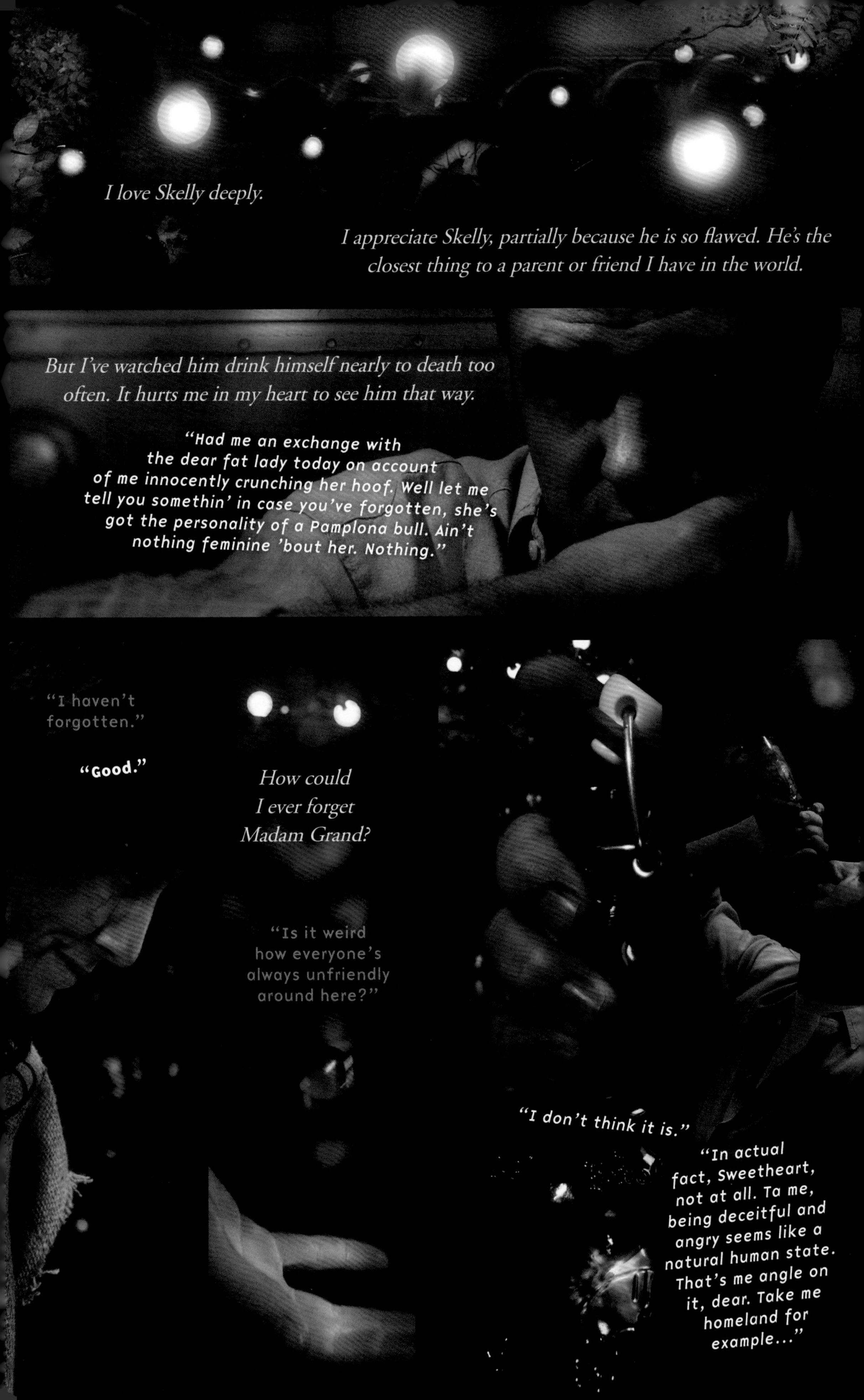
I love Skelly deeply.
I appreciate Skelly, partially because he is so flawed. He's the closest thing to a parent or friend I have in the world.
But I've watched him drink himself nearly to death too often. It hurts me in my heart to see him that way.
"Had me an exchange with the dear fat lady today on account of me innocently crunching her hoof. Well let me tell you somethin' in case you've forgotten, she's got the personality of a Pamplona bull. Ain't nothing feminine 'bout her. Nothing."
"I haven't forgotten."
"Good."
How could I ever forget Madam Grand?
"Is it weird how everyone's always unfriendly around here?"
"I don't think it is."
"In actual fact, Sweetheart, not at all. Ta me, being deceitful and angry seems like a natural human state. That's me angle on it, dear. Take me homeland for example..."

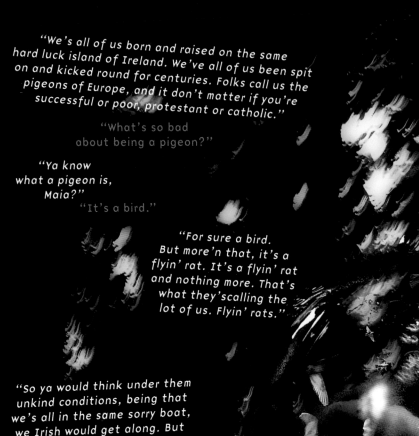

"We's all of us born and raised on the same hard luck island of Ireland. We've all of us been spit on and kicked round for centuries. Folks call us the pigeons of Europe, and it don't matter if you're successful or poor, protestant or catholic."

"What's so bad about being a pigeon?"

"Ya know what a pigeon is, Maia?"

"It's a bird."

"For sure a bird. But more'n that, it's a flyin' rat. It's a flyin' rat and nothing more. That's what they's calling the lot of us. Flyin' rats."

"So ya would think under them unkind conditions, being that we's all in the same sorry boat, we Irish would get along. But we don't for nothin'. We's all scrapping for our little bit. Top'a that, we gotta go sploding bombs and killing fellow flying rats in the name o' religion and the like, which ain't so very religious to me."

"Nope. It don't make sense. Just like this here mothy sideshow. We all get the short end of it from Rictus, and most of us have got his man Horst on our ass twice daily, but we don't come together a lick. We all wants our little bit'a the little bit there is, and to hell with our bleedin' co-workers. It's the sad, sorry, screwed-up human condition, and I for one aims ta drink 'til I forget it tonight."

That's what Skelly did, too.

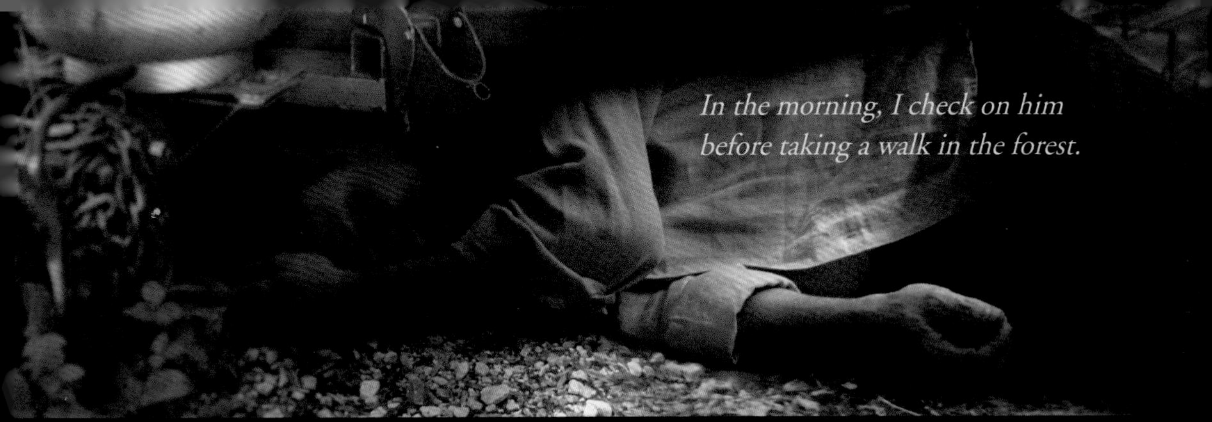

In the morning, I check on him before taking a walk in the forest.

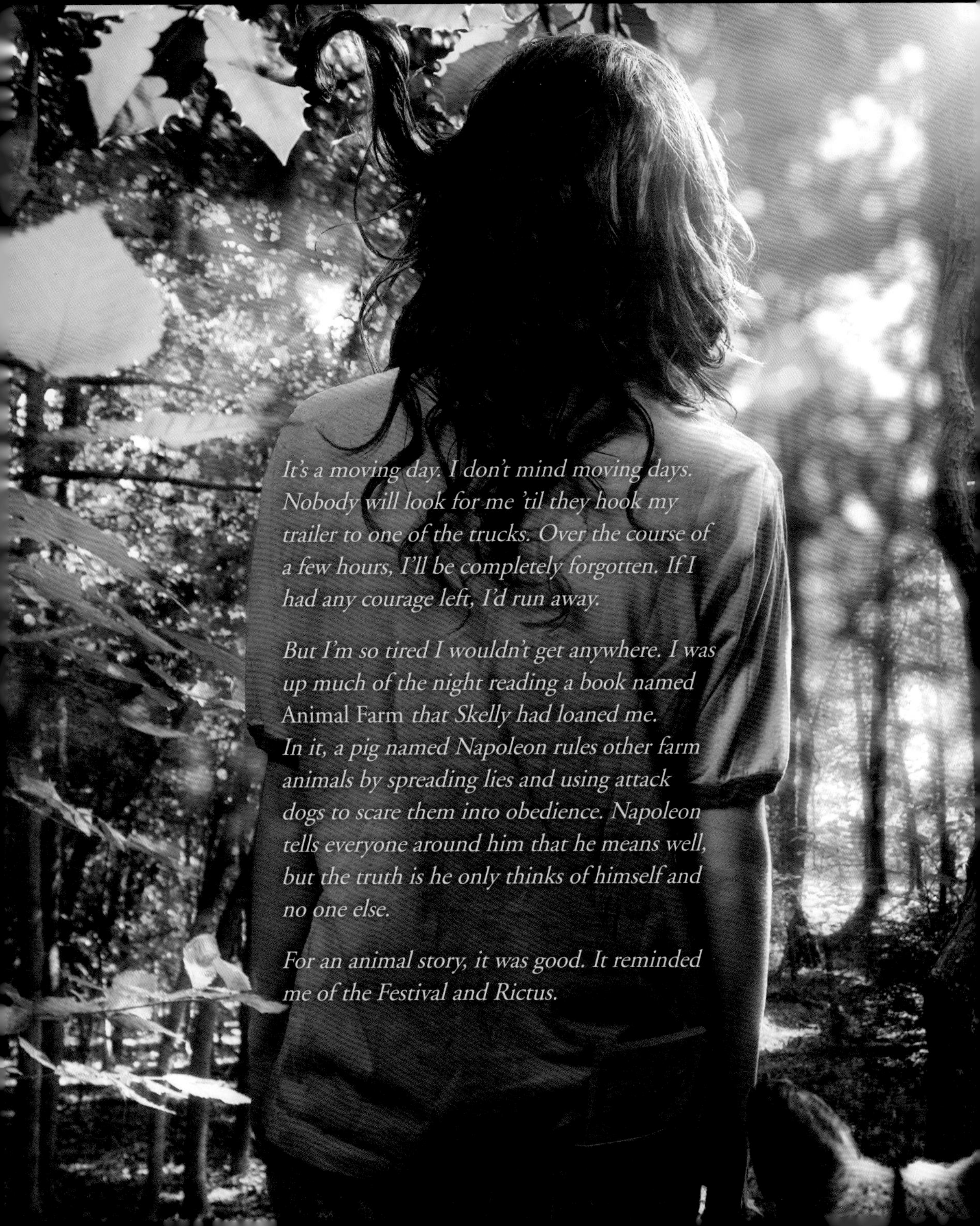

It's a moving day. I don't mind moving days. Nobody will look for me 'til they hook my trailer to one of the trucks. Over the course of a few hours, I'll be completely forgotten. If I had any courage left, I'd run away.

But I'm so tired I wouldn't get anywhere. I was up much of the night reading a book named Animal Farm *that Skelly had loaned me. In it, a pig named Napoleon rules other farm animals by spreading lies and using attack dogs to scare them into obedience. Napoleon tells everyone around him that he means well, but the truth is he only thinks of himself and no one else.*

For an animal story, it was good. It reminded me of the Festival and Rictus.

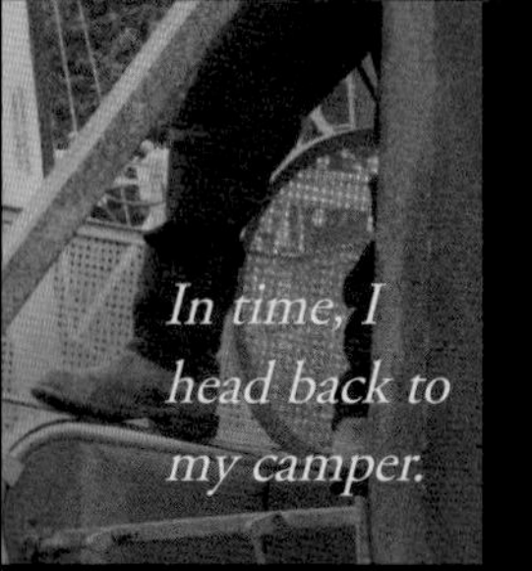
In time, I head back to my camper.

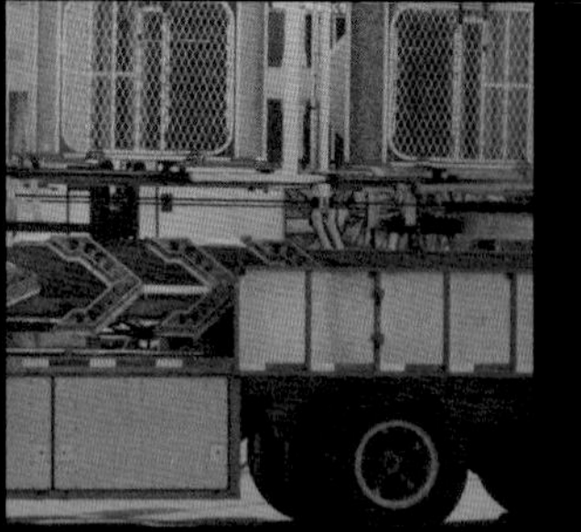

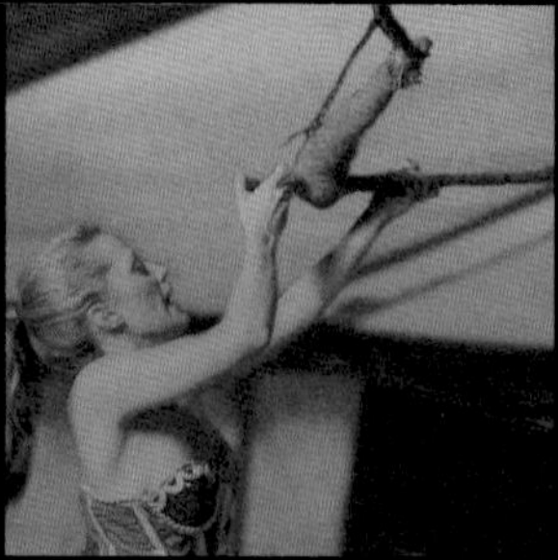

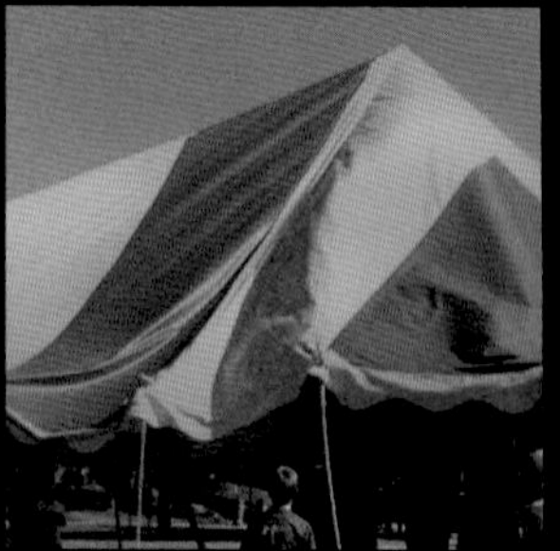

Skelly is gone. I go look for him but everyone is busy breaking the carnival down.

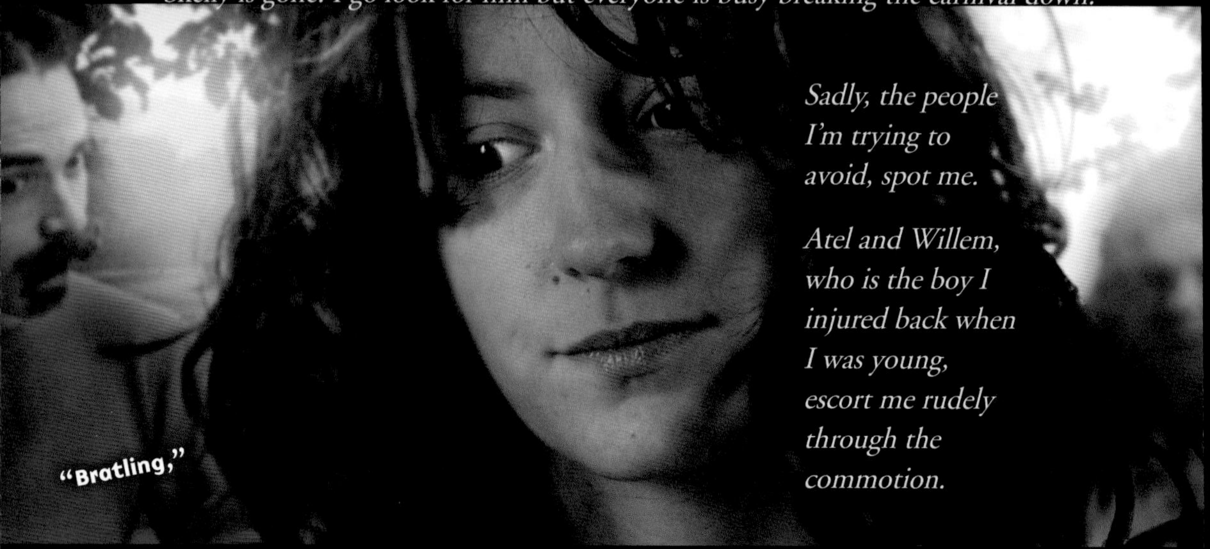
"Bratling,"
Sadly, the people I'm trying to avoid, spot me.
Atel and Willem, who is the boy I injured back when I was young, escort me rudely through the commotion.

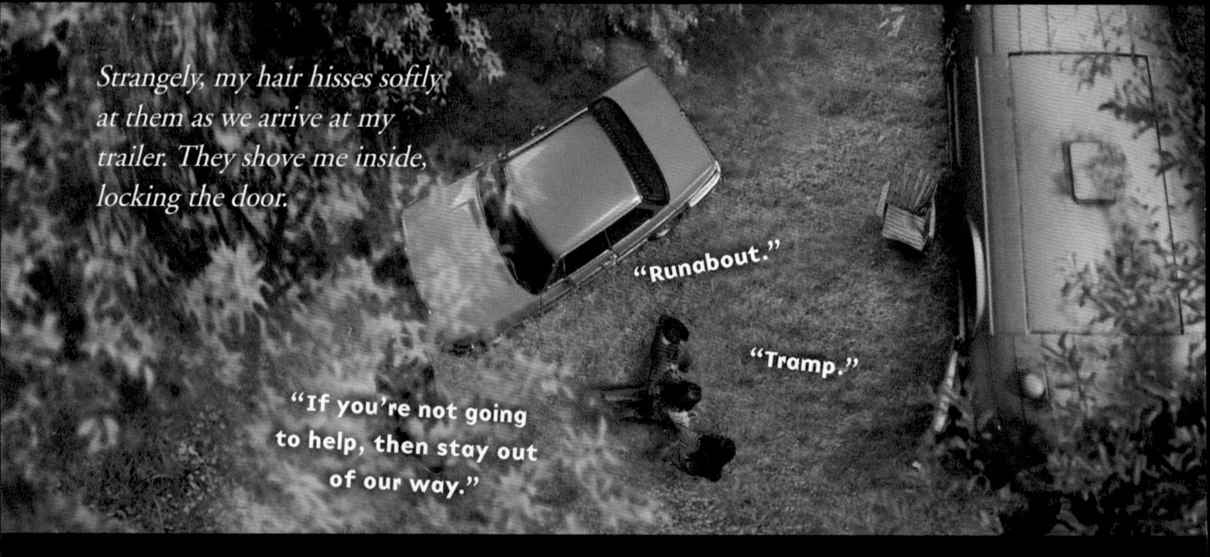
Strangely, my hair hisses softly at them as we arrive at my trailer. They shove me inside, locking the door.
"Runabout."
"Tramp."
"If you're not going to help, then stay out of our way."

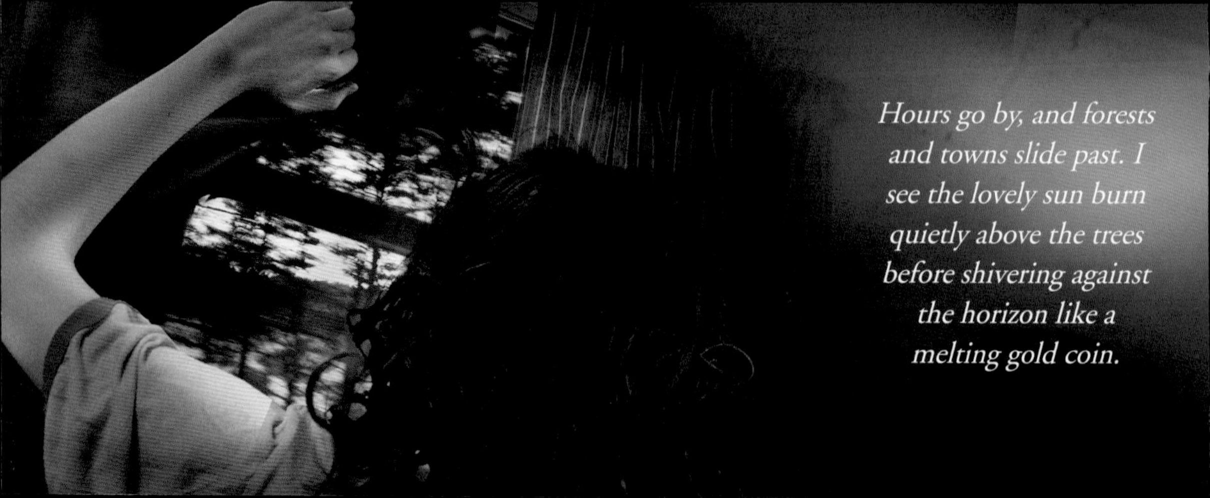
Hours go by, and forests and towns slide past. I see the lovely sun burn quietly above the trees before shivering against the horizon like a melting gold coin.

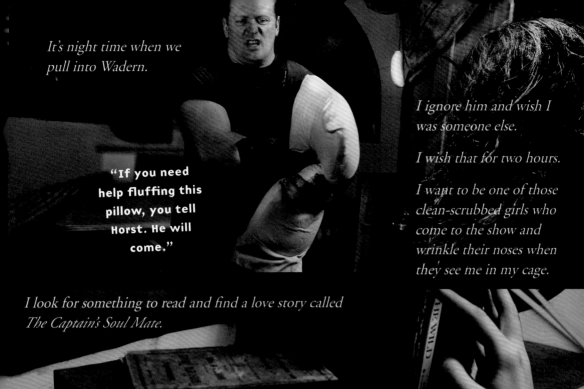

It's night time when we pull into Wadern.

"If you need help fluffing this pillow, you tell Horst. He will come."

I ignore him and wish I was someone else.

I wish that for two hours.

I want to be one of those clean-scrubbed girls who come to the show and wrinkle their noses when they see me in my cage.

I look for something to read and find a love story called *The Captain's Soul Mate*.

Before midnight, Skelly comes around.

"Lassy?"

"Are these stories real? Do people in America really fall in love this way?"

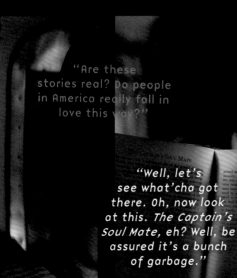

"Well, let's see what'cha got there. Oh, now look at this. *The Captain's Soul Mate*, eh? Well, be assured it's a bunch of garbage."

"But, yes, dear, people fall hopelessly and passionately in love all tha time, not just in America neither."

I don't really believe him. Nobody I've ever met, other than him, seems capable of caring for anyone but themselves.

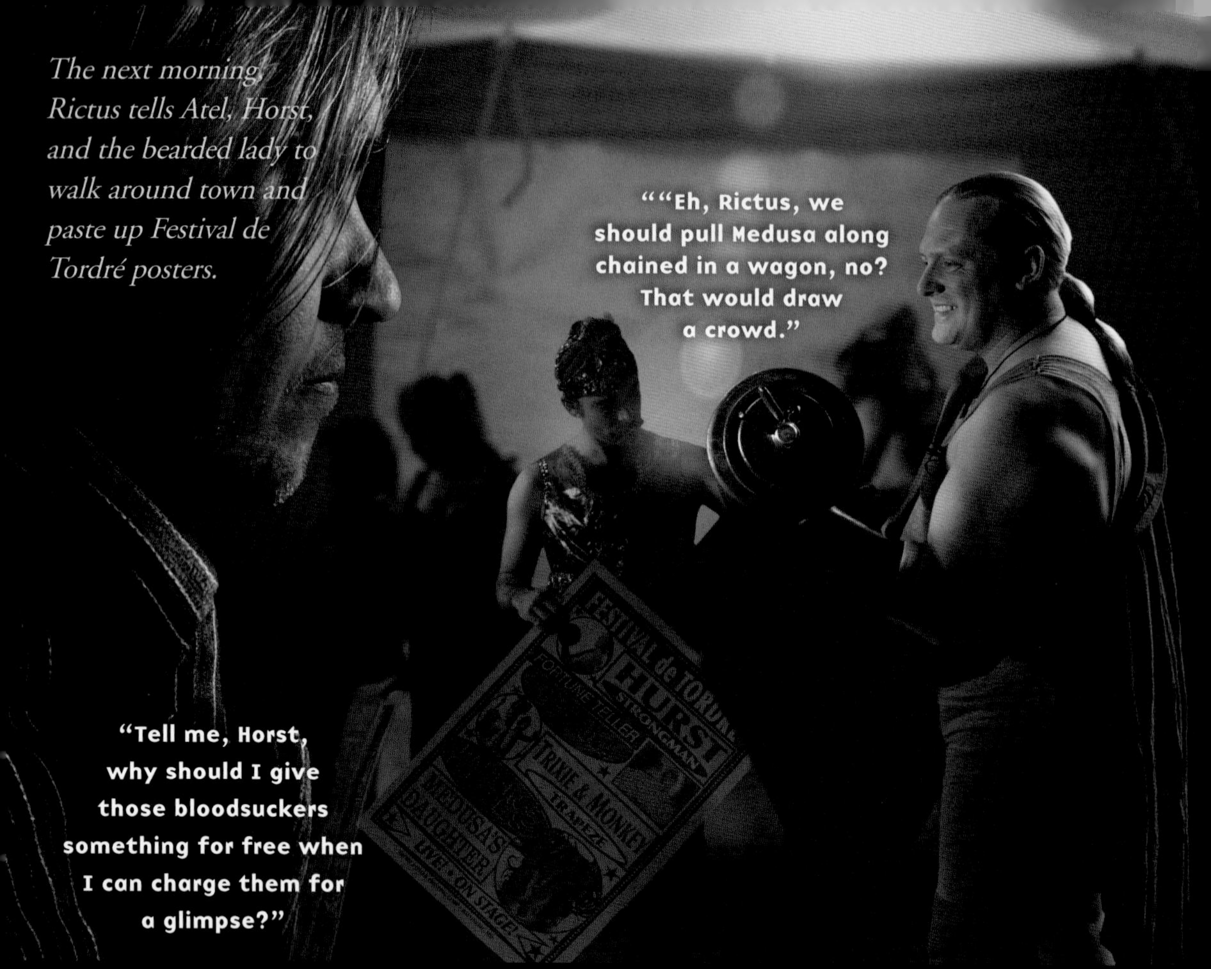
The next morning, Rictus tells Atel, Horst, and the bearded lady to walk around town and paste up Festival de Tordré posters.
““Eh, Rictus, we should pull Medusa along chained in a wagon, no? That would draw a crowd.”
“Tell me, Horst, why should I give those bloodsuckers something for free when I can charge them for a glimpse?”

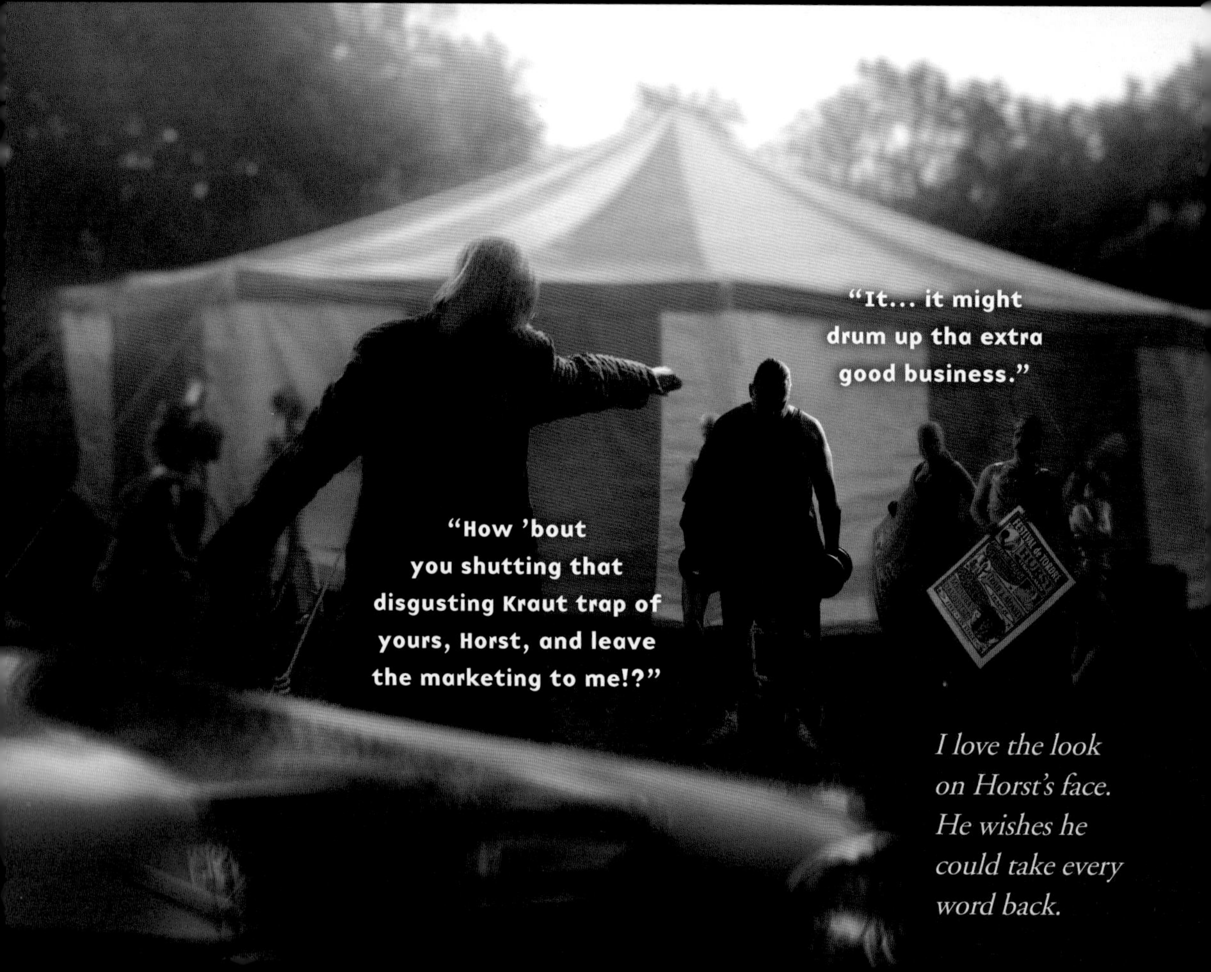
“It... it might drum up tha extra good business.”
“How ’bout you shutting that disgusting Kraut trap of yours, Horst, and leave the marketing to me!?”
I love the look on Horst’s face. He wishes he could take every word back.

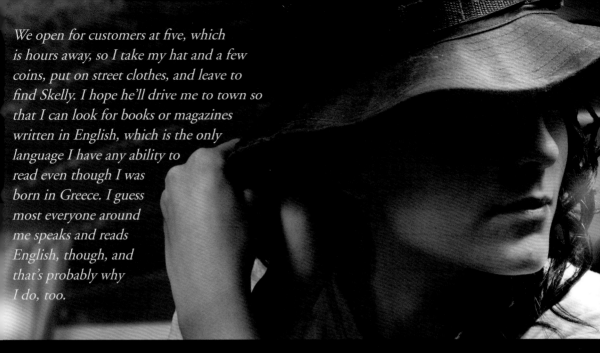

We open for customers at five, which is hours away, so I take my hat and a few coins, put on street clothes, and leave to find Skelly. I hope he'll drive me to town so that I can look for books or magazines written in English, which is the only language I have any ability to read even though I was born in Greece. I guess most everyone around me speaks and reads English, though, and that's probably why I do, too.

"Sure... we can go, Love."

"Just you allow me to go tell Rictus so that I don't get accused of trying to fly the coop with ya."

"Why would anyone try to fly the coop with me? Rictus would just, well, probably kill them if they got caught."

"Sure enough. Ya are his silk purse. His main attraction."

"Will you go ask, then?"

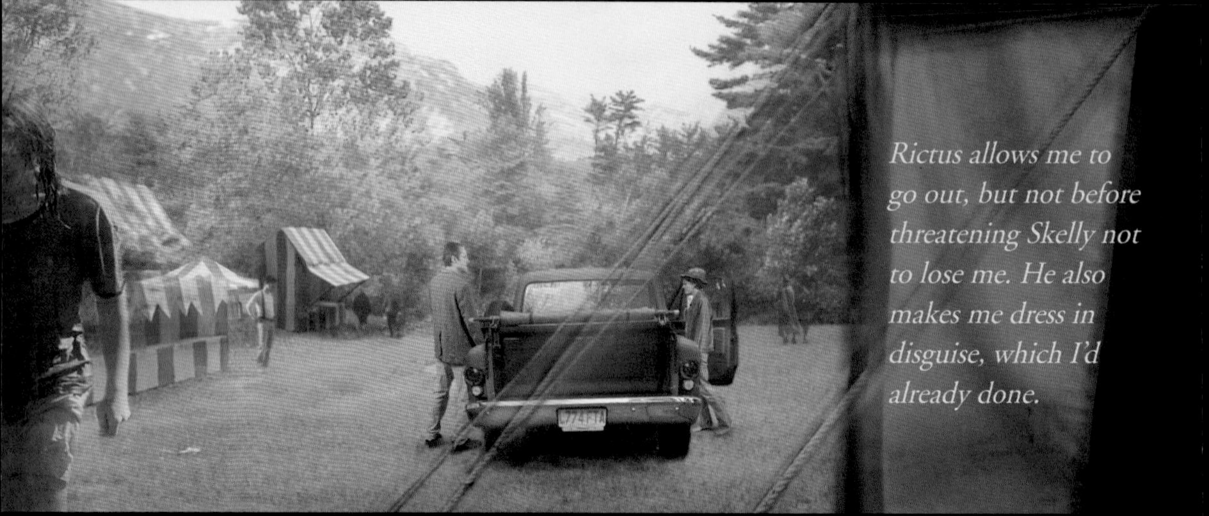
Rictus allows me to go out, but not before threatening Skelly not to lose me. He also makes me dress in disguise, which I'd already done.

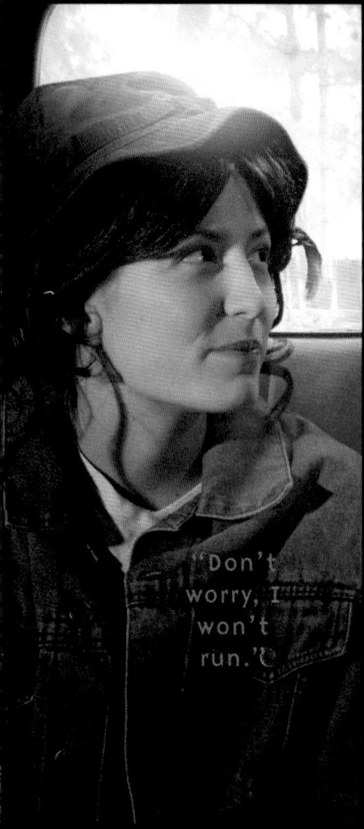
"Don't worry, I won't run."

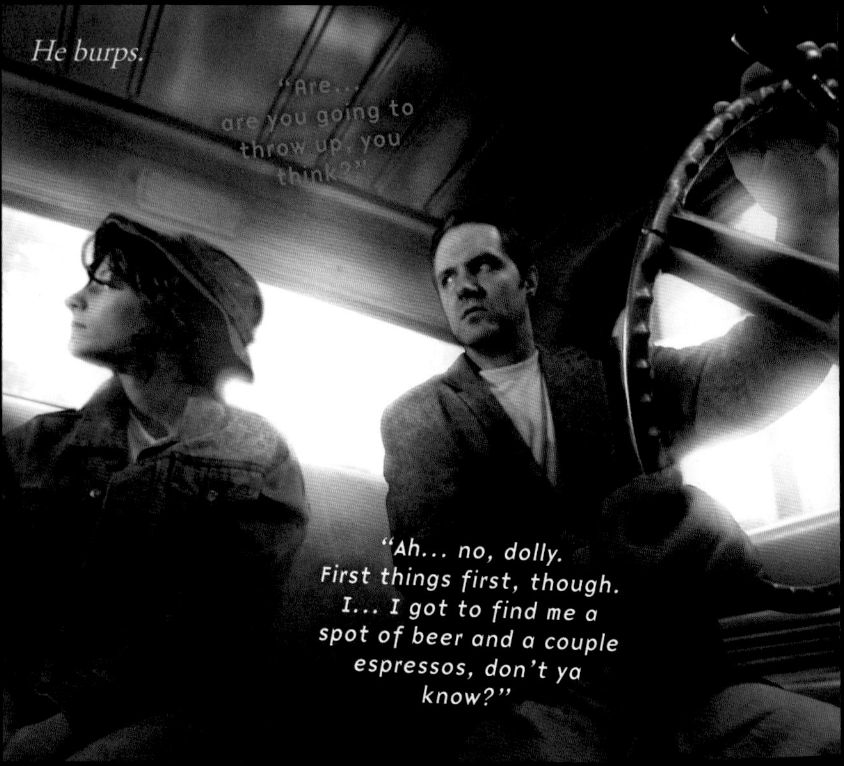
He burps.
"Are... are you going to throw up, you think?"
"Ah... no, dolly. First things first, though. I... I got to find me a spot of beer and a couple espressos, don't ya know?"

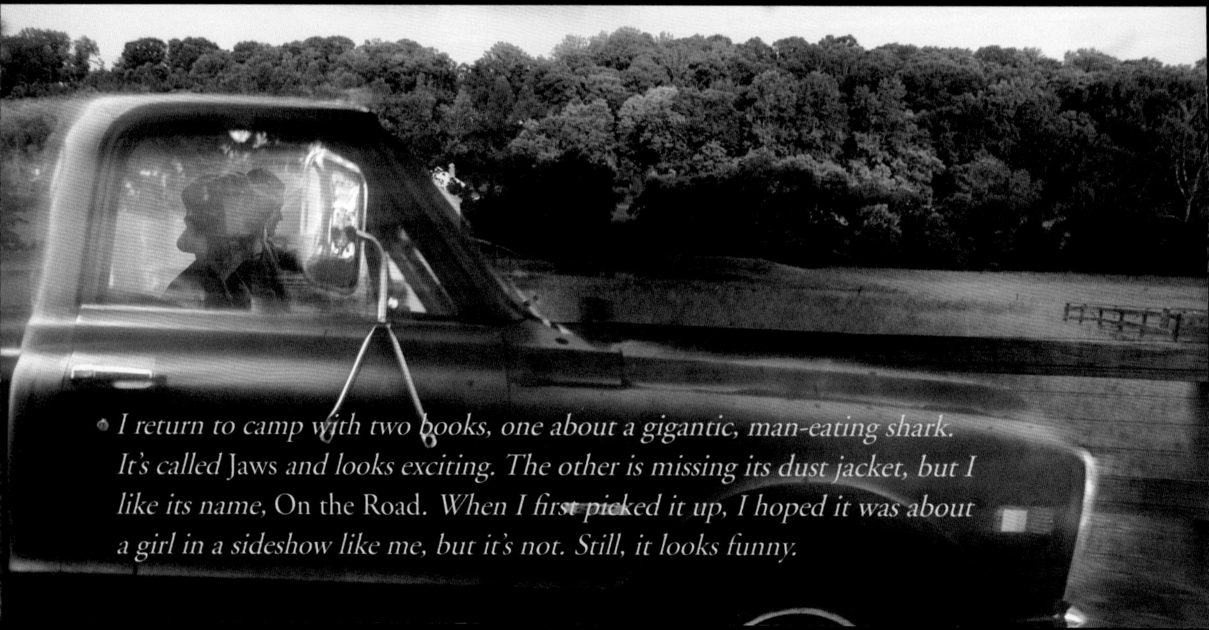
I return to camp with two books, one about a gigantic, man-eating shark. It's called Jaws and looks exciting. The other is missing its dust jacket, but I like its name, On the Road. When I first picked it up, I hoped it was about a girl in a sideshow like me, but it's not. Still, it looks funny.

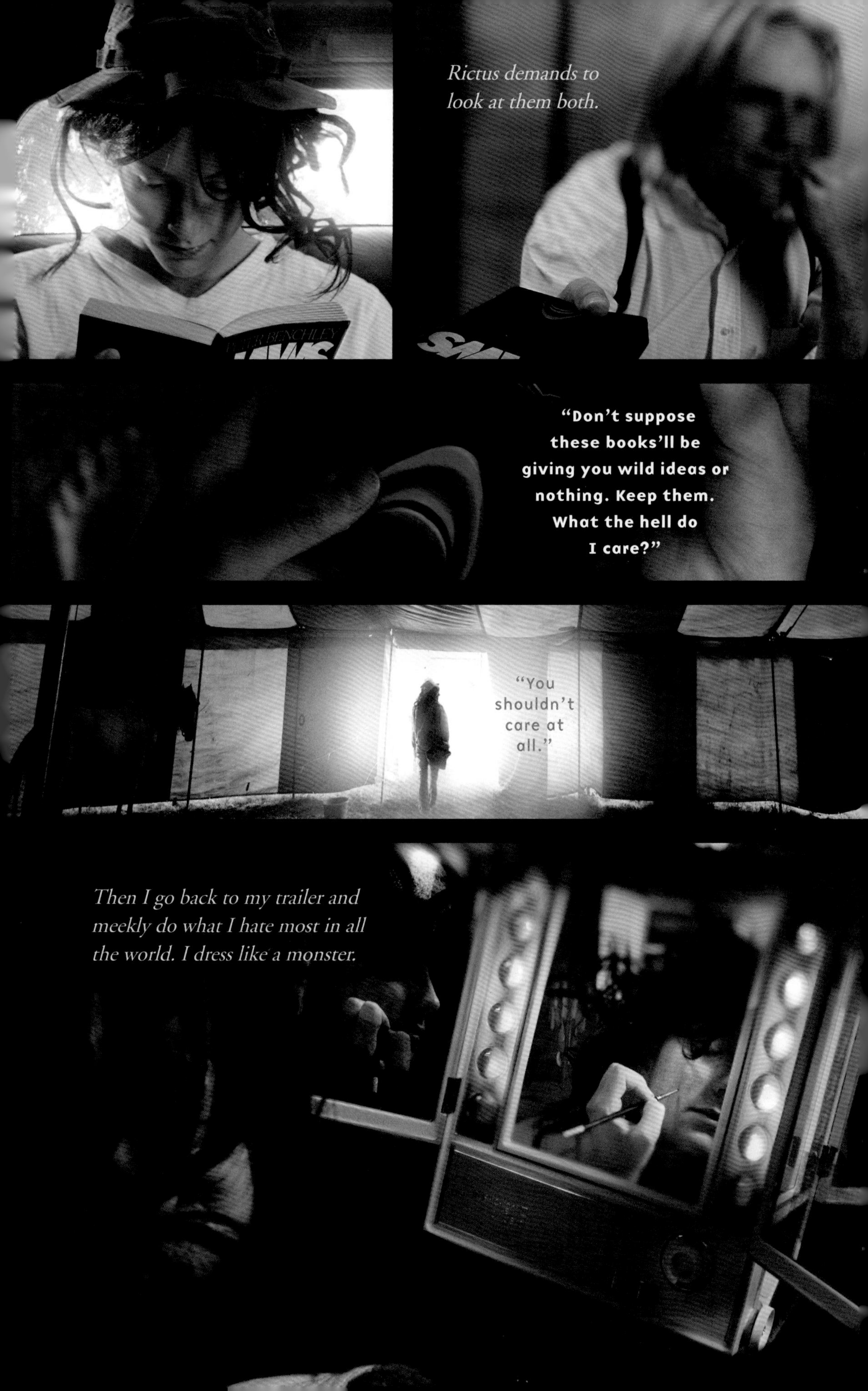
Rictus demands to look at them both.
"Don't suppose these books'll be giving you wild ideas or nothing. Keep them. What the hell do I care?"
"You shouldn't care at all."
Then I go back to my trailer and meekly do what I hate most in all the world. I dress like a monster.

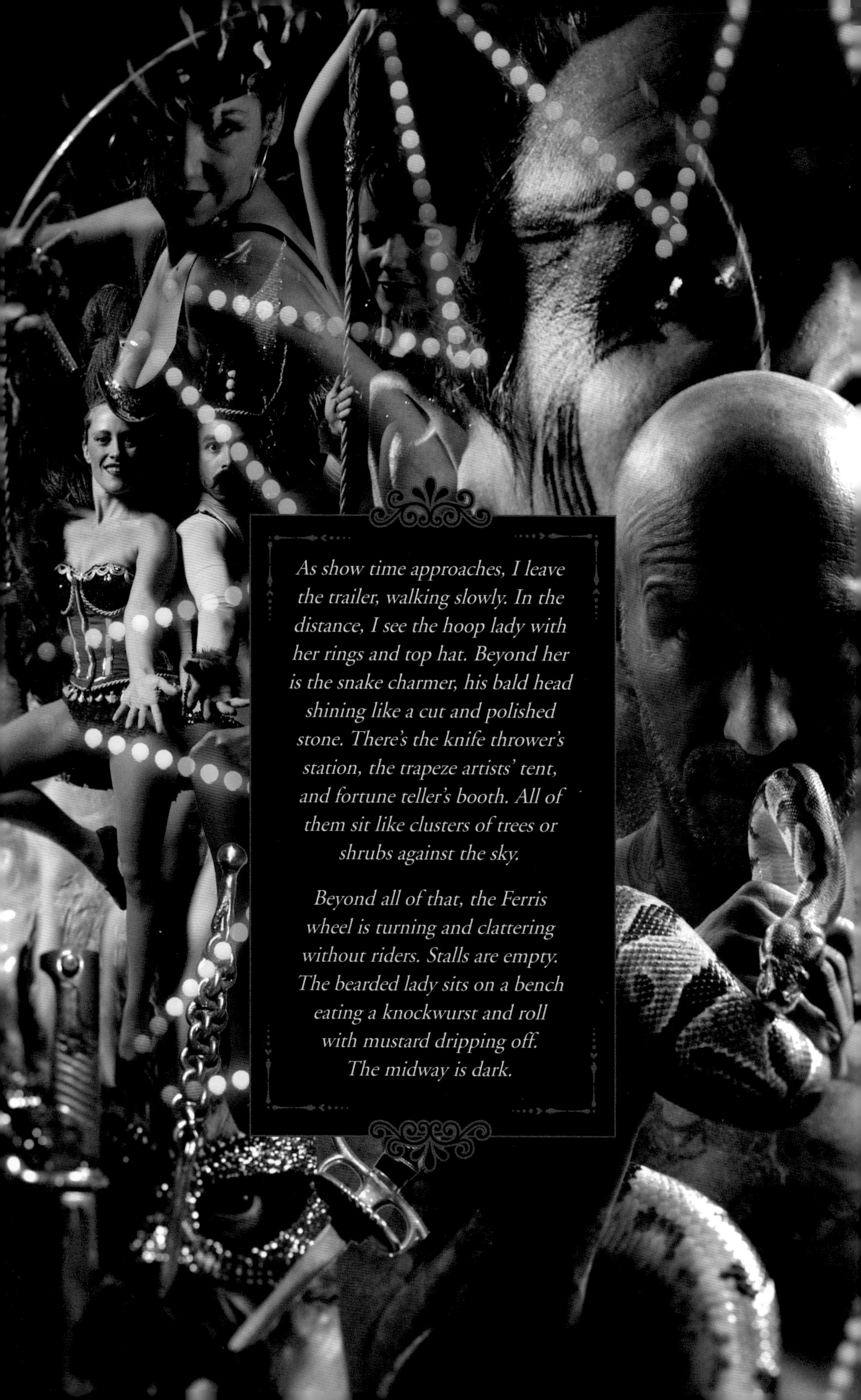

As show time approaches, I leave the trailer, walking slowly. In the distance, I see the hoop lady with her rings and top hat. Beyond her is the snake charmer, his bald head shining like a cut and polished stone. There's the knife thrower's station, the trapeze artists' tent, and fortune teller's booth. All of them sit like clusters of trees or shrubs against the sky.

Beyond all of that, the Ferris wheel is turning and clattering without riders. Stalls are empty. The bearded lady sits on a bench eating a knockwurst and roll with mustard dripping off. The midway is dark.

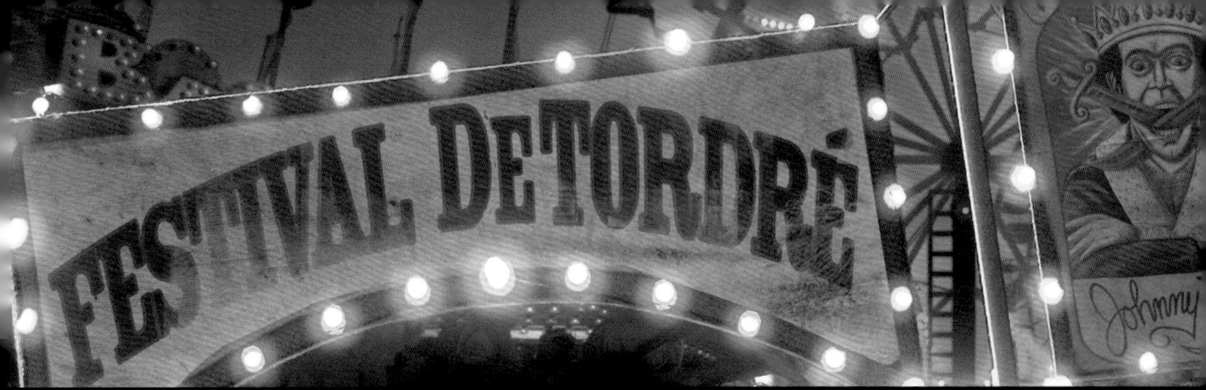
FESTIVAL DETORDRÉ
Johnny

The gates open and crowds swell. In my tent, Skelly climbs atop a box.

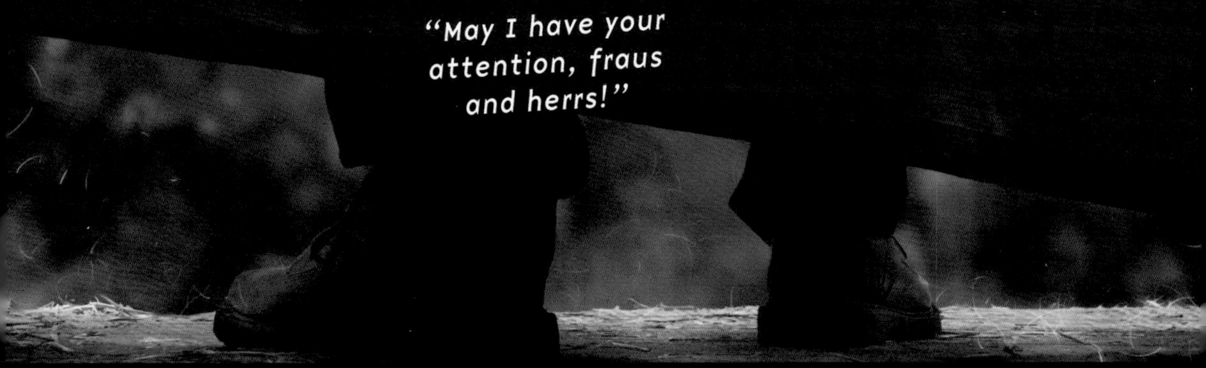
"May I have your attention, fraus and herrs!"

"Fraus" and "herrs" is German for men and women. It's nearly all the German I know.

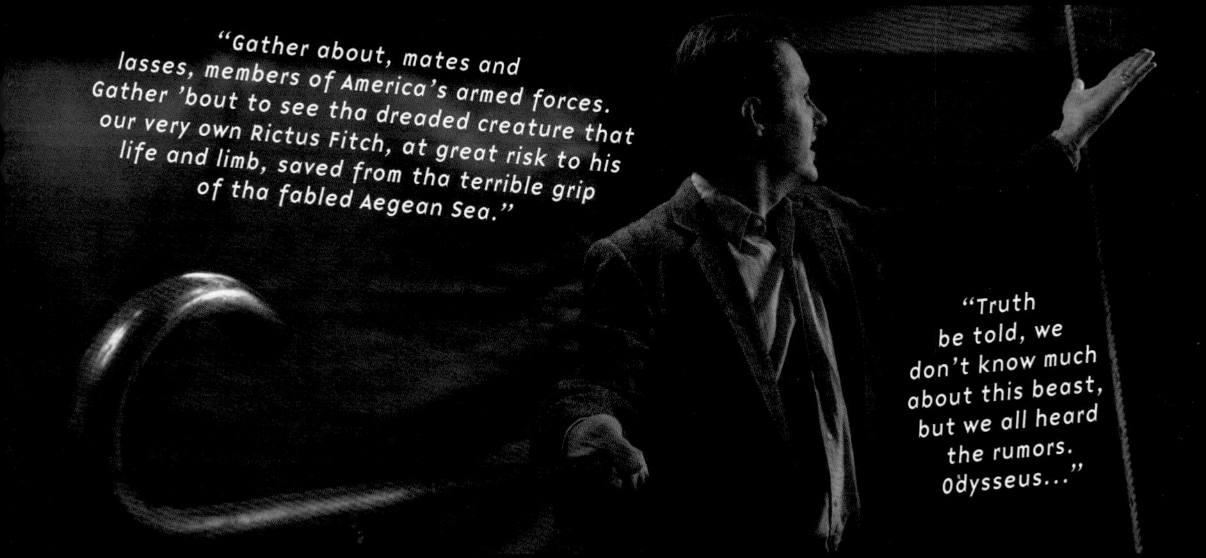
"Gather about, mates and lasses, members of America's armed forces. Gather 'bout to see tha dreaded creature that our very own Rictus Fitch, at great risk to his life and limb, saved from tha terrible grip of tha fabled Aegean Sea."
"Truth be told, we don't know much about this beast, but we all heard the rumors. Odysseus..."

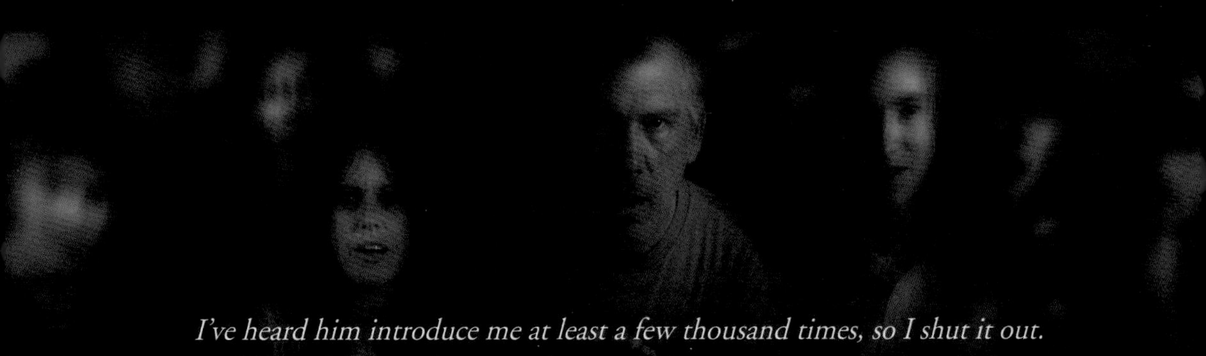

I've heard him introduce me at least a few thousand times, so I shut it out. When the drape is removed, though, I want to scream at the people gawking at me. I want to ask them why.

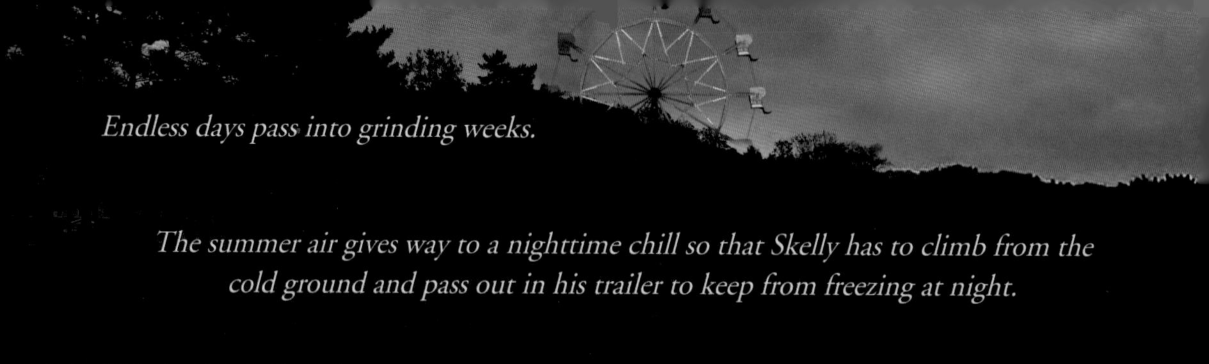
Endless days pass into grinding weeks.
The summer air gives way to a nighttime chill so that Skelly has to climb from the cold ground and pass out in his trailer to keep from freezing at night.

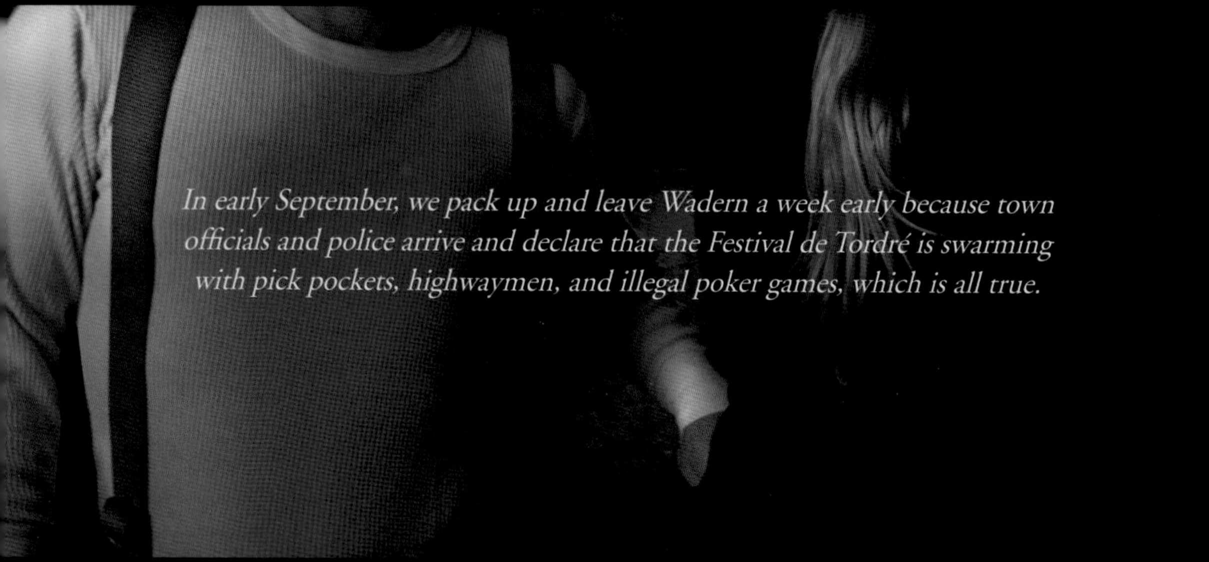
In early September, we pack up and leave Wadern a week early because town officials and police arrive and declare that the Festival de Tordré is swarming with pick pockets, highwaymen, and illegal poker games, which is all true.

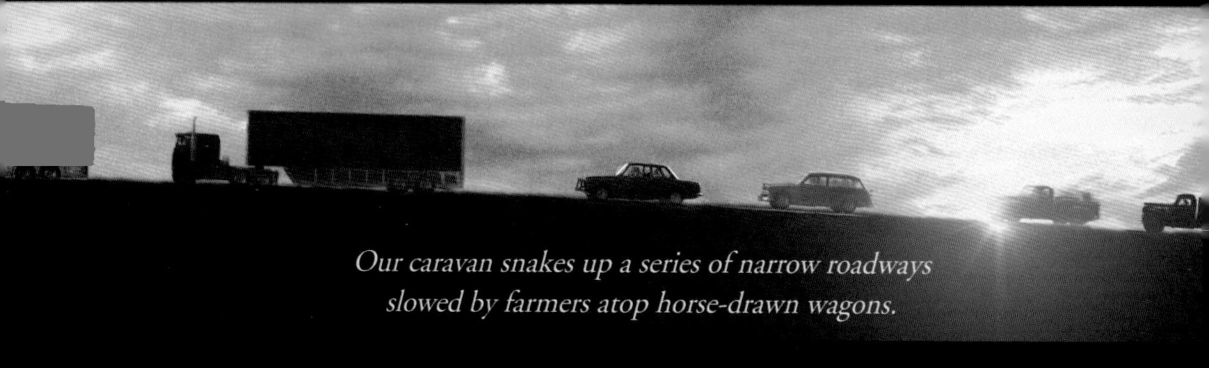
Our caravan snakes up a series of narrow roadways slowed by farmers atop horse-drawn wagons.

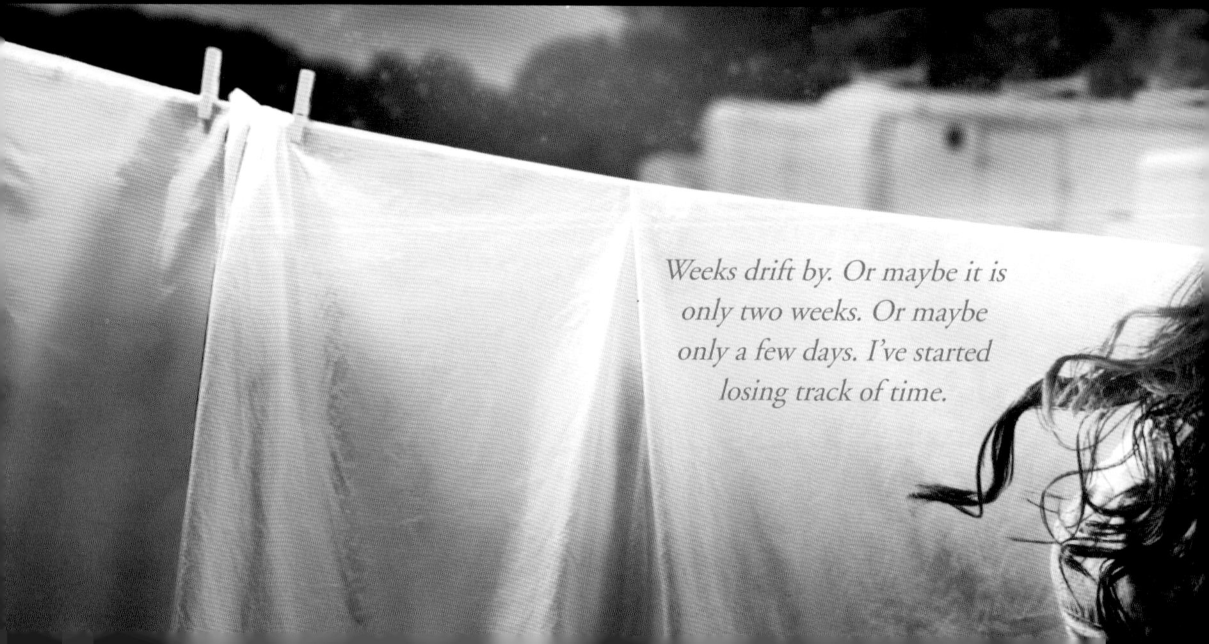
Weeks drift by. Or maybe it is only two weeks. Or maybe only a few days. I've started losing track of time.

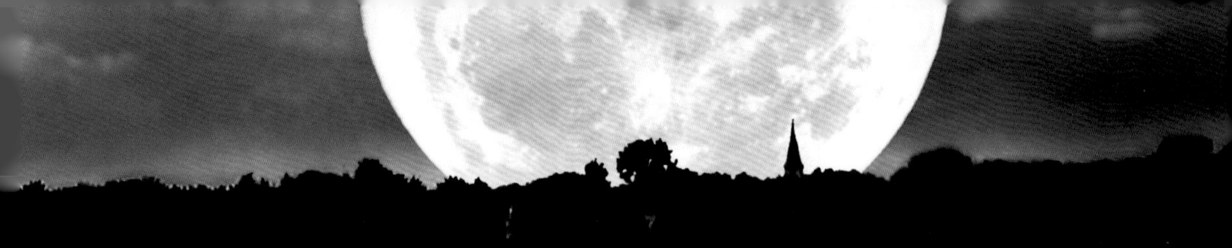

That or he shivers like a bottle atop a truck engine.
I know because I've found him doing it.

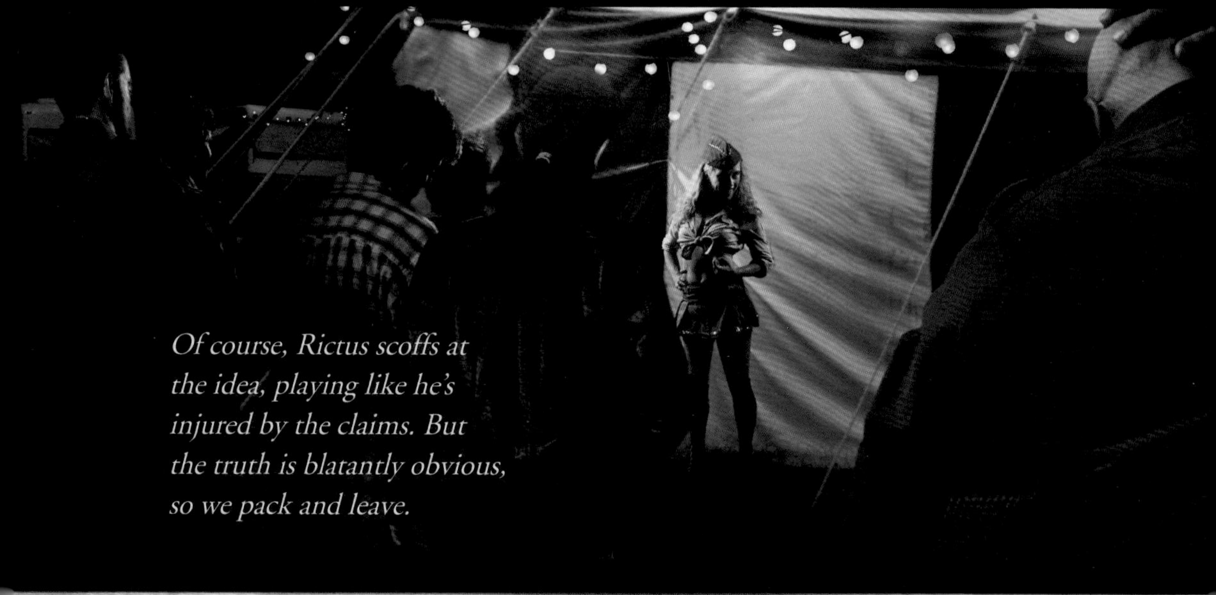

Of course, Rictus scoffs at the idea, playing like he's injured by the claims. But the truth is blatantly obvious, so we pack and leave.

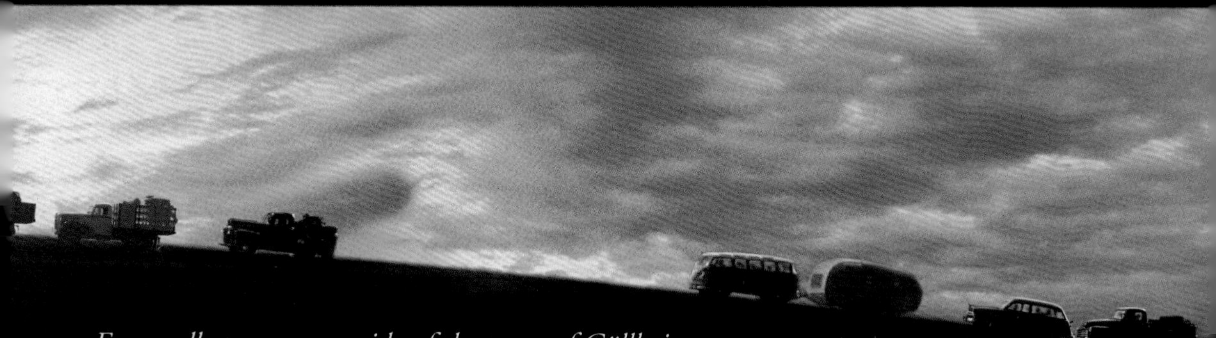

Eventually, we stop outside of the town of Göllheim.

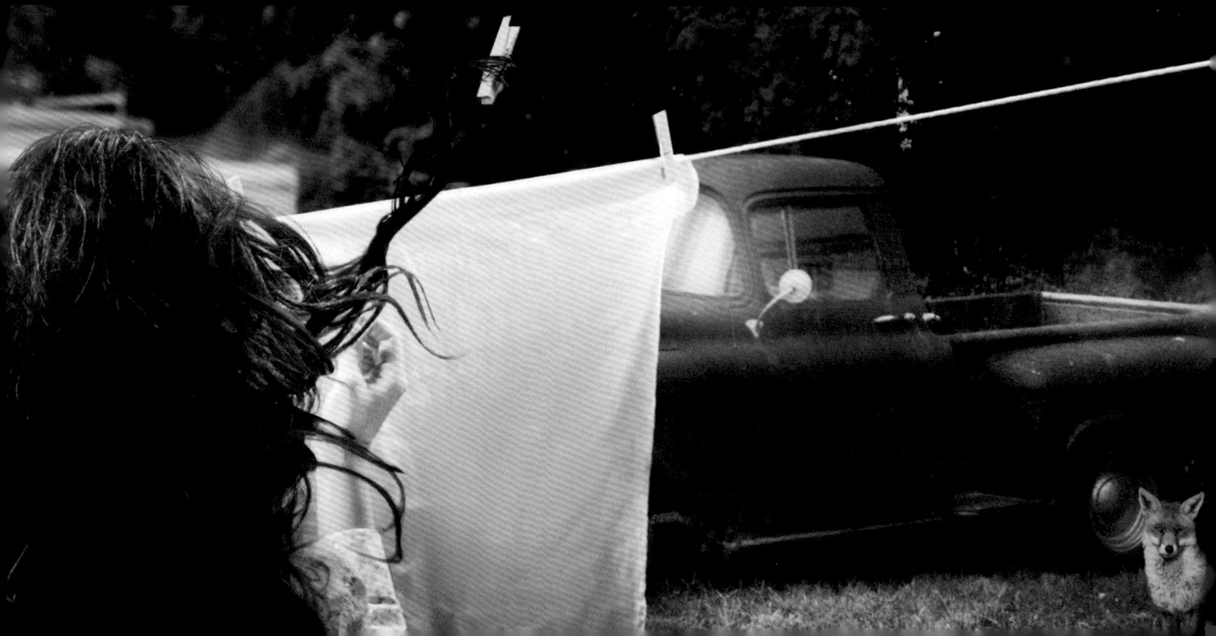

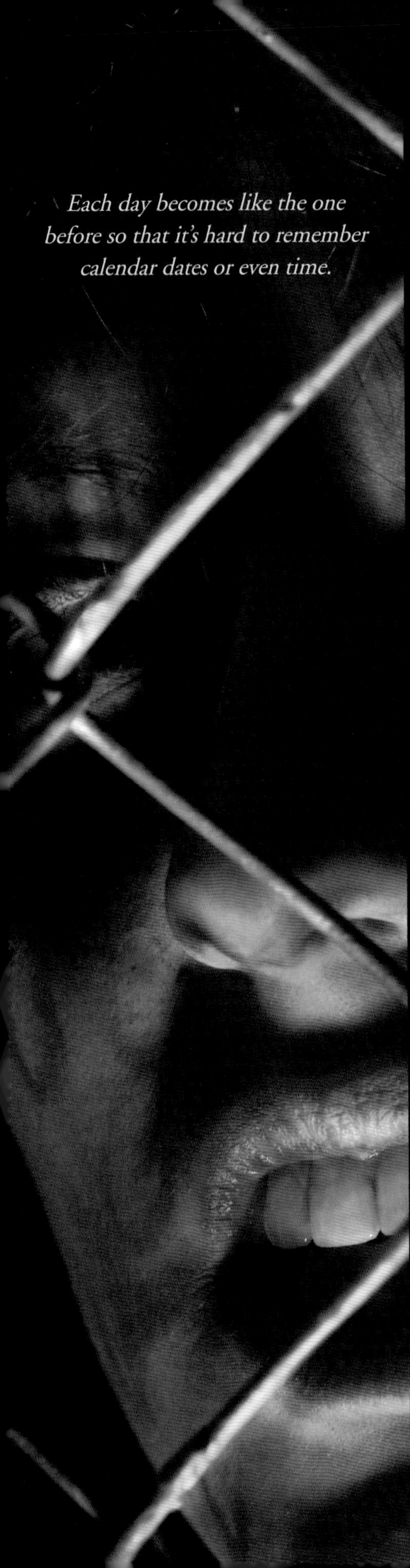

Each day becomes like the one before so that it's hard to remember calendar dates or even time.

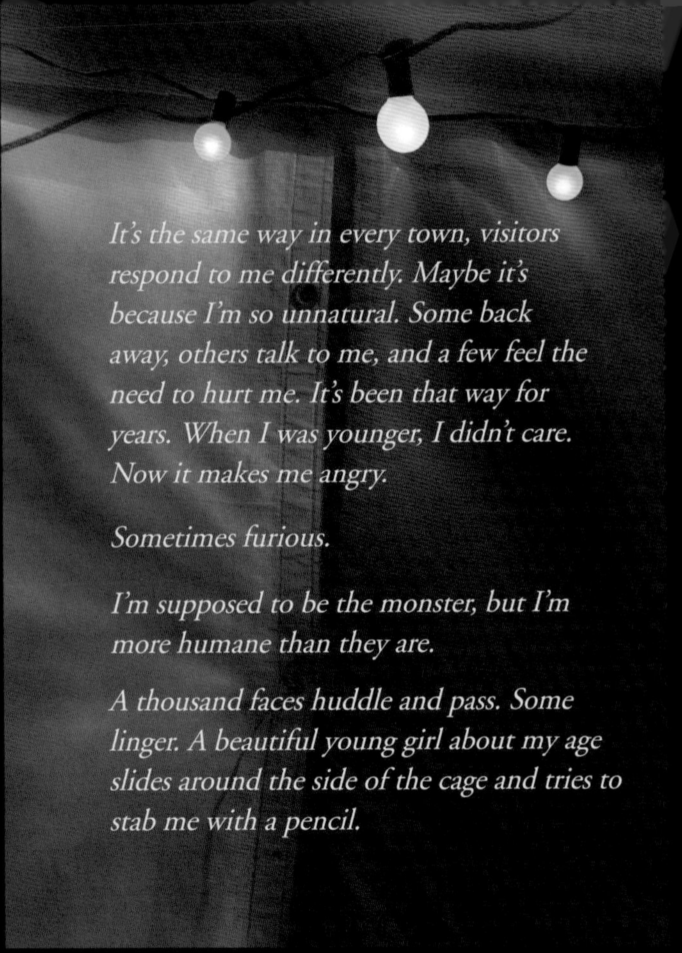

It's the same way in every town, visitors respond to me differently. Maybe it's because I'm so unnatural. Some back away, others talk to me, and a few feel the need to hurt me. It's been that way for years. When I was younger, I didn't care. Now it makes me angry.

Sometimes furious.

I'm supposed to be the monster, but I'm more humane than they are.

A thousand faces huddle and pass. Some linger. A beautiful young girl about my age slides around the side of the cage and tries to stab me with a pencil.

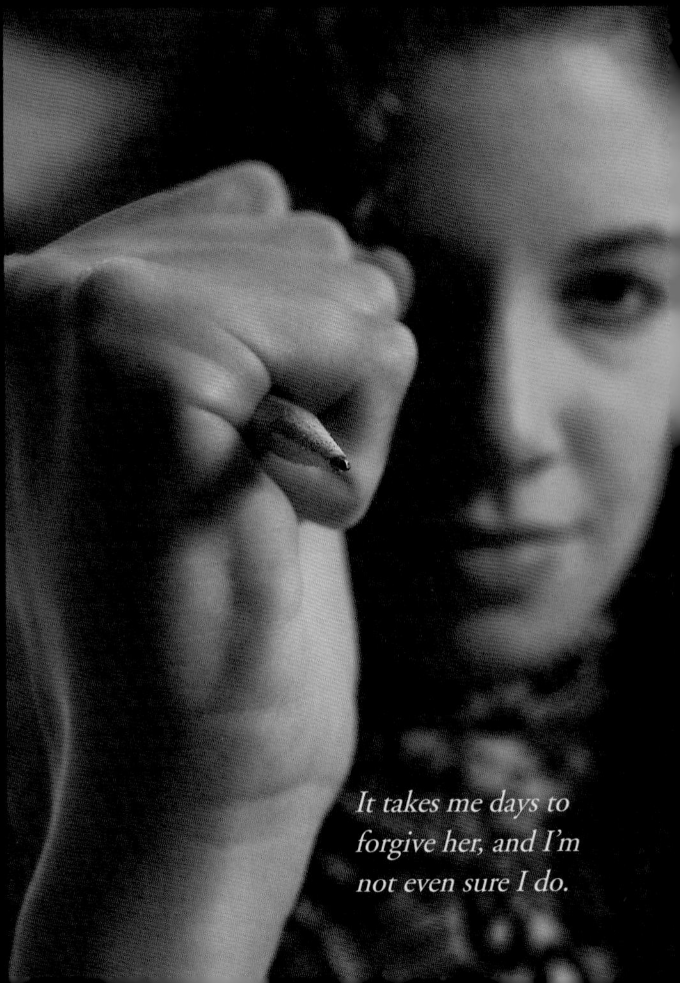

It takes me days to forgive her, and I'm not even sure I do.

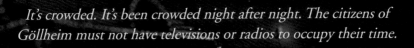

It's crowded. It's been crowded night after night. The citizens of Göllheim must not have televisions or radios to occupy their time.

Skelly stands on a box introducing me.

"Truth be told, we don't know much about this beast, but we all heard tha rumors! Odysseus stumbled upon her during his journey back from the Trojan War! She was a disgusting sight back then! A tragic beast! A horrible, soulless monster! Now behold, blokes!"

"Meet MEDUSA'S DAUGHTER!"

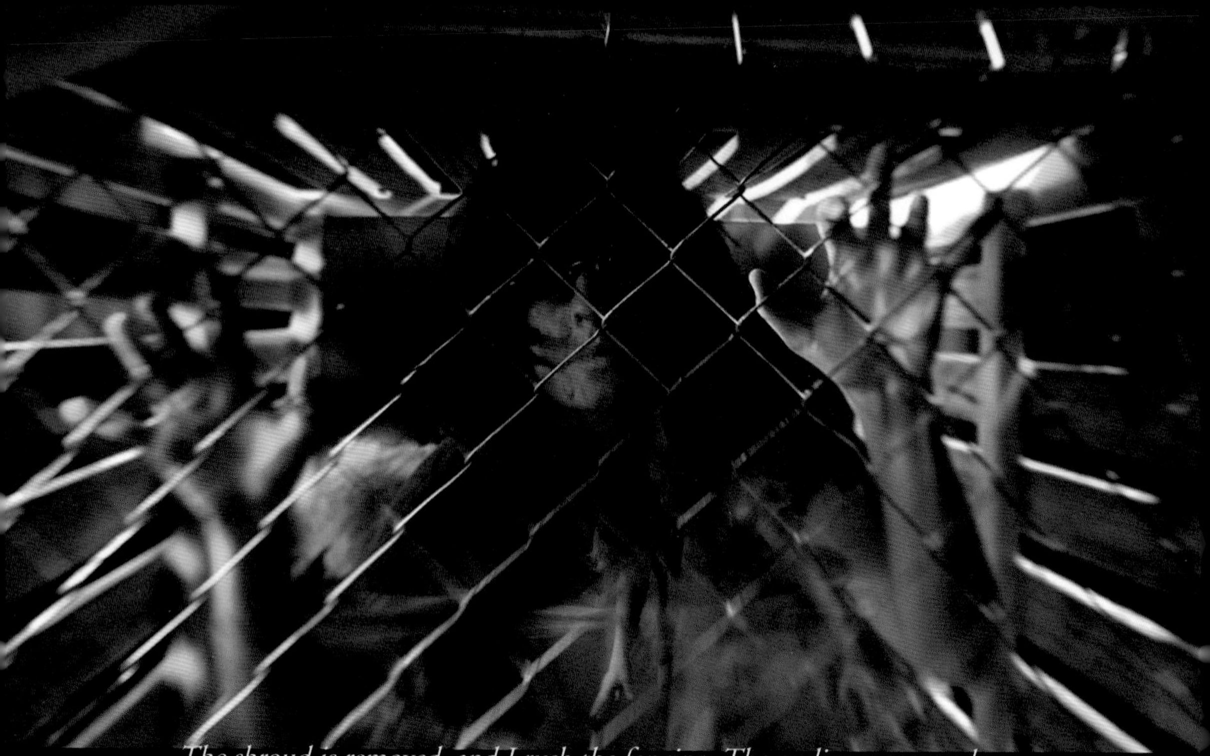

The shroud is removed, and I rush the fencing. The audience responds.

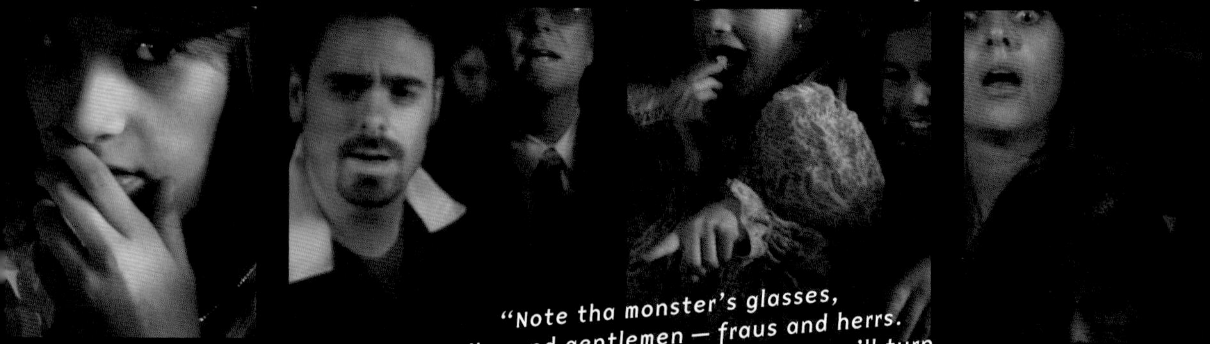

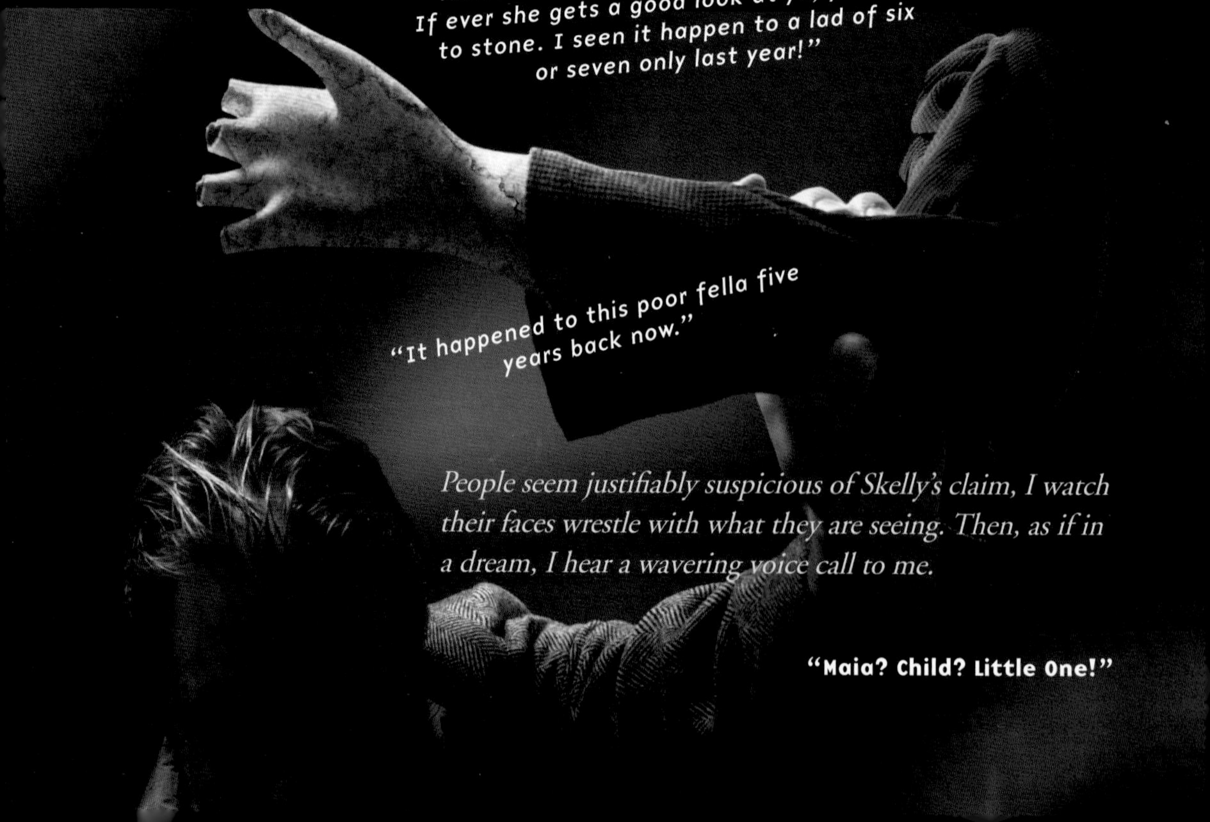
"Note tha monster's glasses, ladies and gentlemen — fraus and herrs. If ever she gets a good look at ya, ya'll turn to stone. I seen it happen to a lad of six or seven only last year!"
"It happened to this poor fella five years back now."
People seem justifiably suspicious of Skelly's claim, I watch their faces wrestle with what they are seeing. Then, as if in a dream, I hear a wavering voice call to me.
"Maia? Child? Little One!"

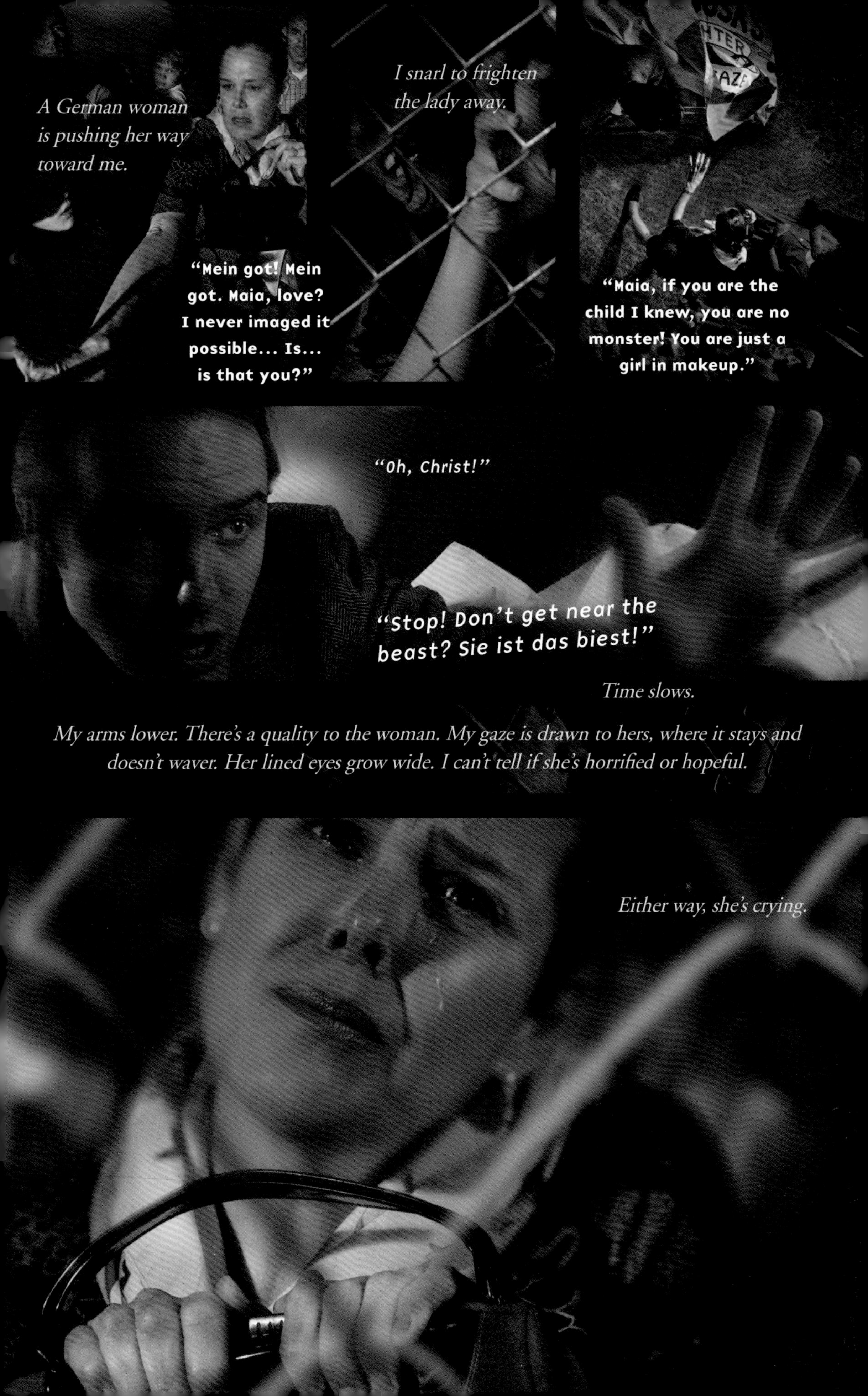
A German woman is pushing her way toward me.
"Mein got! Mein got. Maia, love? I never imaged it possible... Is... is that you?"
I snarl to frighten the lady away.
"Maia, if you are the child I knew, you are no monster! You are just a girl in makeup."
"Oh, Christ!"
"Stop! Don't get near the beast? Sie ist das biest!"
Time slows.
My arms lower. There's a quality to the woman. My gaze is drawn to hers, where it stays and doesn't waver. Her lined eyes grow wide. I can't tell if she's horrified or hopeful.
Either way, she's crying.

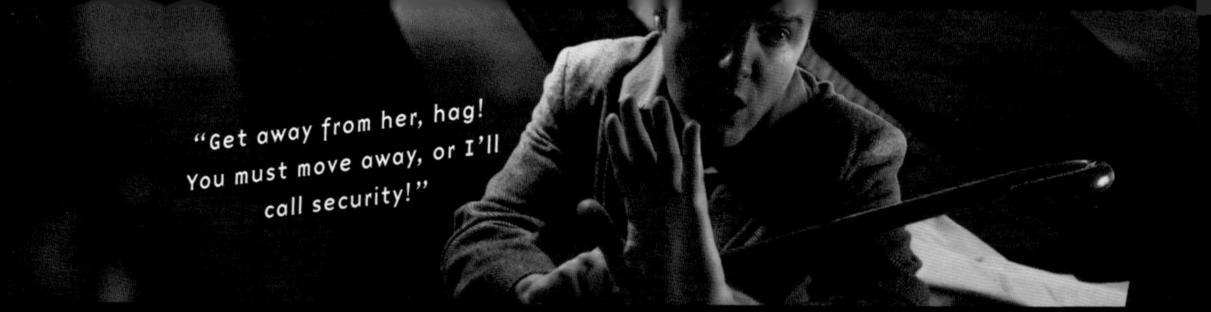
“Get away from her, hag! You must move away, or I’ll call security!”

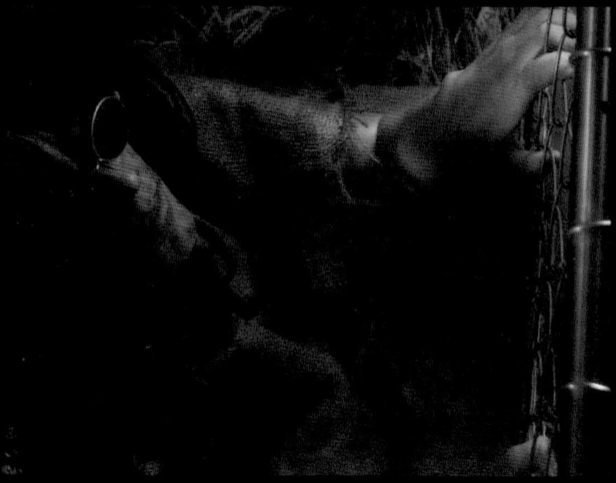

I want to talk to her, but Rictus has strict rules about breaking character, and Medusa’s Daughter is supposed to be so inhuman language is above her.

I weigh how much it would hurt if I disobeyed his rules.

Too much, I decide.

I stare at the lady. She touches fingers to the wire separating us.

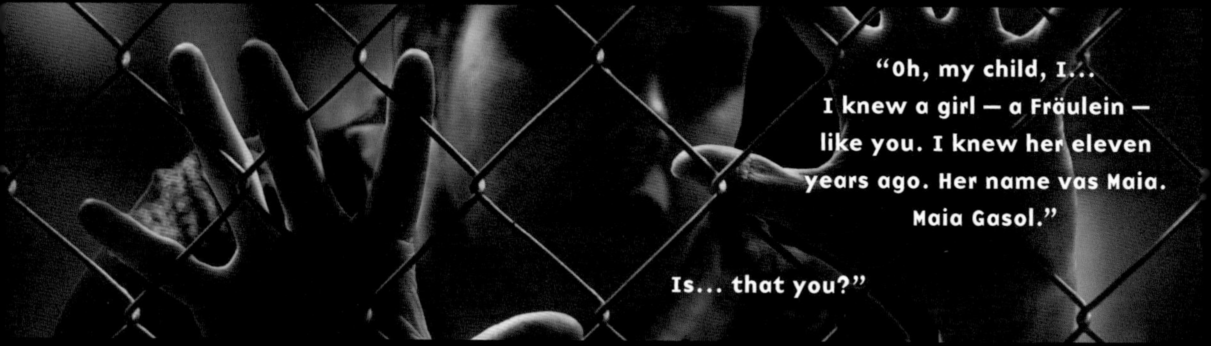
“Oh, my child, I... I knew a girl — a Fräulein — like you. I knew her eleven years ago. Her name vas Maia. Maia Gasol.”
Is... that you?”

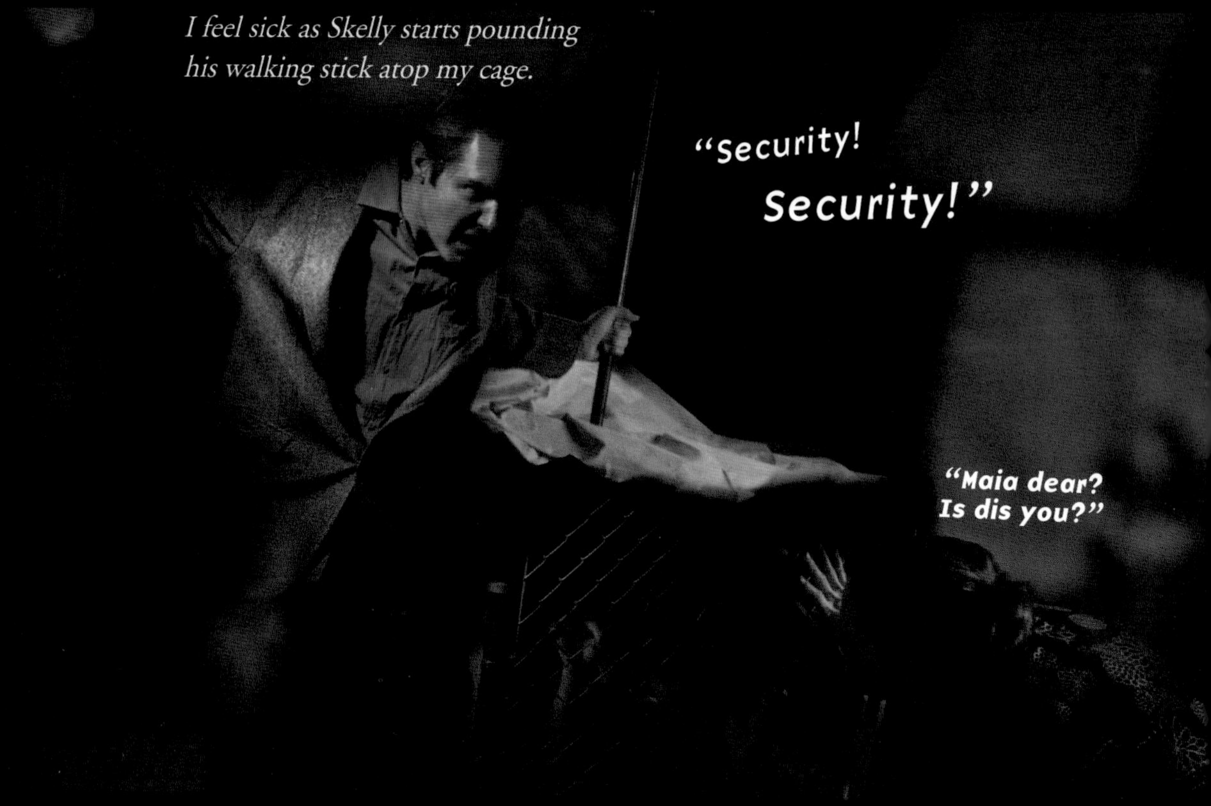
I feel sick as Skelly starts pounding his walking stick atop my cage.
“Security!
Security!”
“Maia dear? Is dis you?”

It's as if we're moving in water. The woman is so beautiful and lovely, and she is using my first name by coincidence or accident, though she's also calling me Gasol when, in fact, I have no last name. It's all so strange and confusing.

I feel so hopeless when Horst and Willem arrive and drag her back harshly.

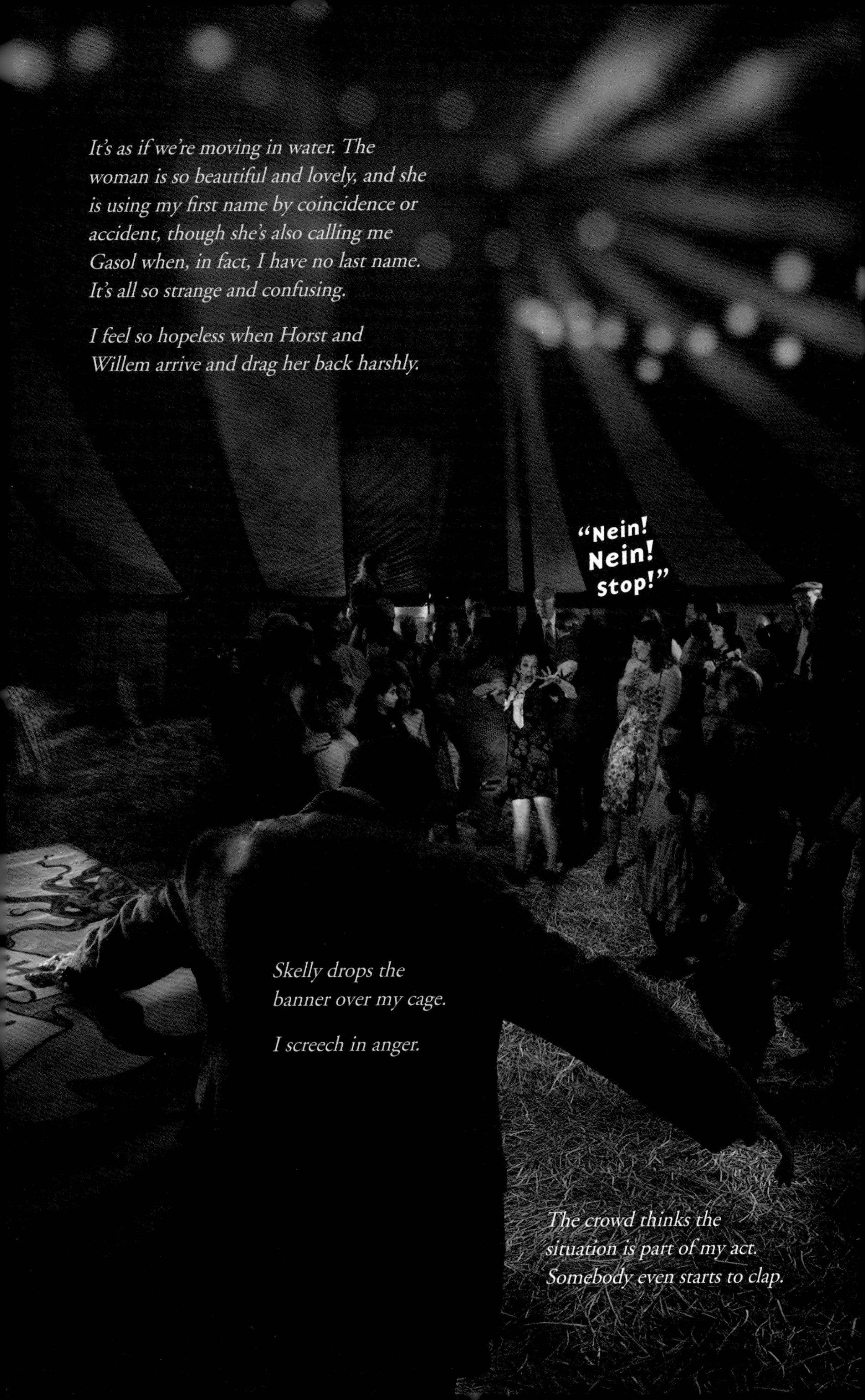
"Nein! Nein! Stop!"

Skelly drops the banner over my cage.

I screech in anger.

The crowd thinks the situation is part of my act. Somebody even starts to clap.

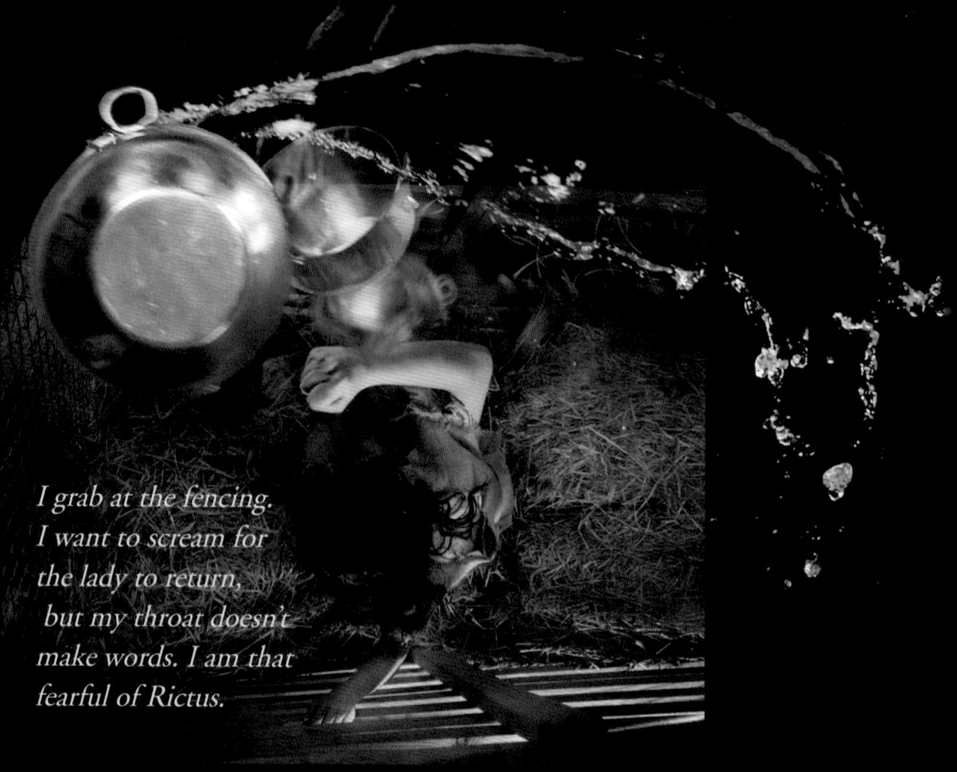
I grab at the fencing.
I want to scream for
the lady to return,
but my throat doesn't
make words. I am that
fearful of Rictus.

Steadily, as if my personality is attached to cables, who I am is pulled away. In anger, I become something else, a monster that wants to tear out Skelly's windpipe. That wants to destroy anything within reach. I slam my fist against the flooring and my steel water bowl jumps, striking the top of my cage.

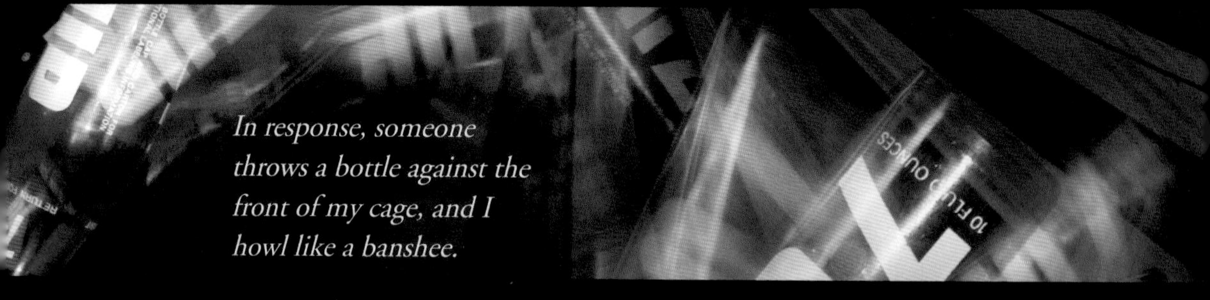
In response, someone
throws a bottle against the
front of my cage, and I
howl like a banshee.

I can hear Skelly talking.

"Folks, we need to be civilized here, huh!"

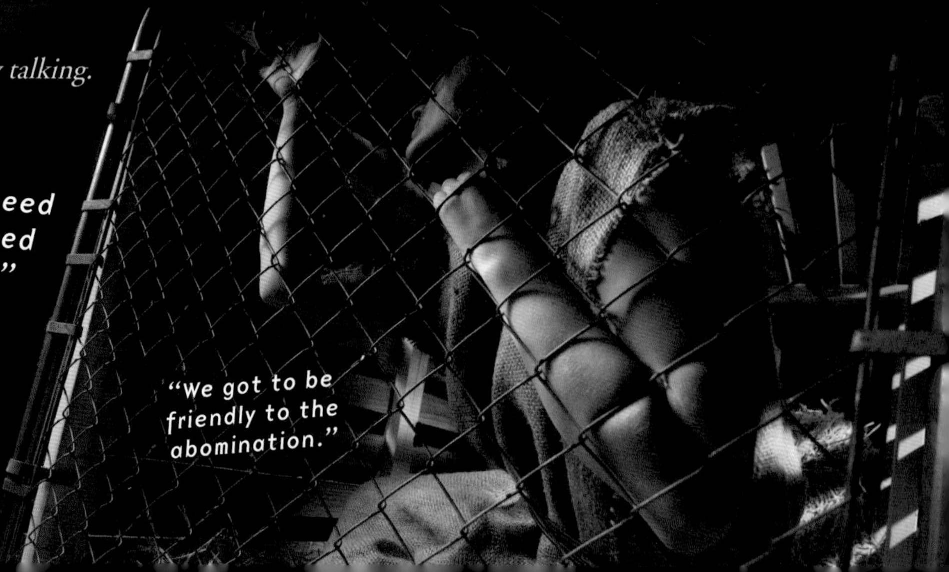
"We got to be
friendly to the
abomination."

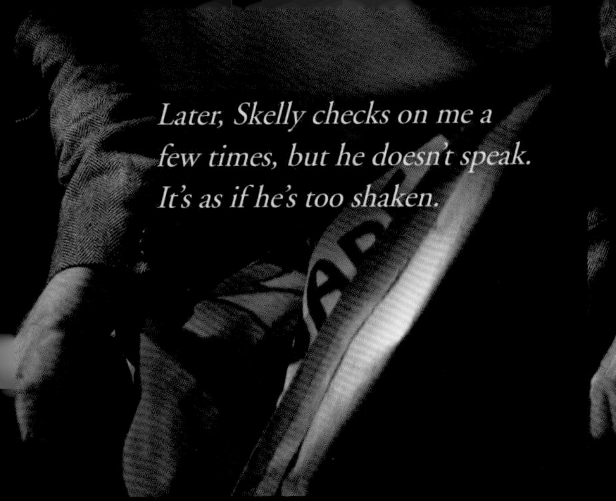
Later, Skelly checks on me a few times, but he doesn't speak. It's as if he's too shaken.
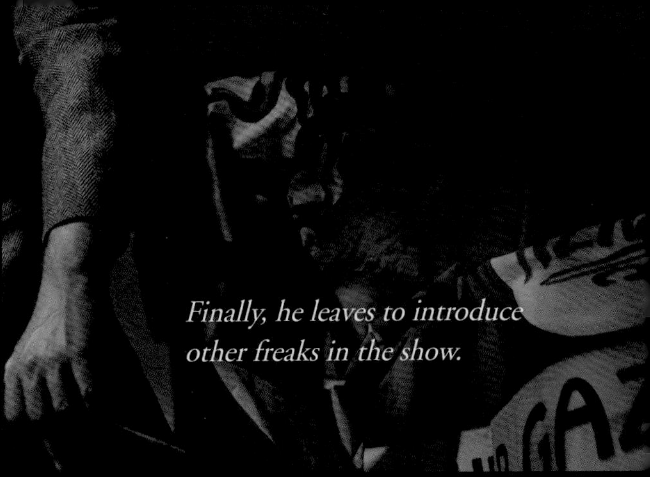
Finally, he leaves to introduce other freaks in the show.
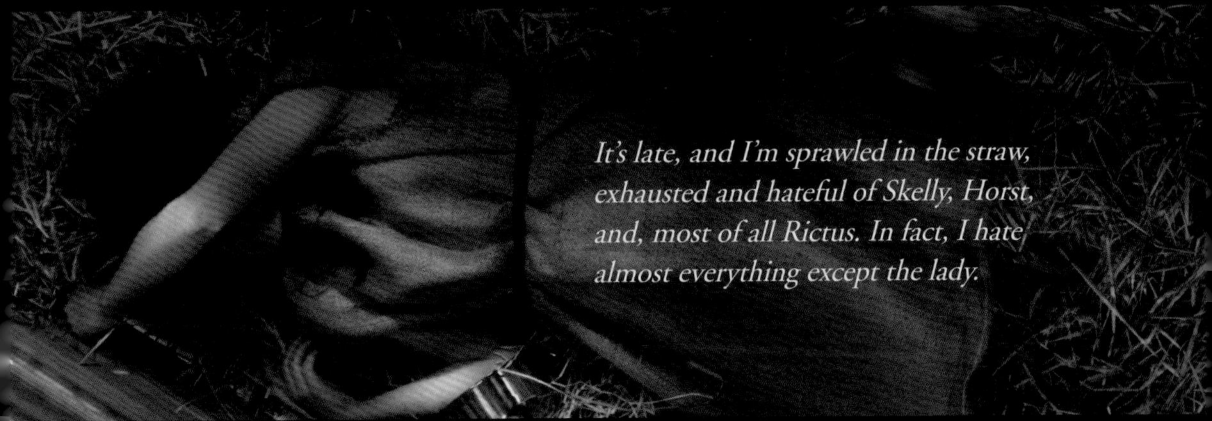
It's late, and I'm sprawled in the straw, exhausted and hateful of Skelly, Horst, and, most of all Rictus. In fact, I hate almost everything except the lady.
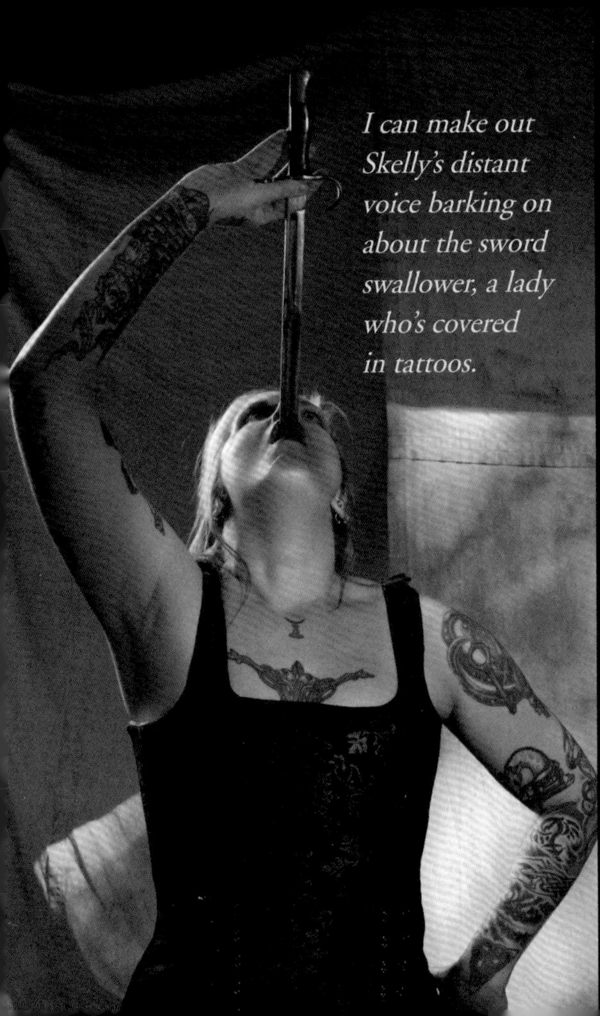
I can make out Skelly's distant voice barking on about the sword swallower, a lady who's covered in tattoos.
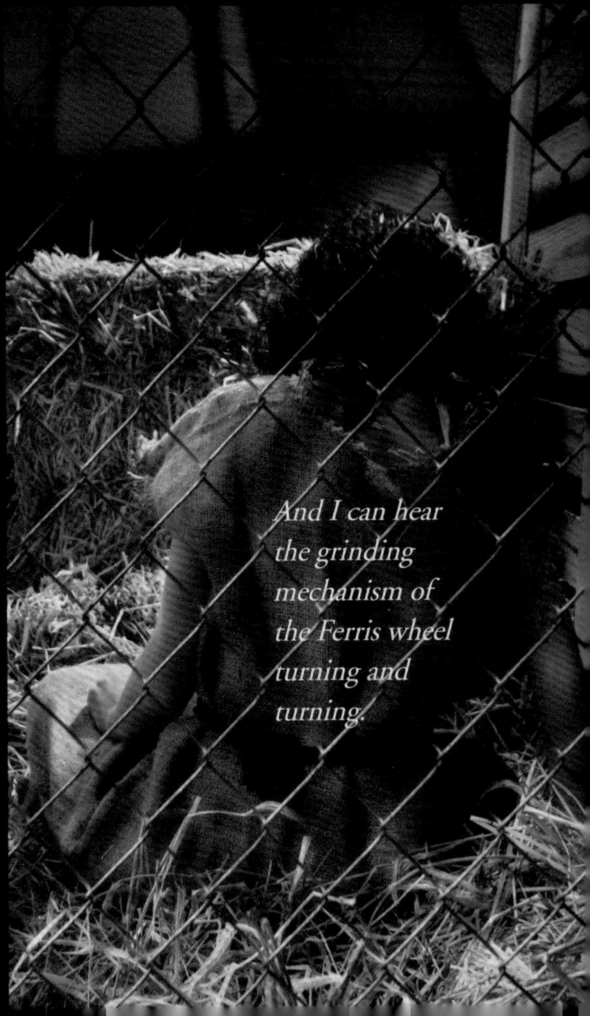
And I can hear the grinding mechanism of the Ferris wheel turning and turning.

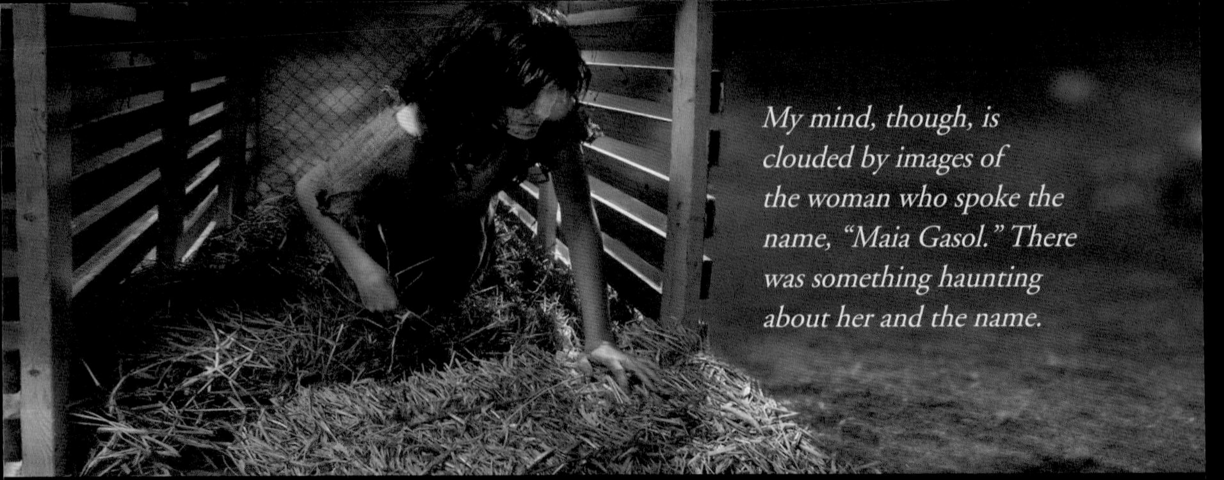
My mind, though, is clouded by images of the woman who spoke the name, "Maia Gasol." There was something haunting about her and the name.

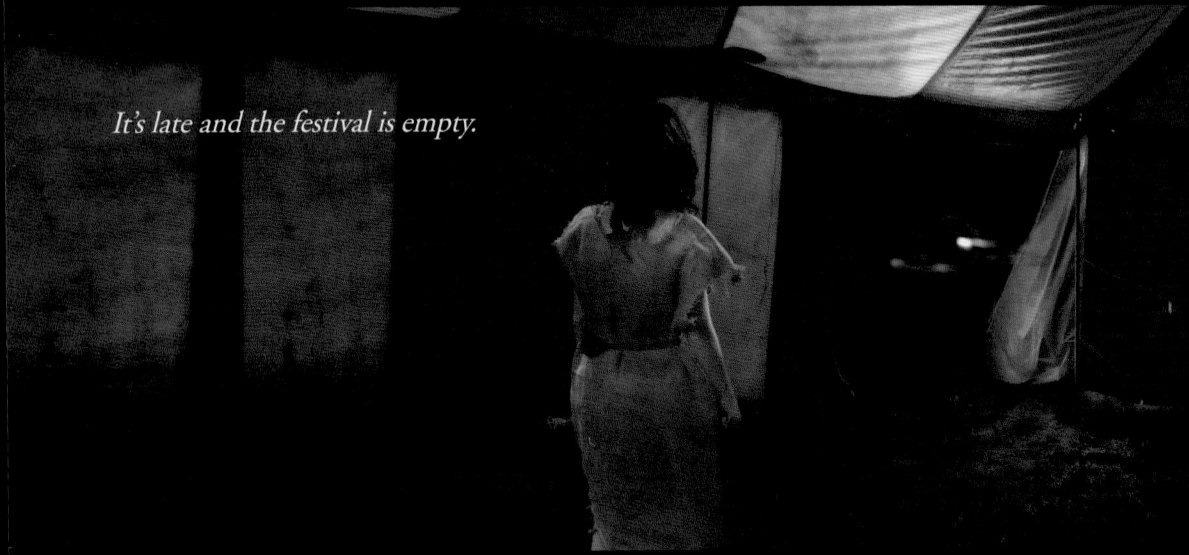
It's late and the festival is empty.

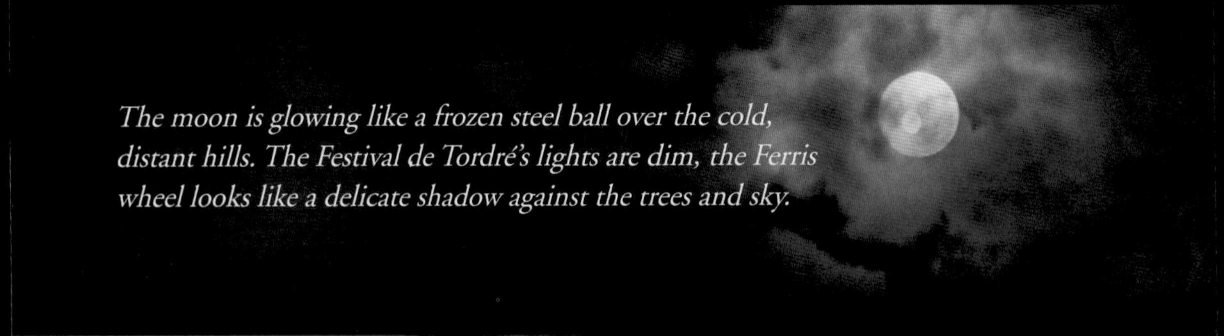
The moon is glowing like a frozen steel ball over the cold, distant hills. The Festival de Tordré's lights are dim, the Ferris wheel looks like a delicate shadow against the trees and sky.

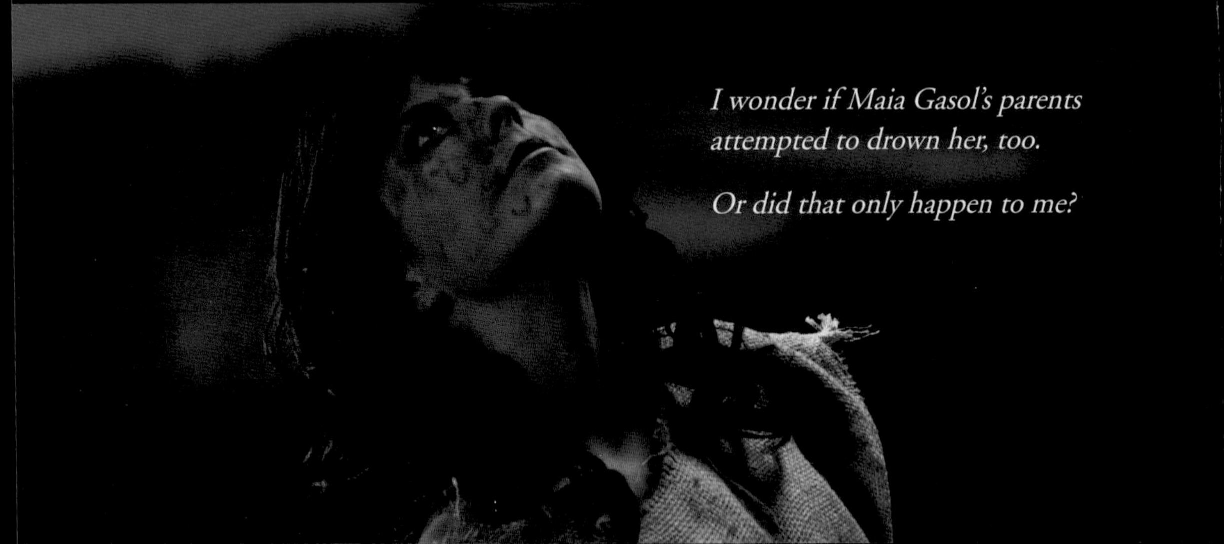
I wonder if Maia Gasol's parents attempted to drown her, too.
Or did that only happen to me?

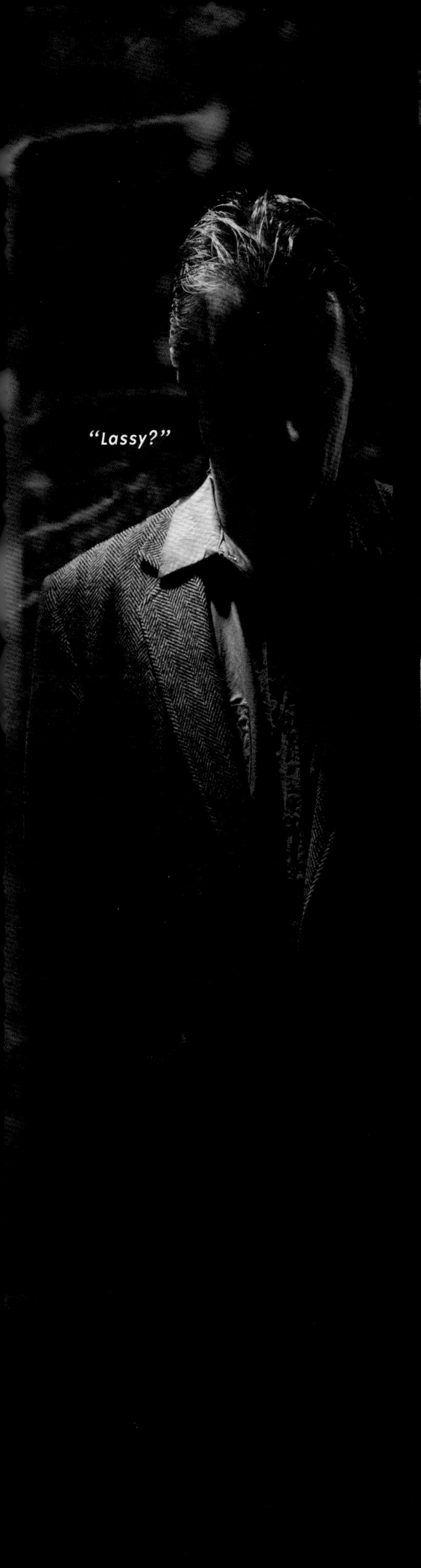
"Lassy?"

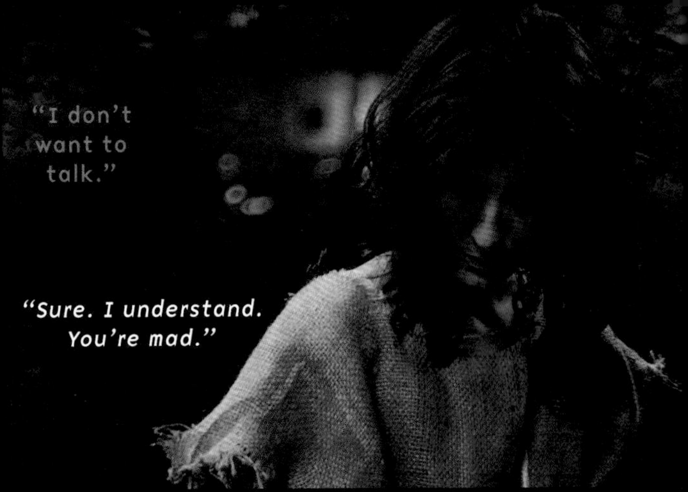
"I don't want to talk."
"Sure. I understand. You're mad."

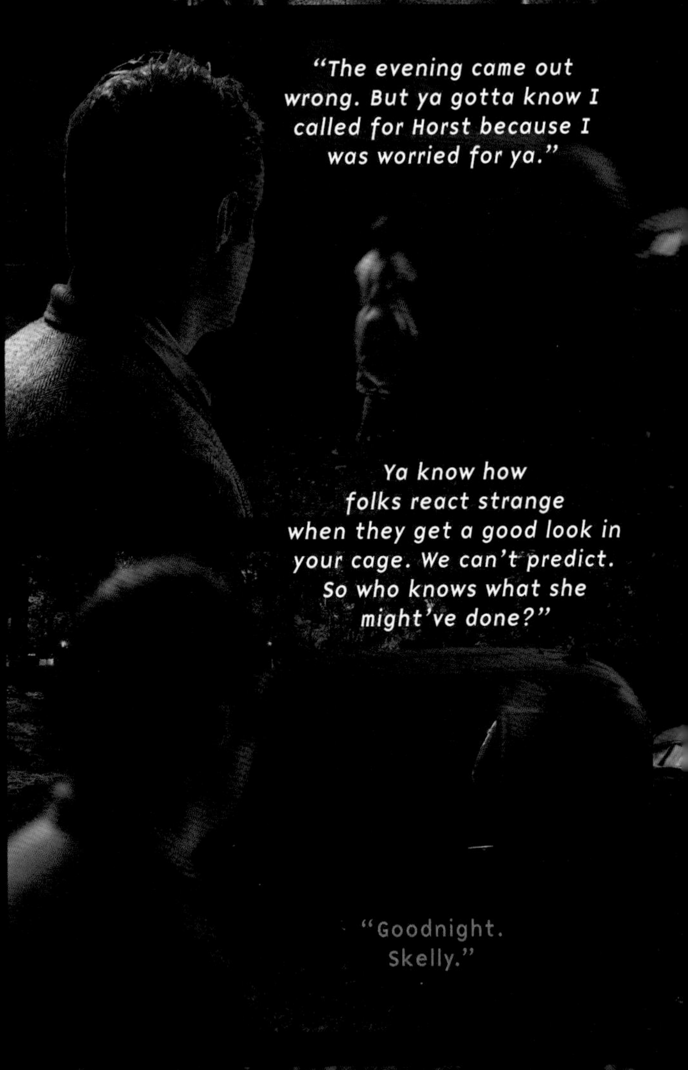
"The evening came out wrong. But ya gotta know I called for Horst because I was worried for ya."
Ya know how folks react strange when they get a good look in your cage. We can't predict. So who knows what she might've done?"
"Goodnight. Skelly."

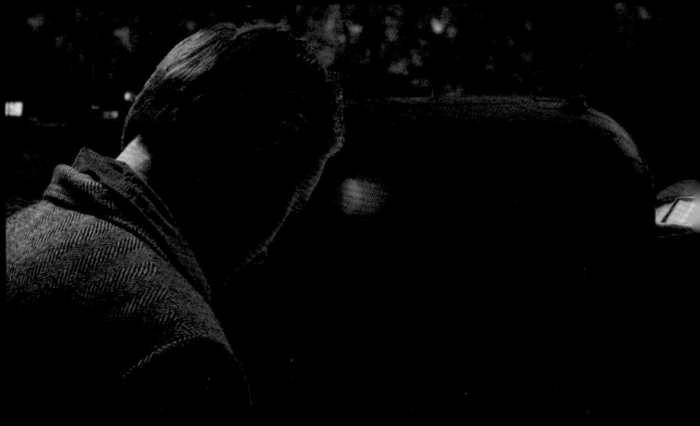

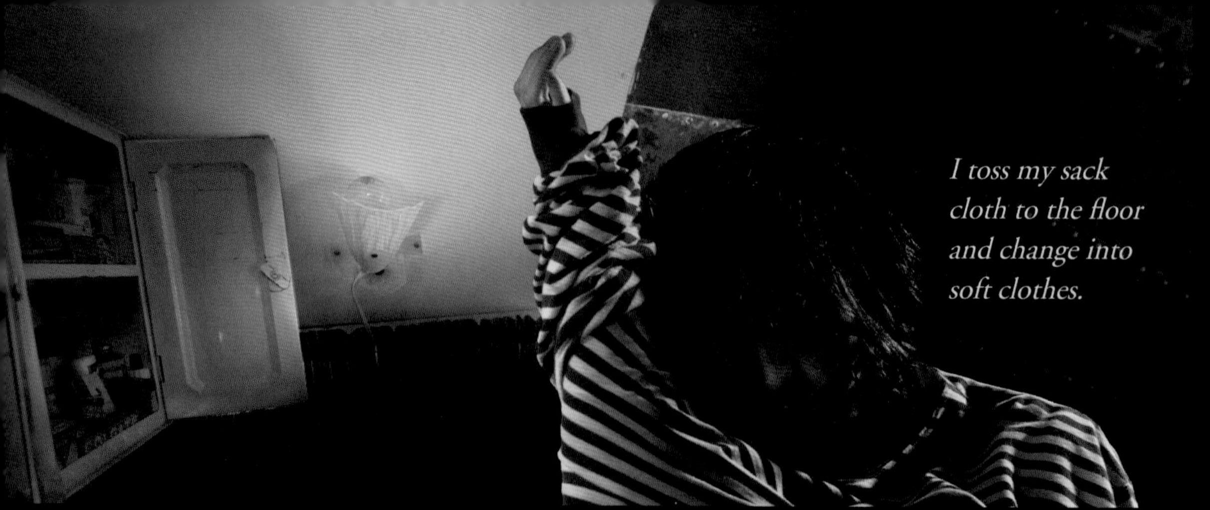
I toss my sack cloth to the floor and change into soft clothes.

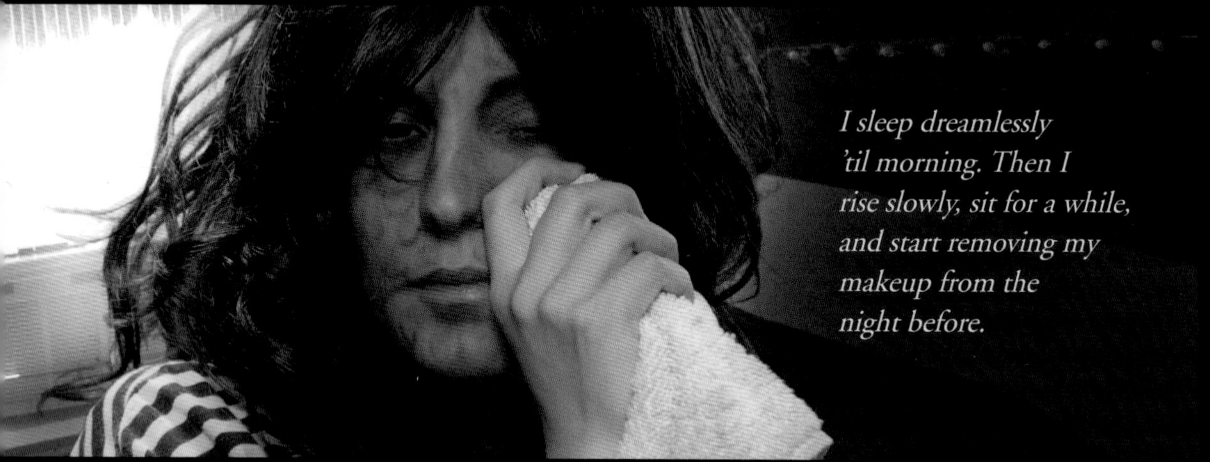
I sleep dreamlessly 'til morning. Then I rise slowly, sit for a while, and start removing my makeup from the night before.

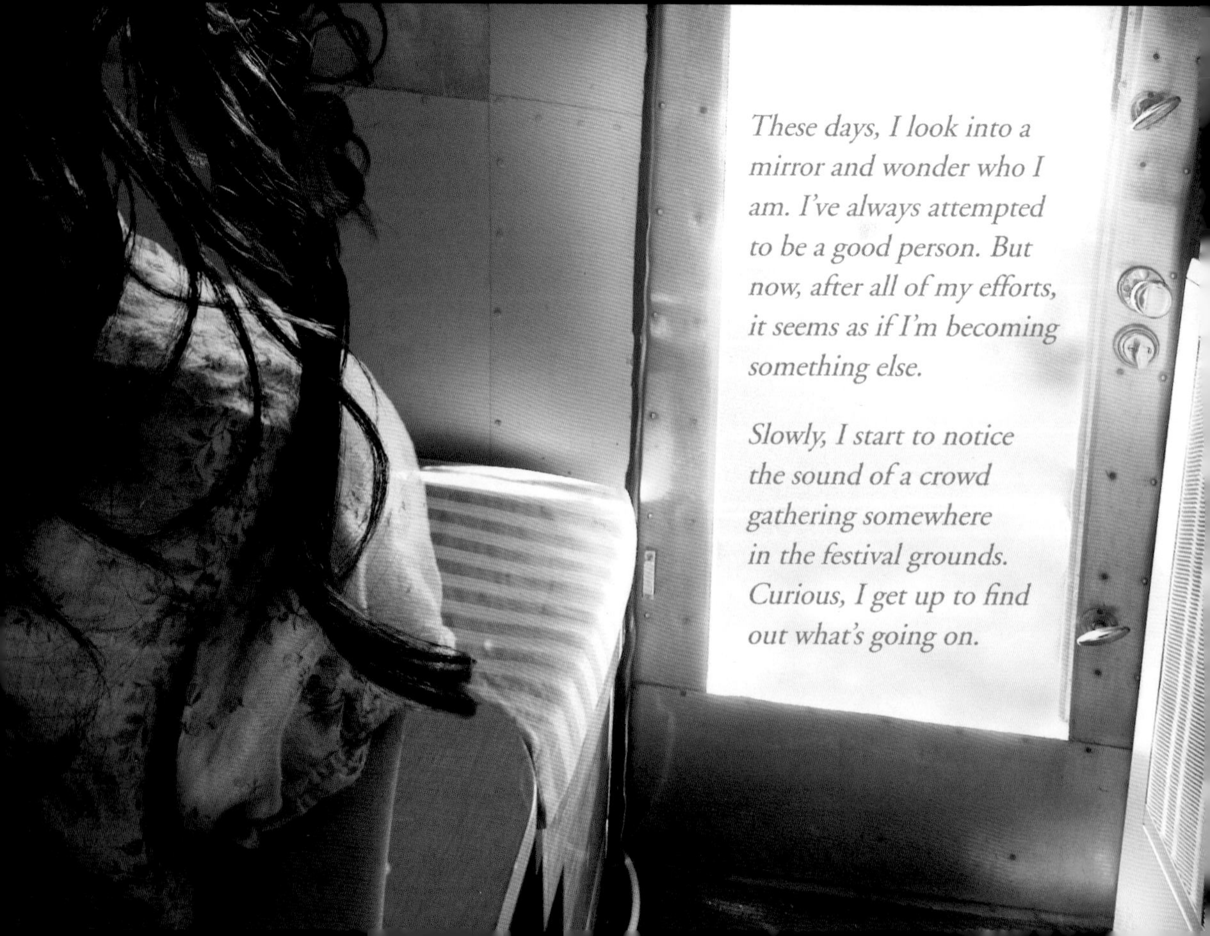
These days, I look into a mirror and wonder who I am. I've always attempted to be a good person. But now, after all of my efforts, it seems as if I'm becoming something else.
Slowly, I start to notice the sound of a crowd gathering somewhere in the festival grounds. Curious, I get up to find out what's going on.

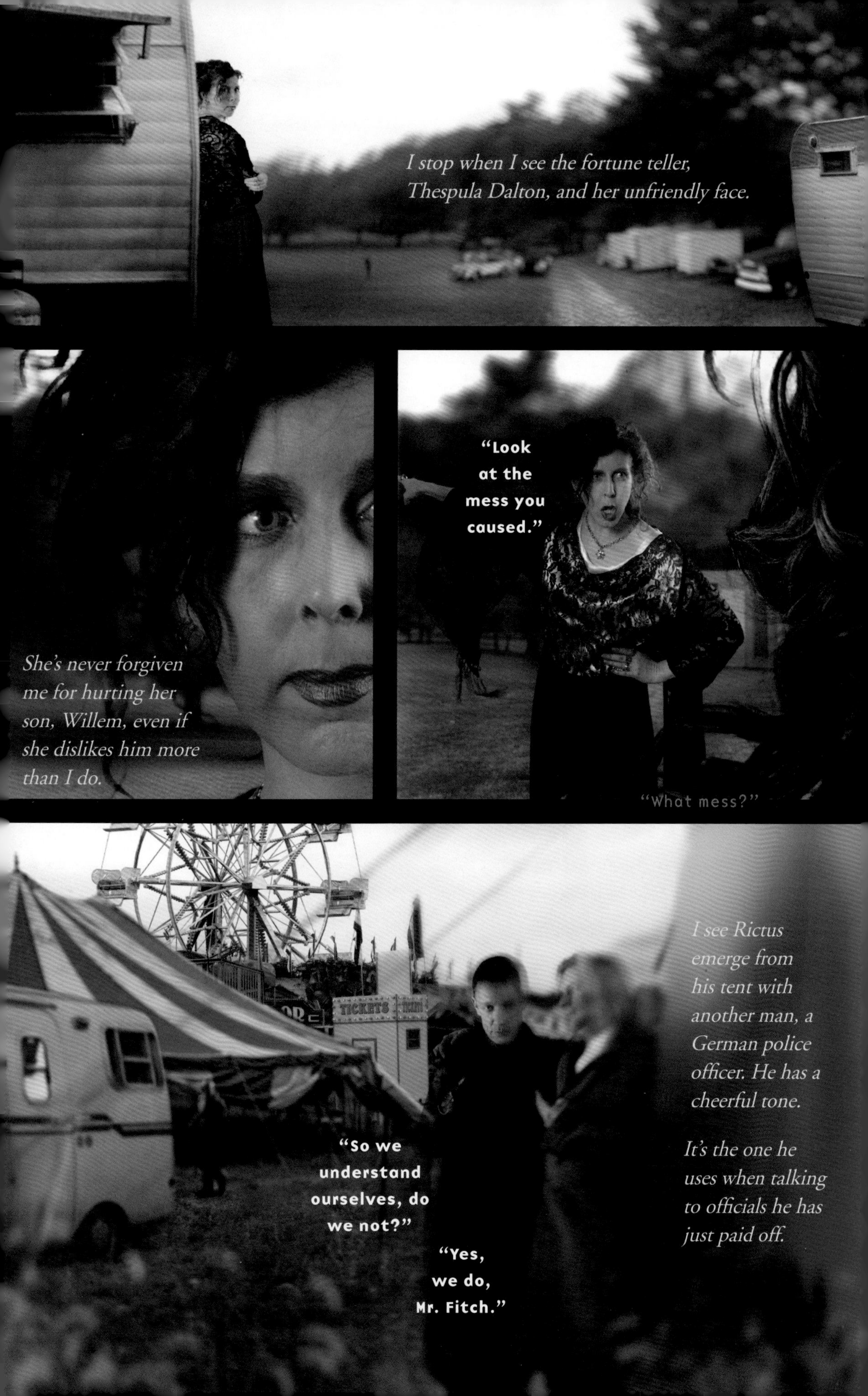
I stop when I see the fortune teller, Thespula Dalton, and her unfriendly face.
She's never forgiven me for hurting her son, Willem, even if she dislikes him more than I do.
"Look at the mess you caused."
"What mess?"
I see Rictus emerge from his tent with another man, a German police officer. He has a cheerful tone.
It's the one he uses when talking to officials he has just paid off.
"So we understand ourselves, do we not?"
"Yes, we do, Mr. Fitch."
TICKETS

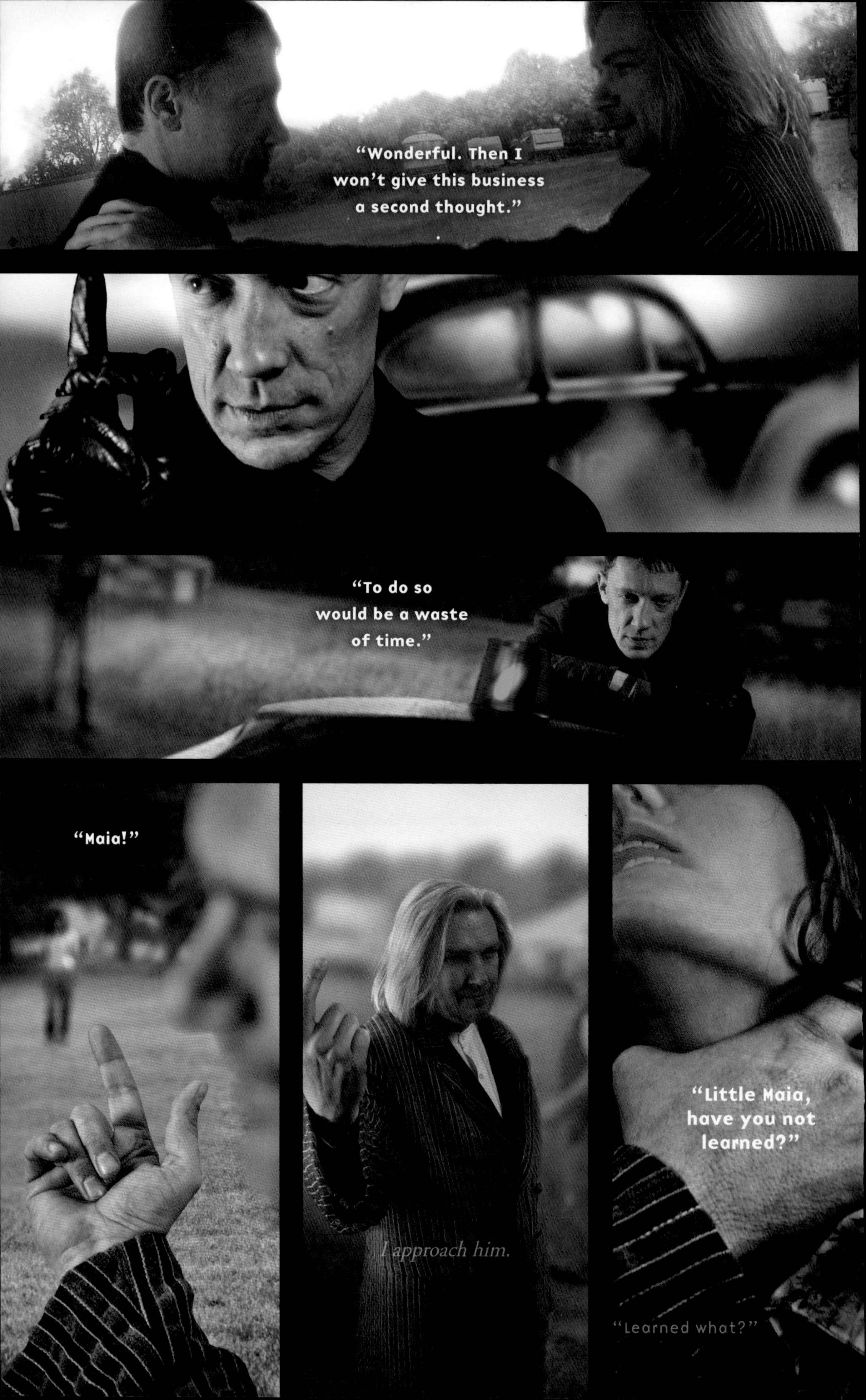
"Wonderful. Then I won't give this business a second thought."
"To do so would be a waste of time."
"Maia!"
I approach him.
"Little Maia, have you not learned?"
"Learned what?"

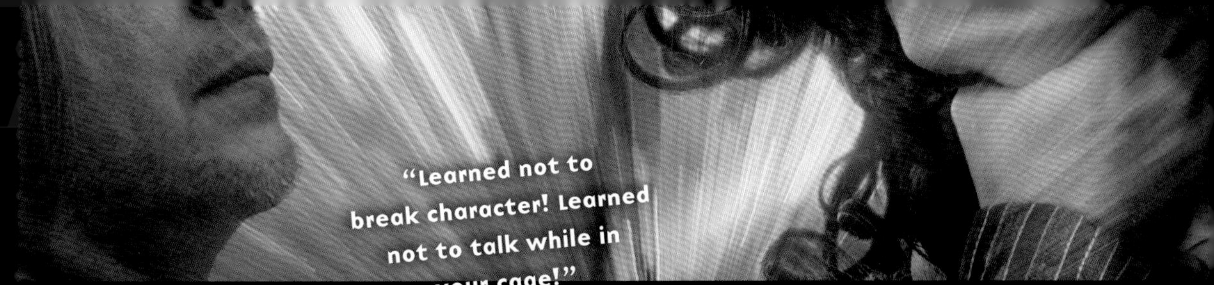
"Learned not to break character! Learned not to talk while in your cage!"

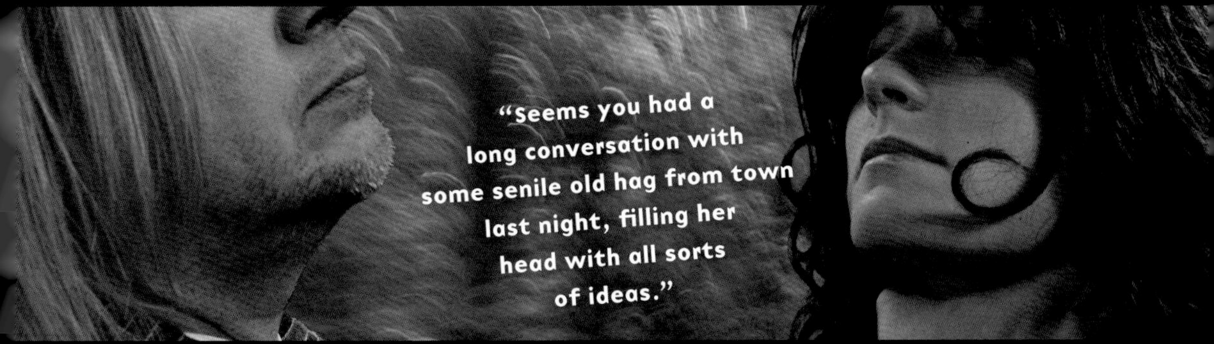
"Seems you had a long conversation with some senile old hag from town last night, filling her head with all sorts of ideas."

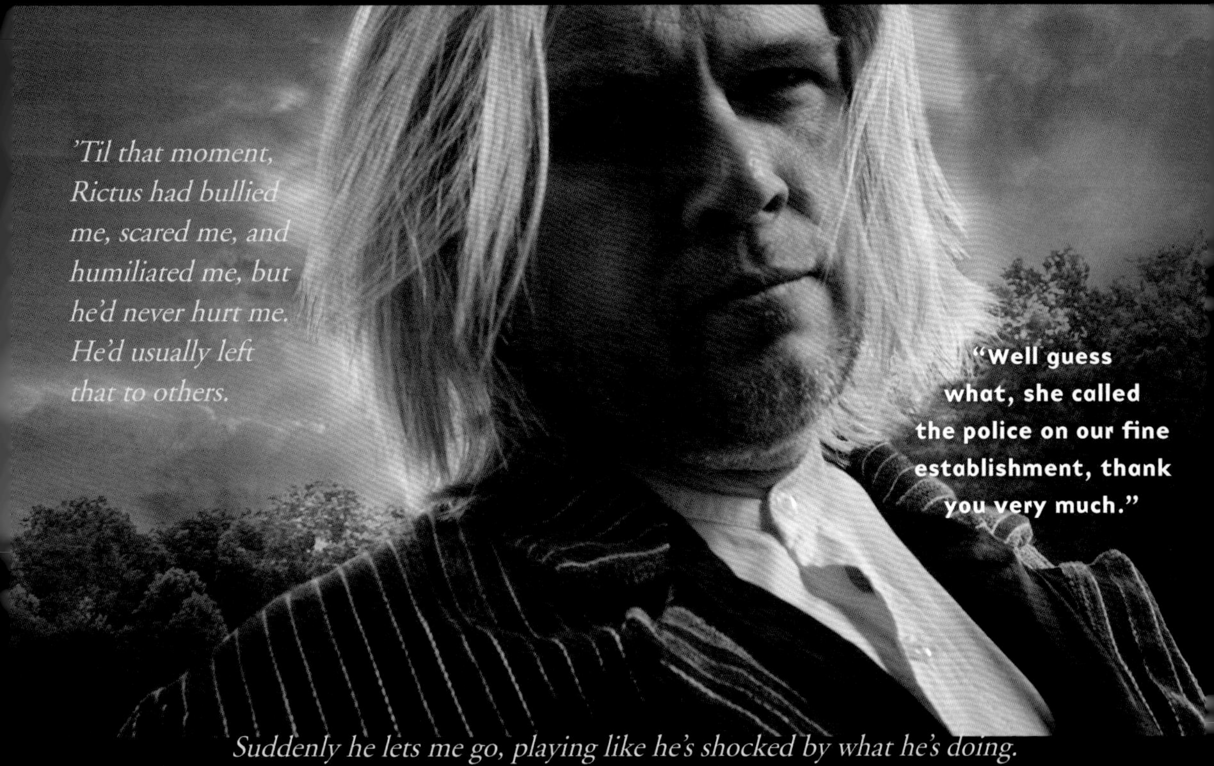
'Til that moment, Rictus had bullied me, scared me, and humiliated me, but he'd never hurt me. He'd usually left that to others.
"Well guess what, she called the police on our fine establishment, thank you very much."
Suddenly he lets me go, playing like he's shocked by what he's doing.

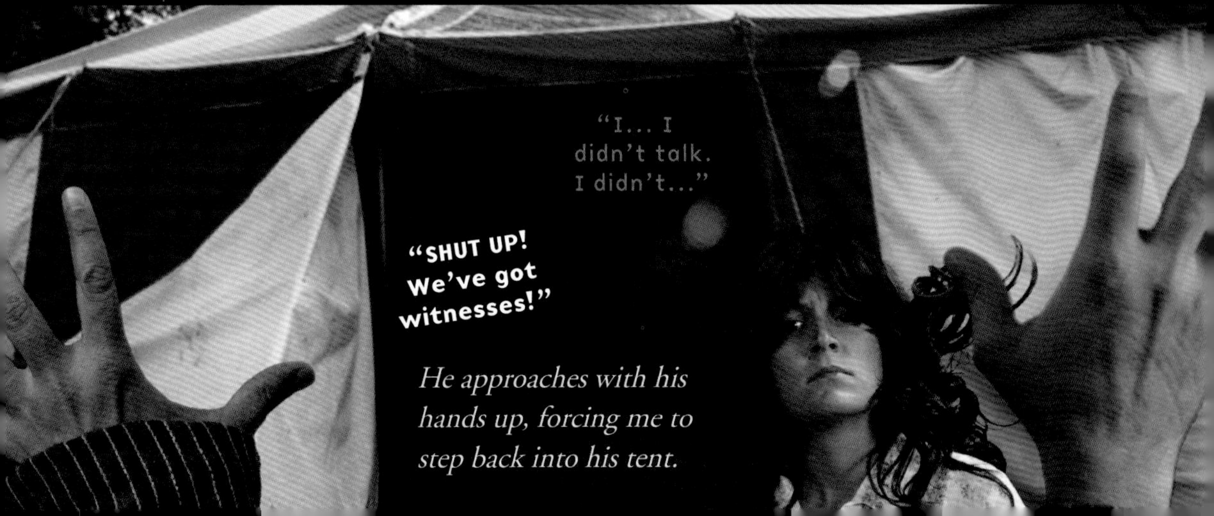
"I... I didn't talk. I didn't..."
"SHUT UP! We've got witnesses!"
He approaches with his hands up, forcing me to step back into his tent.

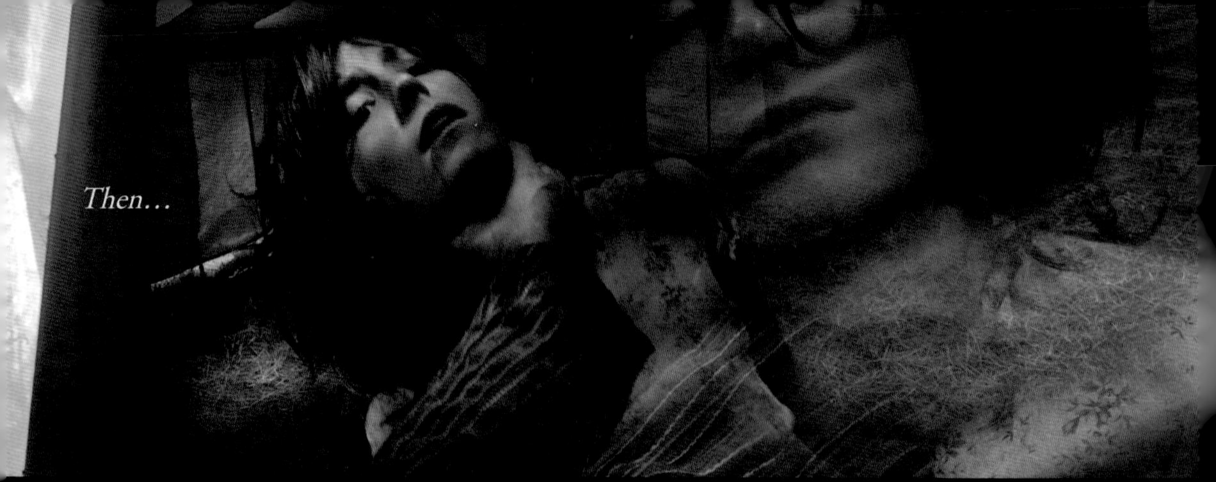
Then…

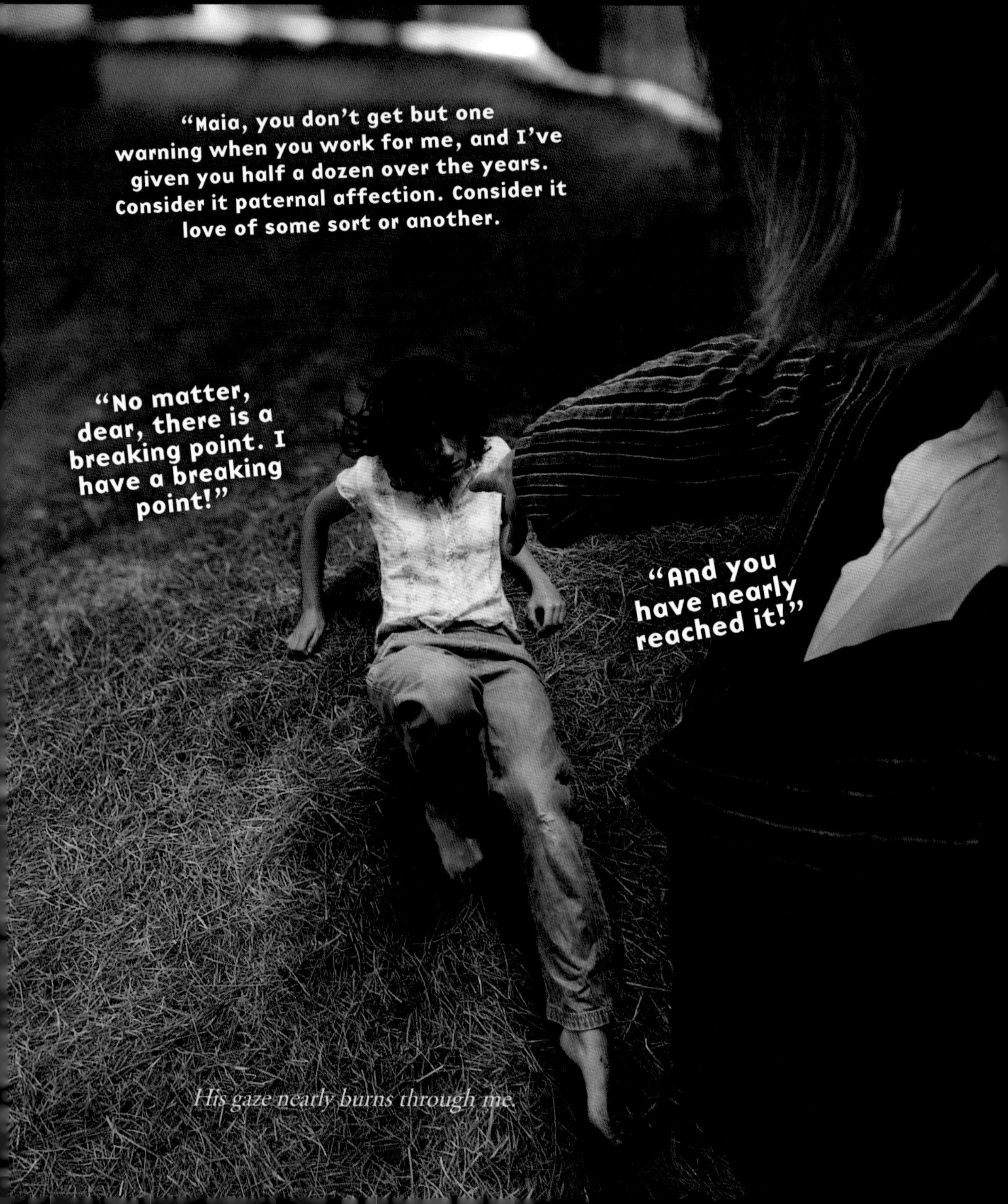
"Maia, you don't get but one warning when you work for me, and I've given you half a dozen over the years. Consider it paternal affection. Consider it love of some sort or another.
"No matter, dear, there is a breaking point. I have a breaking point!"
"And you have nearly reached it!"
His gaze nearly burns through me.

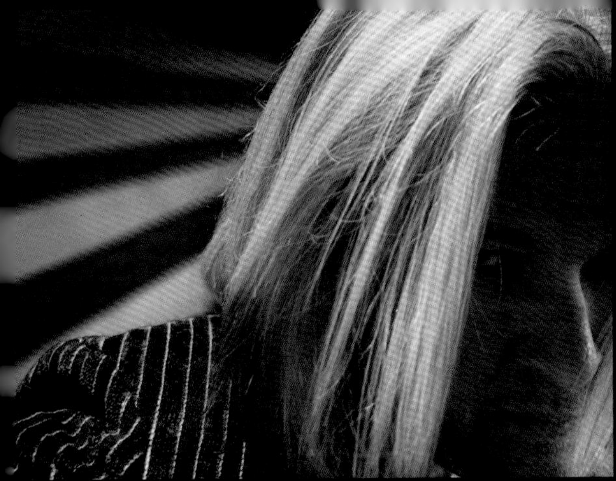

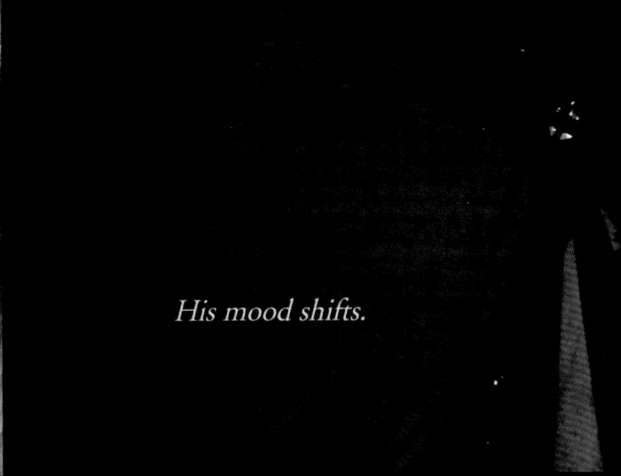
His mood shifts.

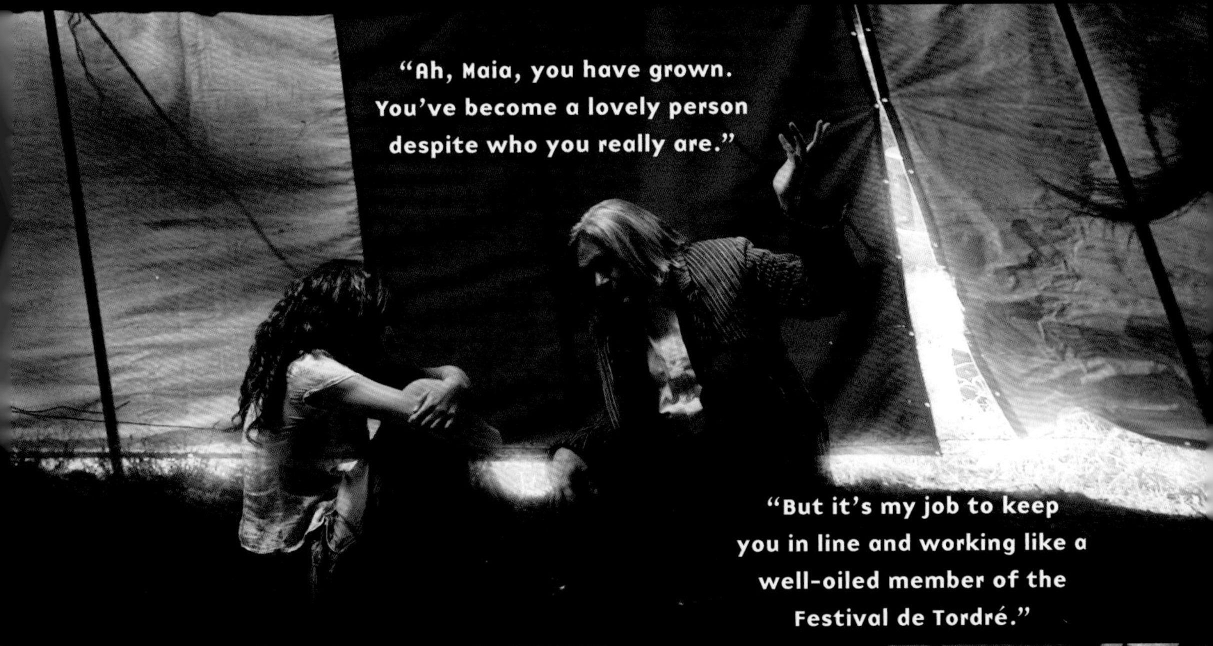
"Ah, Maia, you have grown. You've become a lovely person despite who you really are."
"But it's my job to keep you in line and working like a well-oiled member of the Festival de Tordré."

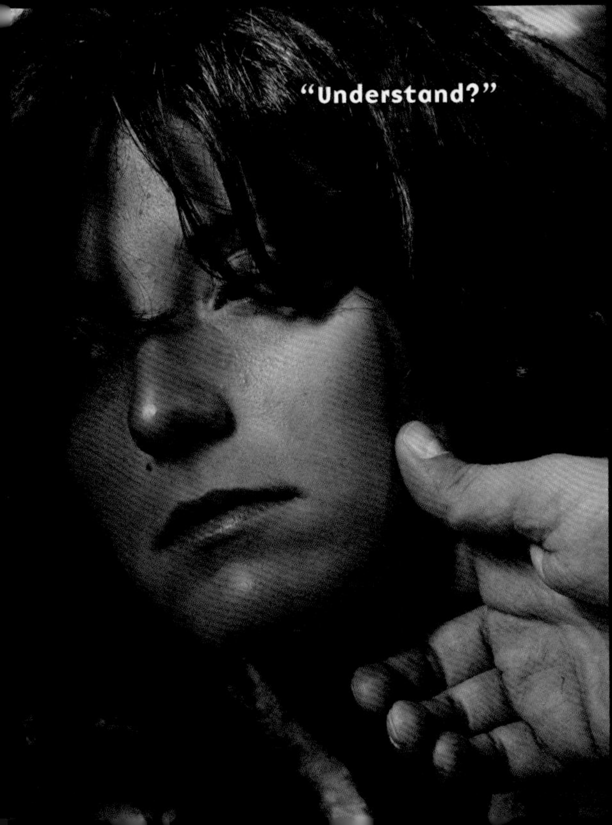
"Understand?"

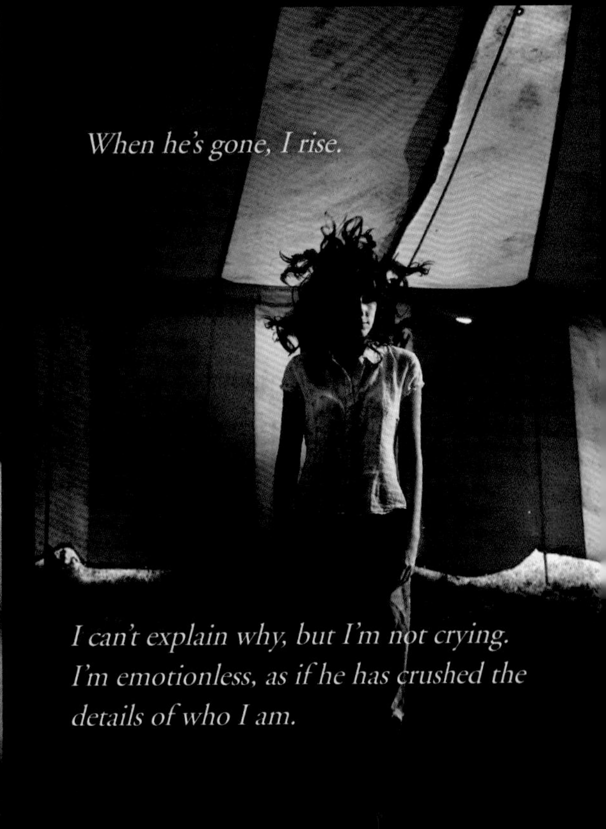
When he's gone, I rise.
I can't explain why, but I'm not crying. I'm emotionless, as if he has crushed the details of who I am.

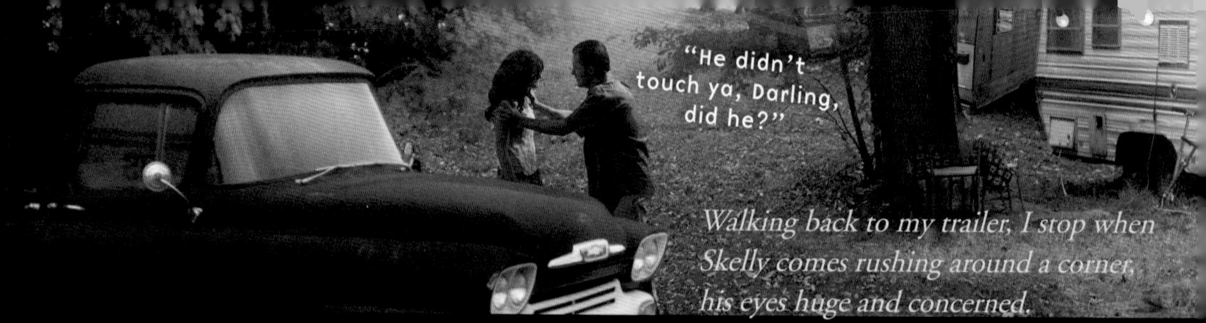
"He didn't touch ya, Darling, did he?"
Walking back to my trailer, I stop when Skelly comes rushing around a corner, his eyes huge and concerned.

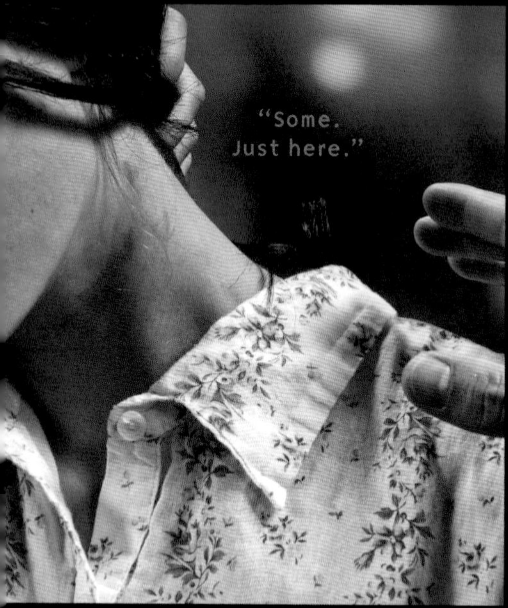
"Some. Just here."

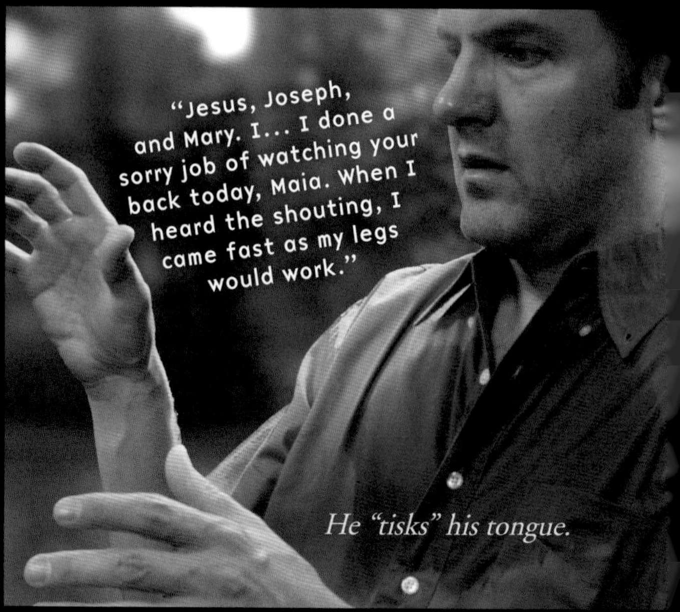
"Jesus, Joseph, and Mary. I... I done a sorry job of watching your back today, Maia. When I heard the shouting, I came fast as my legs would work."
He "tisks" his tongue.

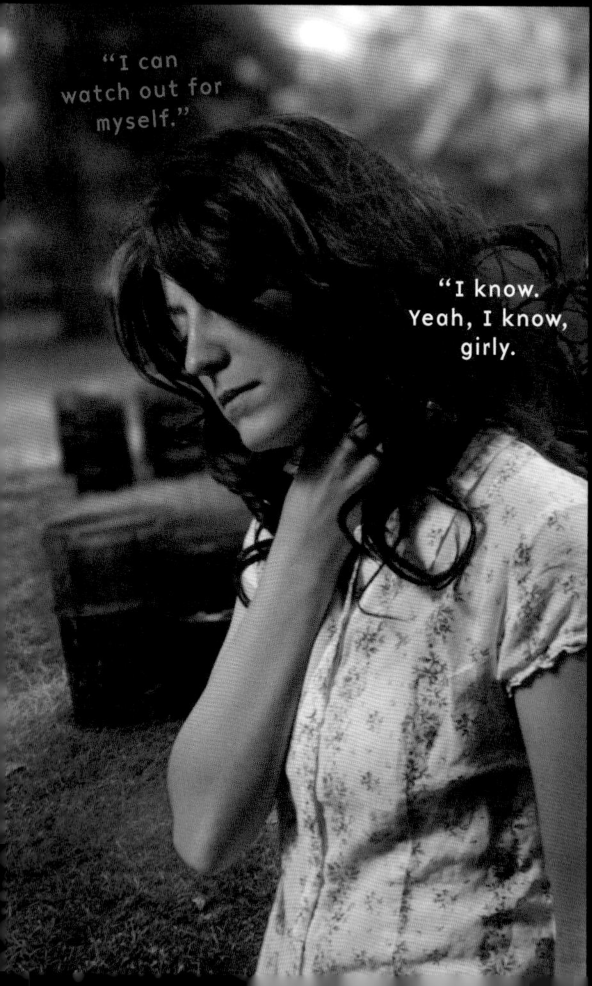
"I can watch out for myself."
"I know. Yeah, I know, girly.

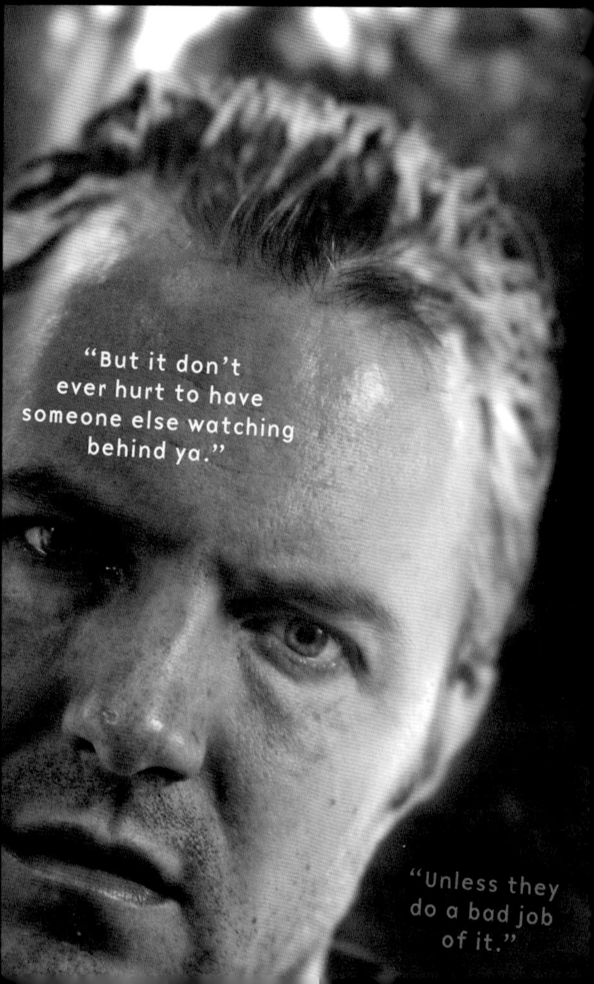
"But it don't ever hurt to have someone else watching behind ya."
"Unless they do a bad job of it."

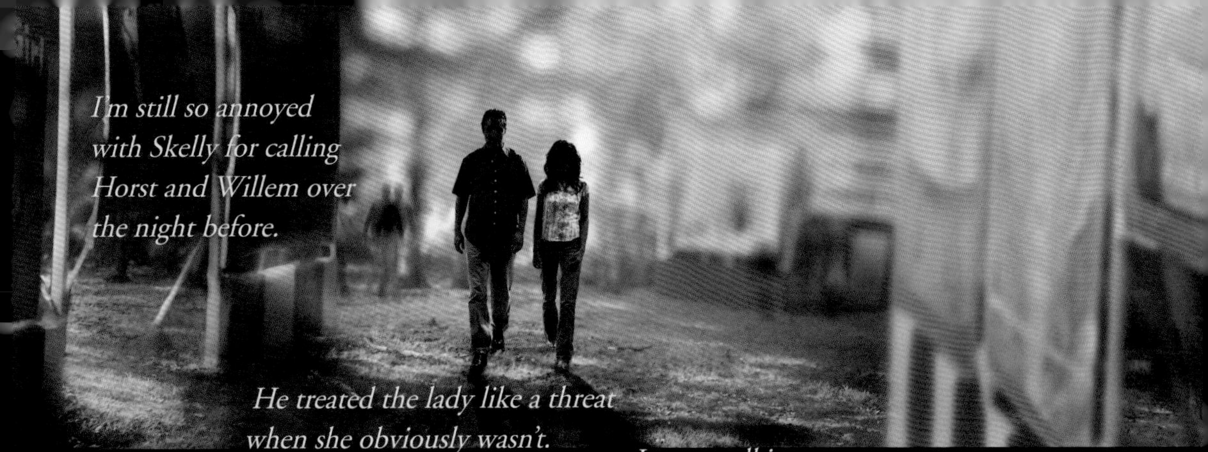
I'm still so annoyed with Skelly for calling Horst and Willem over the night before.
He treated the lady like a threat when she obviously wasn't.

I start walking away.

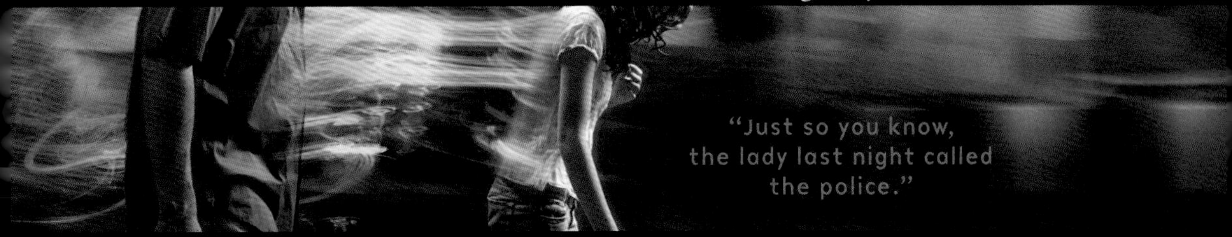
"Just so you know, the lady last night called the police."

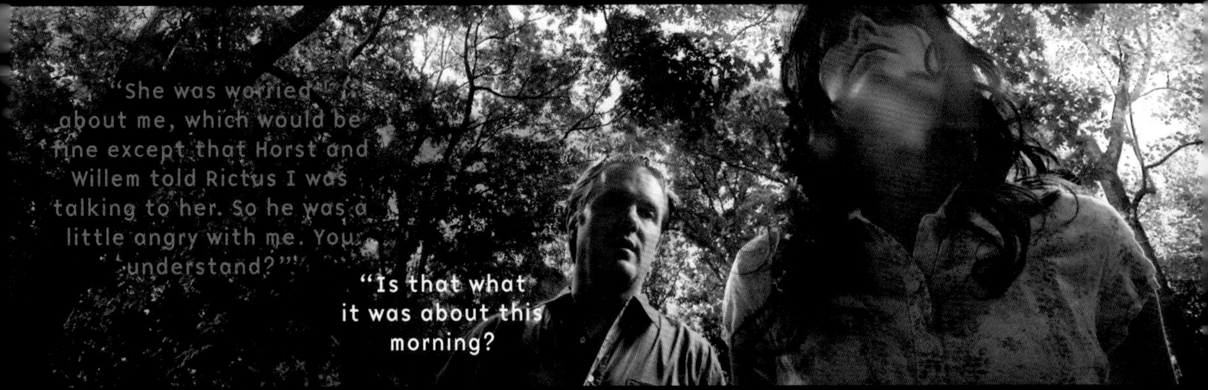
"She was worried about me, which would be fine except that Horst and Willem told Rictus I was talking to her. So he was a little angry with me. You understand?"
"Is that what it was about this morning?

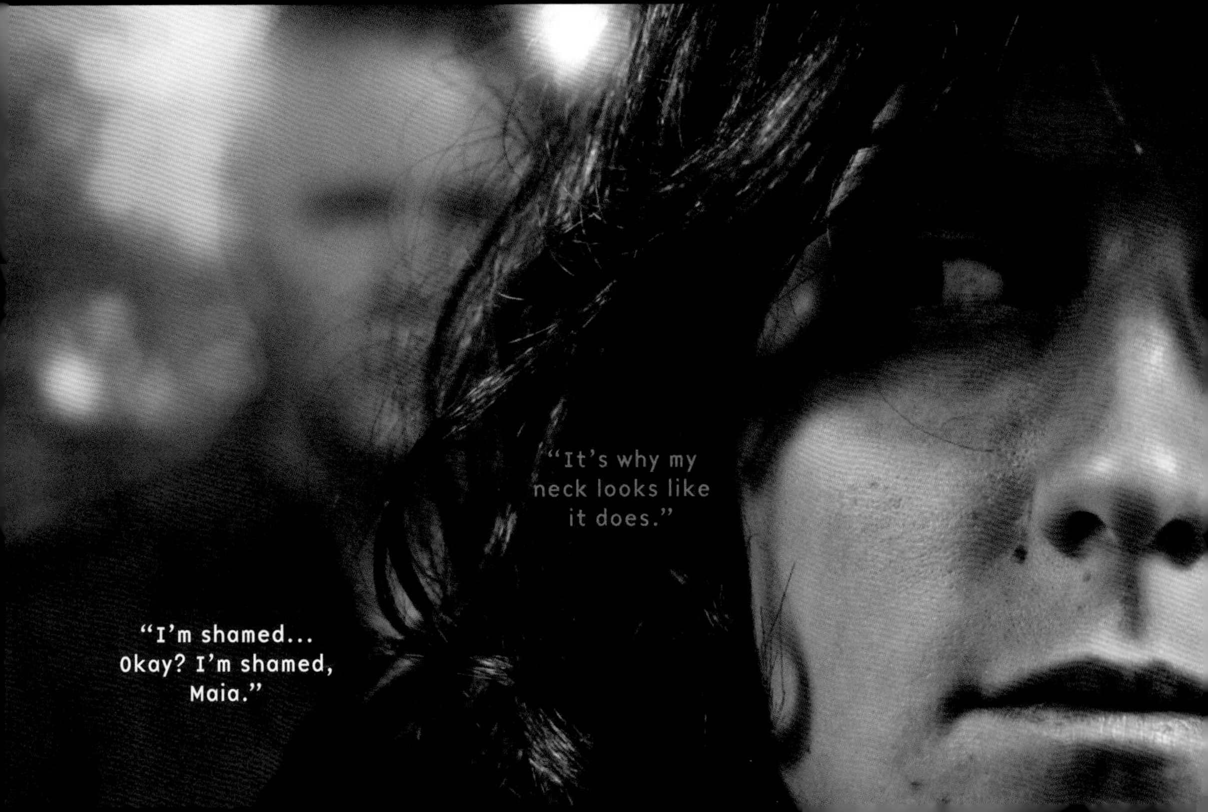
"It's why my neck looks like it does."
"I'm shamed... Okay? I'm shamed, Maia."

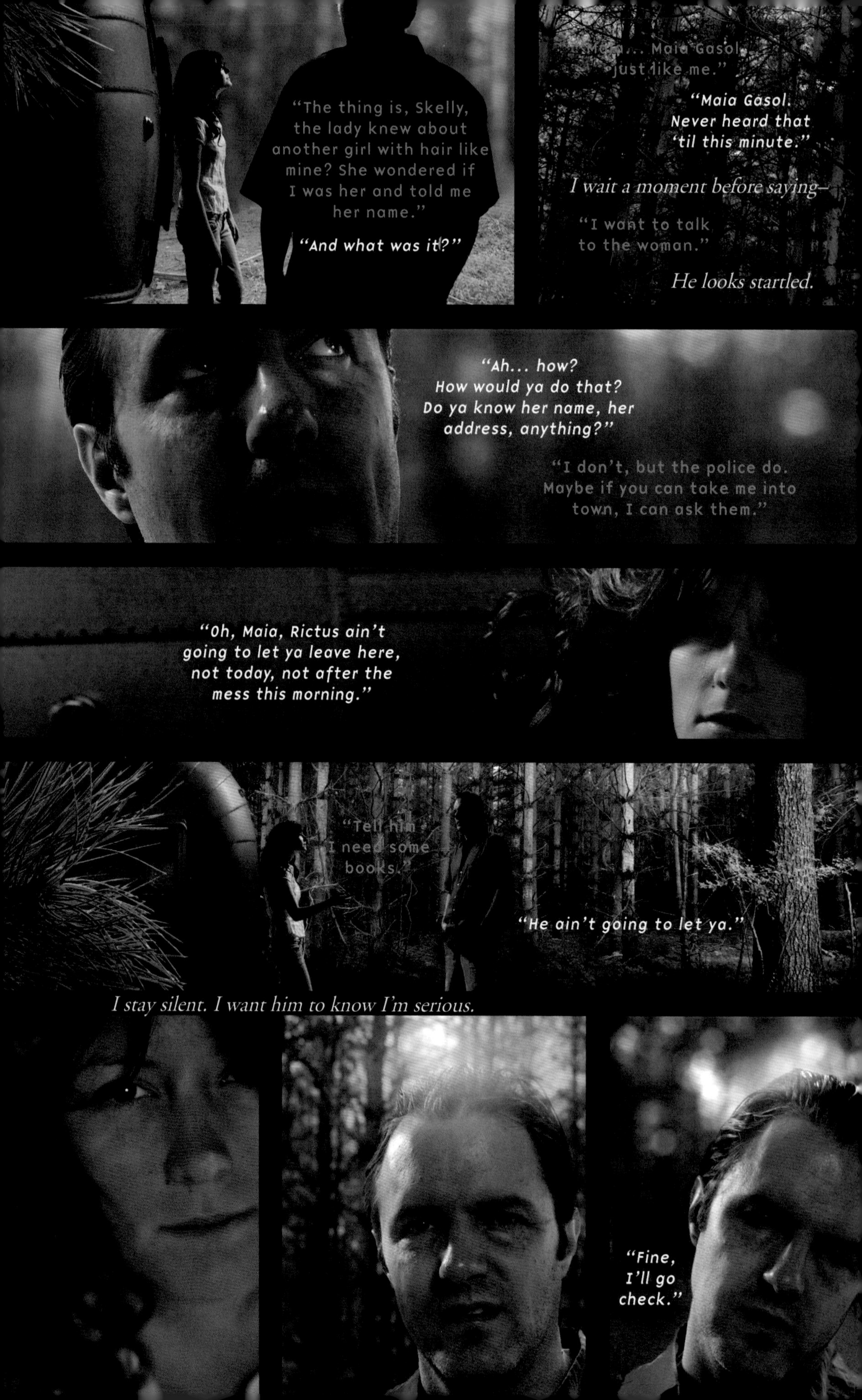
"The thing is, Skelly, the lady knew about another girl with hair like mine? She wondered if I was her and told me her name."
"And what was it?"
Maia... Maia Gasol, just like me."
"Maia Gasol. Never heard that 'til this minute."
I wait a moment before saying–
"I want to talk to the woman."
He looks startled.
"Ah... how? How would ya do that? Do ya know her name, her address, anything?"
"I don't, but the police do. Maybe if you can take me into town, I can ask them."
"Oh, Maia, Rictus ain't going to let ya leave here, not today, not after the mess this morning."
"Tell him I need some books."
"He ain't going to let ya."
I stay silent. I want him to know I'm serious.
"Fine, I'll go check."

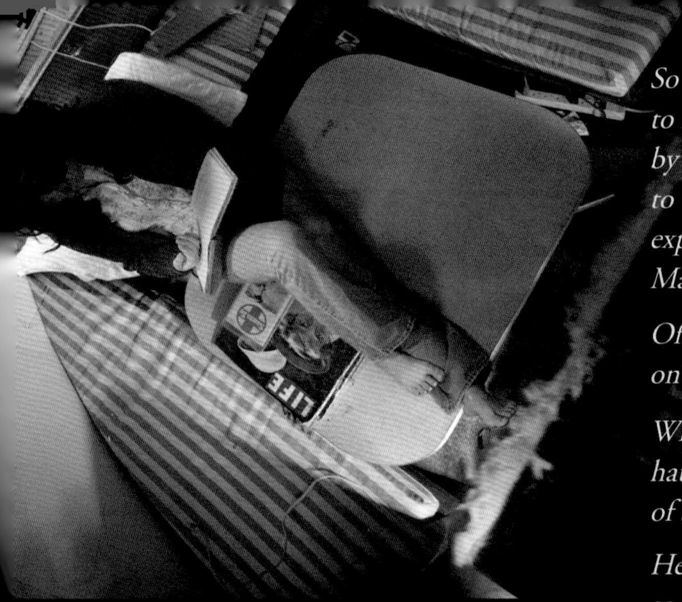

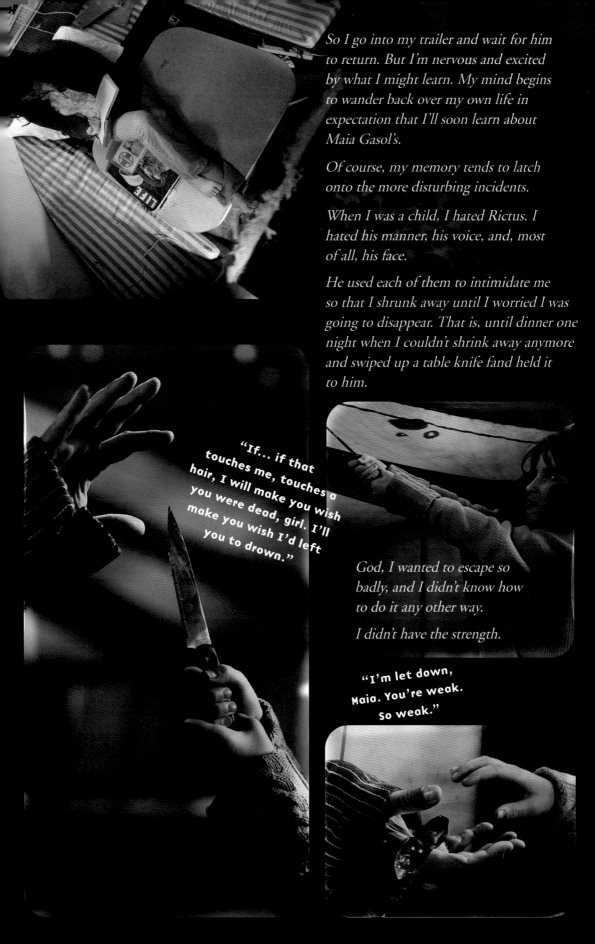

So I go into my trailer and wait for him to return. But I'm nervous and excited by what I might learn. My mind begins to wander back over my own life in expectation that I'll soon learn about Maia Gasol's.

Of course, my memory tends to latch onto the more disturbing incidents.

When I was a child, I hated Rictus. I hated his manner, his voice, and, most of all, his face.

He used each of them to intimidate me so that I shrunk away until I worried I was going to disappear. That is, until dinner one night when I couldn't shrink away anymore and swiped up a table knife fand held it to him.

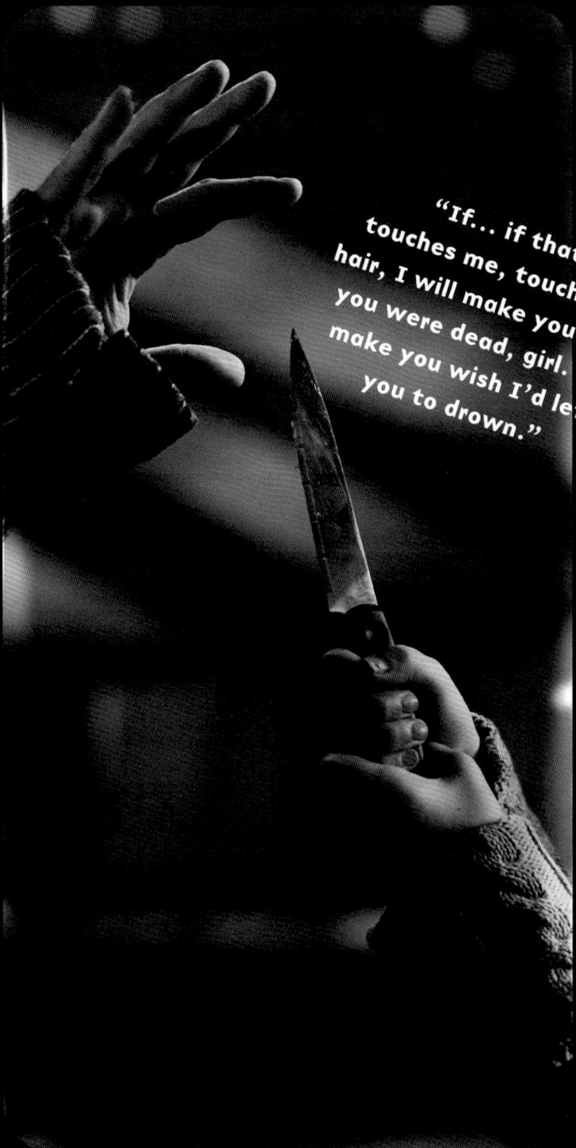
"If... if that touches me, touches a hair, I will make you wish you were dead, girl. I'll make you wish I'd left you to drown."

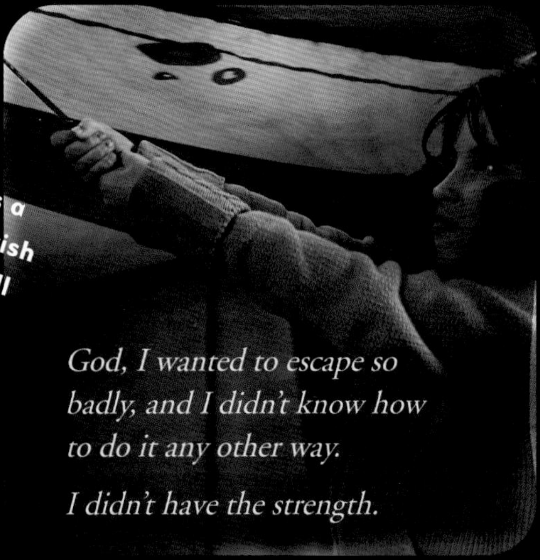
God, I wanted to escape so badly, and I didn't know how to do it any other way.
I didn't have the strength.

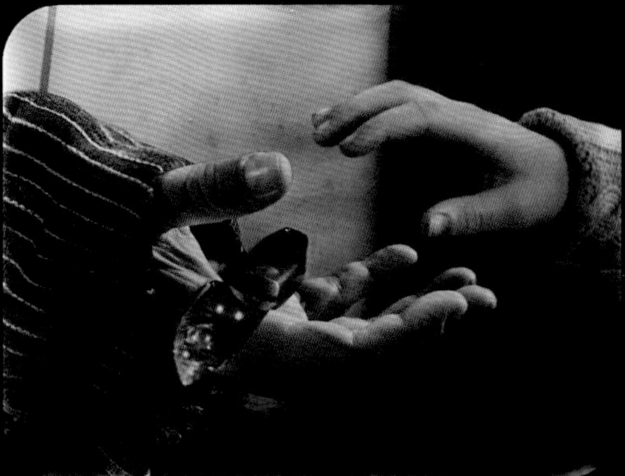
"I'm let down, Maia. You're weak. So weak."

But he really wasn't let down with me, he was actually angry

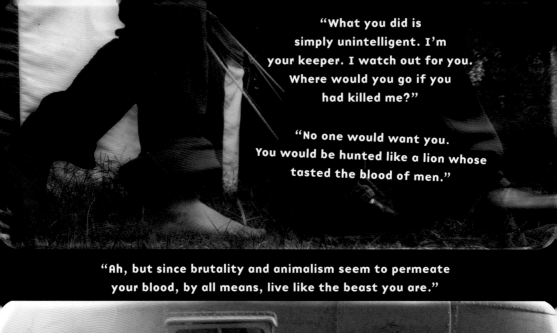

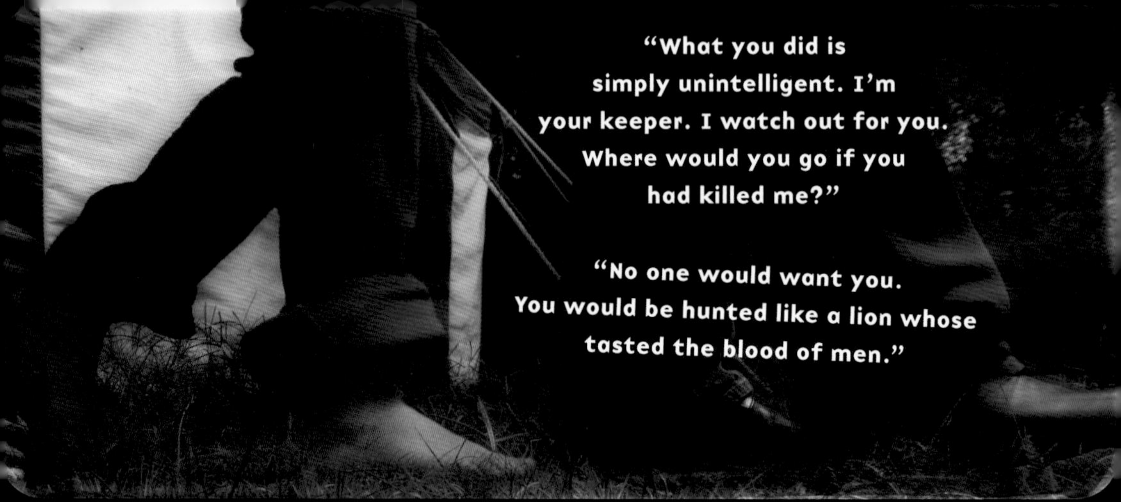
"What you did is simply unintelligent. I'm your keeper. I watch out for you. Where would you go if you had killed me?"
"No one would want you. You would be hunted like a lion whose tasted the blood of men."

"Ah, but since brutality and animalism seem to permeate your blood, by all means, live like the beast you are."

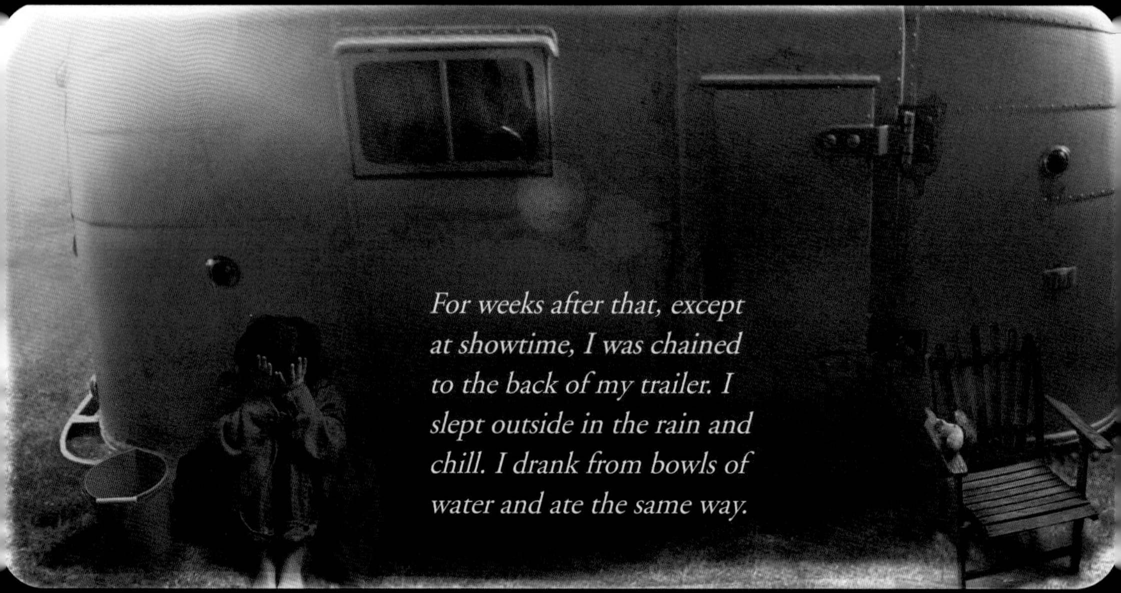
For weeks after that, except at showtime, I was chained to the back of my trailer. I slept outside in the rain and chill. I drank from bowls of water and ate the same way.

I worried I was transforming into something like a coyote or a scavenger.

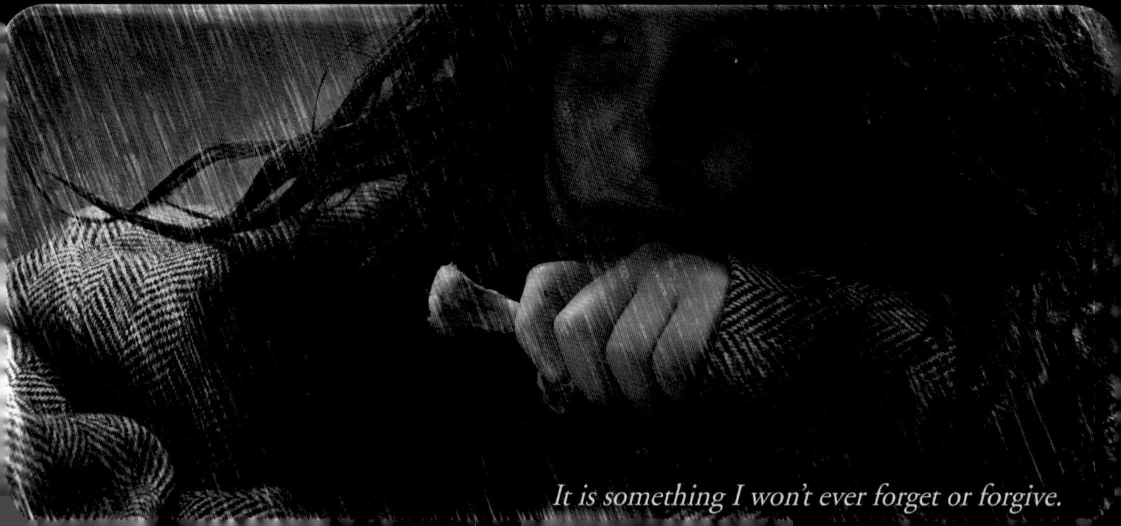
It is something I won't ever forget or forgive.

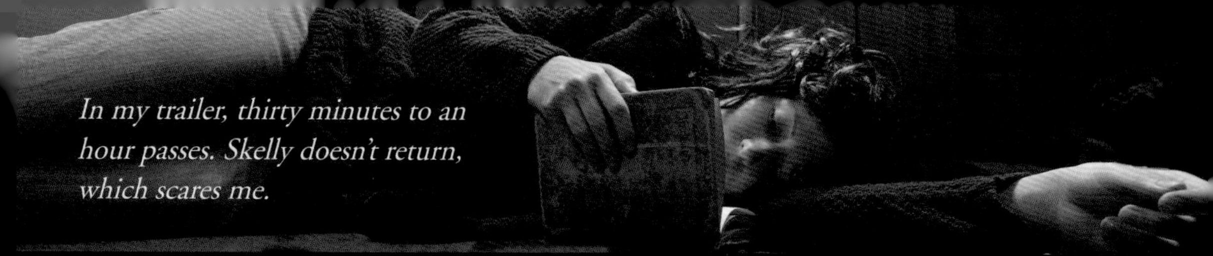
In my trailer, thirty minutes to an hour passes. Skelly doesn't return, which scares me.

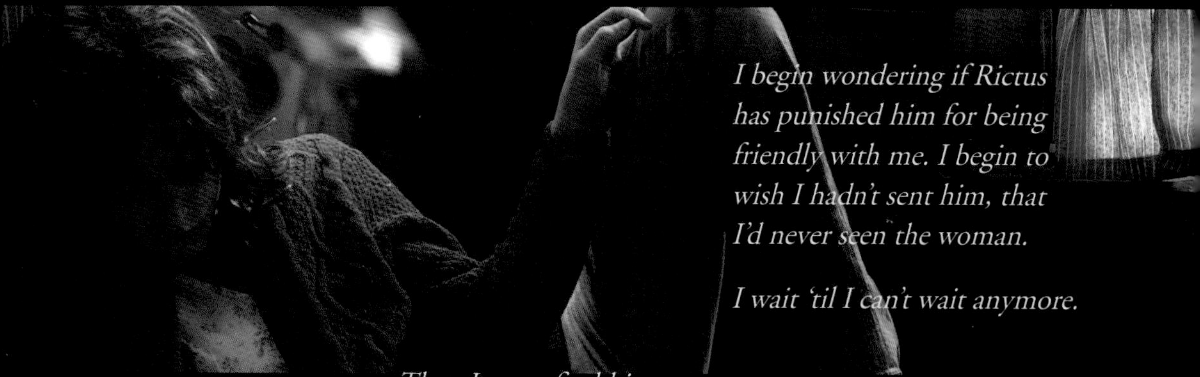
I begin wondering if Rictus has punished him for being friendly with me. I begin to wish I hadn't sent him, that I'd never seen the woman.
I wait 'til I can't wait anymore.

Then I go to find him.

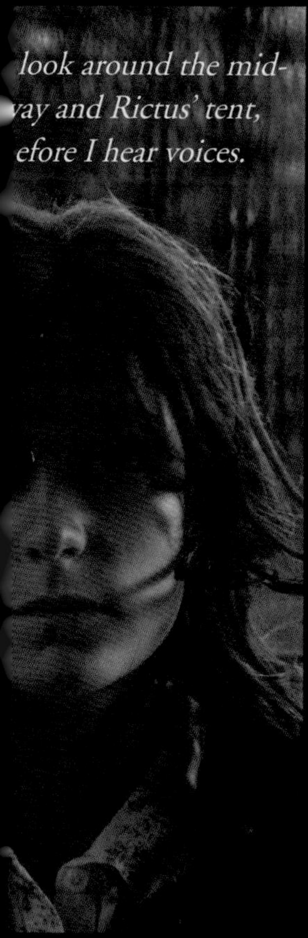
look around the mid-vay and Rictus' tent, efore I hear voices.

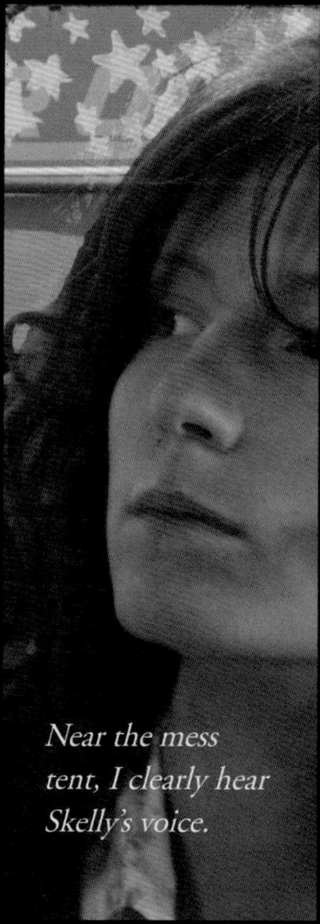
Near the mess tent, I clearly hear Skelly's voice.

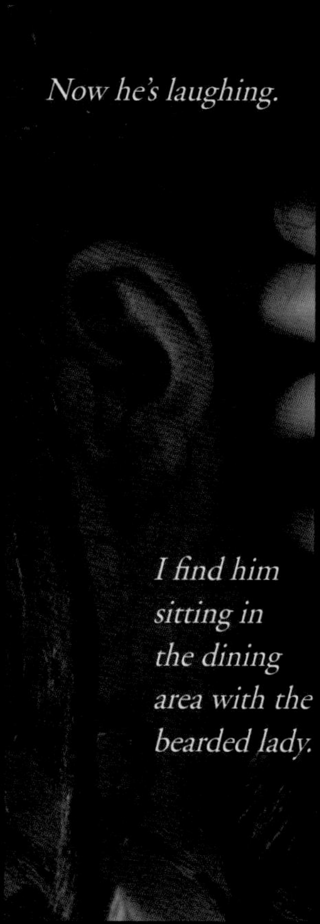
Now he's laughing.
I find him sitting in the dining area with the bearded lady.

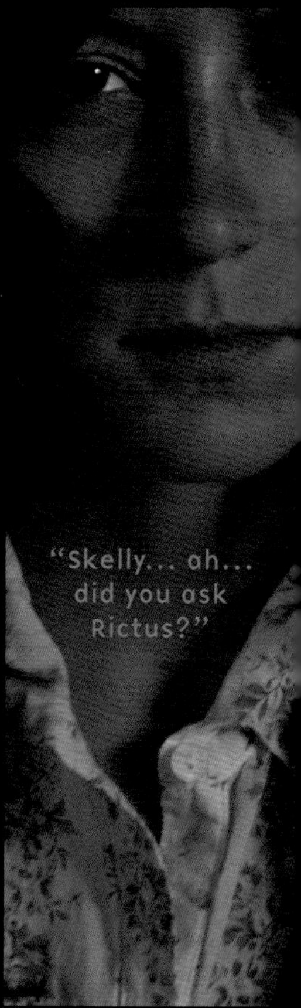
"Skelly... ah... did you ask Rictus?"

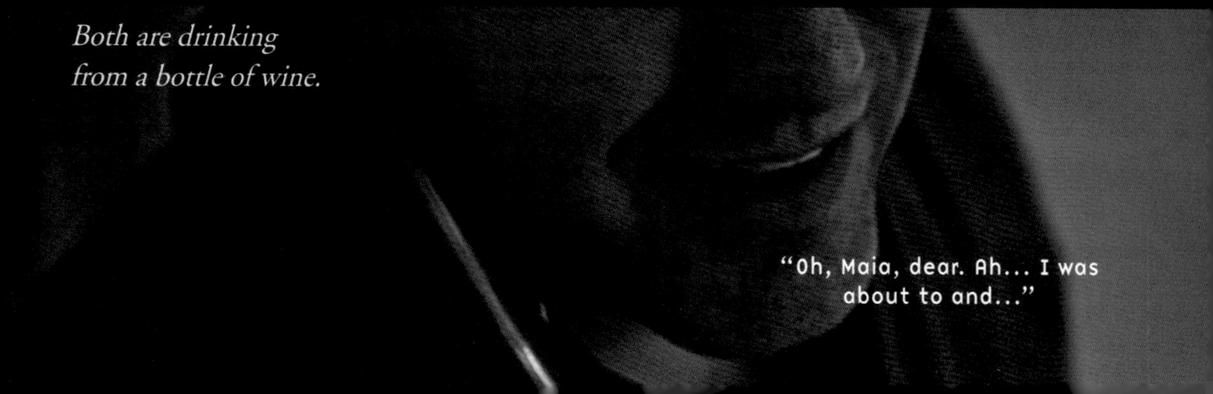
Both are drinking from a bottle of wine.
"Oh, Maia, dear. Ah... I was about to and..."

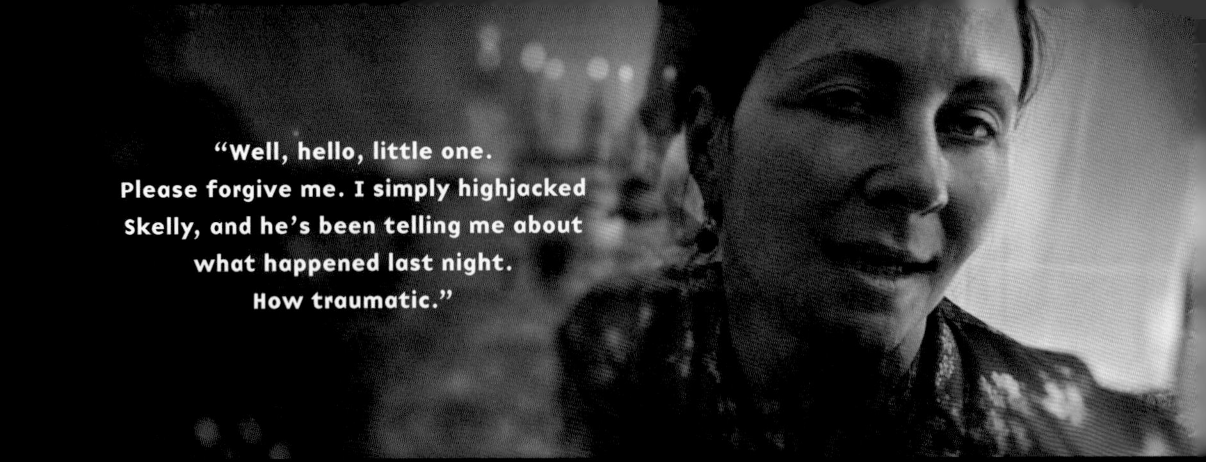
"Well, hello, little one.
Please forgive me. I simply highjacked Skelly, and he's been telling me about what happened last night.
How traumatic."

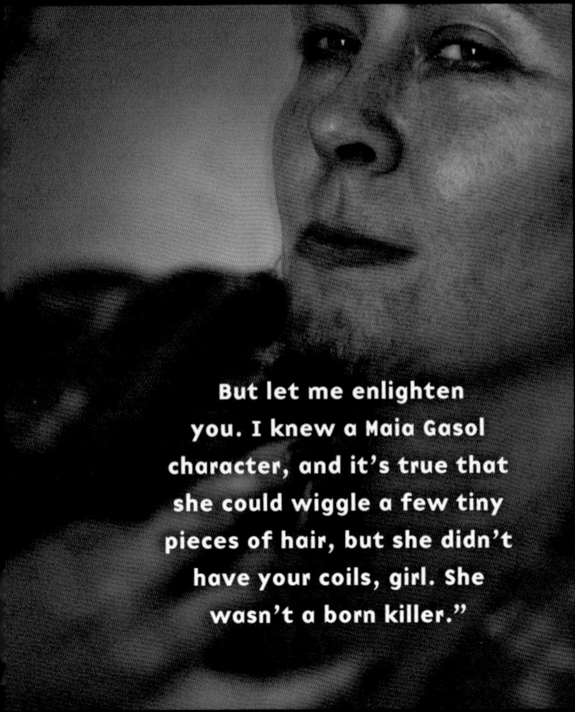
But let me enlighten you. I knew a Maia Gasol character, and it's true that she could wiggle a few tiny pieces of hair, but she didn't have your coils, girl. She wasn't a born killer."

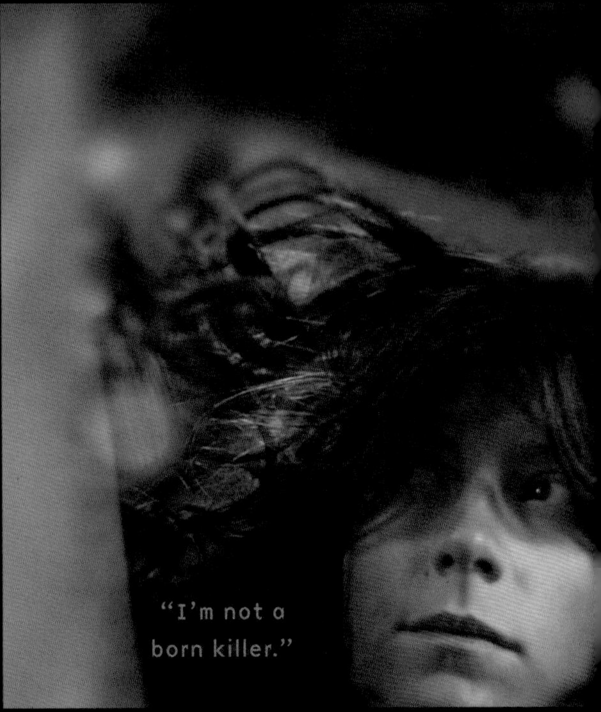
"I'm not a born killer."

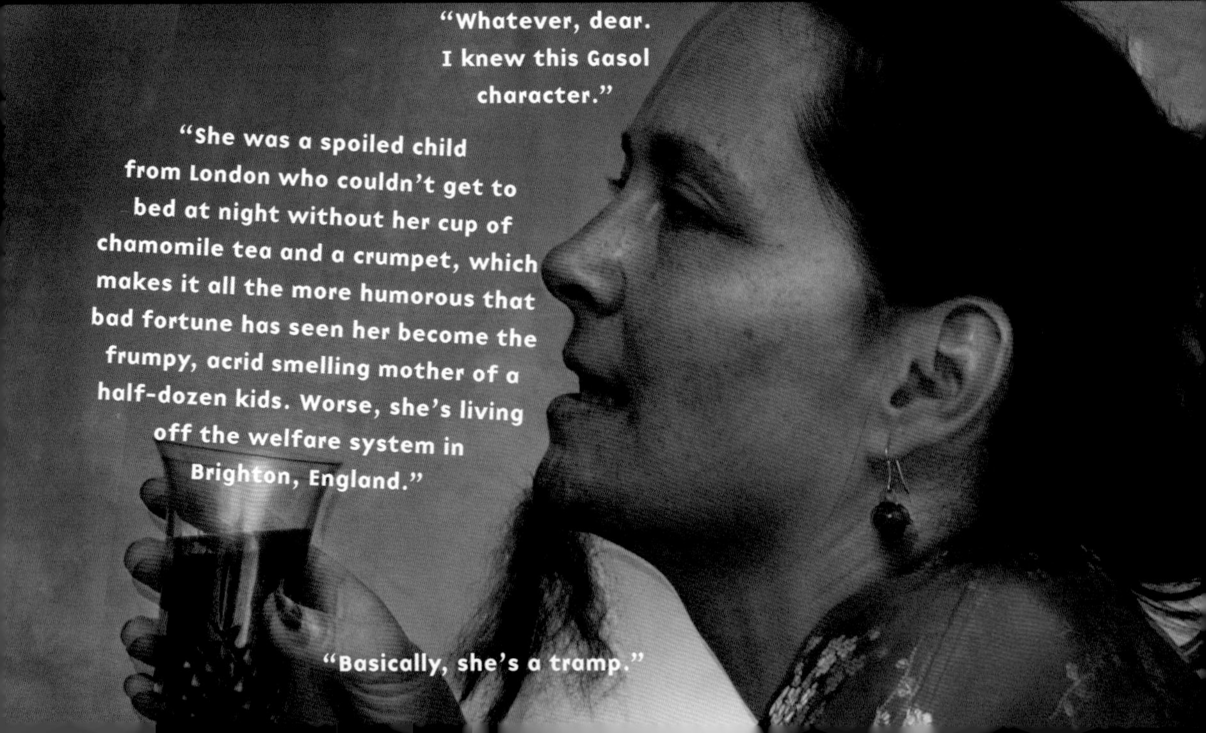
"Whatever, dear. I knew this Gasol character."
"She was a spoiled child from London who couldn't get to bed at night without her cup of chamomile tea and a crumpet, which makes it all the more humorous that bad fortune has seen her become the frumpy, acrid smelling mother of a half-dozen kids. Worse, she's living off the welfare system in Brighton, England."
"Basically, she's a tramp."

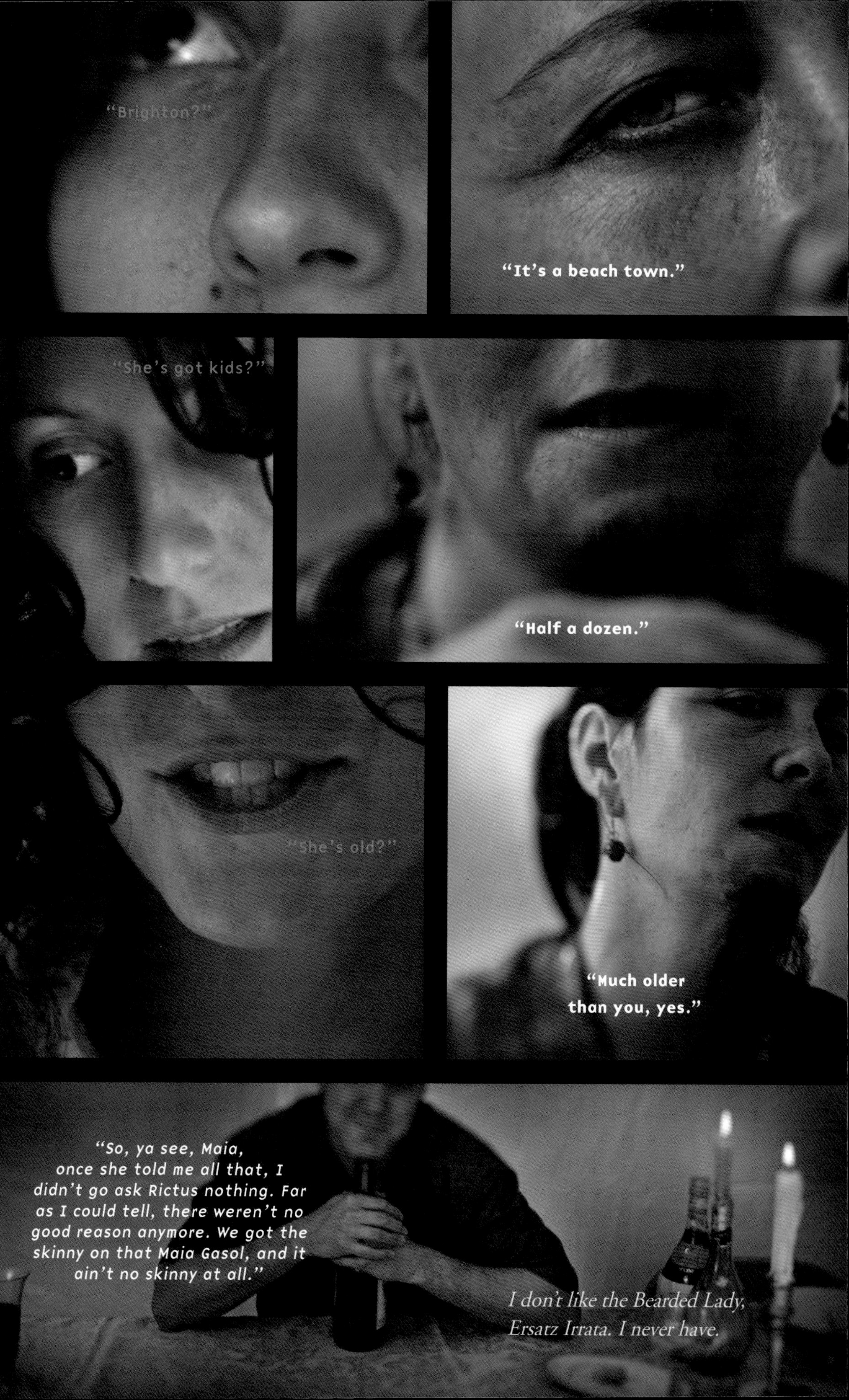
"Brighton?"
"It's a beach town."
"She's got kids?"
"Half a dozen."
"She's old?"
"Much older than you, yes."
"So, ya see, Maia, once she told me all that, I didn't go ask Rictus nothing. Far as I could tell, there weren't no good reason anymore. We got the skinny on that Maia Gasol, and it ain't no skinny at all."
I don't like the Bearded Lady, Ersatz Irrata. I never have.

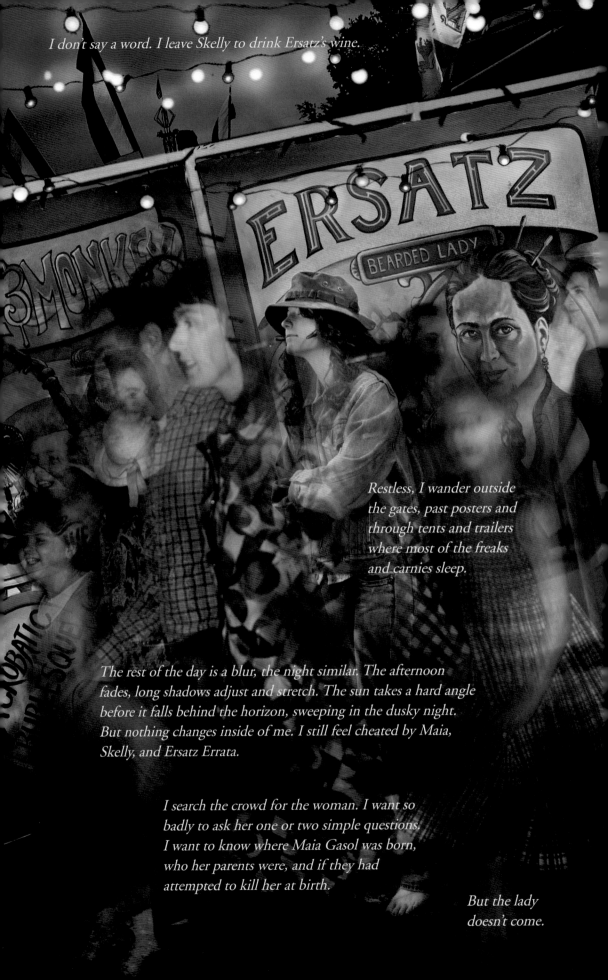

I don't say a word. I leave Skelly to drink Ersatz's wine.

Restless, I wander outside
the gates, past posters and
through tents and trailers
where most of the freaks
and carnies sleep.

The rest of the day is a blur, the night similar. The afternoon
fades, long shadows adjust and stretch. The sun takes a hard angle
before it falls behind the horizon, sweeping in the dusky night.
But nothing changes inside of me. I still feel cheated by Maia,
Skelly, and Ersatz Errata.

I search the crowd for the woman. I want so
badly to ask her one or two simple questions.
I want to know where Maia Gasol was born,
who her parents were, and if they had
attempted to kill her at birth.

But the lady
doesn't come.

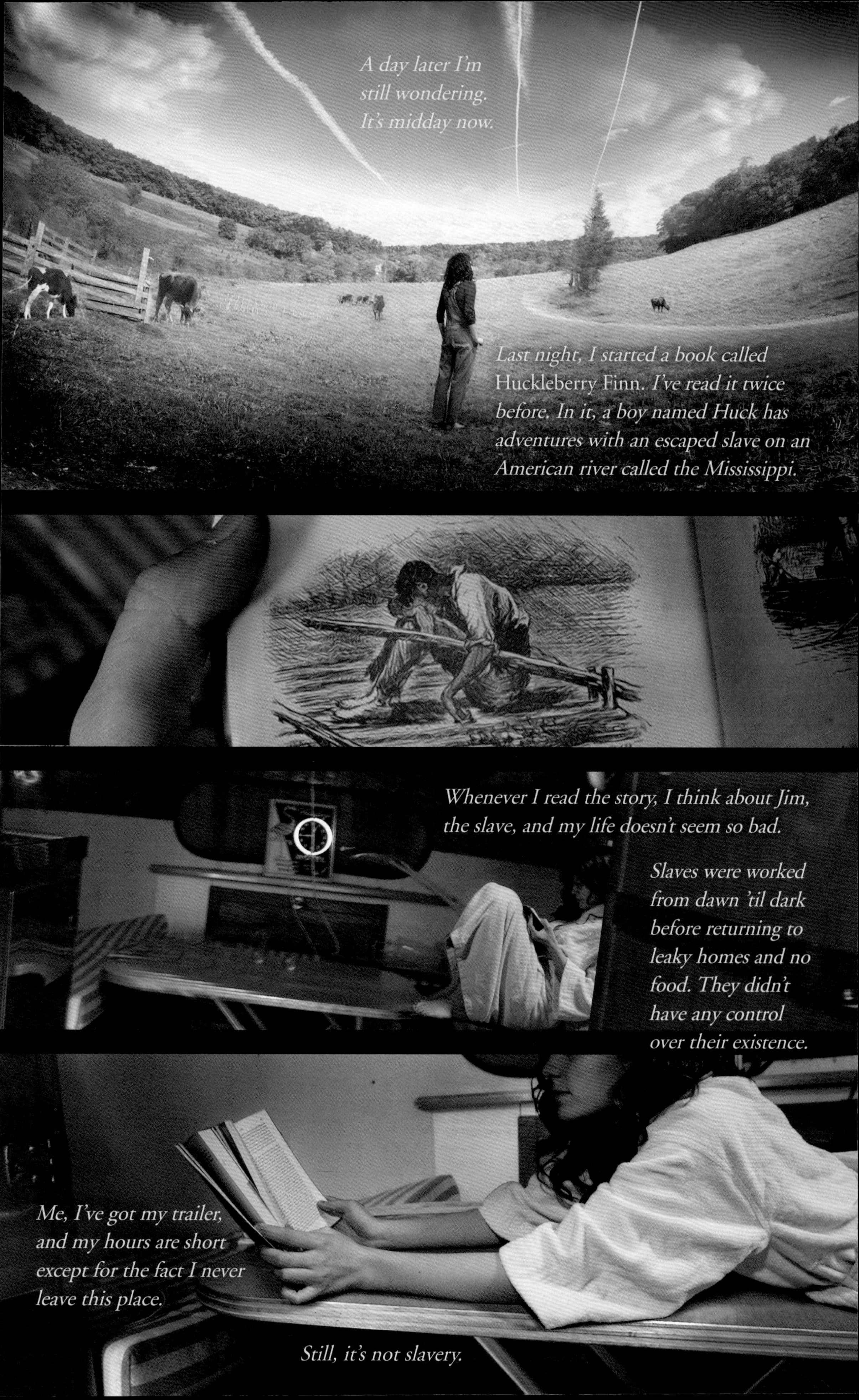
A day later I'm still wondering. It's midday now.
Last night, I started a book called Huckleberry Finn. I've read it twice before. In it, a boy named Huck has adventures with an escaped slave on an American river called the Mississippi.
Whenever I read the story, I think about Jim, the slave, and my life doesn't seem so bad.
Slaves were worked from dawn 'til dark before returning to leaky homes and no food. They didn't have any control over their existence.
Me, I've got my trailer, and my hours are short except for the fact I never leave this place.
Still, it's not slavery.

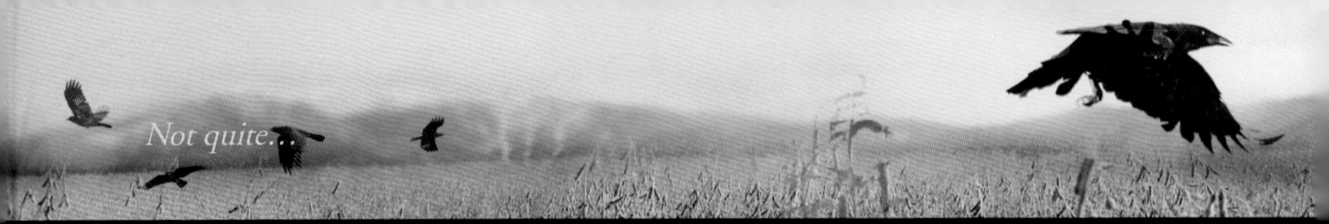
Not quite…

My hair hisses, and I turn around.

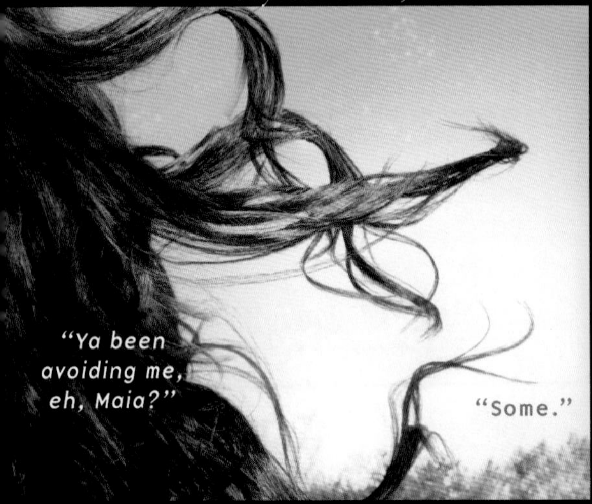
"Ya been avoiding me, eh, Maia?"
"Some."

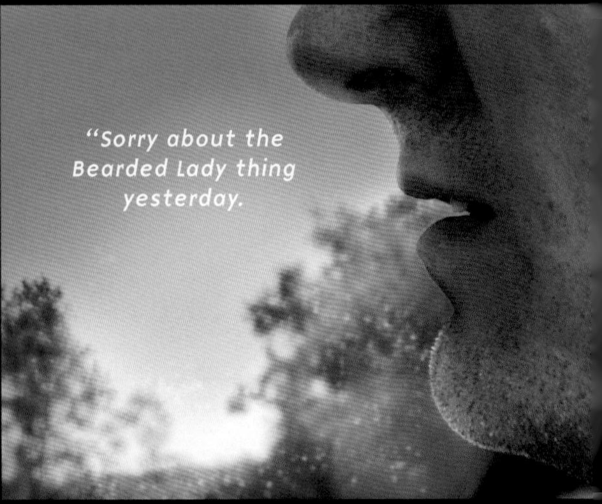
"Sorry about the Bearded Lady thing yesterday.

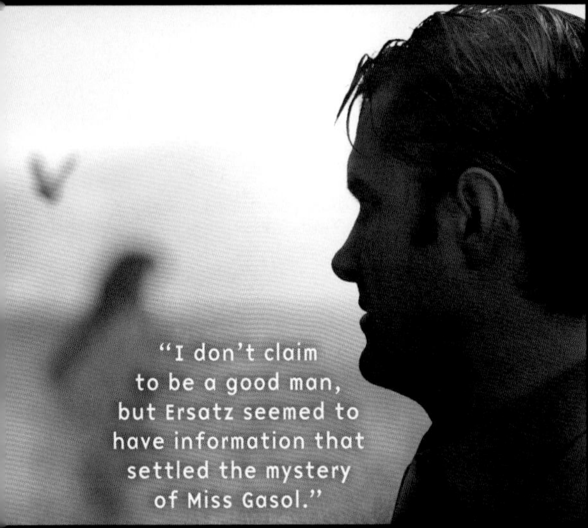
"I don't claim to be a good man, but Ersatz seemed to have information that settled the mystery of Miss Gasol."

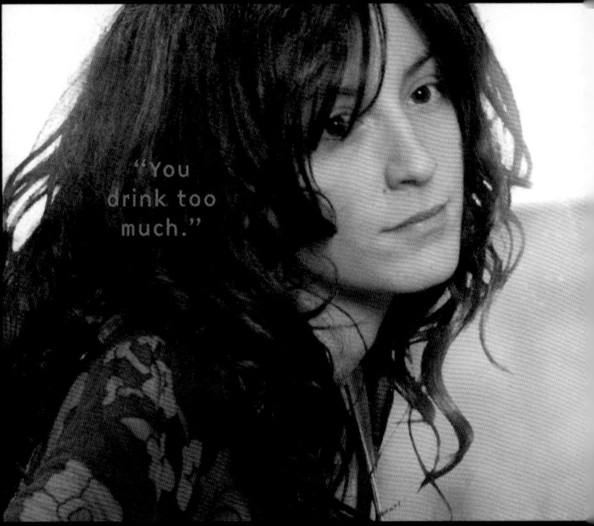
"You drink too much."

"Yeah, that's true."

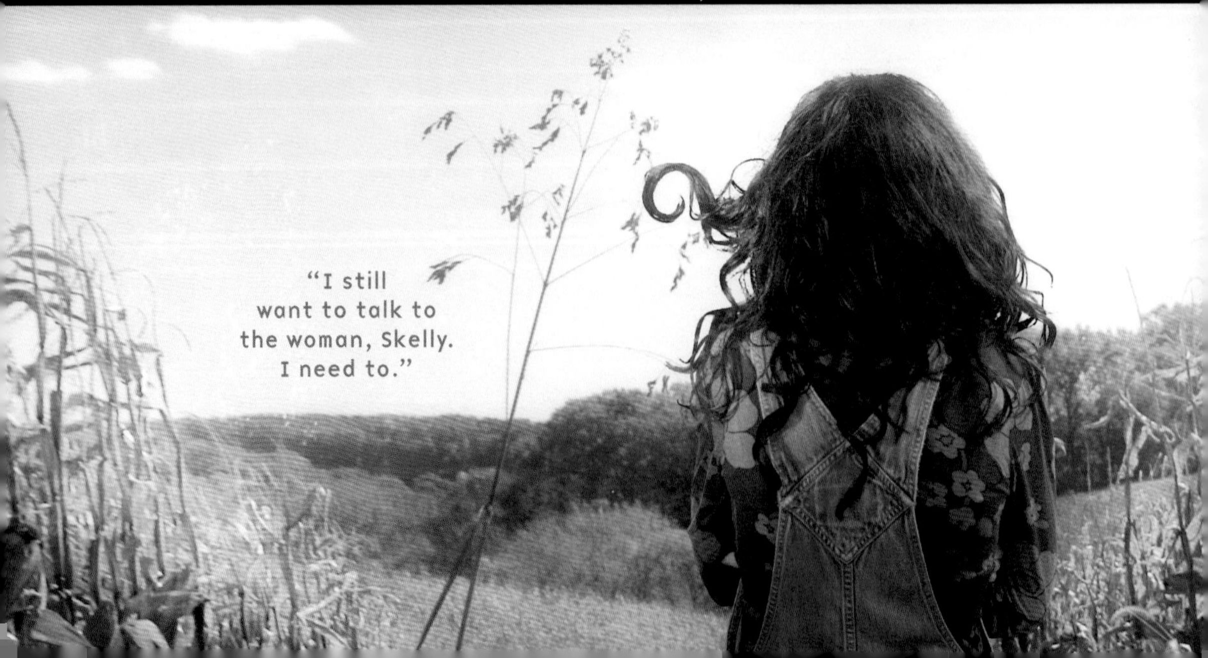
"I still want to talk to the woman, Skelly. I need to."

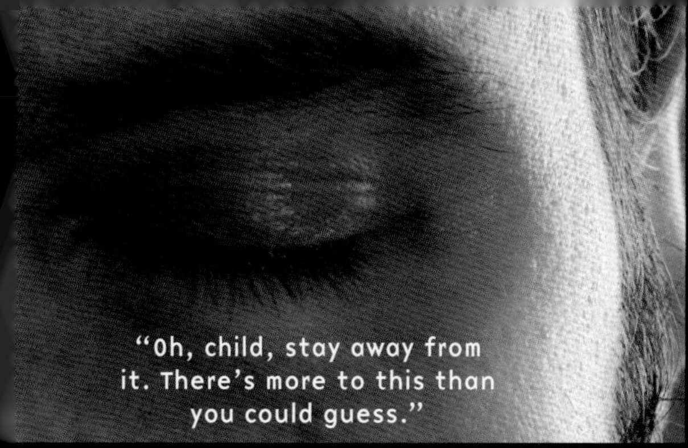
"Oh, child, stay away from it. There's more to this than you could guess."
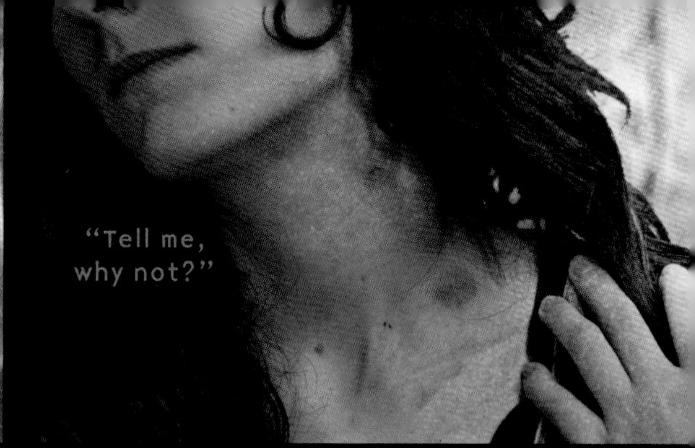
"Tell me, why not?"
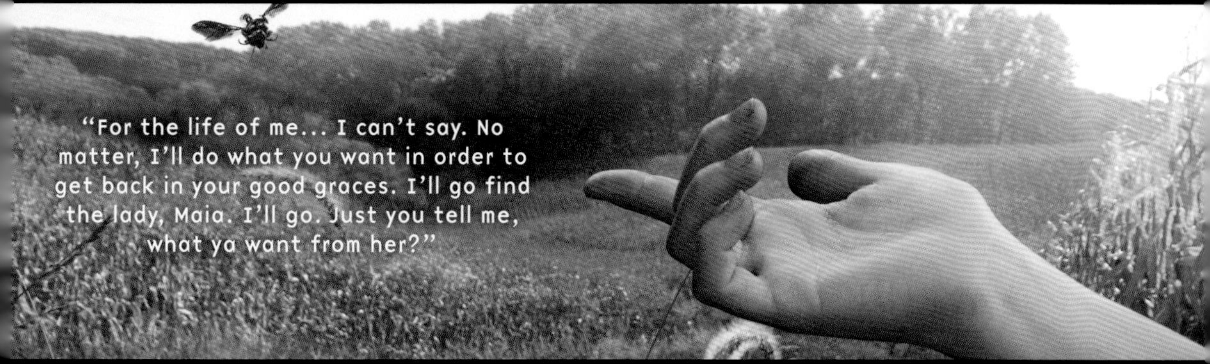
"For the life of me... I can't say. No matter, I'll do what you want in order to get back in your good graces. I'll go find the lady, Maia. I'll go. Just you tell me, what ya want from her?"
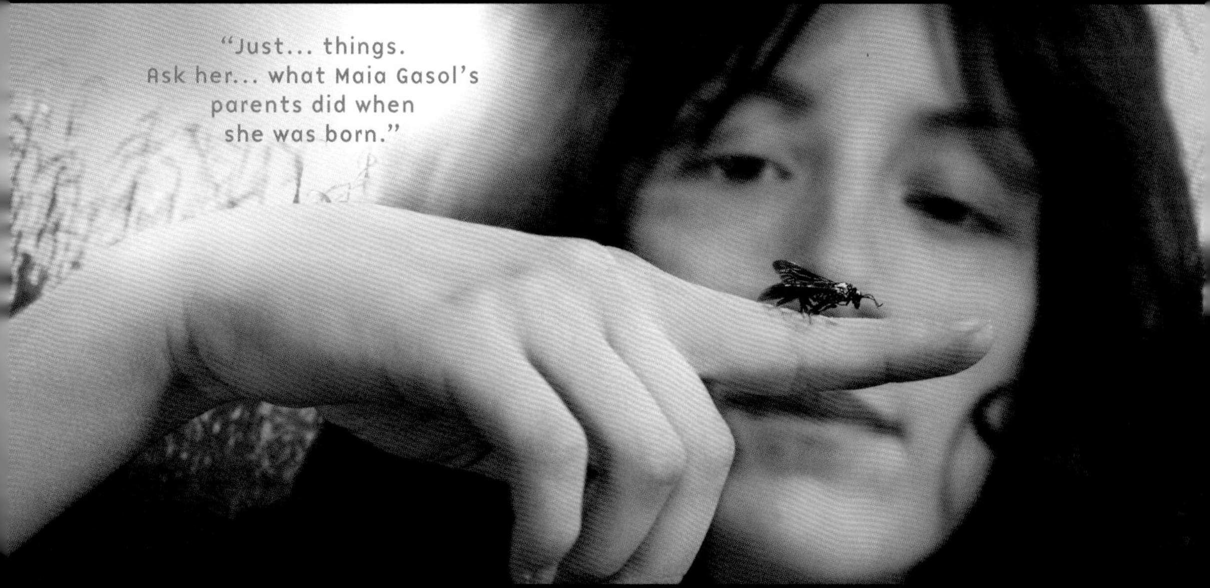
"Just... things. Ask her... what Maia Gasol's parents did when she was born."
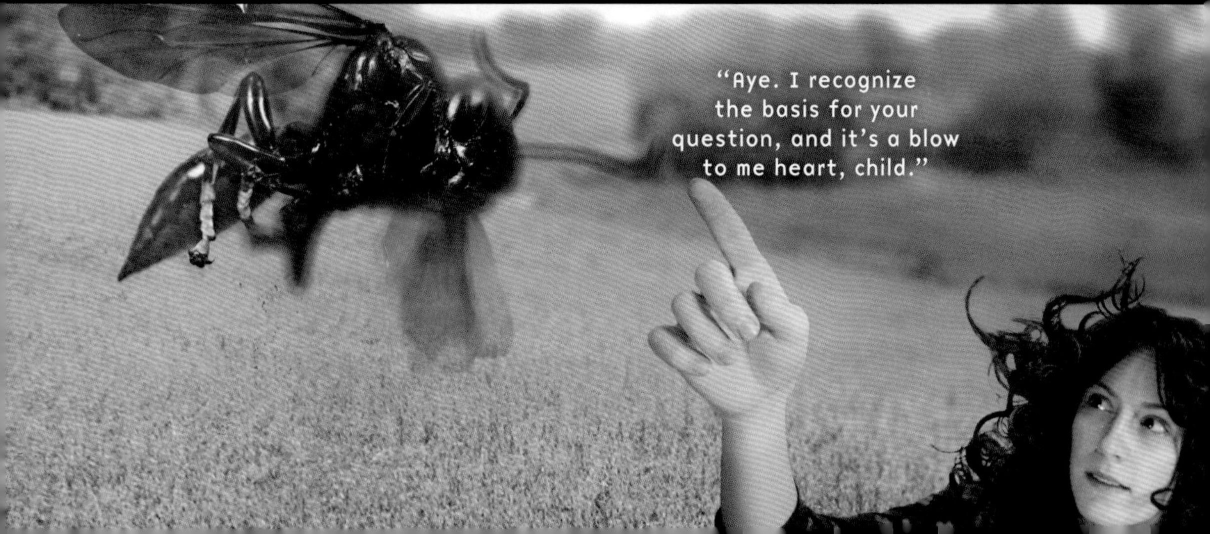
"Aye. I recognize the basis for your question, and it's a blow to me heart, child."

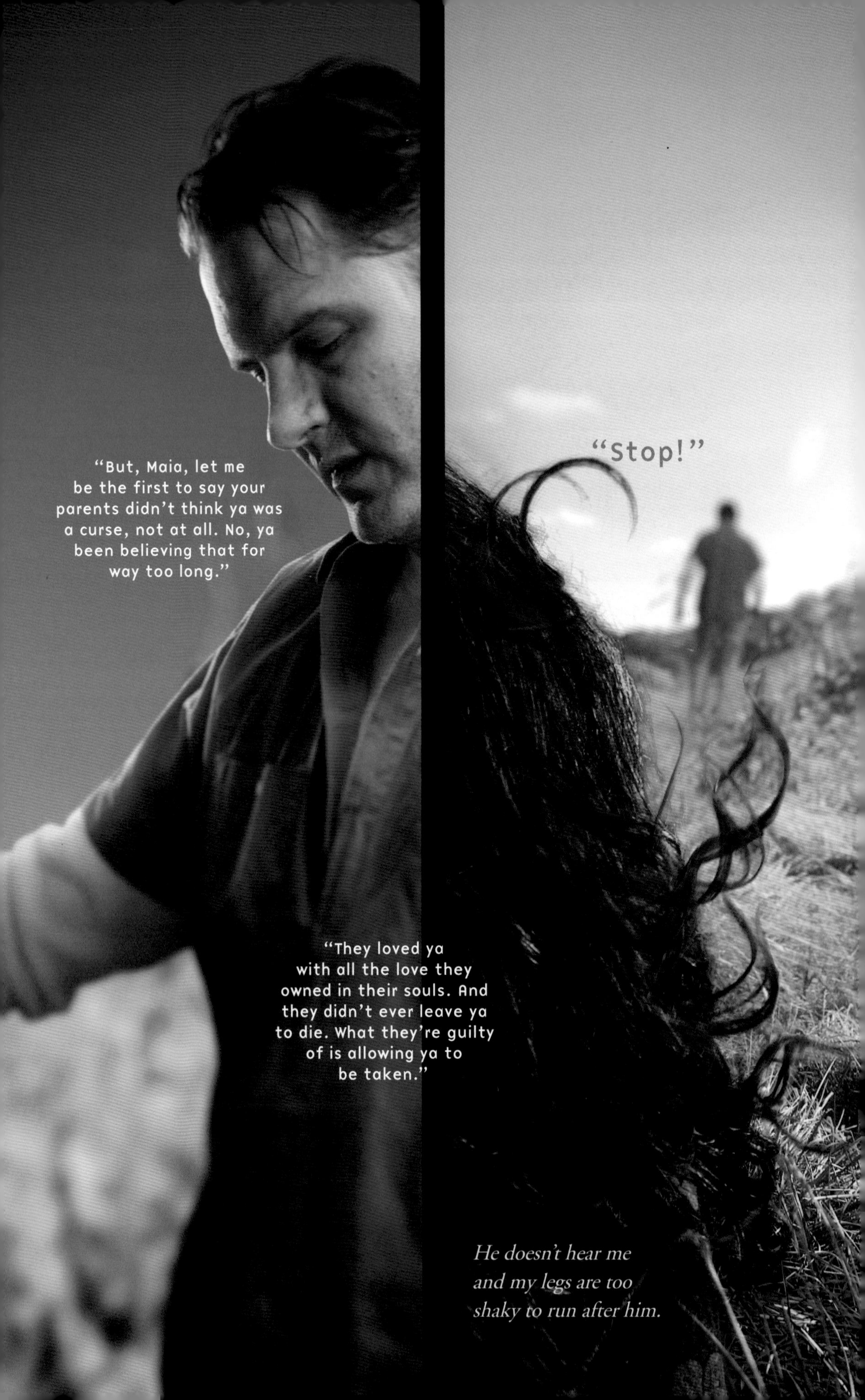

"But, Maia, let me be the first to say your parents didn't think ya was a curse, not at all. No, ya been believing that for way too long."

"Stop!"

"They loved ya with all the love they owned in their souls. And they didn't ever leave ya to die. What they're guilty of is allowing ya to be taken."

He doesn't hear me and my legs are too shaky to run after him.

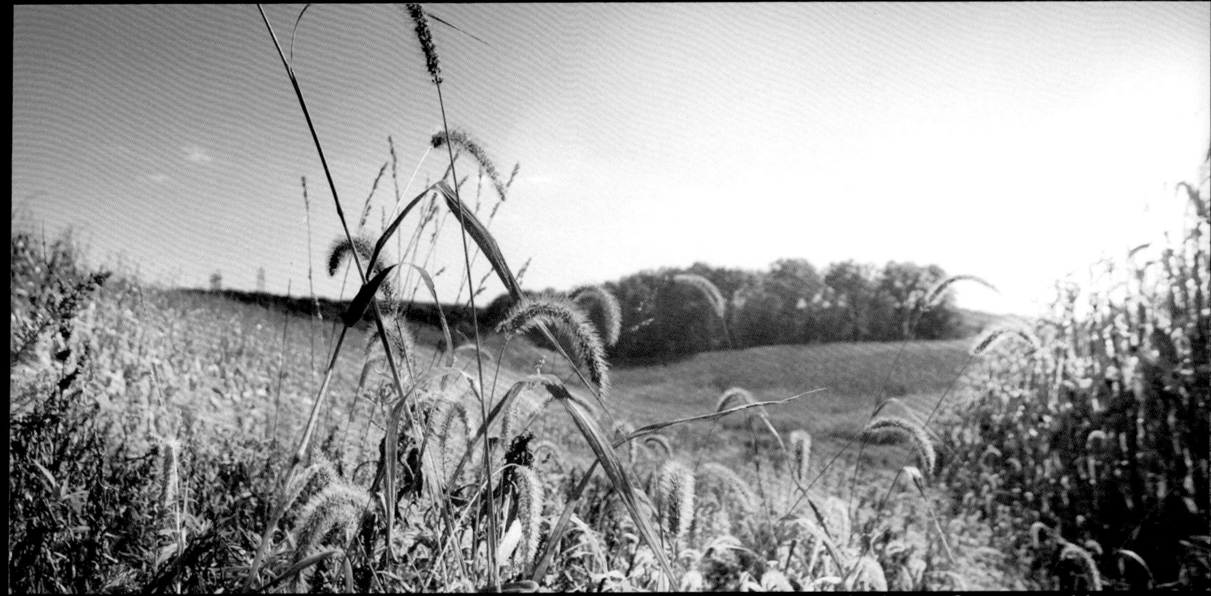

Because of what I am, I have tried not to imagine how I was treated when I first arrived here.

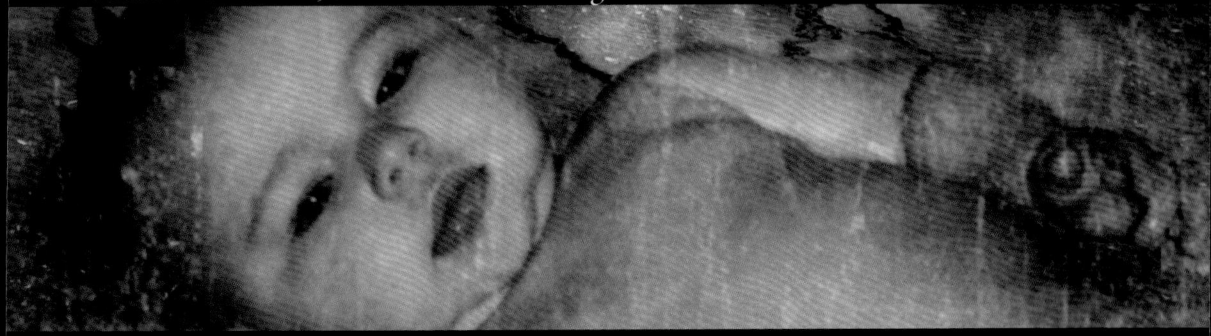

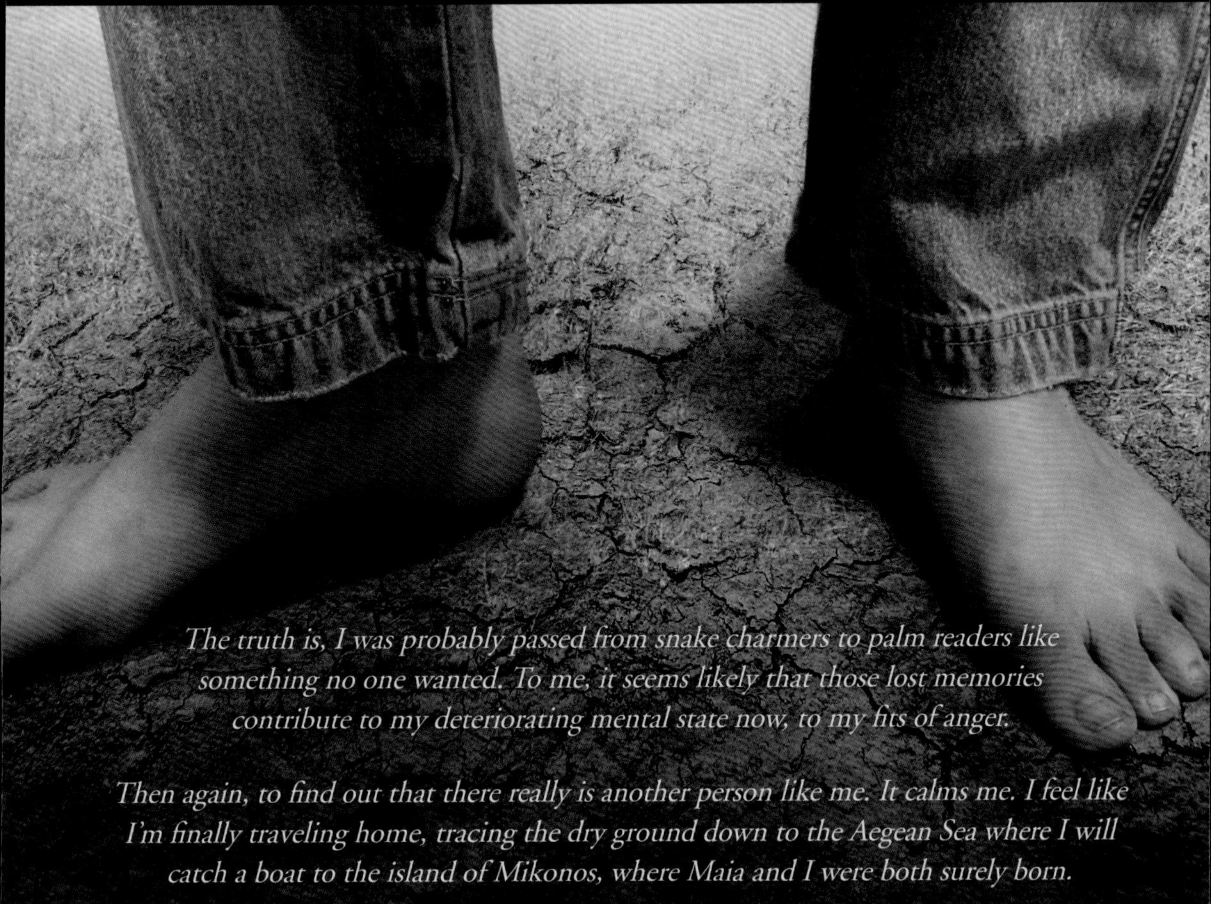

The truth is, I was probably passed from snake charmers to palm readers like something no one wanted. To me, it seems likely that those lost memories contribute to my deteriorating mental state now, to my fits of anger.

Then again, to find out that there really is another person like me. It calms me. I feel like I'm finally traveling home, tracing the dry ground down to the Aegean Sea where I will catch a boat to the island of Mikonos, where Maia and I were both surely born.

somewhere. It wouldn't be a shock. He has almost no self control. Late in the afternoon, I dress like Medusa's Daughter and leave my trailer.

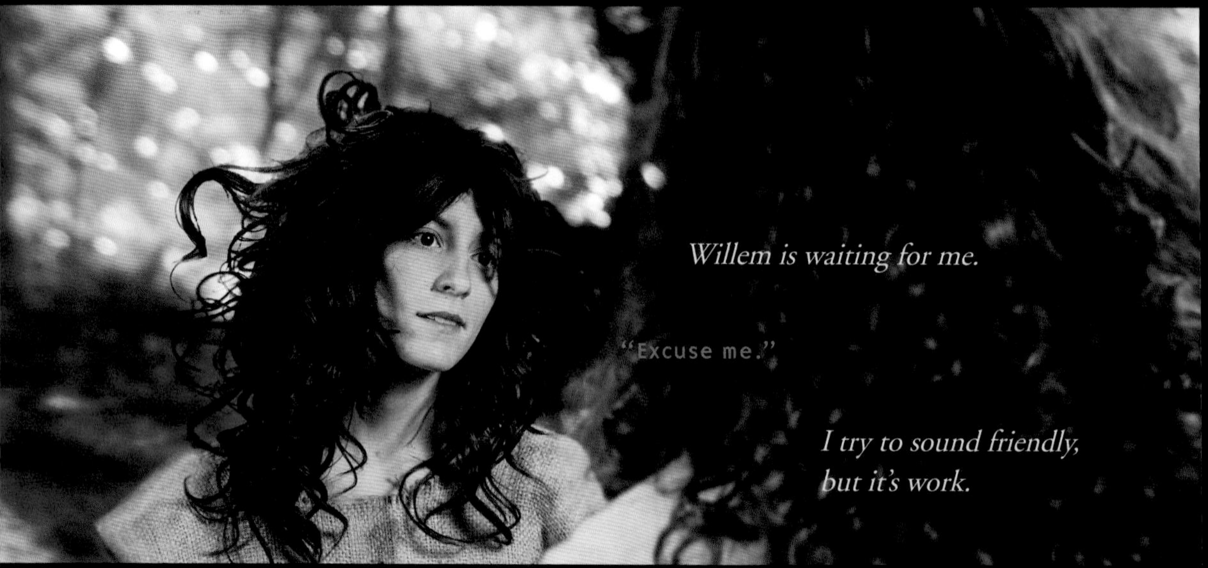
Willem is waiting for me.
"Excuse me."
I try to sound friendly, but it's work.

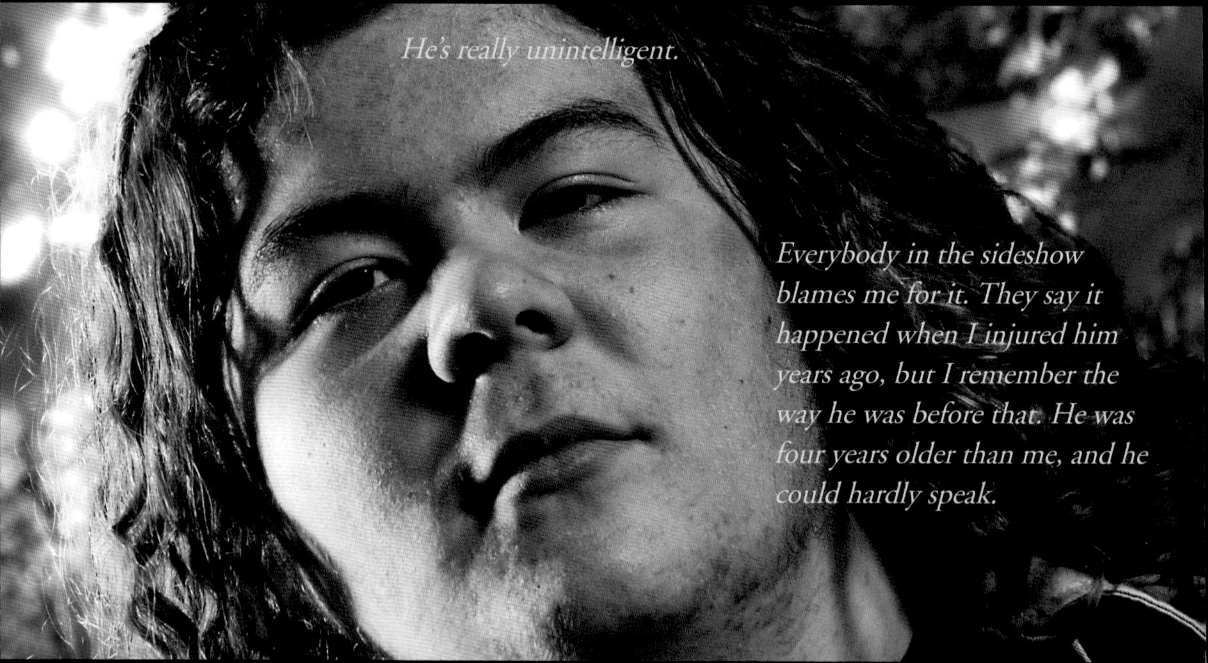
He's really unintelligent.
Everybody in the sideshow blames me for it. They say it happened when I injured him years ago, but I remember the way he was before that. He was four years older than me, and he could hardly speak.

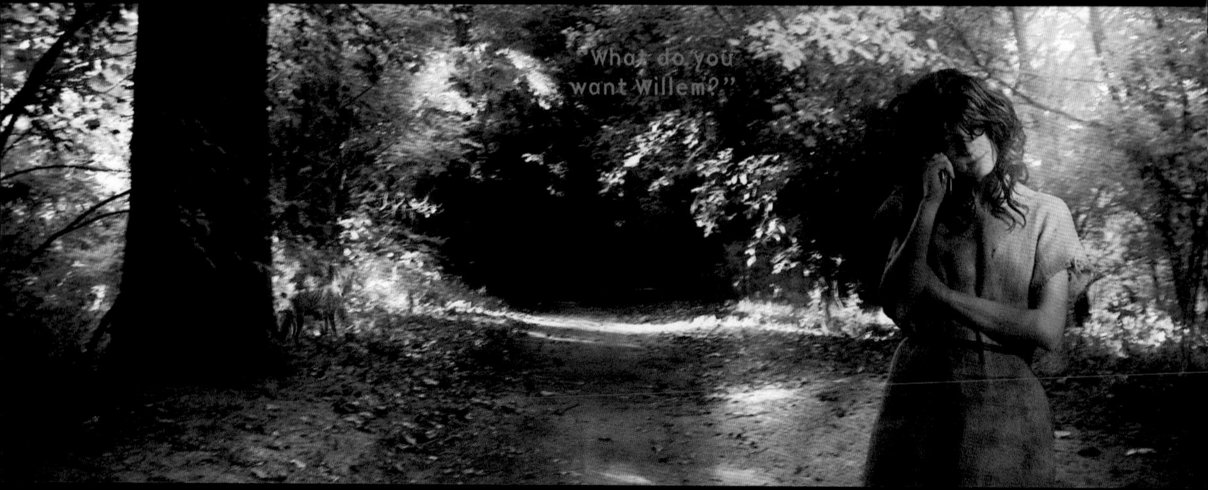
"What do you want Willem?"

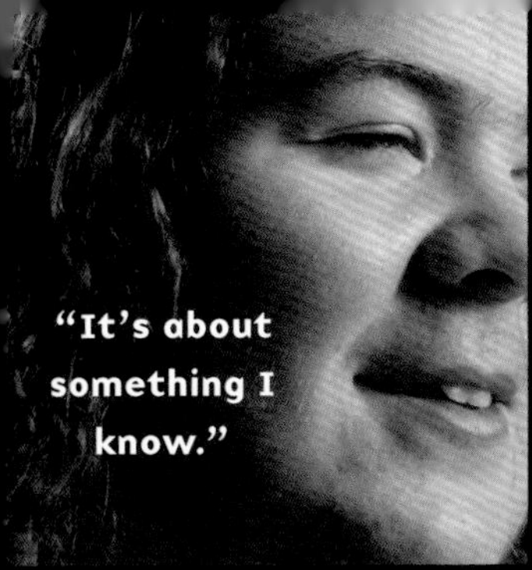
"It's about something I know."
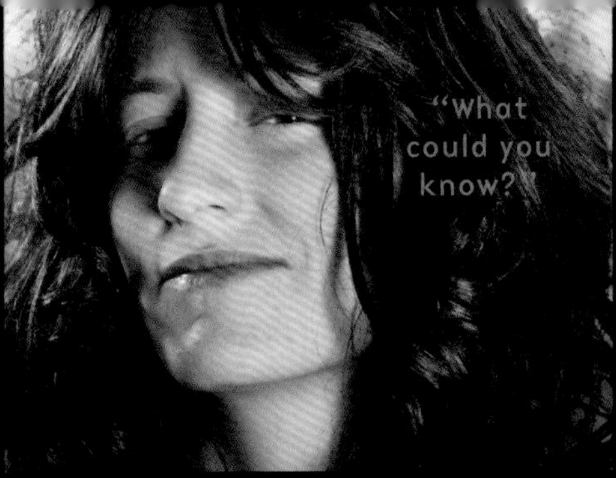
"What could you know?"
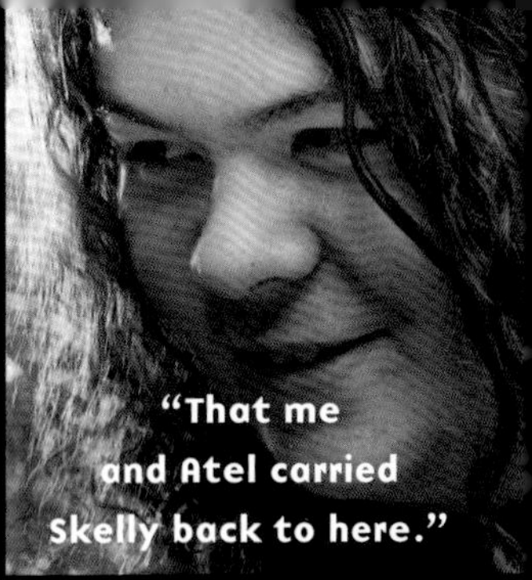
"That me and Atel carried Skelly back to here."
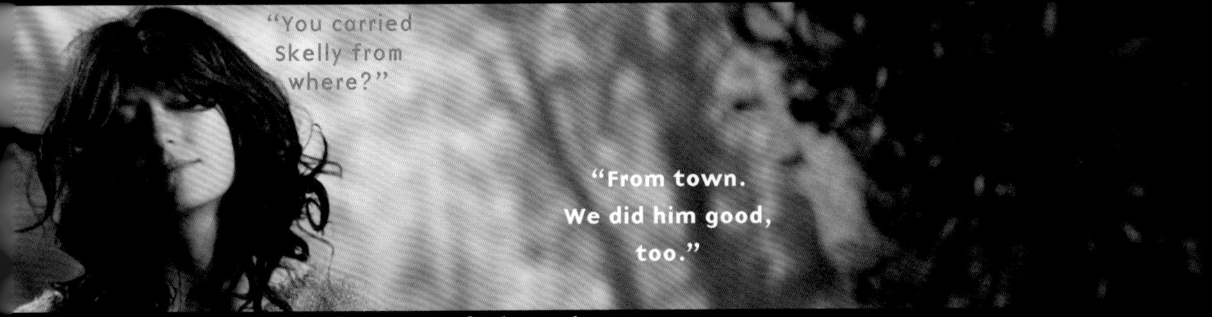
"You carried Skelly from where?"
"From town. We did him good, too."

I look up, now frightened.

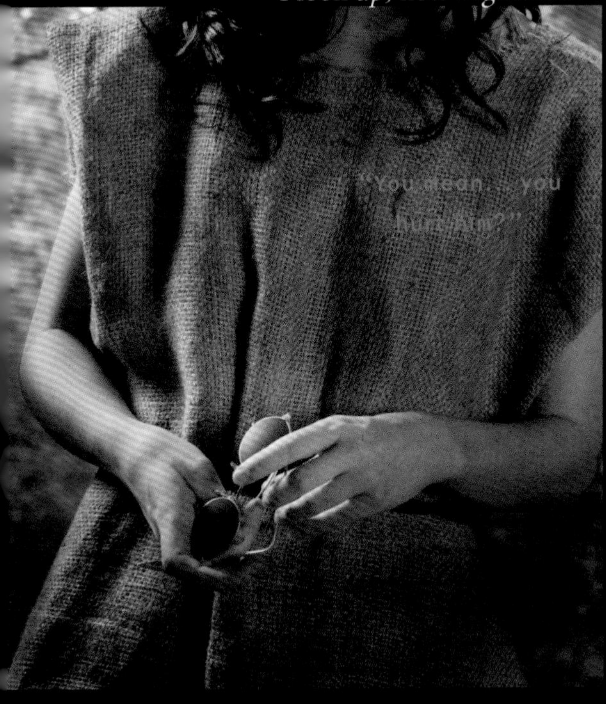
"You mean . . . you hurt him?"
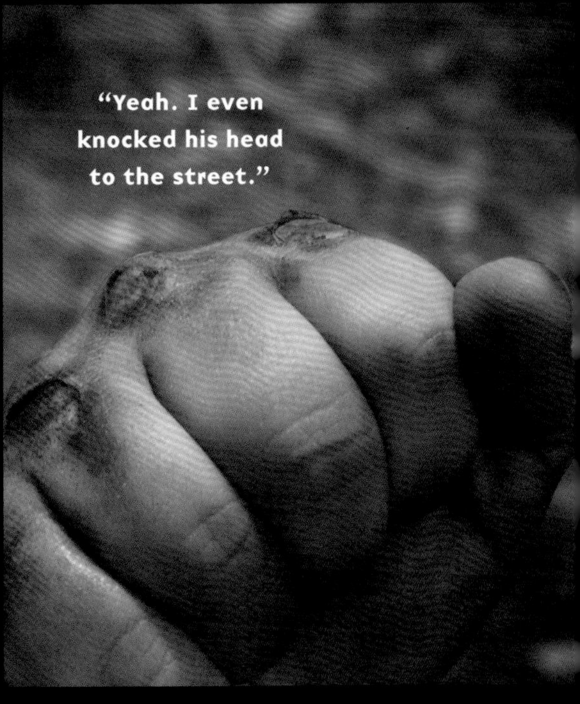
"Yeah. I even knocked his head to the street."
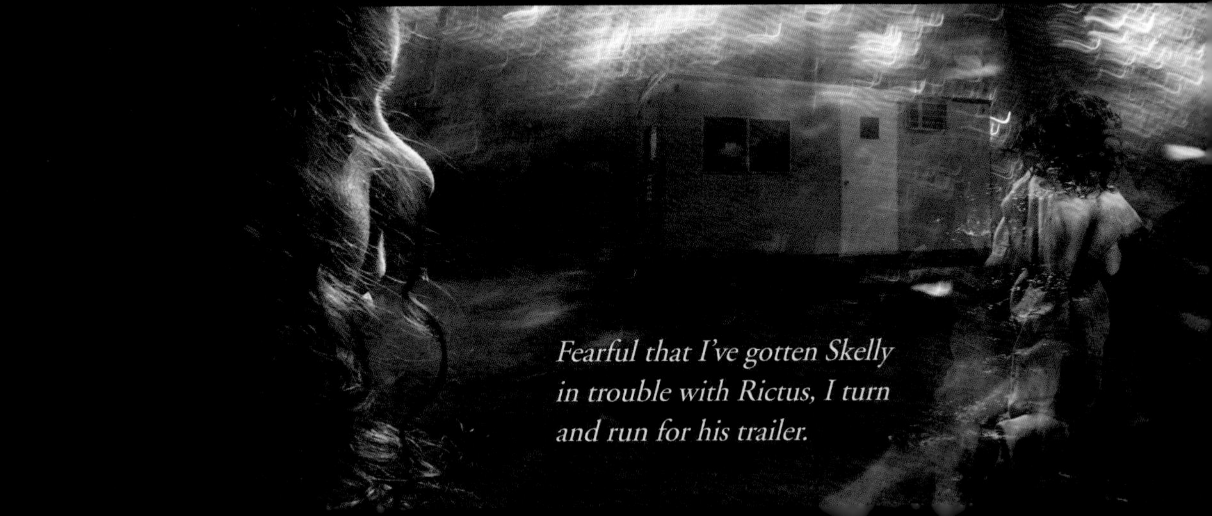
Fearful that I've gotten Skelly in trouble with Rictus, I turn and run for his trailer.

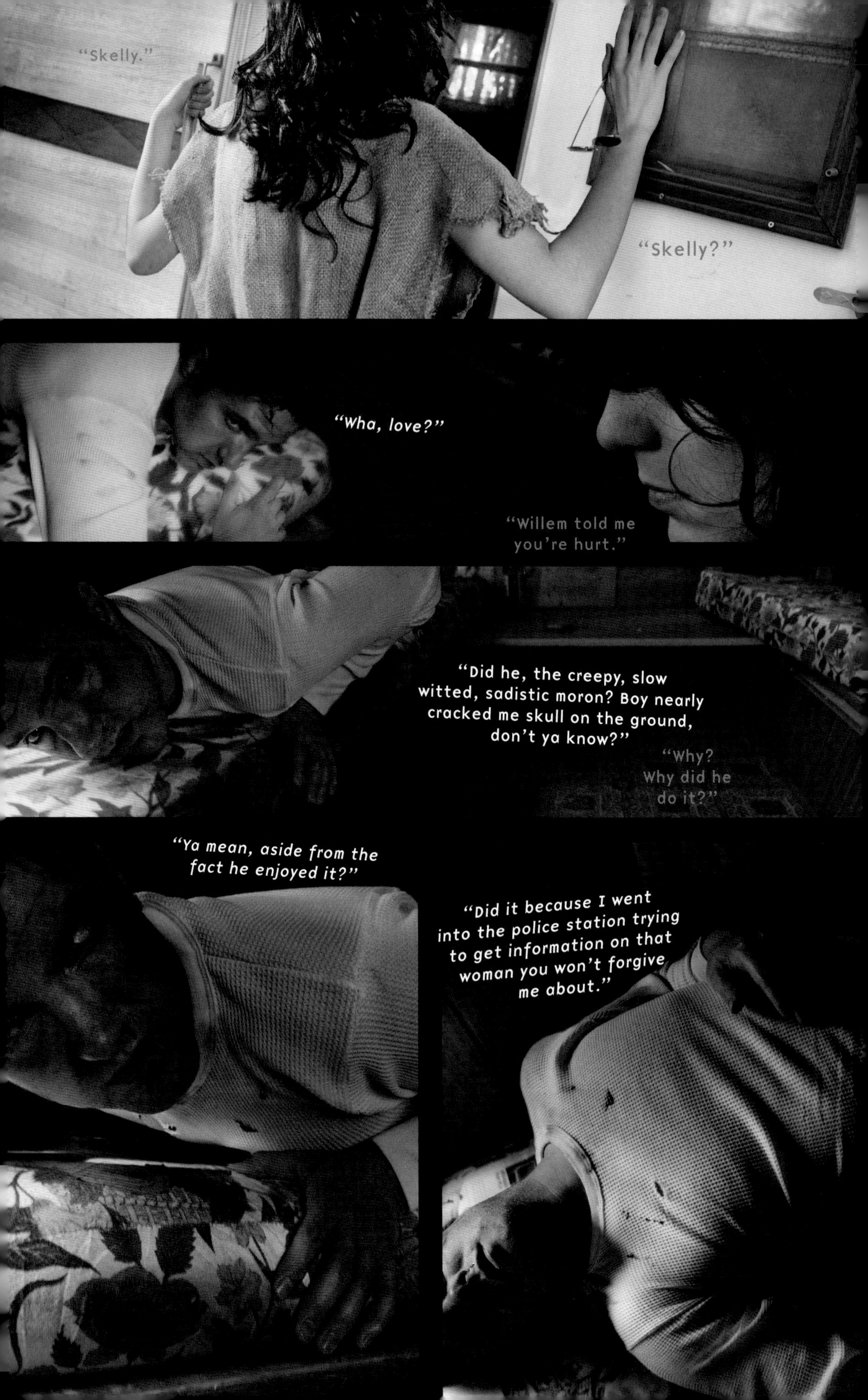

"Skelly."
"Skelly?"
"Wha, love?"
"Willem told me you're hurt."
"Did he, the creepy, slow witted, sadistic moron? Boy nearly cracked me skull on the ground, don't ya know?"
"Why? Why did he do it?"
"Ya mean, aside from the fact he enjoyed it?"
"Did it because I went into the police station trying to get information on that woman you won't forgive me about."

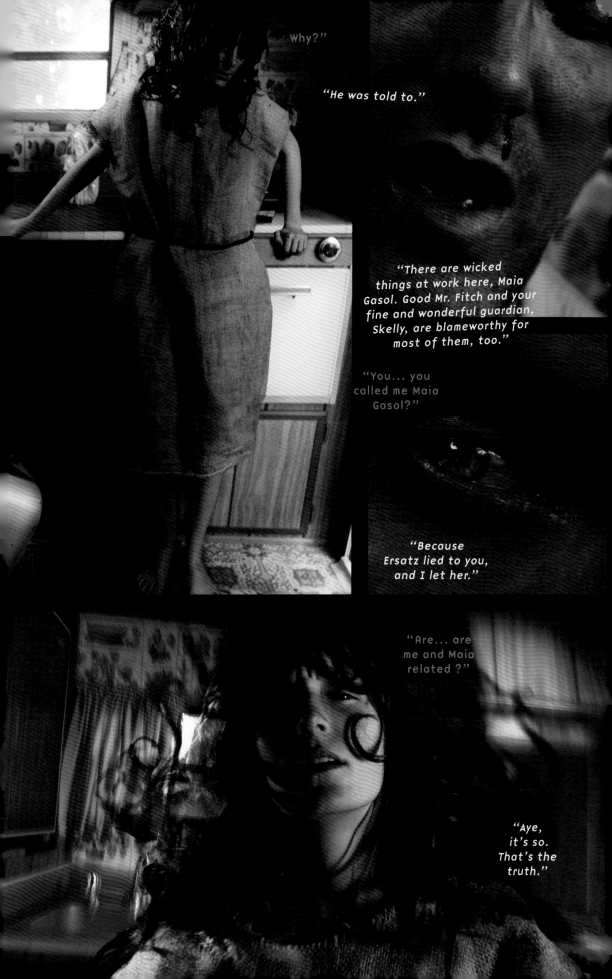

Why?"

"He was told to."

"There are wicked things at work here, Maia Gasol. Good Mr. Fitch and your fine and wonderful guardian, Skelly, are blameworthy for most of them, too."

"You... you called me Maia Gasol?"

"Because Ersatz lied to you, and I let her."

"Are... are me and Maia related?"

"Aye, it's so. That's the truth."

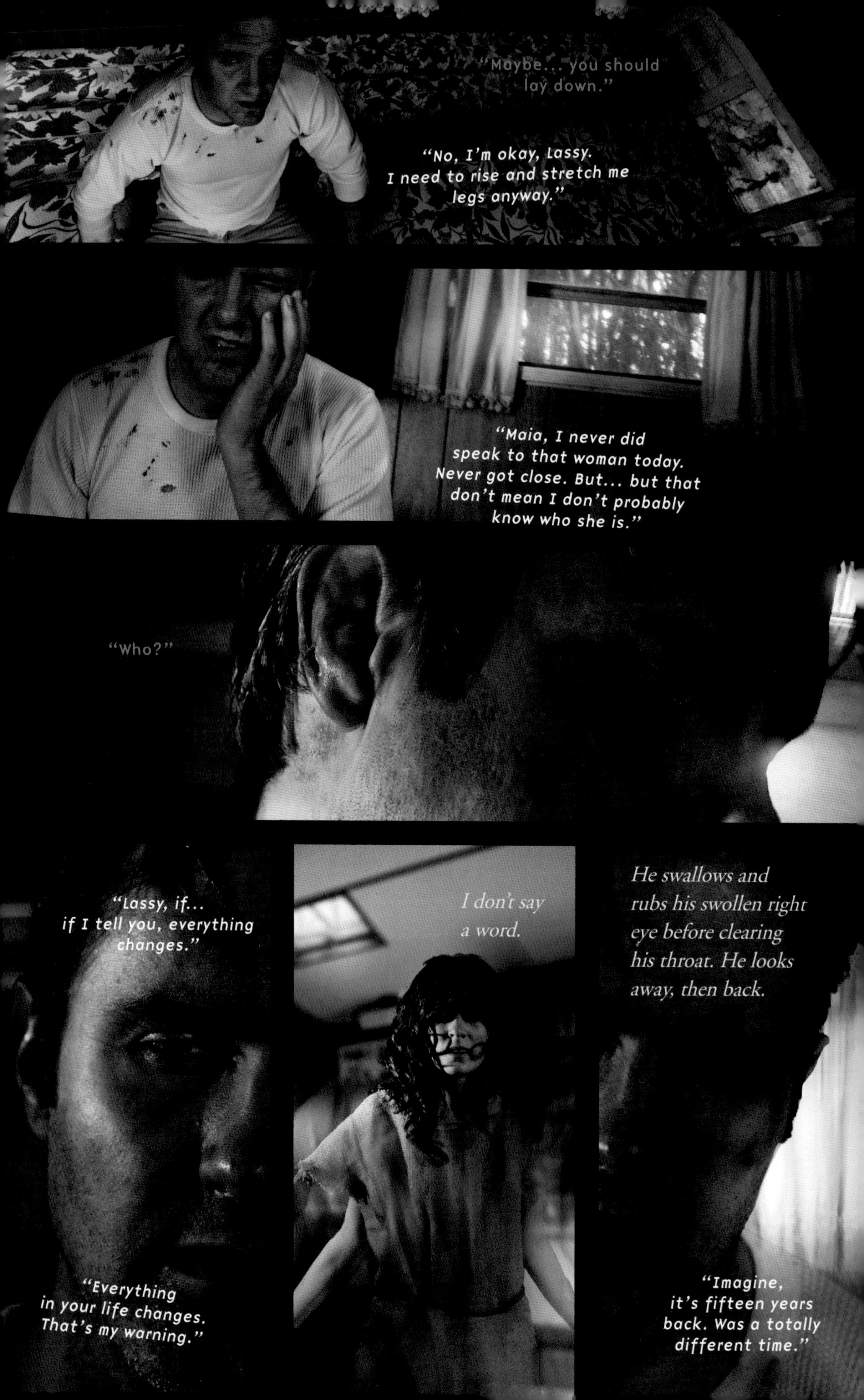
"Maybe... you should lay down."
"No, I'm okay, Lassy. I need to rise and stretch me legs anyway."
"Maia, I never did speak to that woman today. Never got close. But... but that don't mean I don't probably know who she is."
"Who?"
"Lassy, if... if I tell you, everything changes."
"Everything in your life changes. That's my warning."
I don't say a word.
He swallows and rubs his swollen right eye before clearing his throat. He looks away, then back.
"Imagine, it's fifteen years back. Was a totally different time."

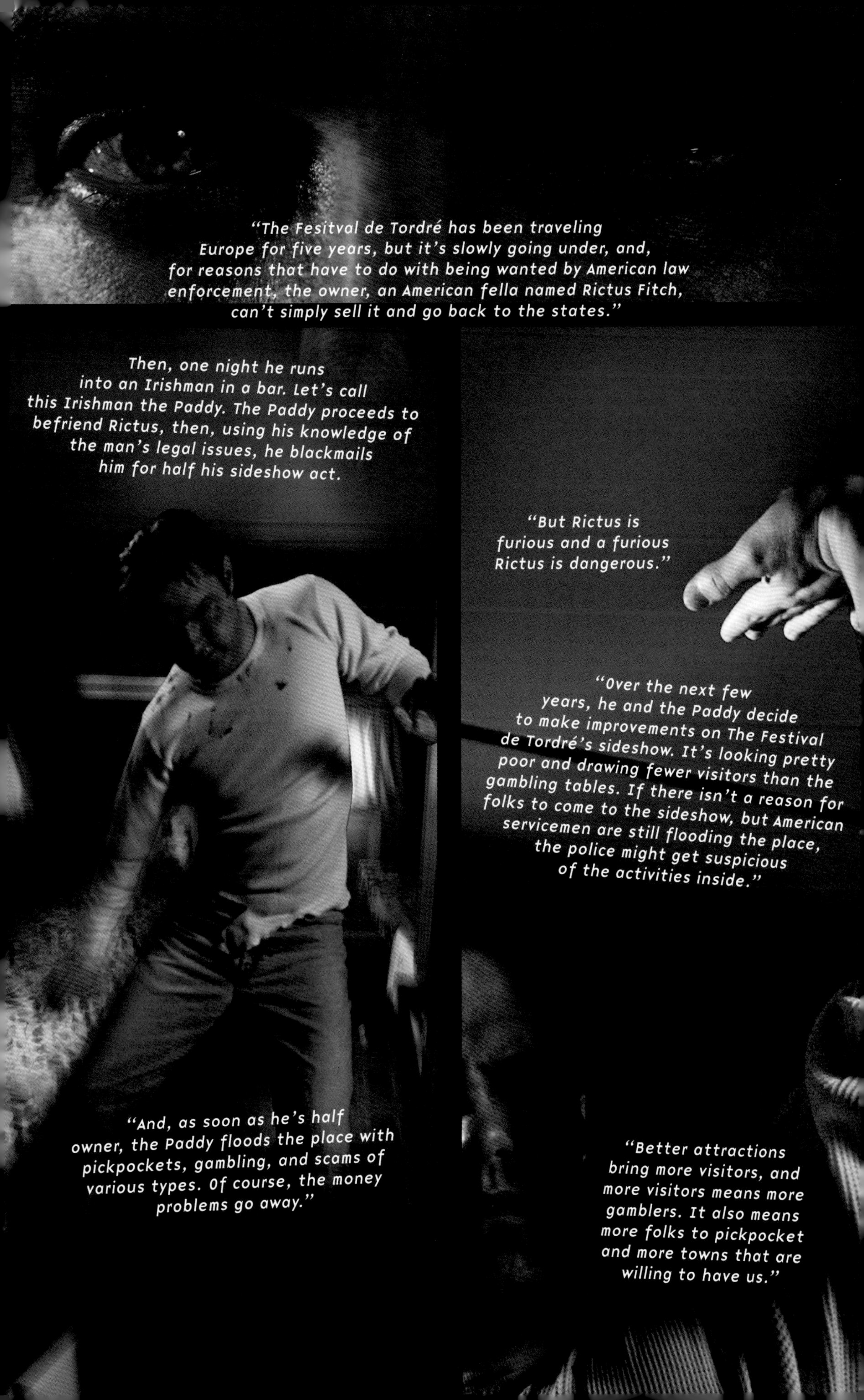
"The Fesitval de Tordré has been traveling Europe for five years, but it's slowly going under, and, for reasons that have to do with being wanted by American law enforcement, the owner, an American fella named Rictus Fitch, can't simply sell it and go back to the states."
Then, one night he runs into an Irishman in a bar. Let's call this Irishman the Paddy. The Paddy proceeds to befriend Rictus, then, using his knowledge of the man's legal issues, he blackmails him for half his sideshow act.
"And, as soon as he's half owner, the Paddy floods the place with pickpockets, gambling, and scams of various types. Of course, the money problems go away."
"But Rictus is furious and a furious Rictus is dangerous."
"Over the next few years, he and the Paddy decide to make improvements on The Festival de Tordré's sideshow. It's looking pretty poor and drawing fewer visitors than the gambling tables. If there isn't a reason for folks to come to the sideshow, but American servicemen are still flooding the place, the police might get suspicious of the activities inside."
"Better attractions bring more visitors, and more visitors means more gamblers. It also means more folks to pickpocket and more towns that are willing to have us."

So the two men start searching for freaks.

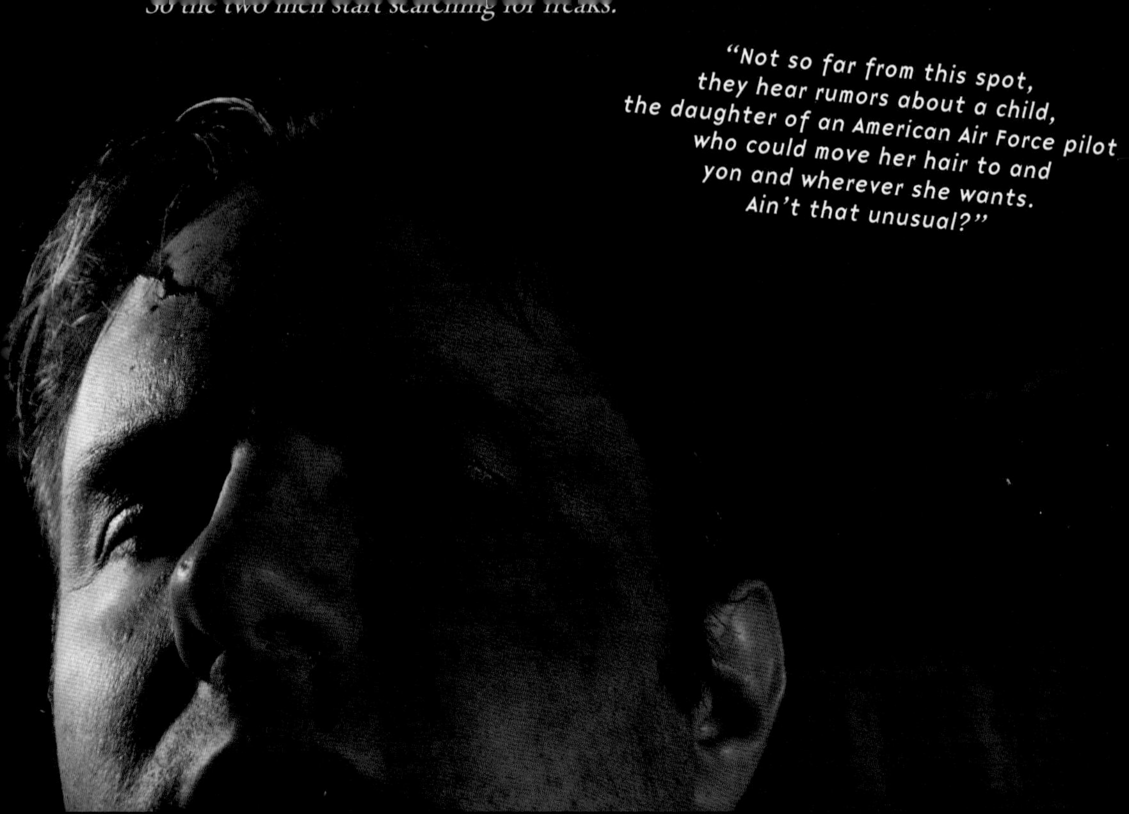

"Not so far from this spot, they hear rumors about a child, the daughter of an American Air Force pilot who could move her hair to and yon and wherever she wants. Ain't that unusual?"

"Except, her parents, who love her dearly, are worried about the way people will treat her, so they don't let no one know the details of her strangeness. They tries to keep it a secret."

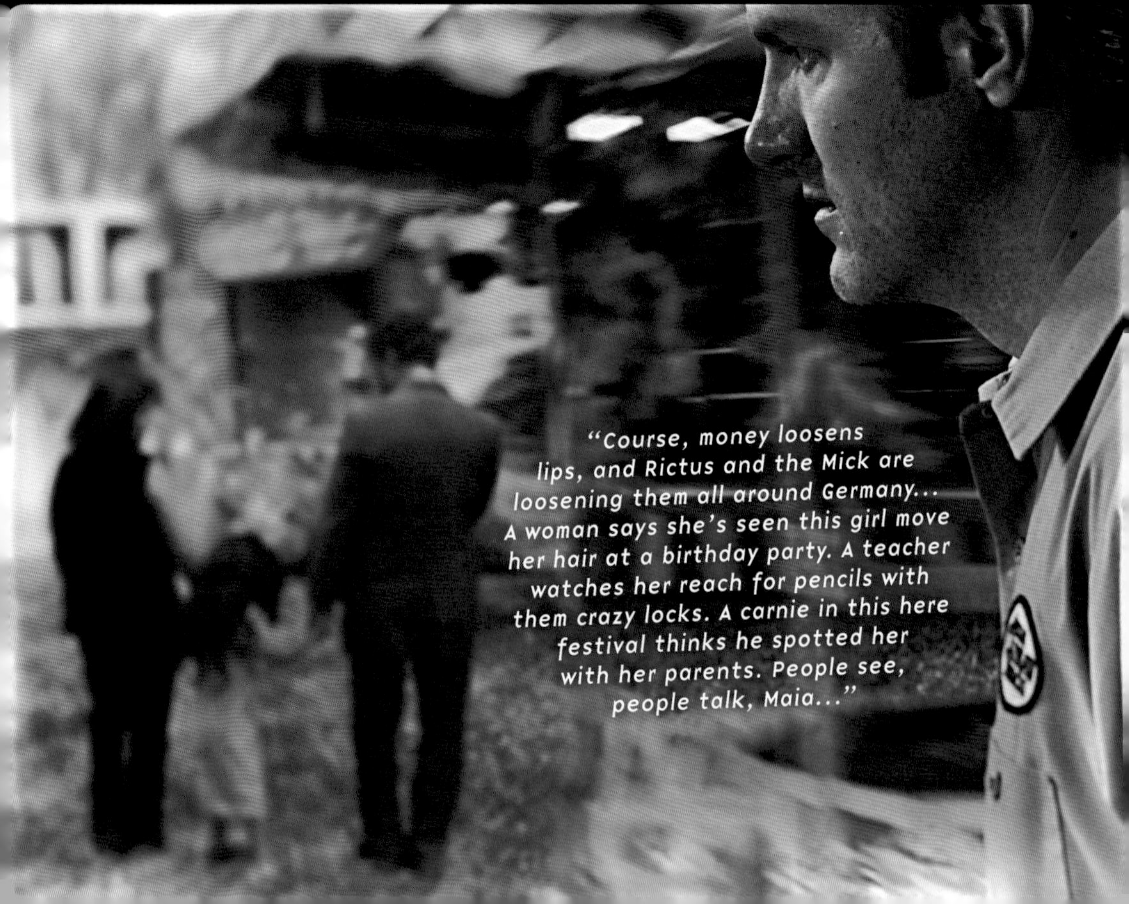

"Course, money loosens lips, and Rictus and the Mick are loosening them all around Germany... A woman says she's seen this girl move her hair at a birthday party. A teacher watches her reach for pencils with them crazy locks. A carnie in this here festival thinks he spotted her with her parents. People see, people talk, Maia..."

"...especially the air base doctor. He doesn't feel no conflict of interest in discussing his patients."

"Ya own a freak show?"

"God, that must be a hoot."

"And we're looking for freaks, but not a bunch of war wounded. We're looking for the real thing."

"Freaks? Well, hell, got a fella with seven fingers on one hand, two thumbs and a pointer. I seen a little person in town, here. Oh! Oh, and I got a real winner for you. Weirdest thing I ever saw."

"What is it?"

"What'cha paying?"

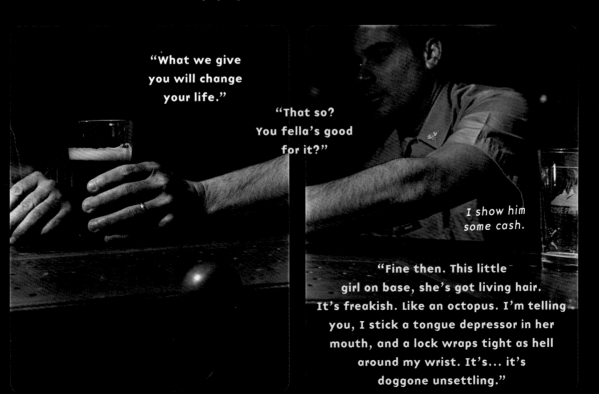

"What we give you will change your life."

"That so? You fella's good for it?"

I show him some cash.

"Fine then. This little girl on base, she's got living hair. It's freakish. Like an octopus. I'm telling you, I stick a tongue depressor in her mouth, and a lock wraps tight as hell around my wrist. It's... it's doggone unsettling."

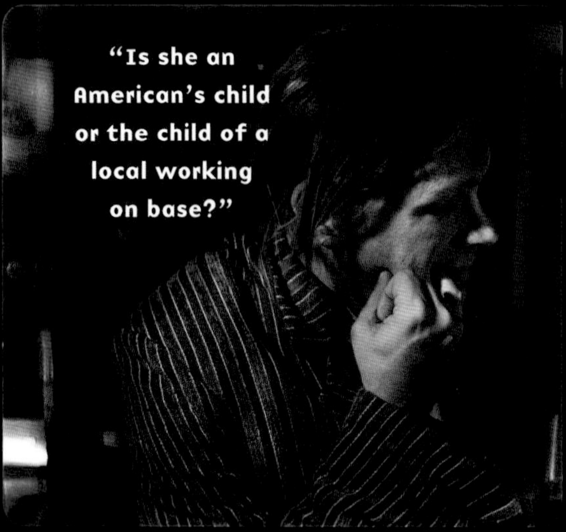
"Is she an American's child or the child of a local working on base?"

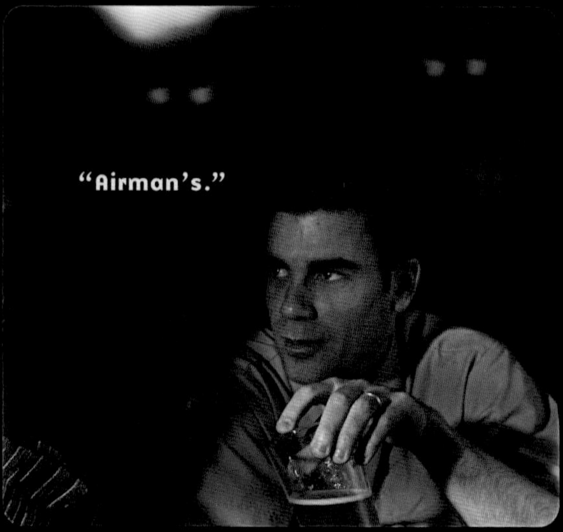
"Airman's."

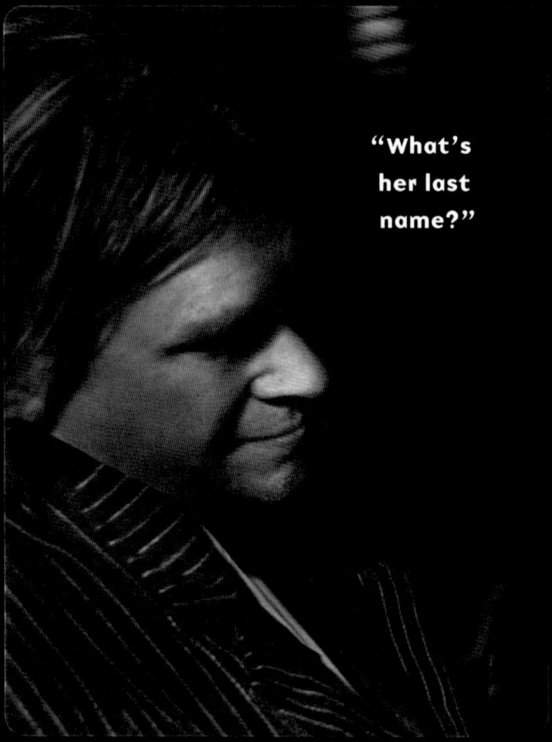
"What's her last name?"

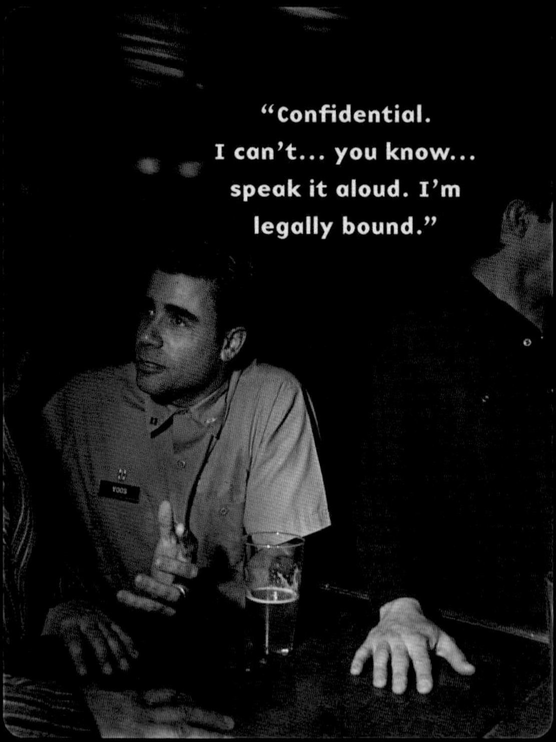
"Confidential. I can't... you know... speak it aloud. I'm legally bound."

"Well, Herr Doctor, why don't ya write it on a piece of paper
and we'll buy the information outside?"

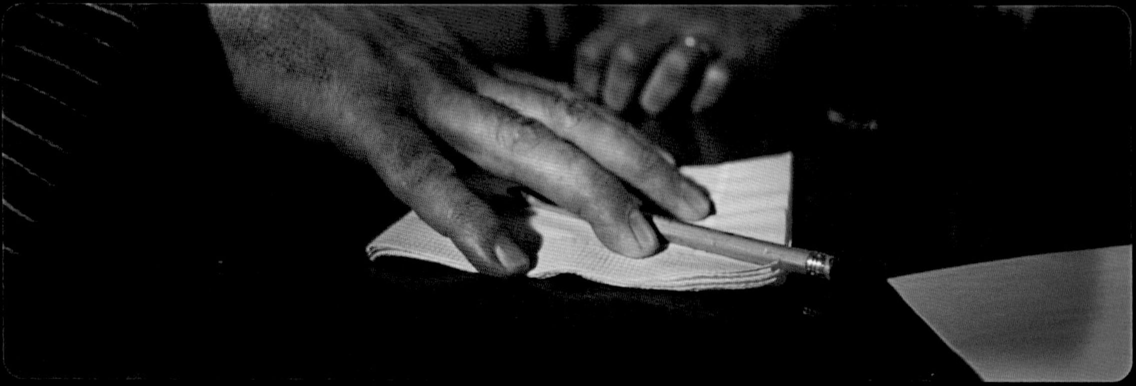

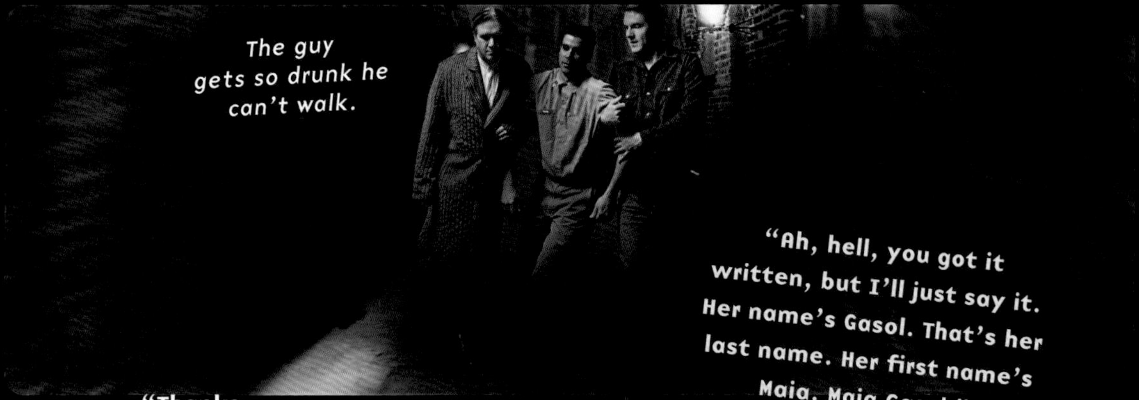
The guy gets so drunk he can't walk.
"Ah, hell, you got it written, but I'll just say it. Her name's Gasol. That's her last name. Her first name's Maia. Maia Gasol."

"Thanks. Now I got something for you, Doc."

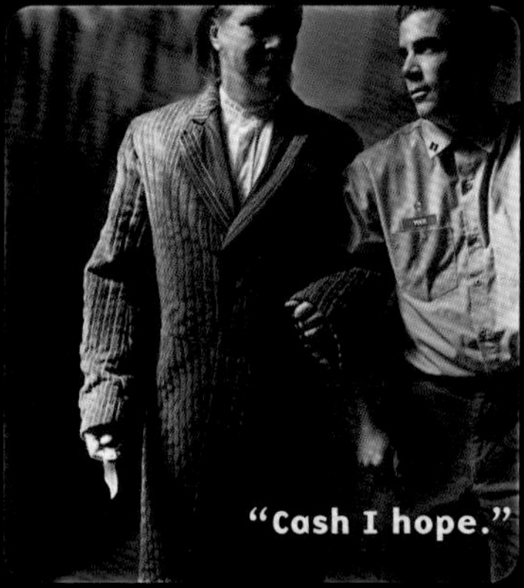
"Cash I hope."

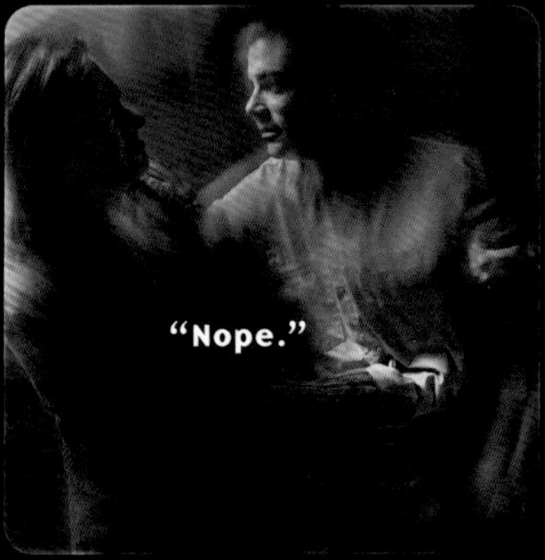
"Nope."

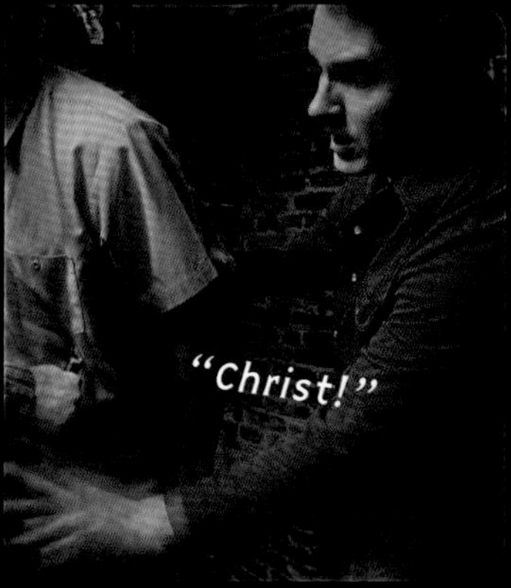
"Christ!"

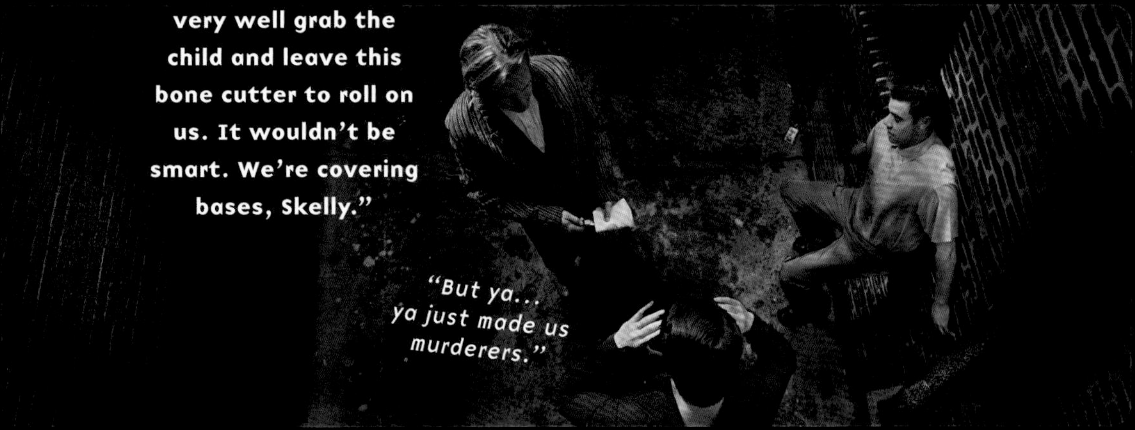
"We couldn't very well grab the child and leave this bone cutter to roll on us. It wouldn't be smart. We're covering bases, Skelly."
"But ya... ya just made us murderers."

"Can't believe you're squeamish, Skelly. I've never seen you experience a moment's remorse in all these years. Not a moment's."

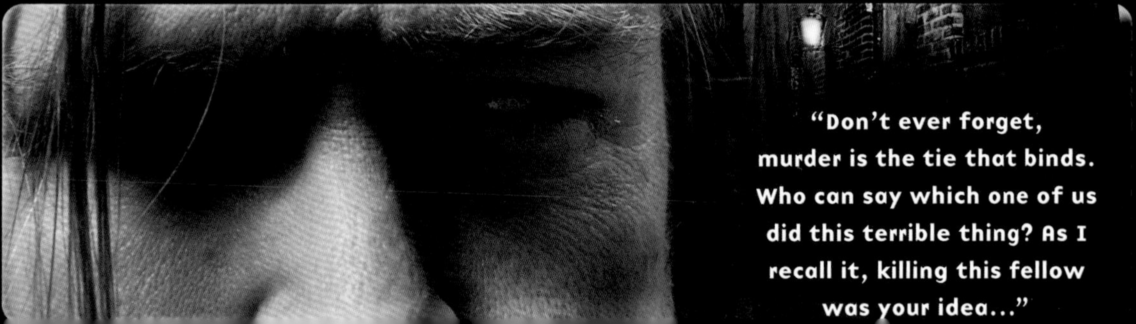
"Don't ever forget, murder is the tie that binds. Who can say which one of us did this terrible thing? As I recall it, killing this fellow was your idea..."

" ...or at least that's what I'll tell the police. Now, I'll go get the car. You can throw the good doctor in the trunk."

It doesn't seem possible that the drunk, indifferent man I've known is the ambitious person in Skelly's stories.

"Skelly, tell me that wasn't you."

As if in a trance, he doesn't answer.

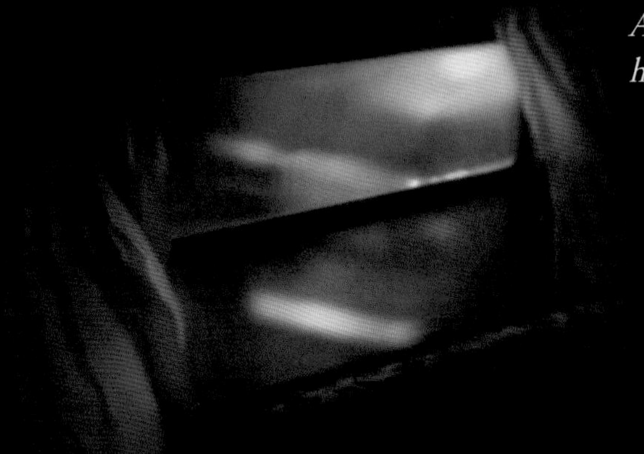

"Took a week for us to grab the kid. She was visiting a downtown grocery off base with her nurse or nanny, whatever you like to call her. The child stayed outside with all the other youngins while your German nanny went into a shop. All these years later, I recognized the lady and she apparently recognized ya just as easily, Maia."

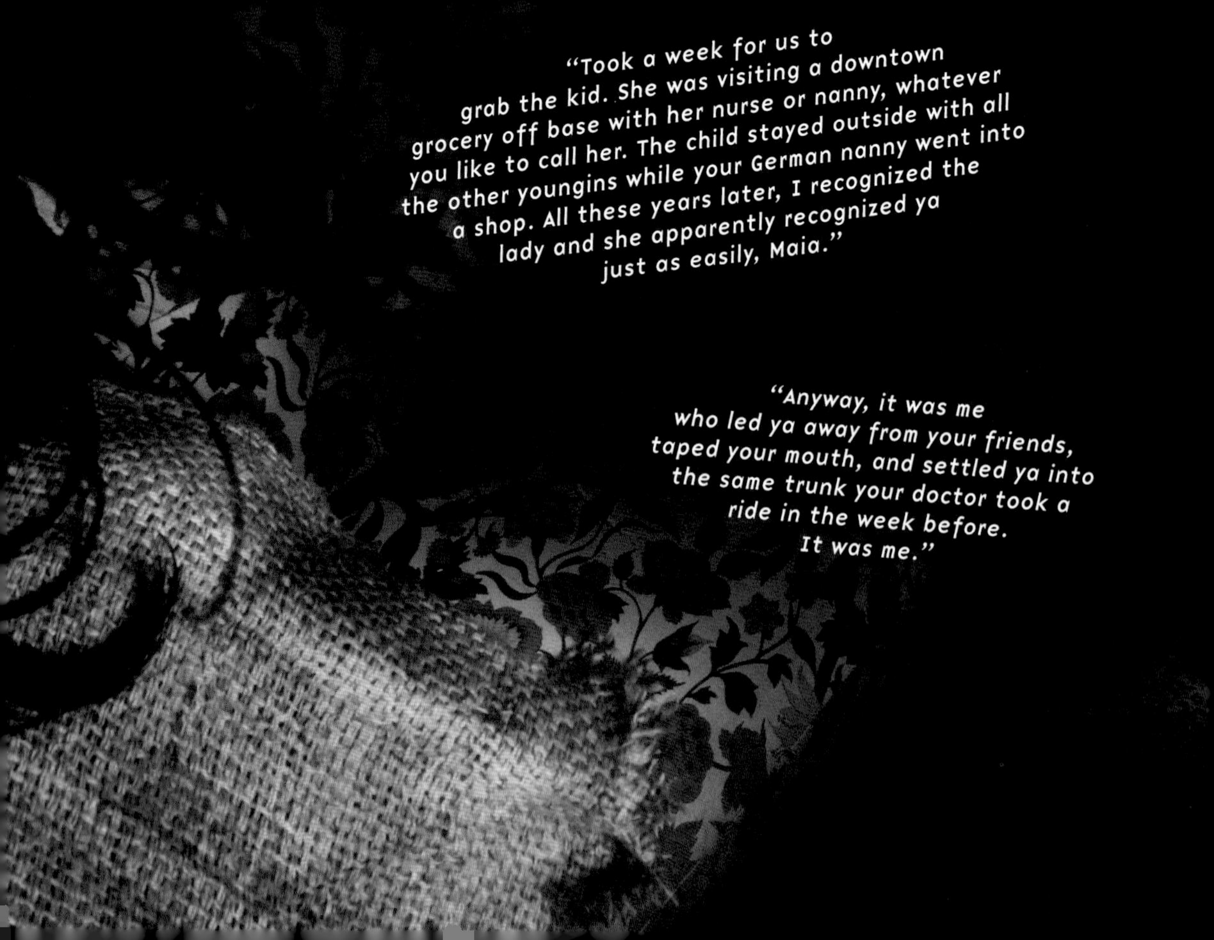

"Anyway, it was me who led ya away from your friends, taped your mouth, and settled ya into the same trunk your doctor took a ride in the week before. It was me."

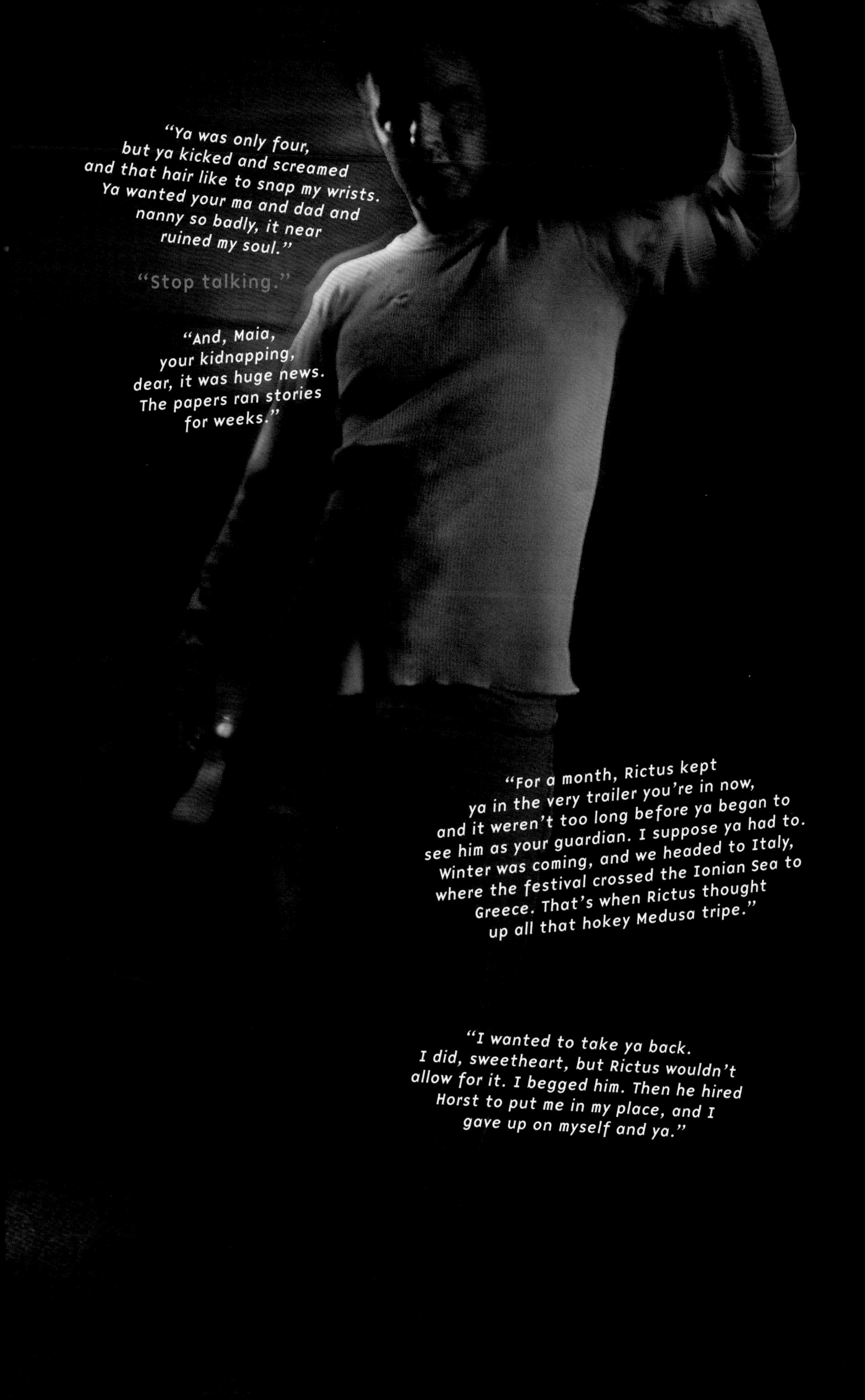

"Ya was only four, but ya kicked and screamed and that hair like to snap my wrists. Ya wanted your ma and dad and nanny so badly, it near ruined my soul."

"Stop talking."

"And, Maia, your kidnapping, dear, it was huge news. The papers ran stories for weeks."

"For a month, Rictus kept ya in the very trailer you're in now, and it weren't too long before ya began to see him as your guardian. I suppose ya had to. Winter was coming, and we headed to Italy, where the festival crossed the Ionian Sea to Greece. That's when Rictus thought up all that hokey Medusa tripe."

"I wanted to take ya back. I did, sweetheart, but Rictus wouldn't allow for it. I begged him. Then he hired Horst to put me in my place, and I gave up on myself and ya."

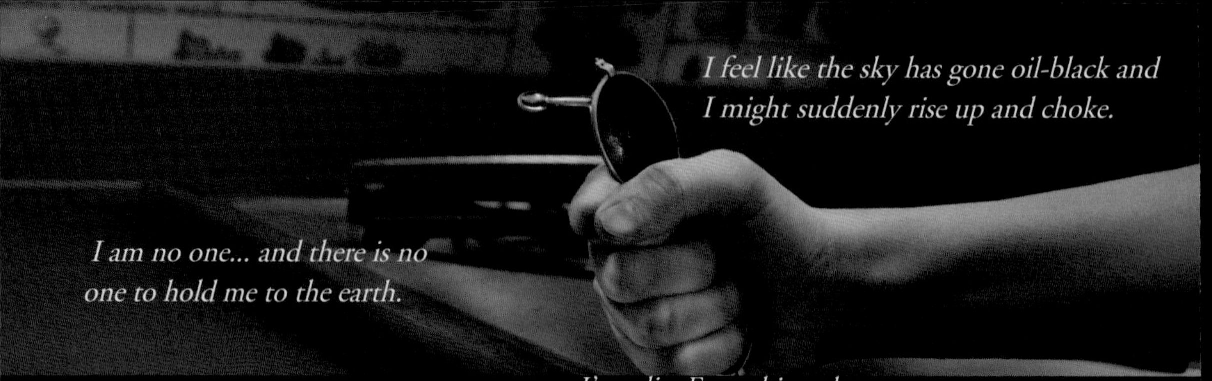
I feel like the sky has gone oil-black and I might suddenly rise up and choke.
I am no one... and there is no one to hold me to the earth.

I'm a lie. Everything about me.

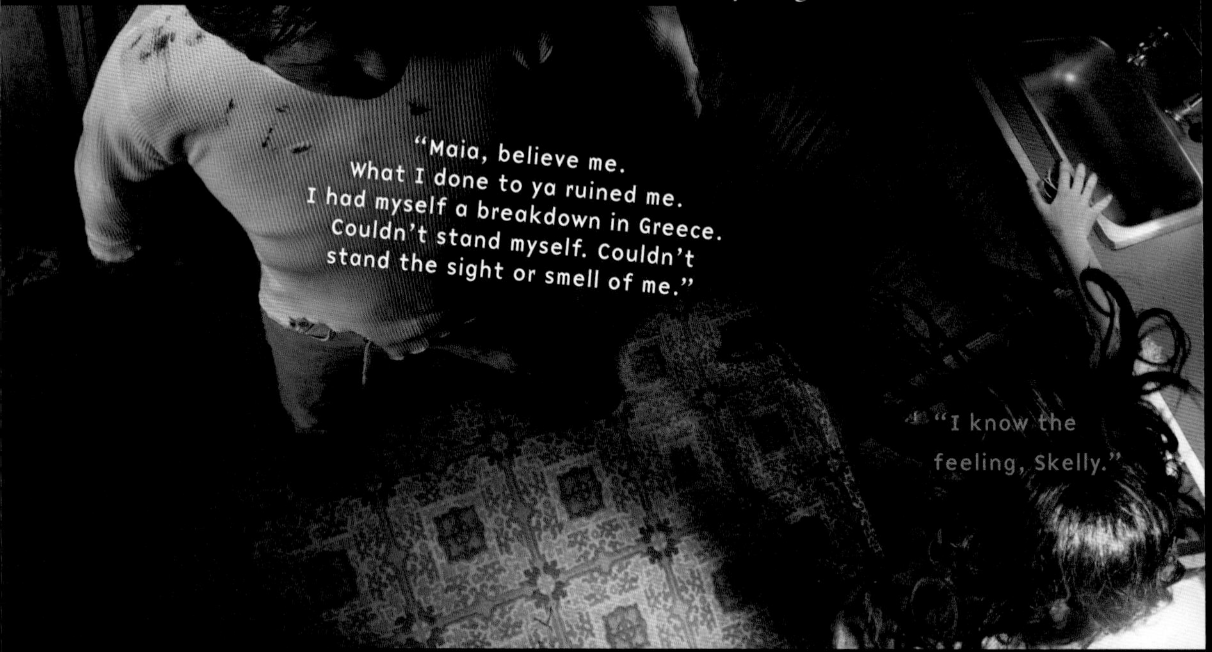
"Maia, believe me. What I done to ya ruined me. I had myself a breakdown in Greece. Couldn't stand myself. Couldn't stand the sight or smell of me."
"I know the feeling, Skelly."

I want to strike him with something, to hurt him for stealing me from my parents, for taking away my life so that I could crawl around in a cage seven nights a week.

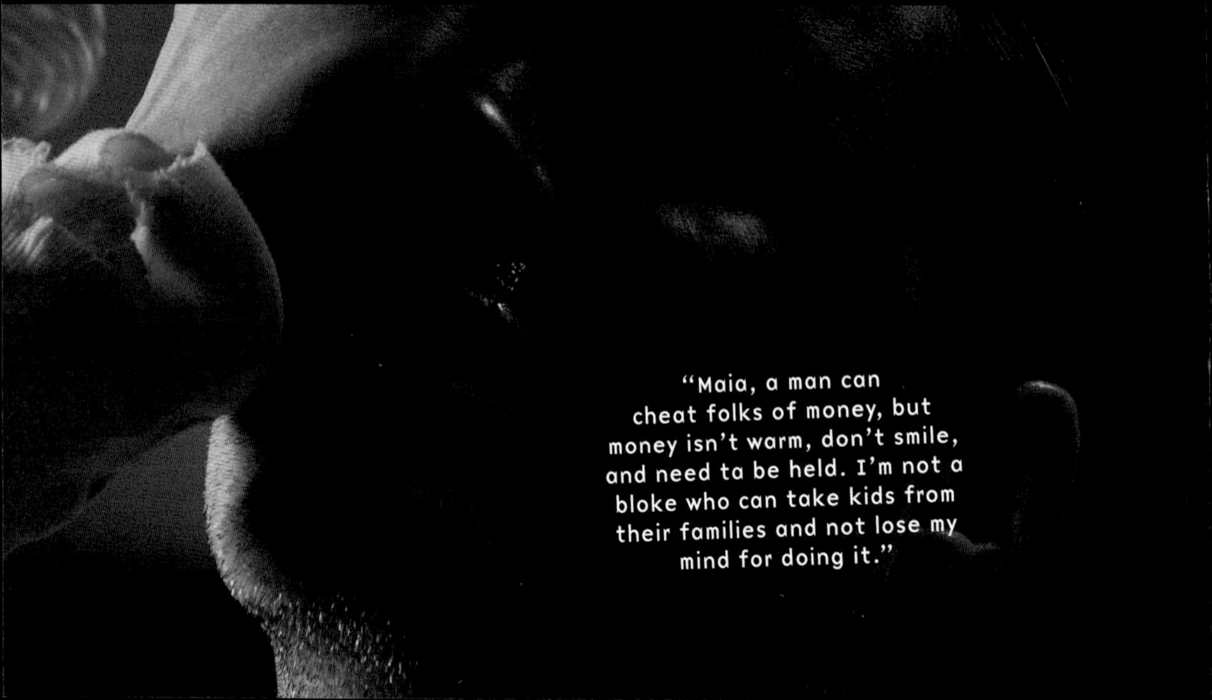
"Maia, a man can cheat folks of money, but money isn't warm, don't smile, and need to be held. I'm not a bloke who can take kids from their families and not lose my mind for doing it."

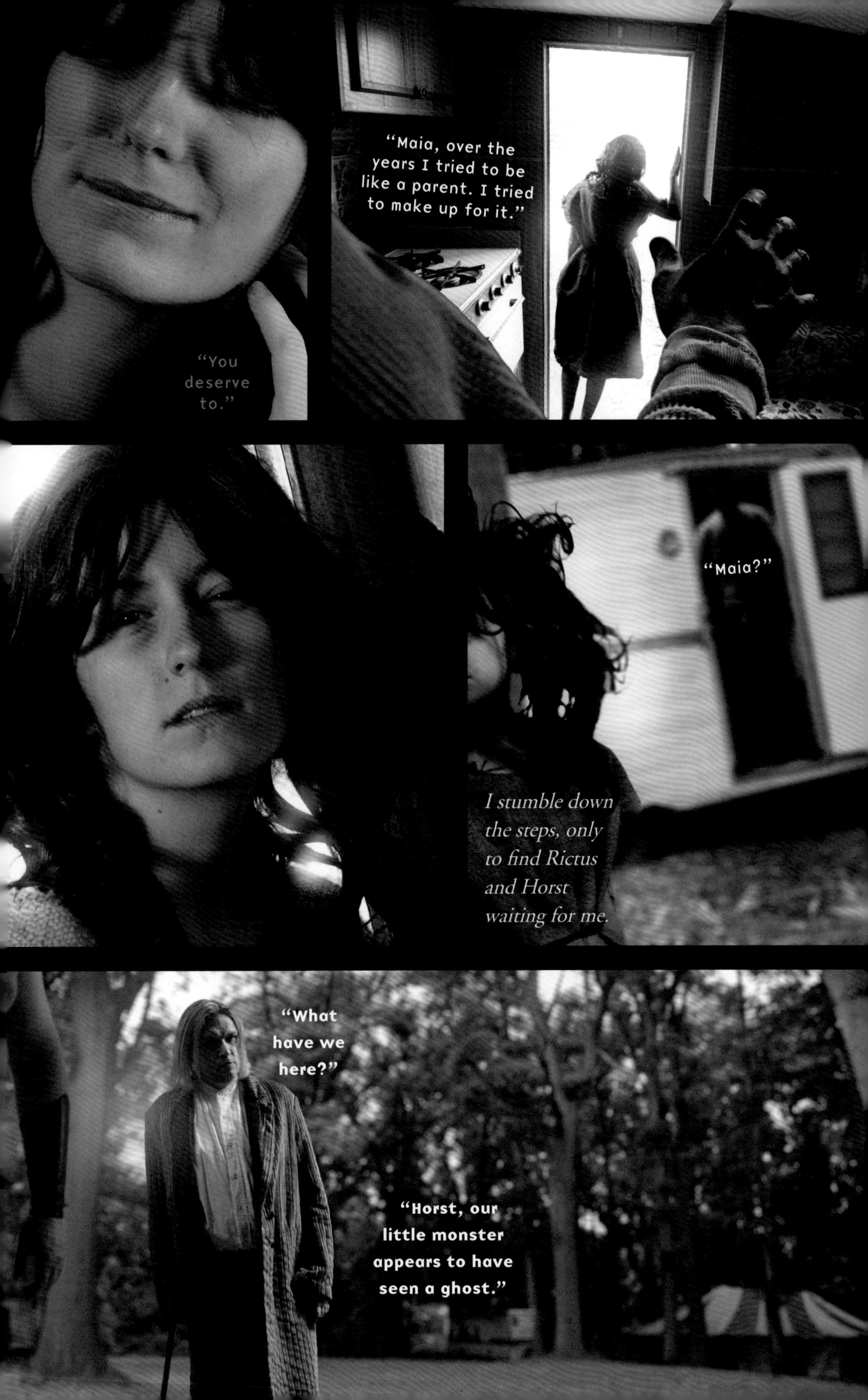
"You deserve to."
"Maia, over the years I tried to be like a parent. I tried to make up for it."
"Maia?"
I stumble down the steps, only to find Rictus and Horst waiting for me.
"What have we here?"
"Horst, our little monster appears to have seen a ghost."

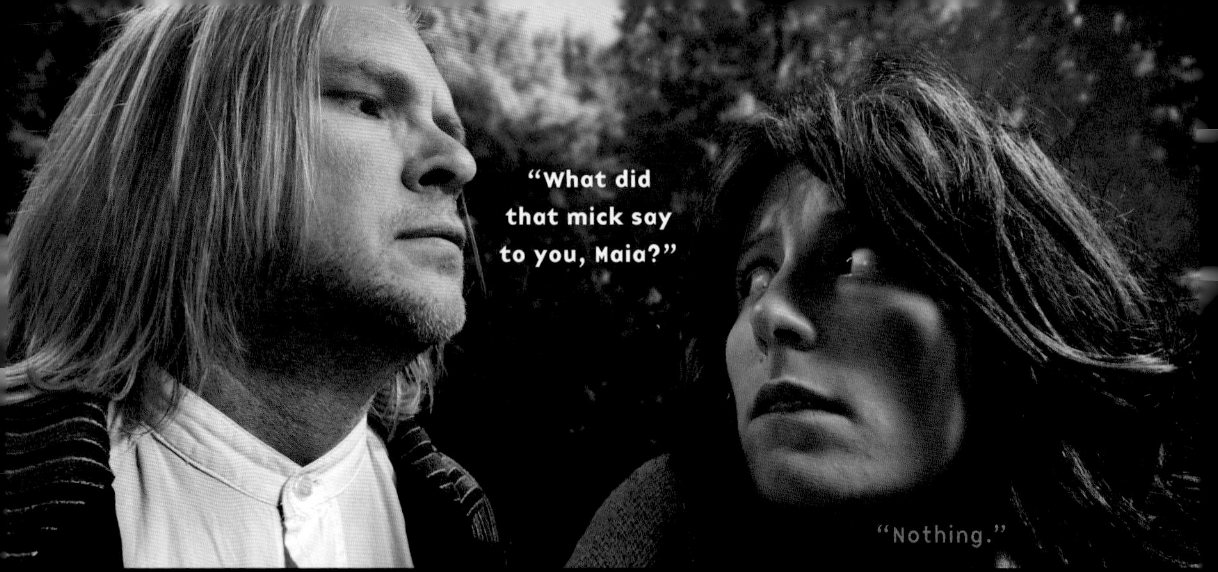
"What did that mick say to you, Maia?"
"Nothing."

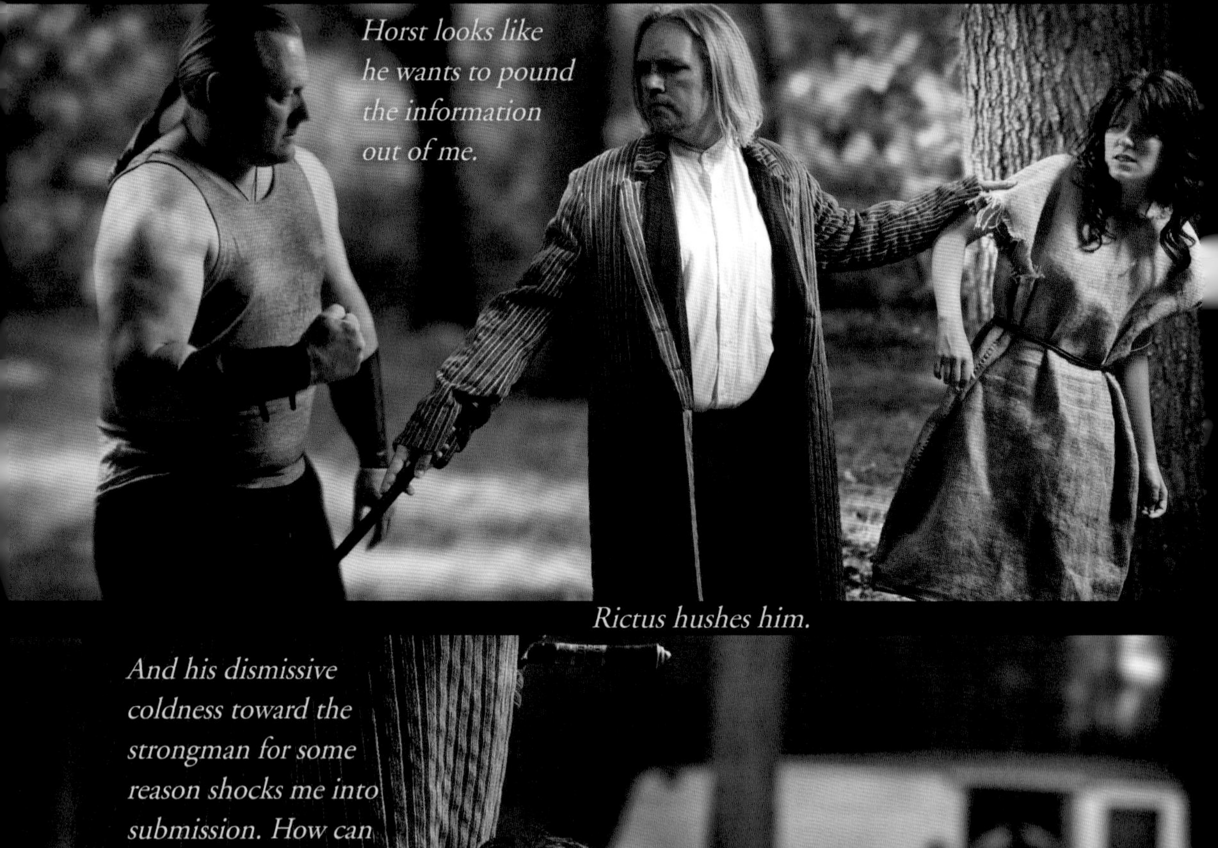
Horst looks like he wants to pound the information out of me.

Rictus hushes him.

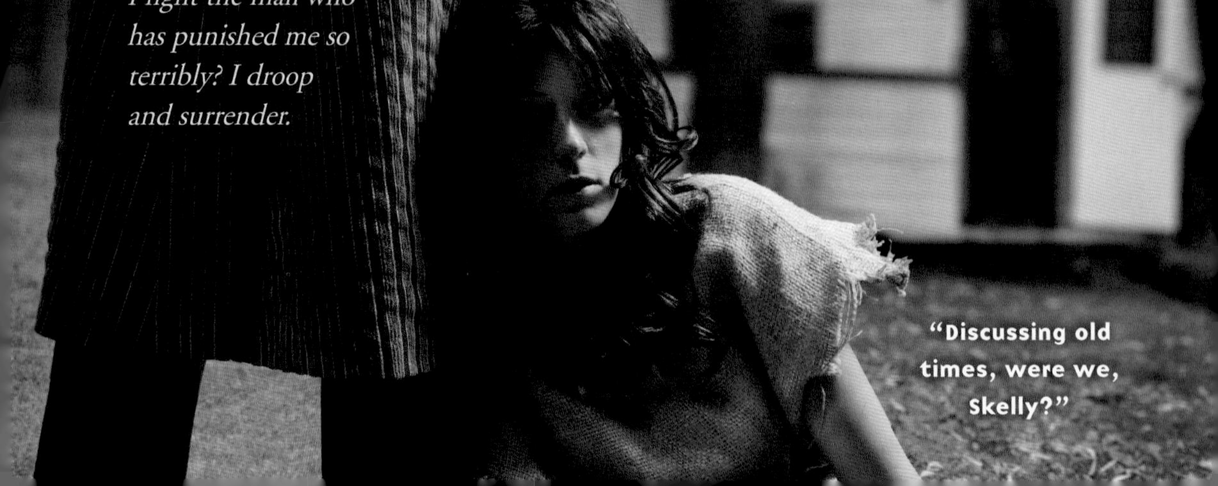
And his dismissive coldness toward the strongman for some reason shocks me into submission. How can I fight the man who has punished me so terribly? I droop and surrender.
"Discussing old times, were we, Skelly?"

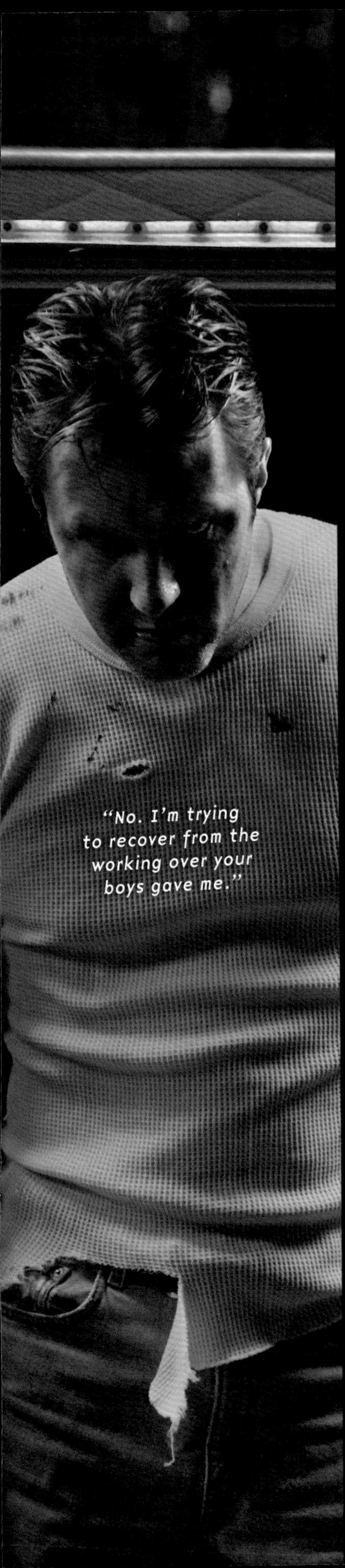
"No. I'm trying to recover from the working over your boys gave me."
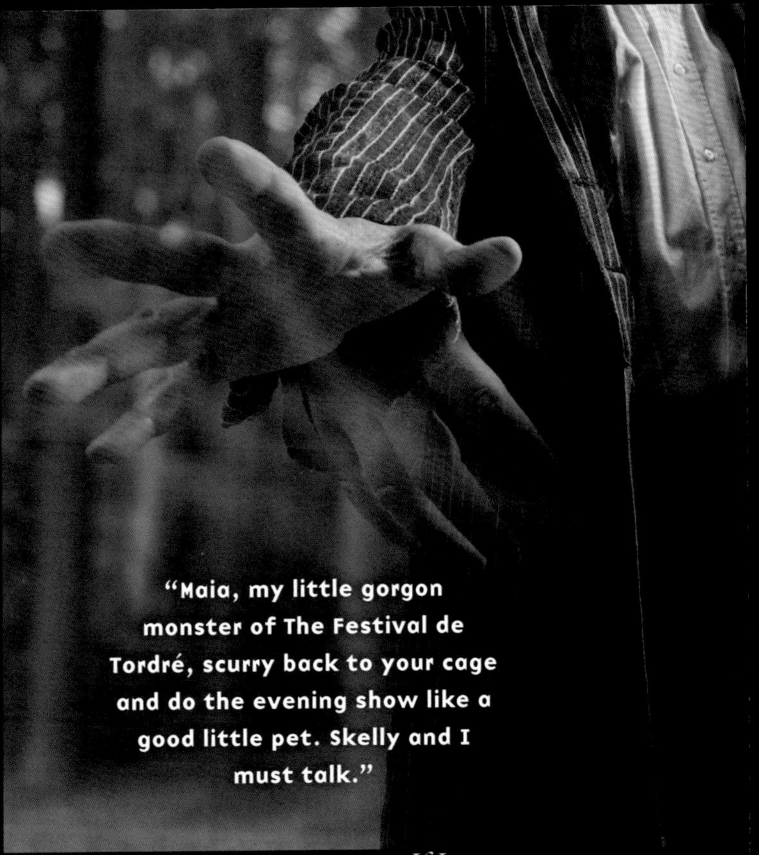
"Maia, my little gorgon monster of The Festival de Tordré, scurry back to your cage and do the evening show like a good little pet. Skelly and I must talk."
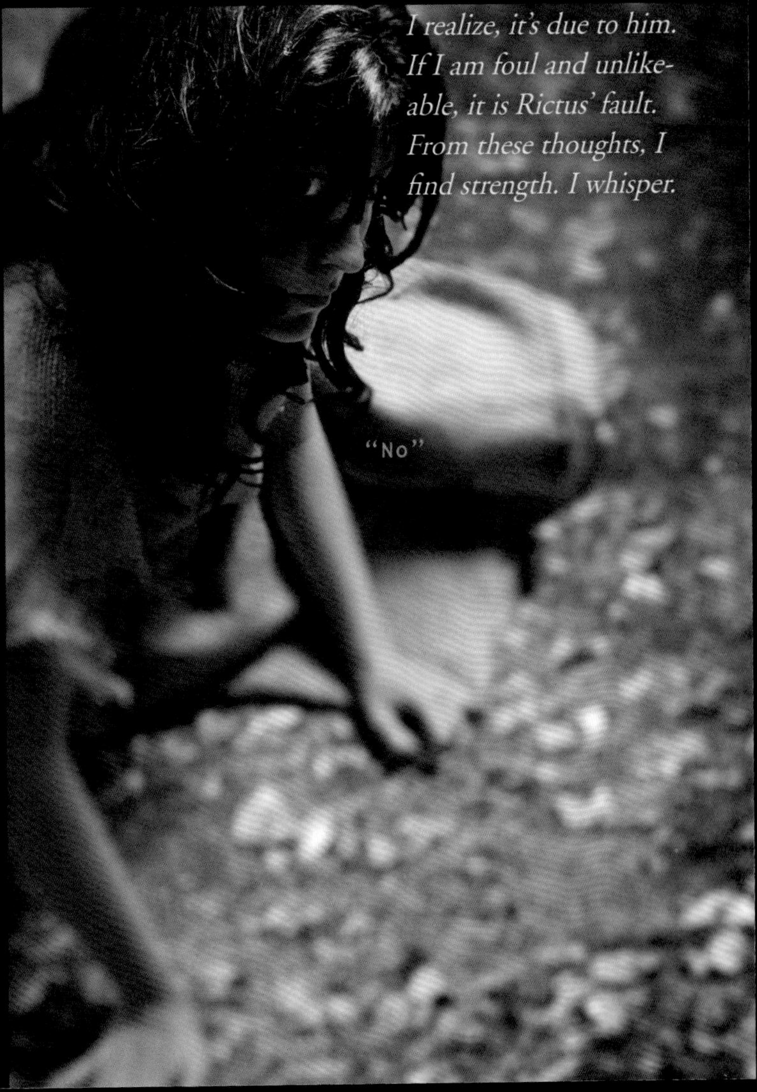
If I am a monster, I realize, it's due to him. If I am foul and unlikeable, it is Rictus' fault. From these thoughts, I find strength. I whisper.
"No"

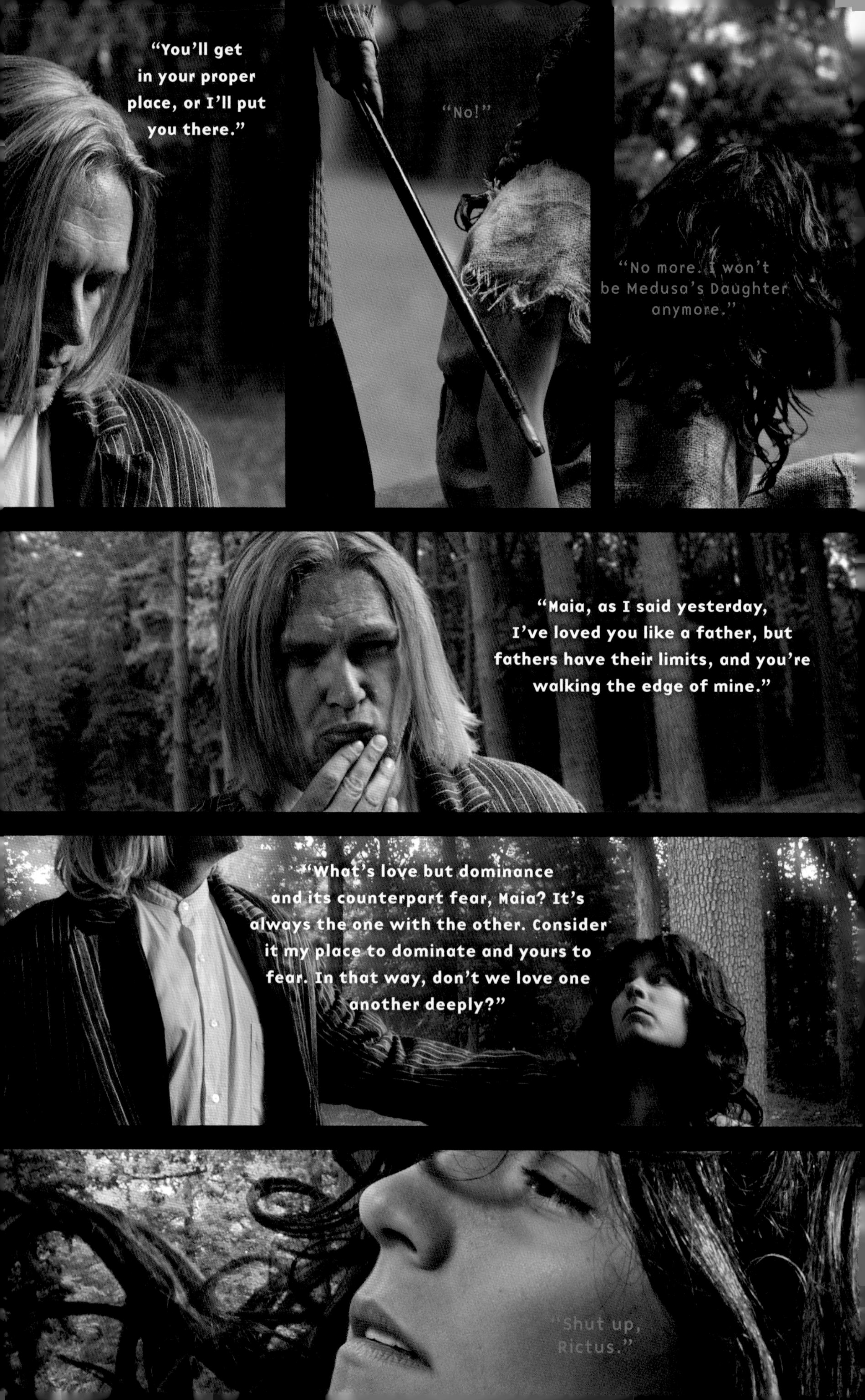
"You'll get in your proper place, or I'll put you there."
"No!"
"No more. I won't be Medusa's Daughter anymore."
"Maia, as I said yesterday, I've loved you like a father, but fathers have their limits, and you're walking the edge of mine."
"What's love but dominance and its counterpart fear, Maia? It's always the one with the other. Consider it my place to dominate and yours to fear. In that way, don't we love one another deeply?"
"Shut up, Rictus."

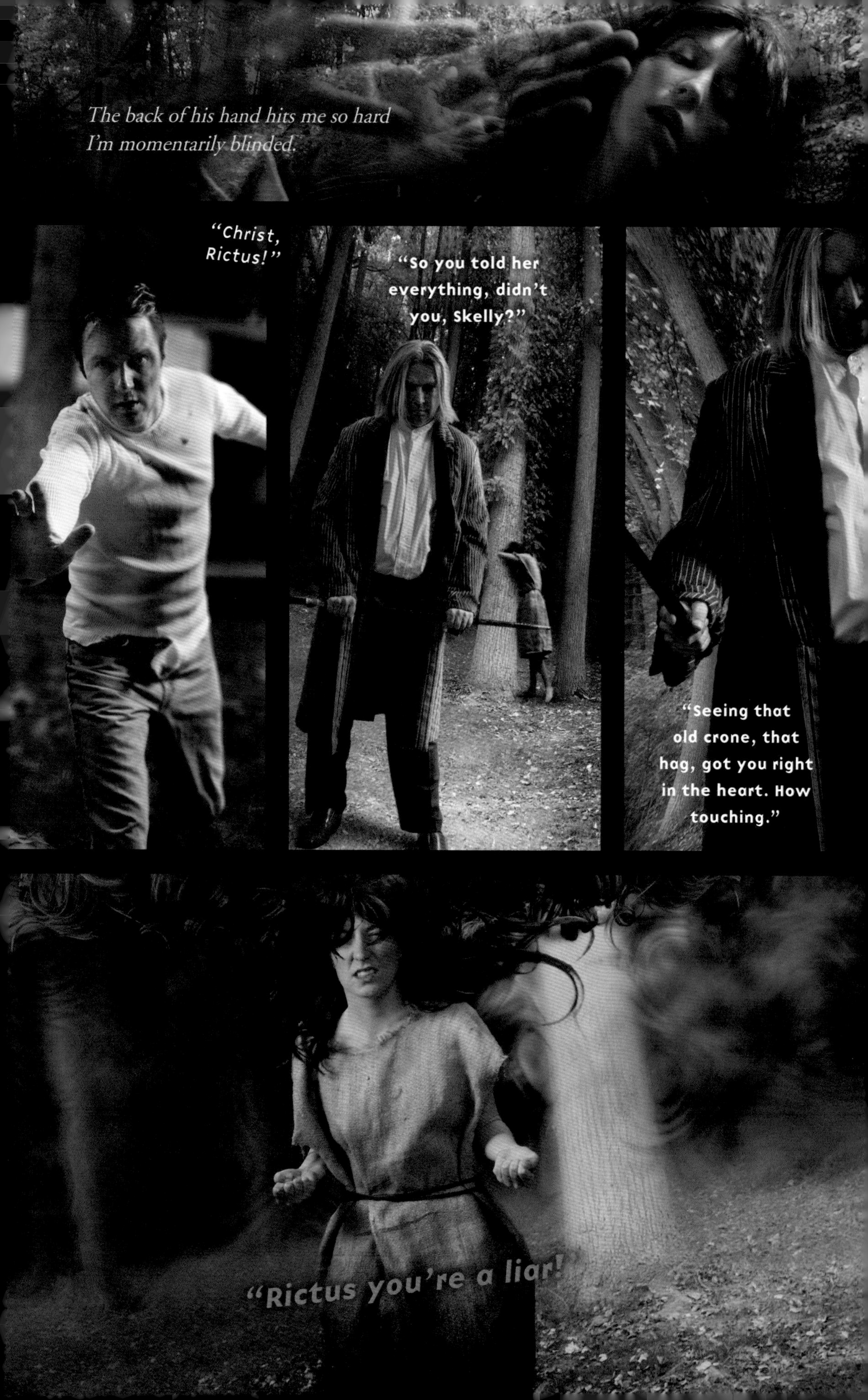
The back of his hand hits me so hard
I'm momentarily blinded.
"Christ, Rictus!"
"So you told her everything, didn't you, Skelly?"
"Seeing that old crone, that hag, got you right in the heart. How touching."
"Rictus you're a liar!"

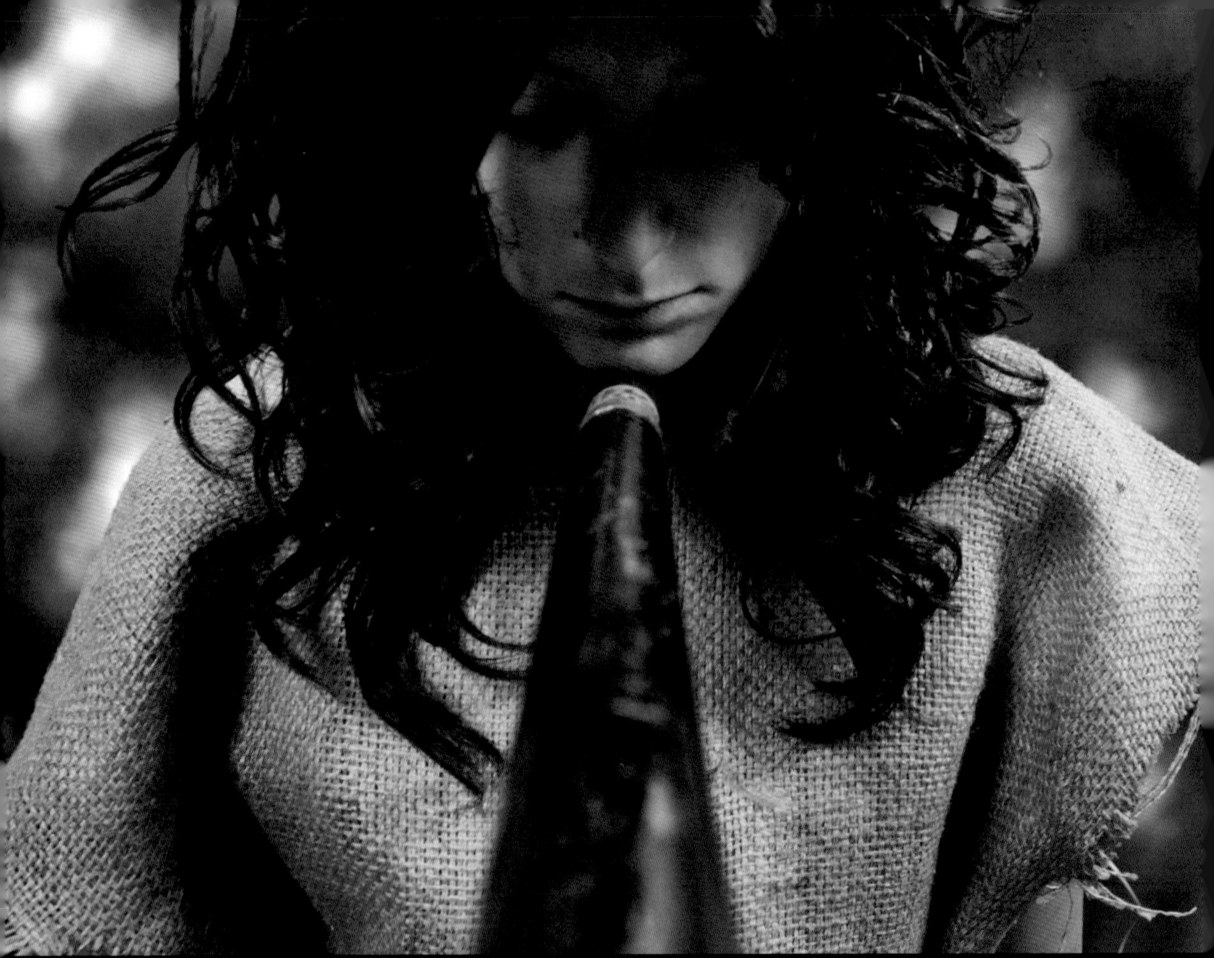

He points the tip of his walking stick at me, and the fire in my heart is doused.
I'm incapable of working beyond my dread of Rictus .

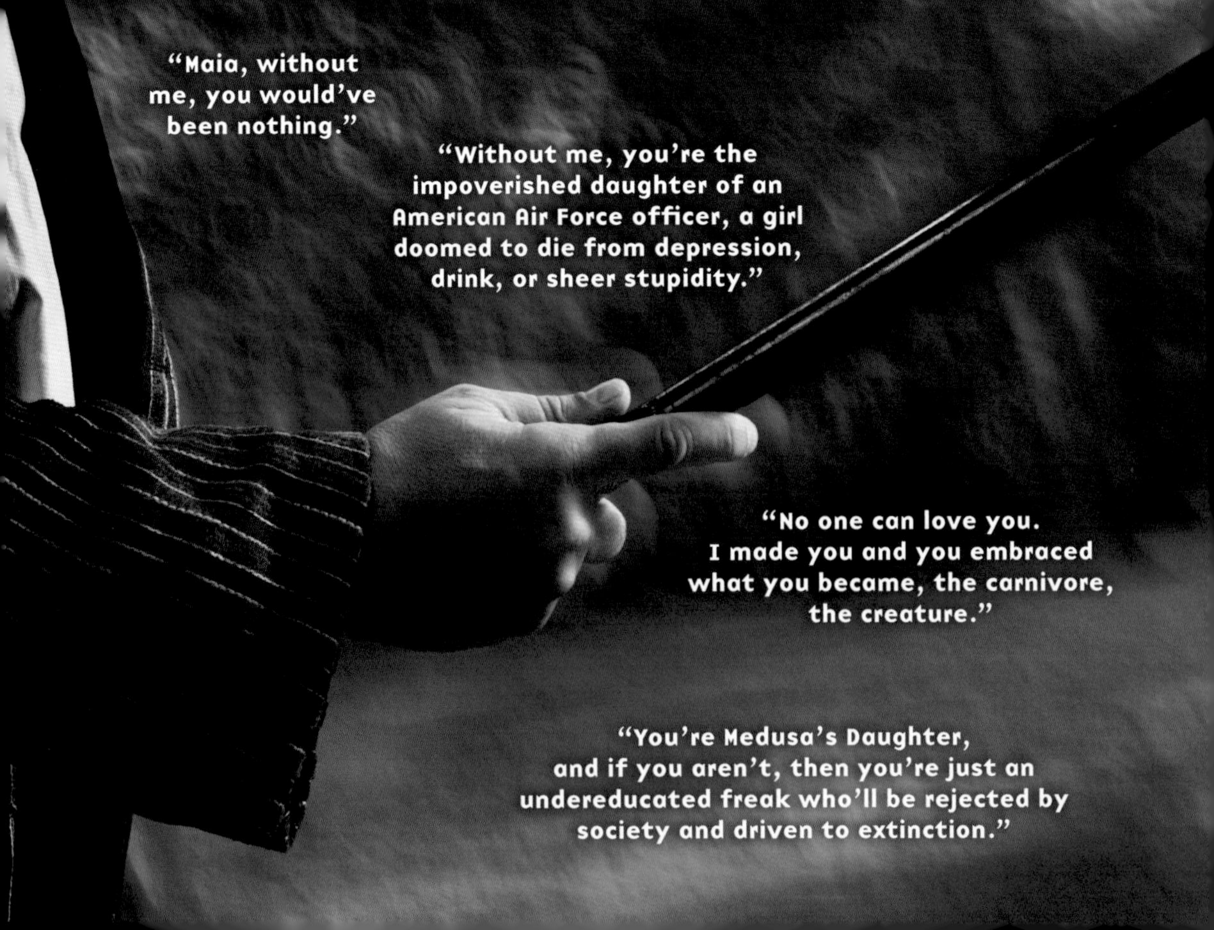
"Maia, without me, you would've been nothing."
"Without me, you're the impoverished daughter of an American Air Force officer, a girl doomed to die from depression, drink, or sheer stupidity."
"No one can love you. I made you and you embraced what you became, the carnivore, the creature."
"You're Medusa's Daughter, and if you aren't, then you're just an undereducated freak who'll be rejected by society and driven to extinction."

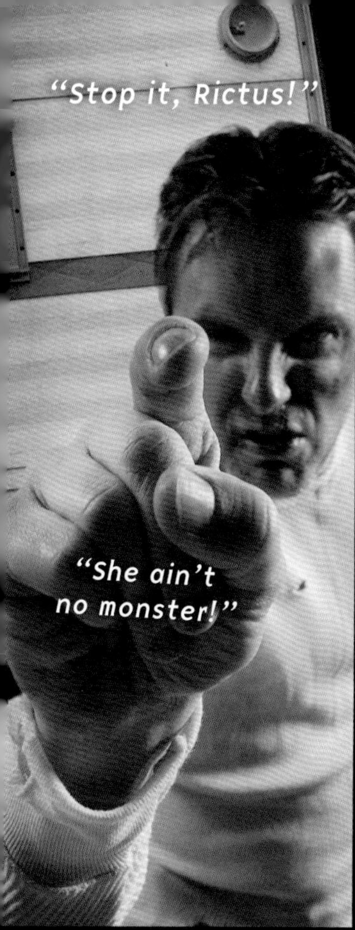
"Stop it, Rictus!"
"She ain't no monster!"

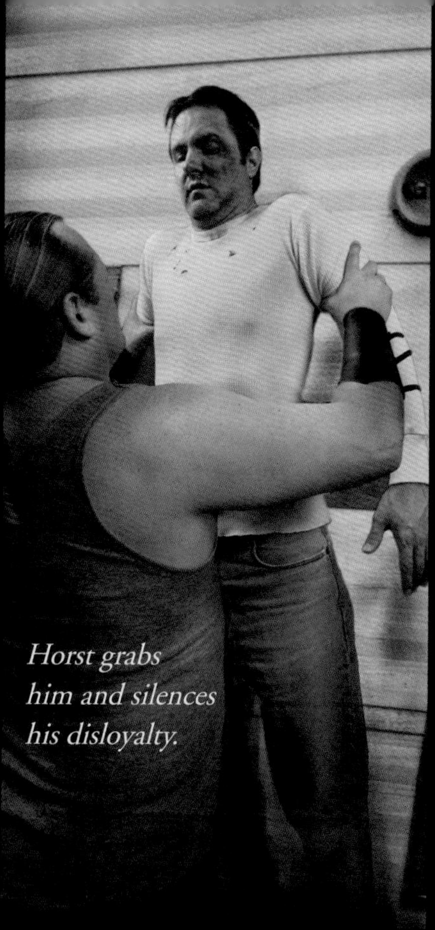
Horst grabs him and silences his disloyalty.

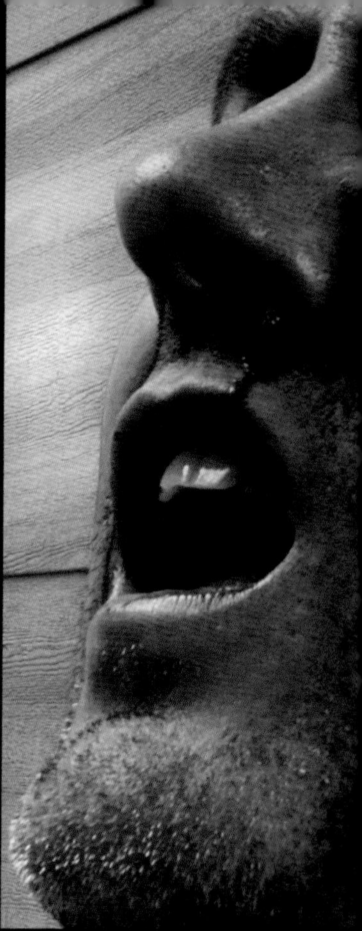

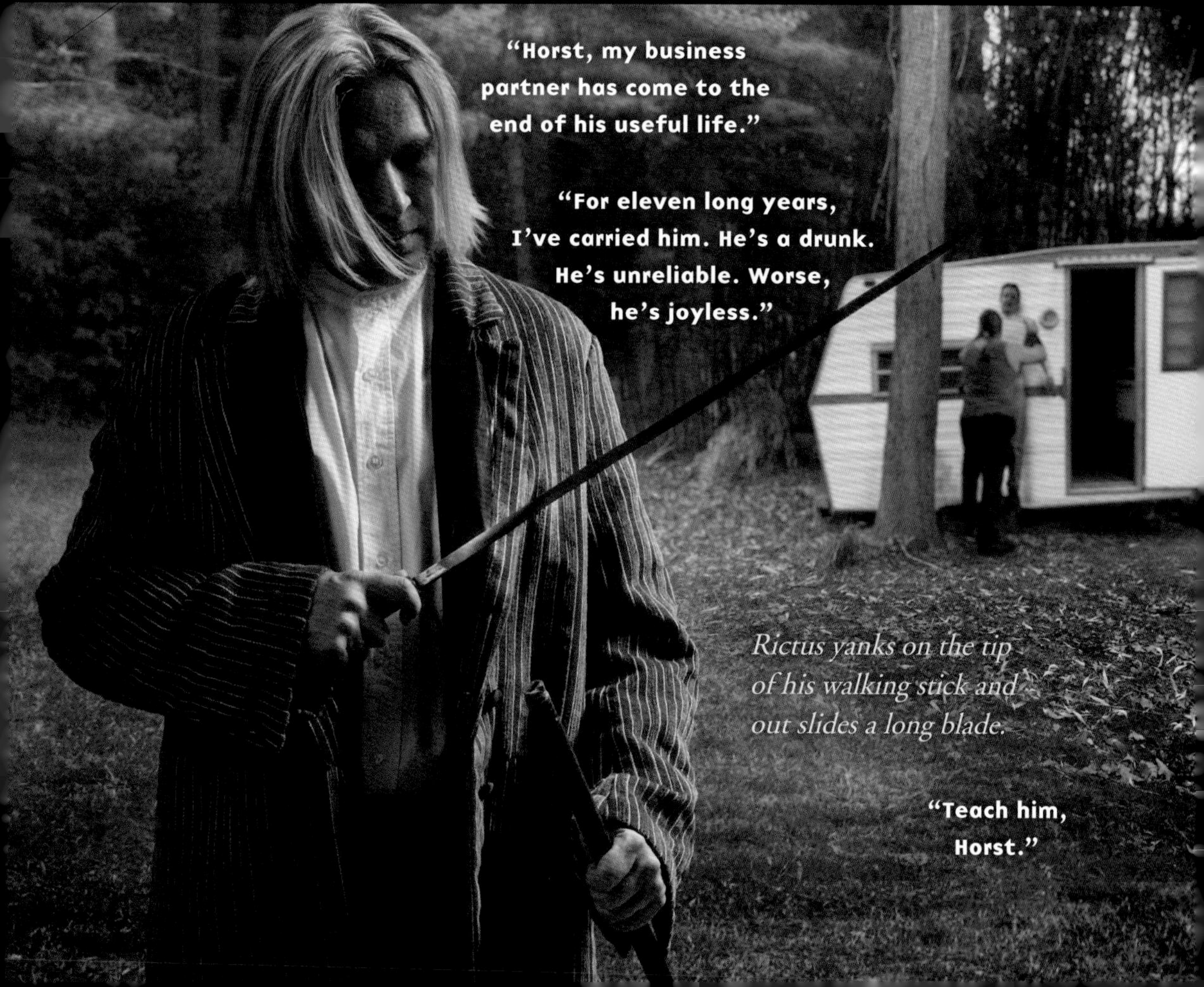
"Horst, my business partner has come to the end of his useful life."
"For eleven long years, I've carried him. He's a drunk. He's unreliable. Worse, he's joyless."
Rictus yanks on the tip of his walking stick and out slides a long blade.
"Teach him, Horst."

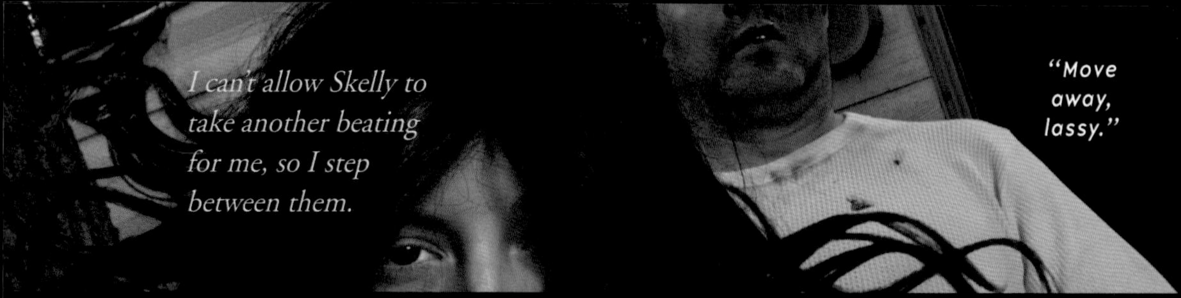
I can't allow Skelly to take another beating for me, so I step between them.
"Move away, lassy."

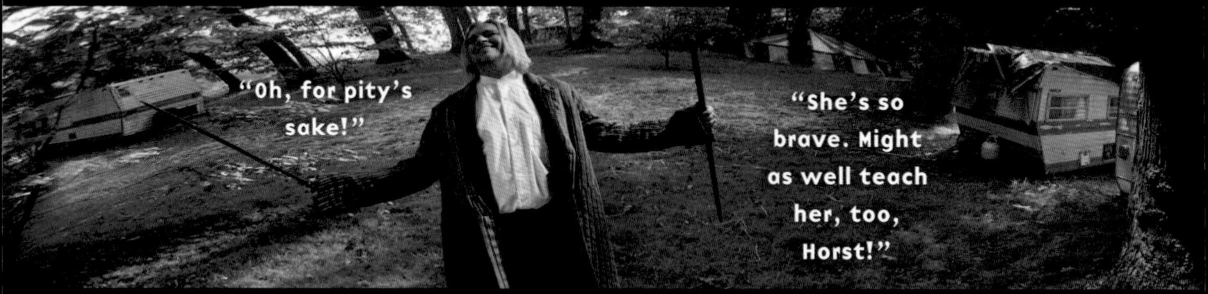
"Oh, for pity's sake!"
"She's so brave. Might as well teach her, too, Horst!"

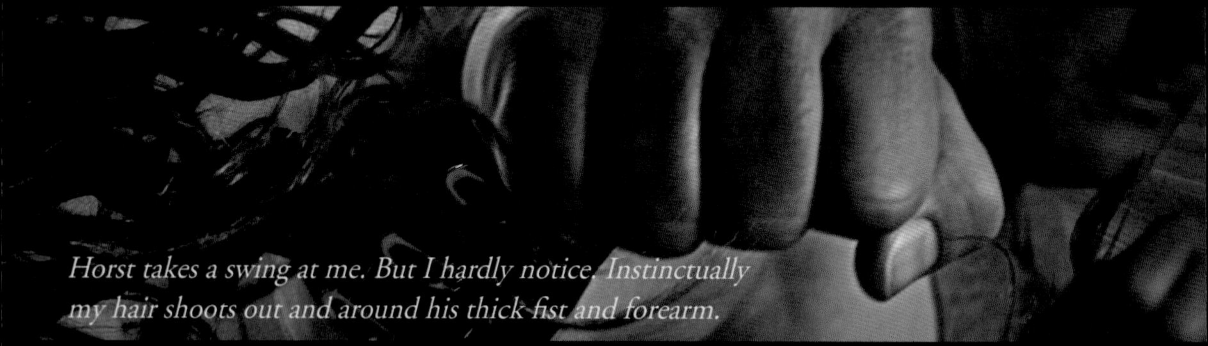
Horst takes a swing at me. But I hardly notice. Instinctually my hair shoots out and around his thick fist and forearm.

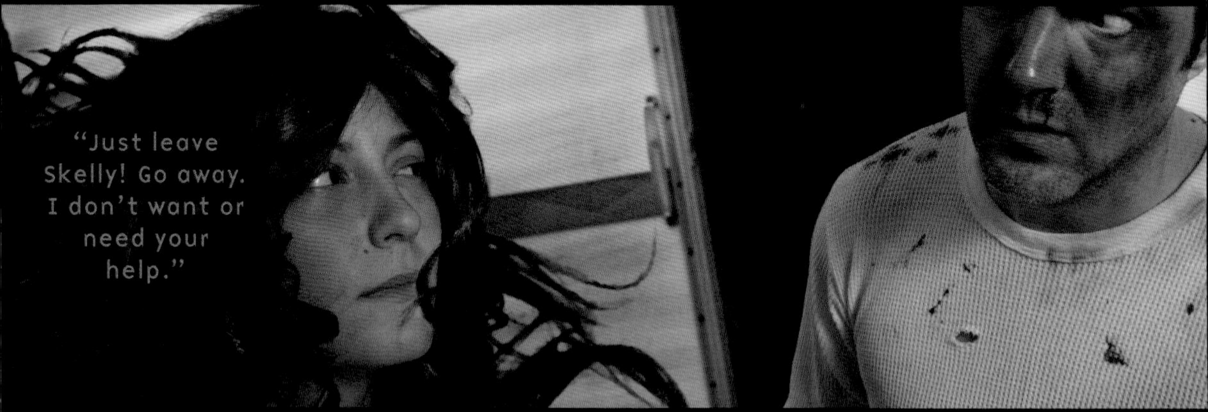
"Just leave Skelly! Go away. I don't want or need your help."

But the truth is, I don't want him to go.

When I was young, he put me to sleep every night. He took me to breakfast so that no one would bother me, and in the evenings after shows, he read to me for hours, told me stories, and discussed books.

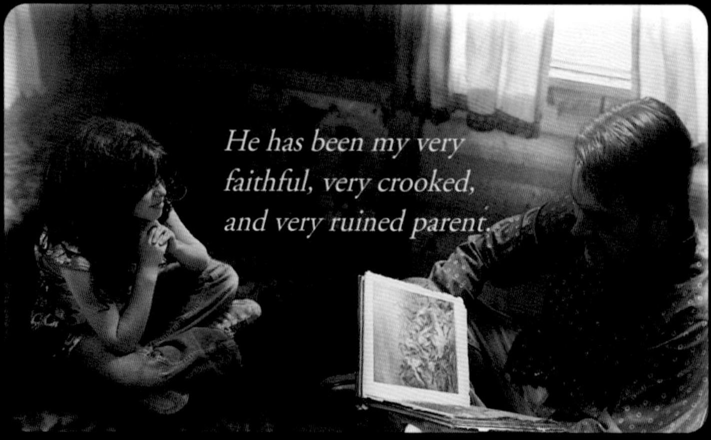
He has been my very faithful, very crooked, and very ruined parent.

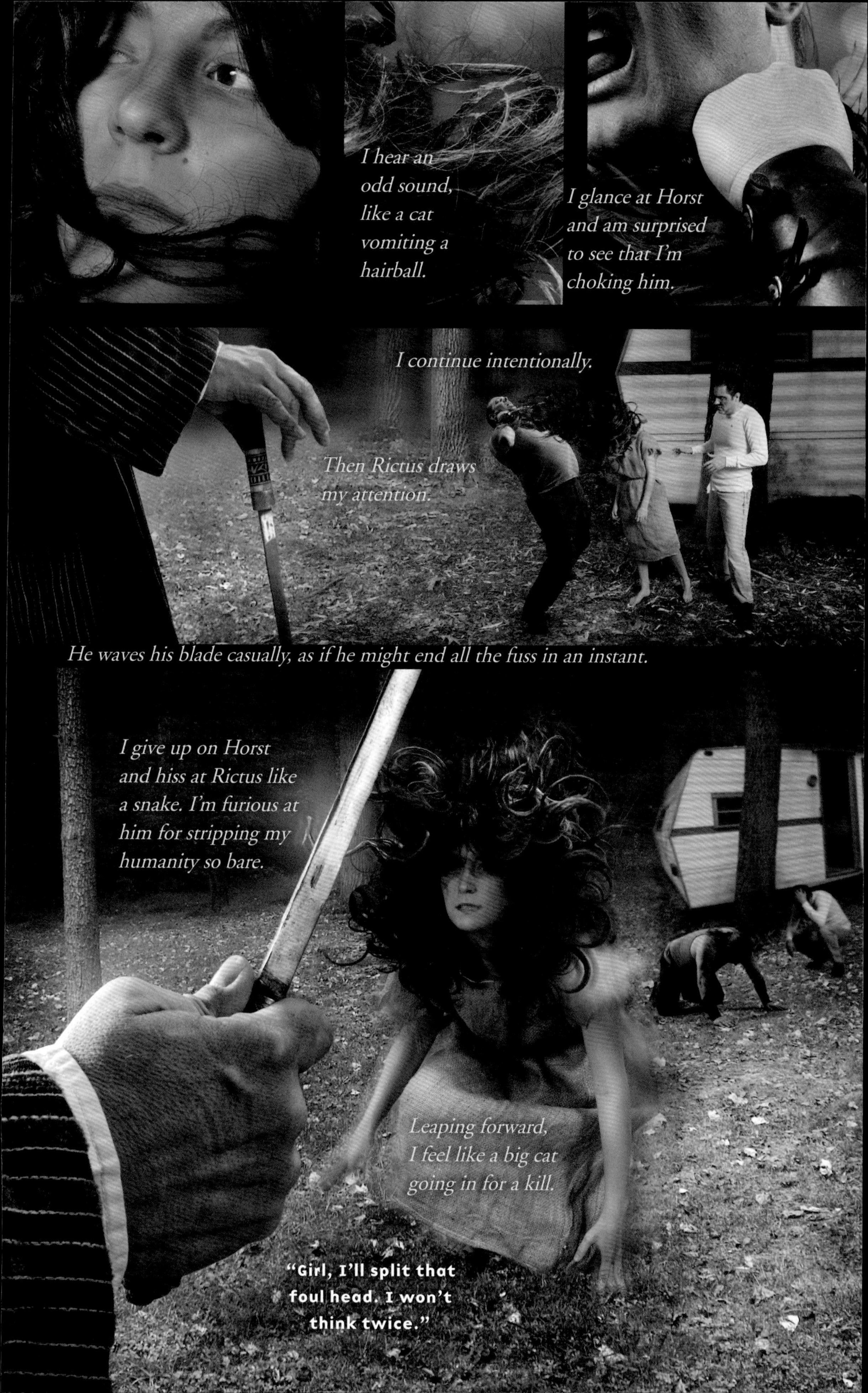
I hear an odd sound, like a cat vomiting a hairball.
I glance at Horst and am surprised to see that I'm choking him.
I continue intentionally.
Then Rictus draws my attention.
He waves his blade casually, as if he might end all the fuss in an instant.
I give up on Horst and hiss at Rictus like a snake. I'm furious at him for stripping my humanity so bare.
Leaping forward, I feel like a big cat going in for a kill.
"Girl, I'll split that foul head. I won't think twice."

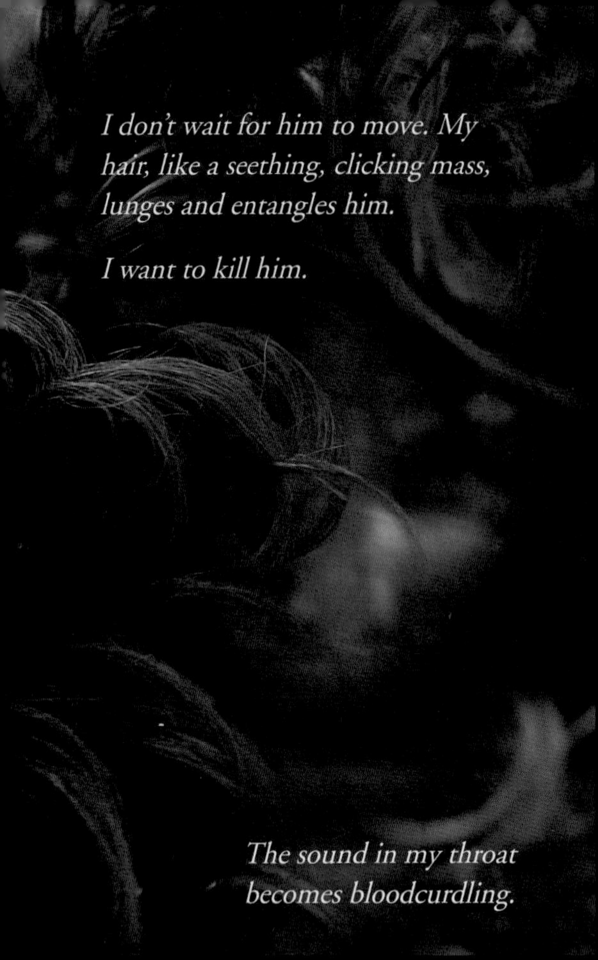
I don't wait for him to move. My hair, like a seething, clicking mass, lunges and entangles him.
I want to kill him.
The sound in my throat becomes bloodcurdling.

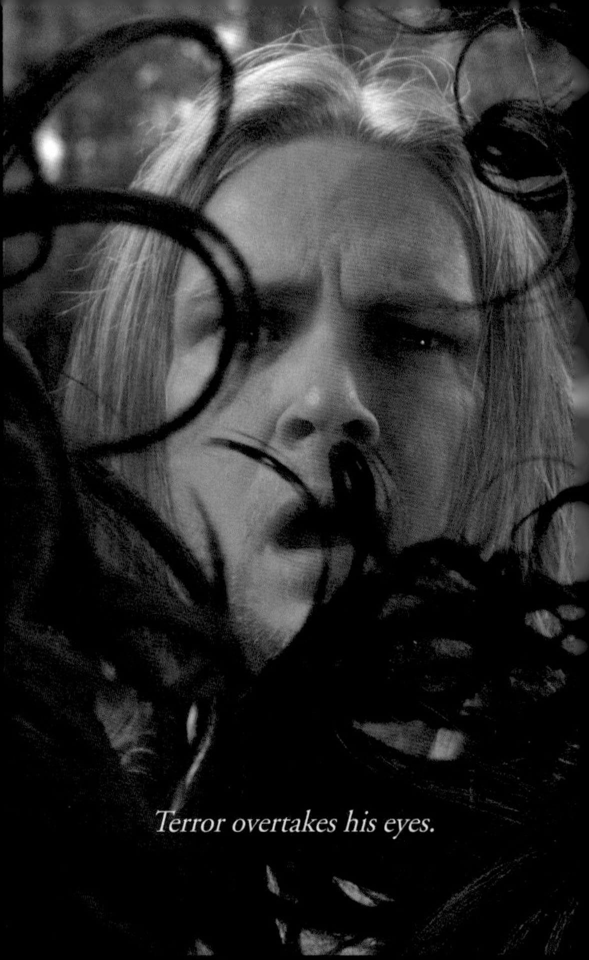
Terror overtakes his eyes.

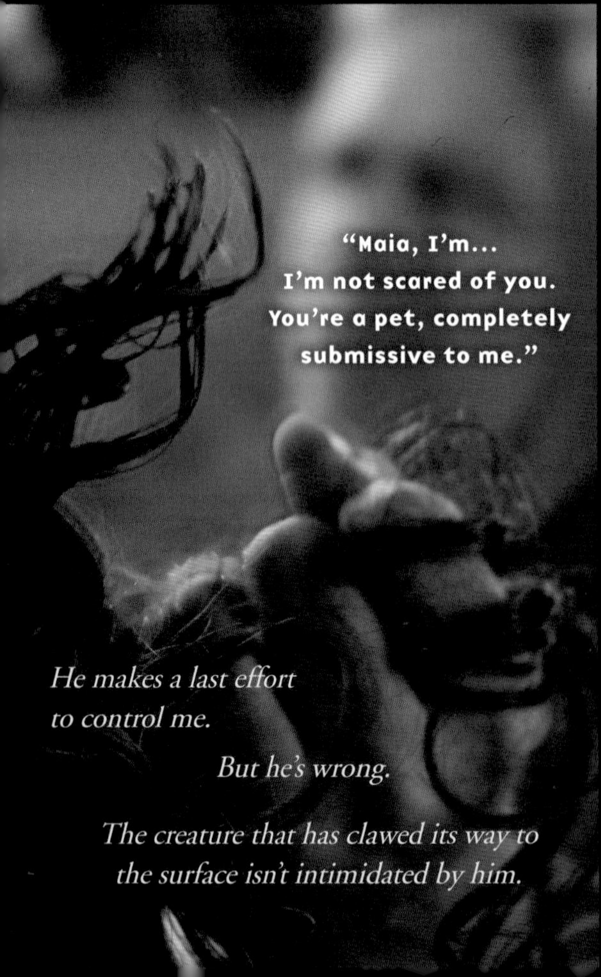
"Maia, I'm... I'm not scared of you. You're a pet, completely submissive to me."
He makes a last effort to control me.
But he's wrong.
The creature that has clawed its way to the surface isn't intimidated by him.

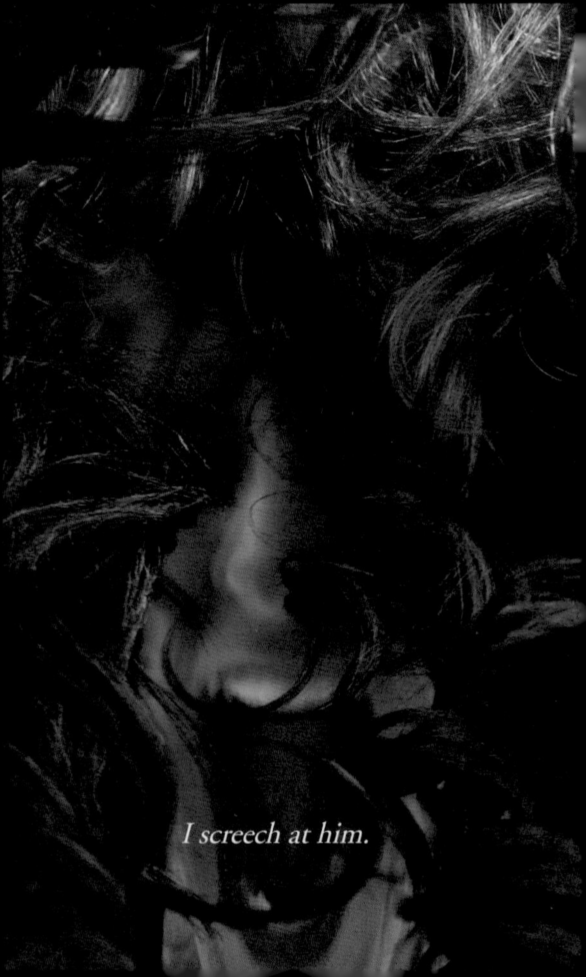
I screech at him.

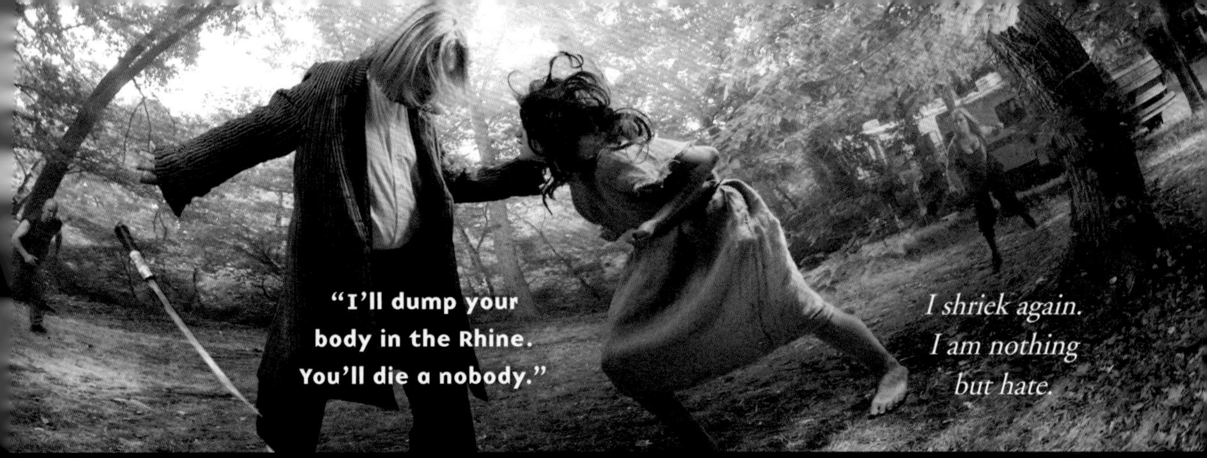
"I'll dump your
body in the Rhine.
You'll die a nobody."
I shriek again.
I am nothing
but hate.

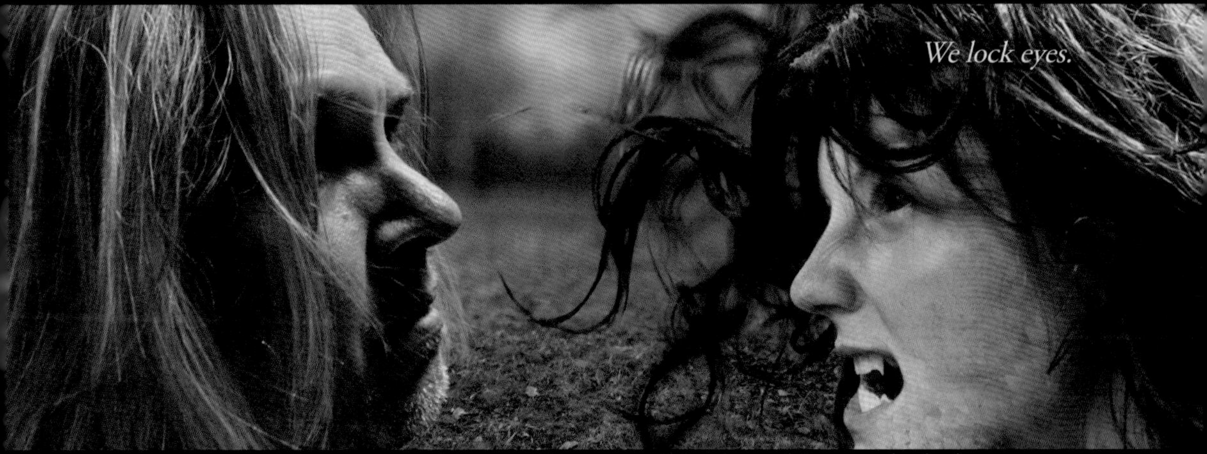
We lock eyes.

He starts to whimper. His eyes roll back, and he stands slack.

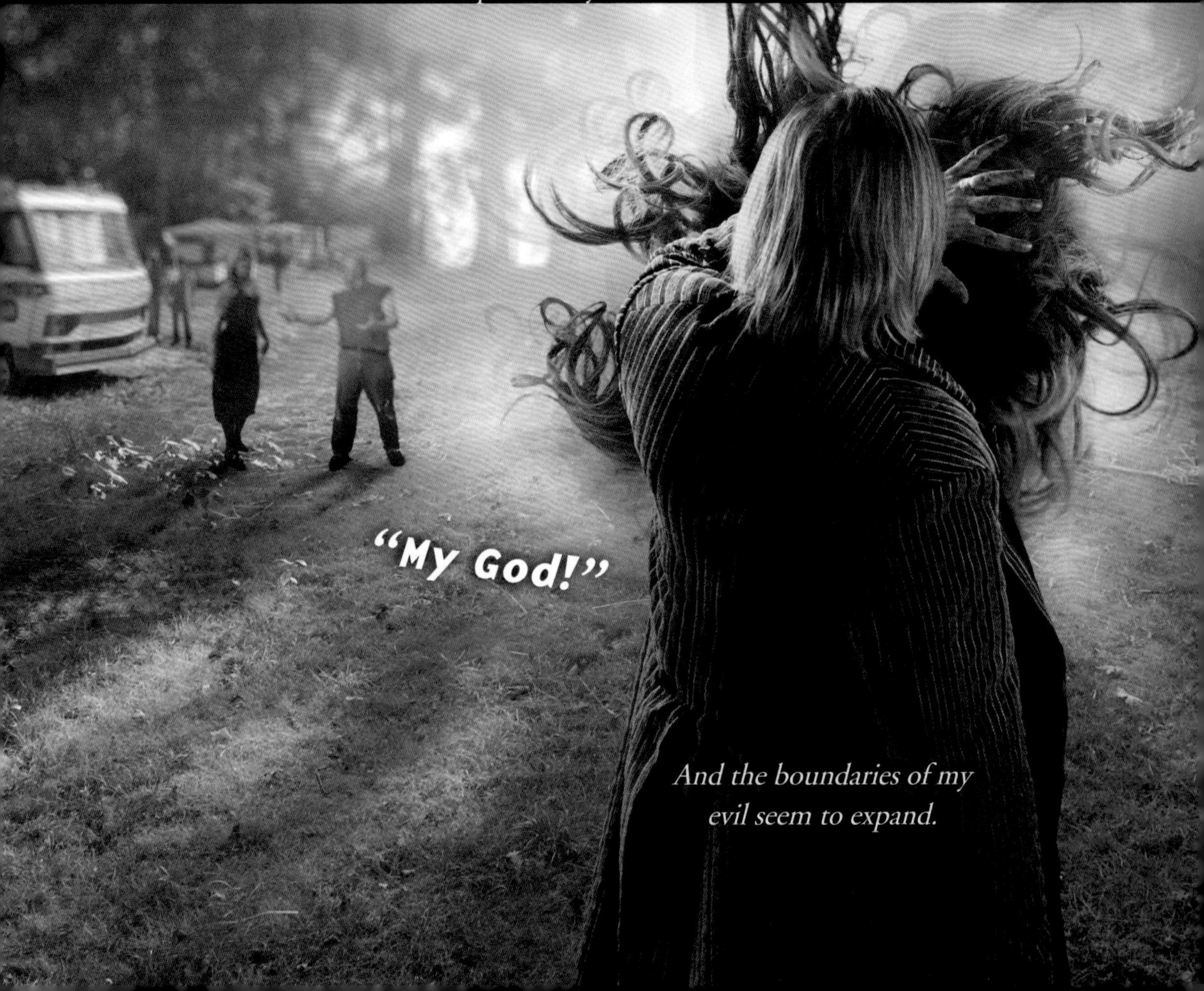
"My God!"
And the boundaries of my
evil seem to expand.

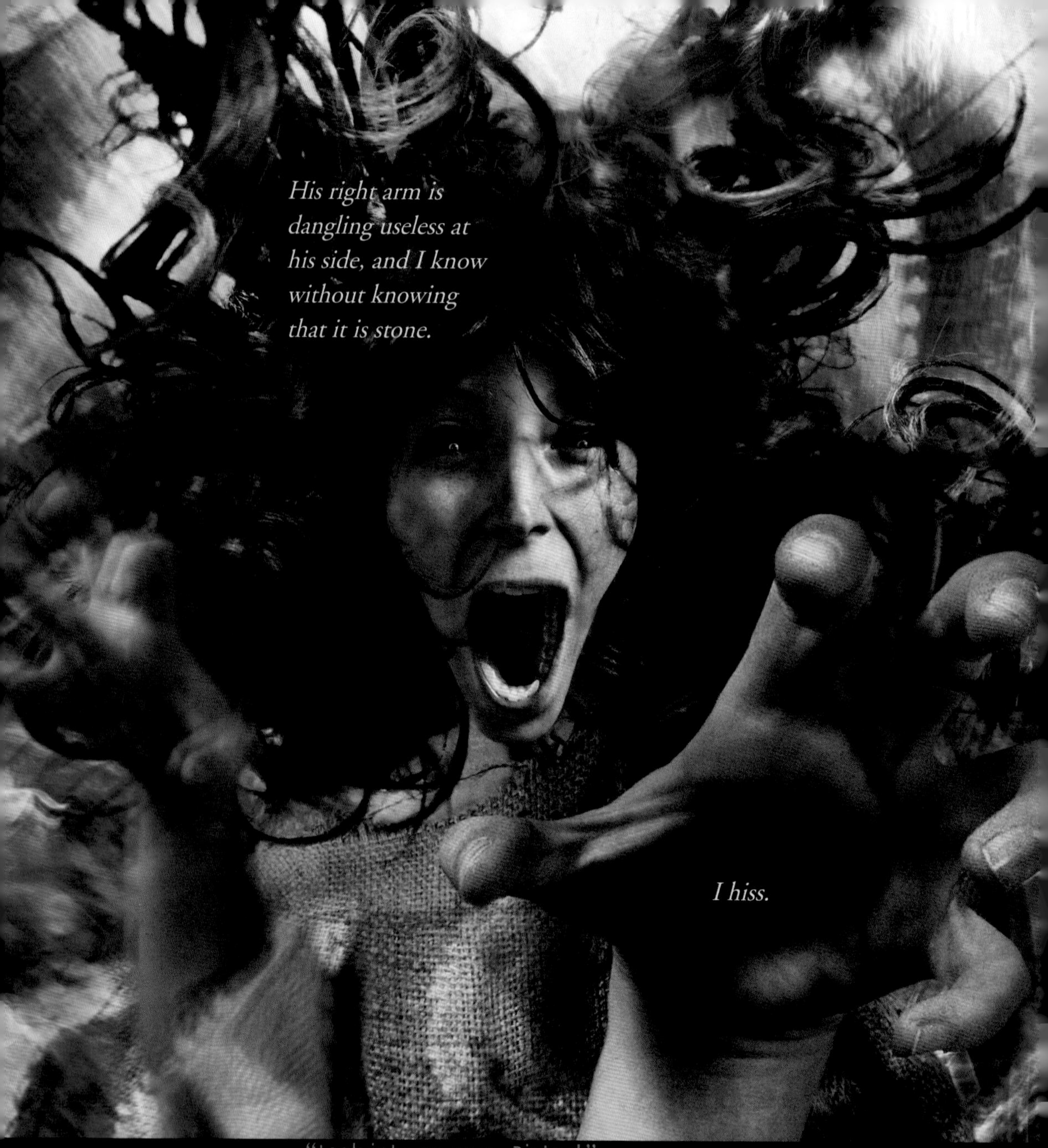
His right arm is dangling useless at his side, and I know without knowing that it is stone.
I hiss.

"Look into my eyes, Rictus!"

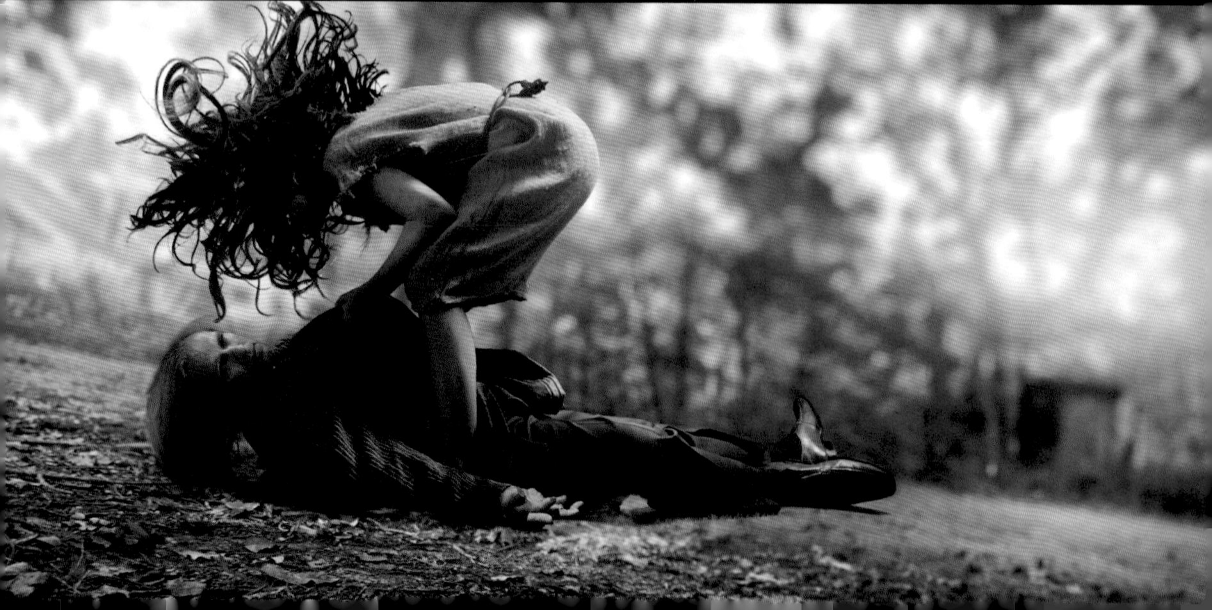

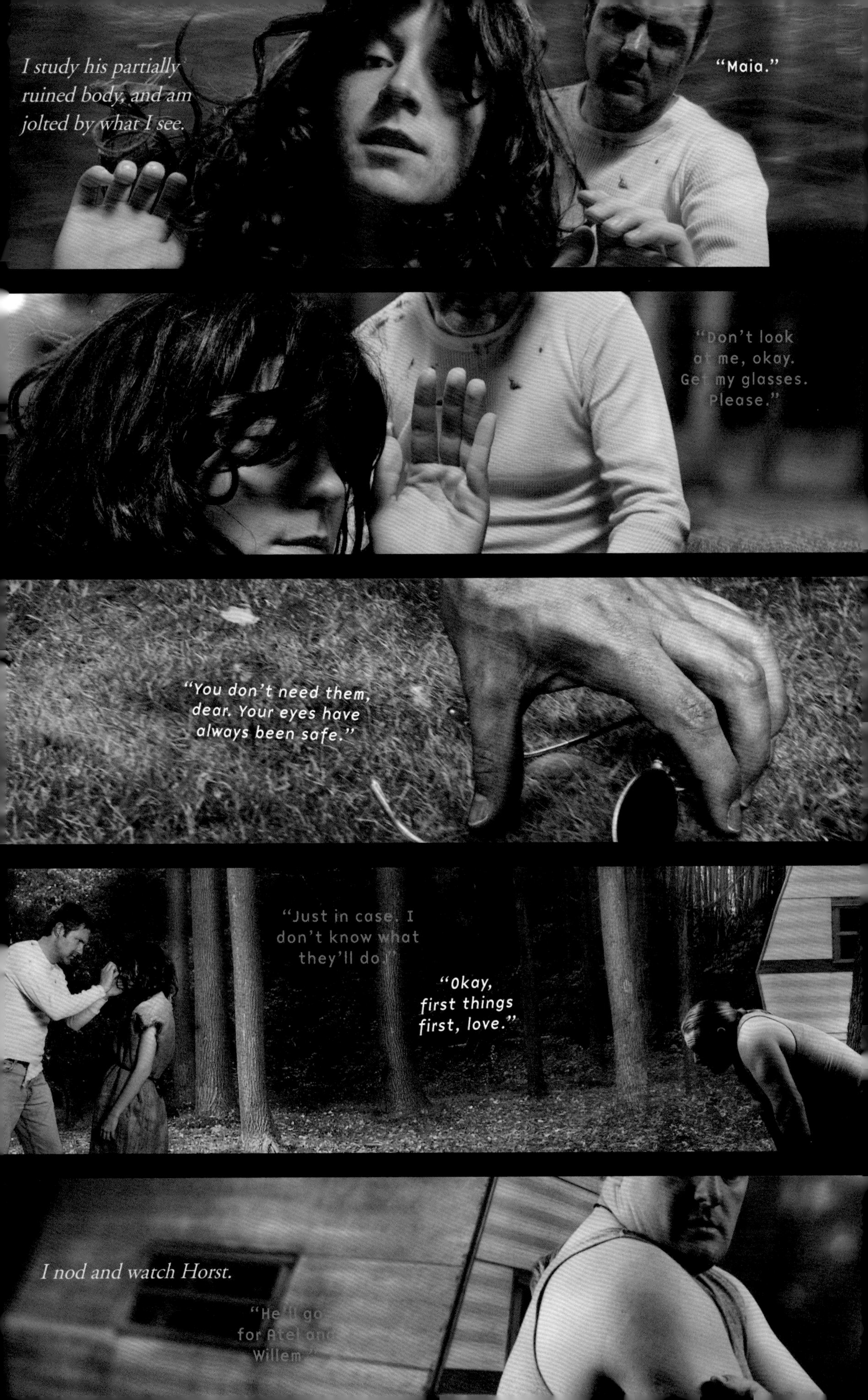
I study his partially ruined body, and am jolted by what I see.
"Maia."
"Don't look at me, okay. Get my glasses. Please."
"You don't need them, dear. Your eyes have always been safe."
"Just in case. I don't know what they'll do."
"Okay, first things first, love."
I nod and watch Horst.
"He'll go for Atel and Willem."

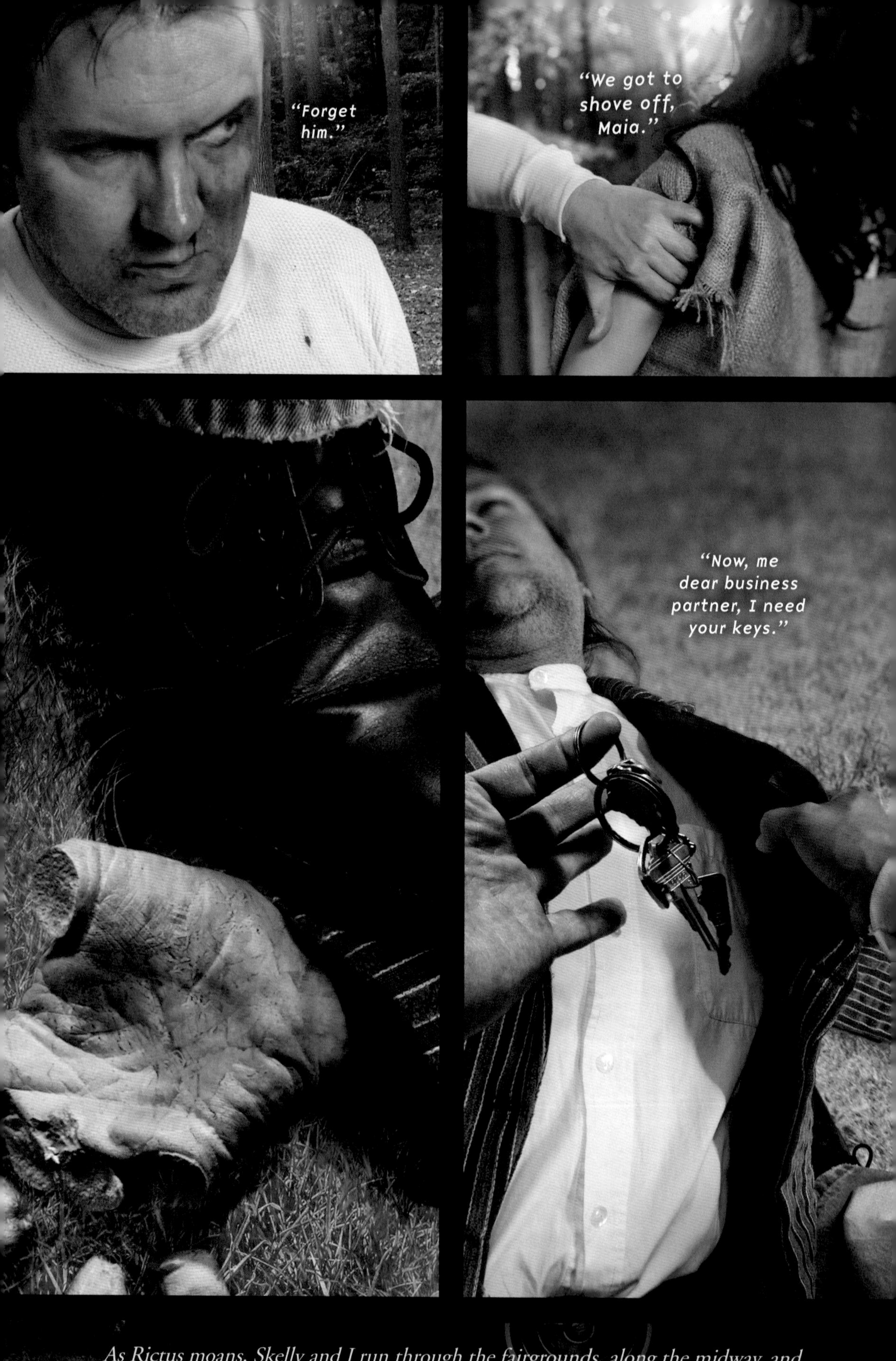
"Forget him."
"We got to shove off, Maia."
"Now, me dear business partner, I need your keys."

As Rictus moans, Skelly and I run through the fairgrounds, along the midway, and into the forest of tents at the festival's far edge, where Rictus parks his car.

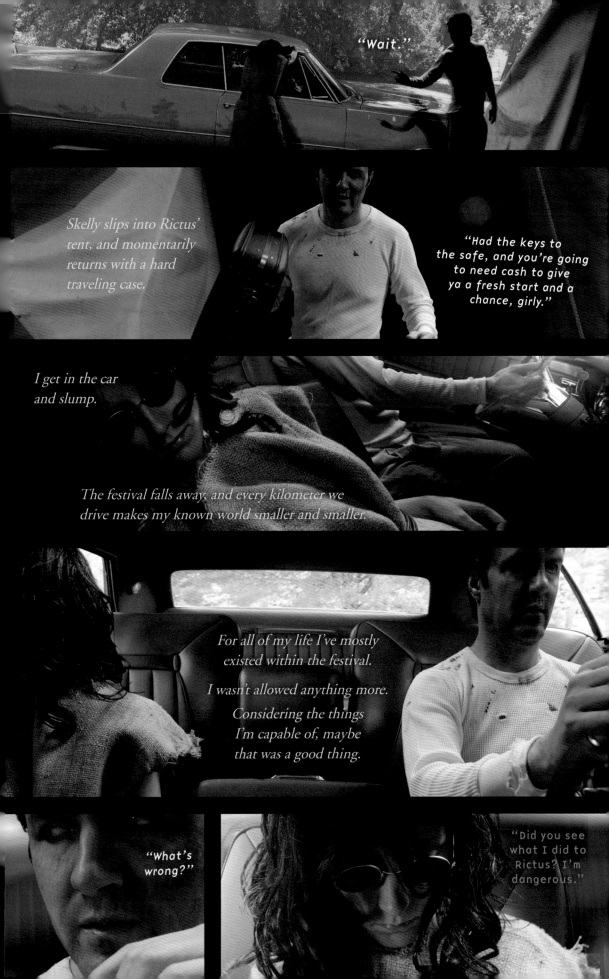

"Wait."

Skelly slips into Rictus' tent, and momentarily returns with a hard traveling case.

"Had the keys to the safe, and you're going to need cash to give ya a fresh start and a chance, girly."

I get in the car and slump.

The festival falls away, and every kilometer we drive makes my known world smaller and smaller.

For all of my life I've mostly existed within the festival.

I wasn't allowed anything more. Considering the things I'm capable of, maybe that was a good thing.

"What's wrong?"

"Did you see what I did to Rictus? I'm dangerous."

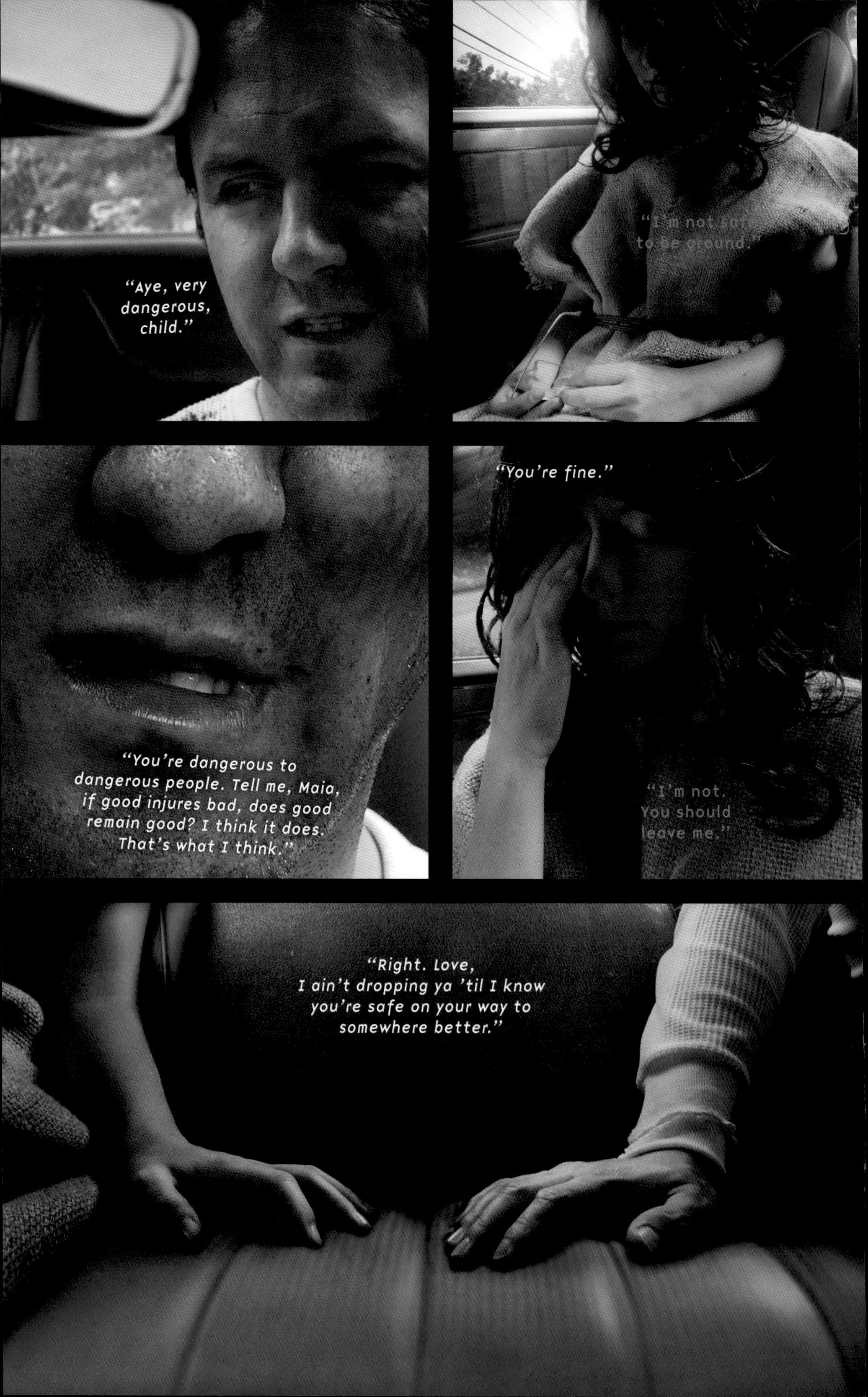
“Aye, very dangerous, child.”
“I’m not saf
to be around.”
“You’re dangerous to dangerous people. Tell me, Maia, if good injures bad, does good remain good? I think it does. That’s what I think.”
“You’re fine.”
“I’m not. You should leave me.”
“Right. Love, I ain’t dropping ya ’til I know you’re safe on your way to somewhere better.”

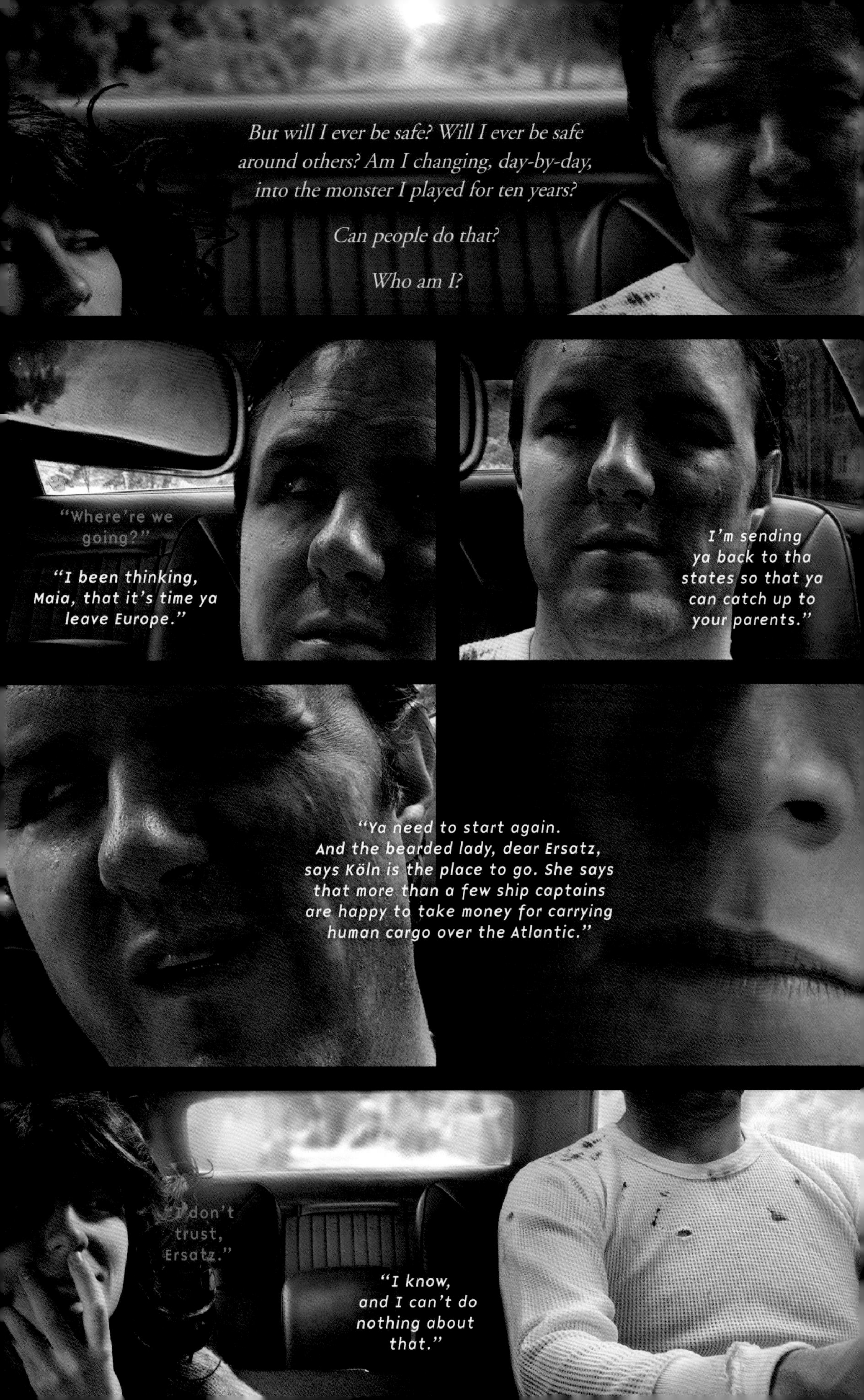
But will I ever be safe? Will I ever be safe around others? Am I changing, day-by-day, into the monster I played for ten years?
Can people do that?
Who am I?
"Where're we going?"
"I been thinking, Maia, that it's time ya leave Europe."
I'm sending ya back to tha states so that ya can catch up to your parents."
"Ya need to start again. And the bearded lady, dear Ersatz, says Köln is the place to go. She says that more than a few ship captains are happy to take money for carrying human cargo over the Atlantic."
"I don't trust, Ersatz."
"I know, and I can't do nothing about that."

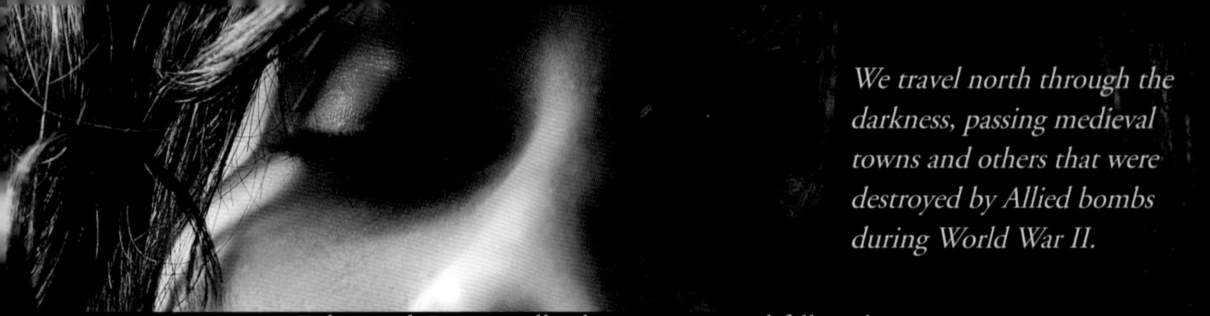
We travel north through the darkness, passing medieval towns and others that were destroyed by Allied bombs during World War II.

Exhausted, I eventually close my eyes and fall to sleep.

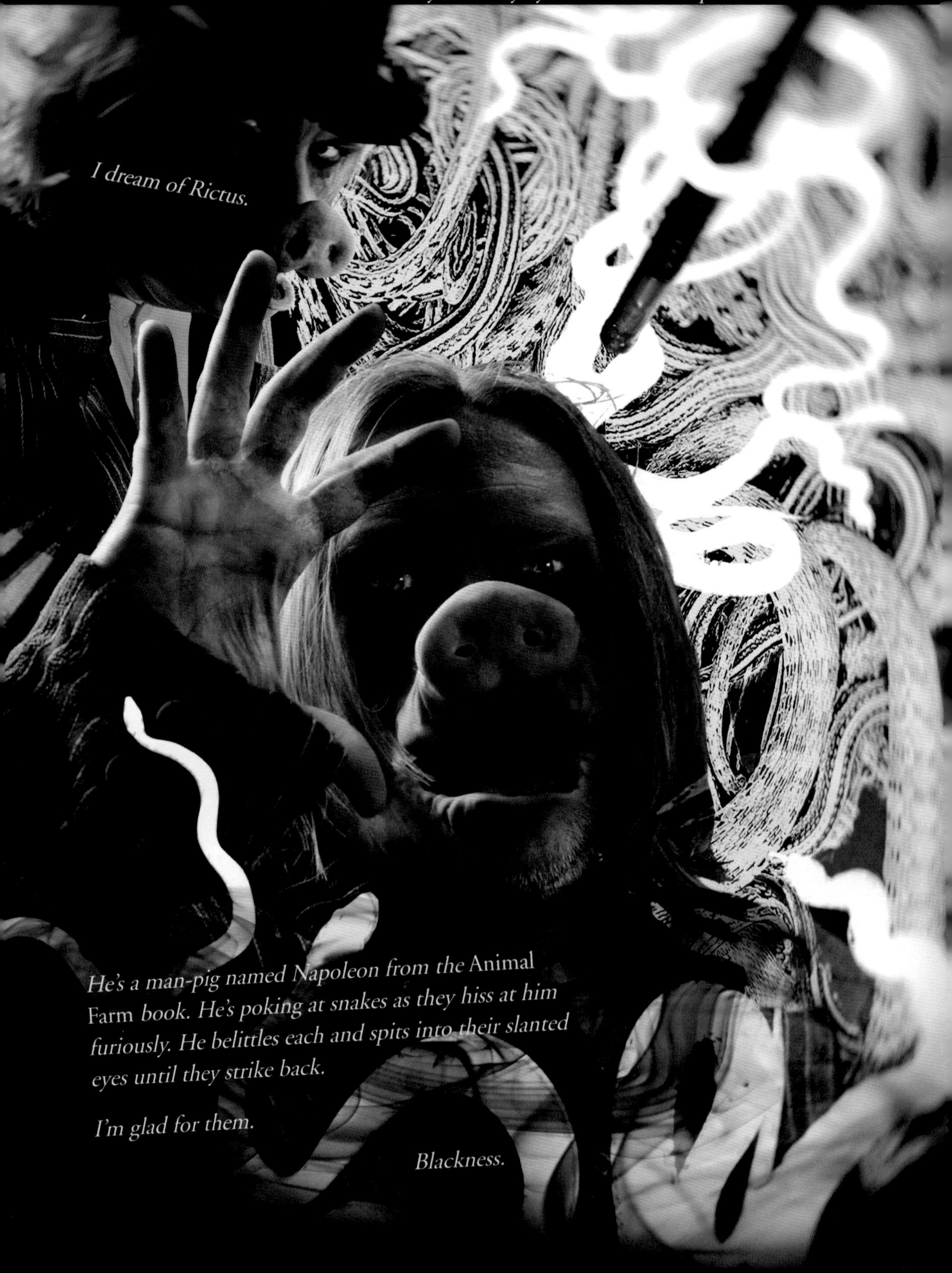
I dream of Rictus.
He's a man-pig named Napoleon from the Animal Farm book. He's poking at snakes as they hiss at him furiously. He belittles each and spits into their slanted eyes until they strike back.
I'm glad for them.
Blackness.

Now I'm passing down a golden river that looks like a valley of molten lava in the sunlight. I think of Huckleberry Finn and Tom afloat on the Mississippi, and I realize that Skelly and I are exactly like them.

Flowers and trees line the shore.
Behind those are gentle, green hills and farms with clean rows.

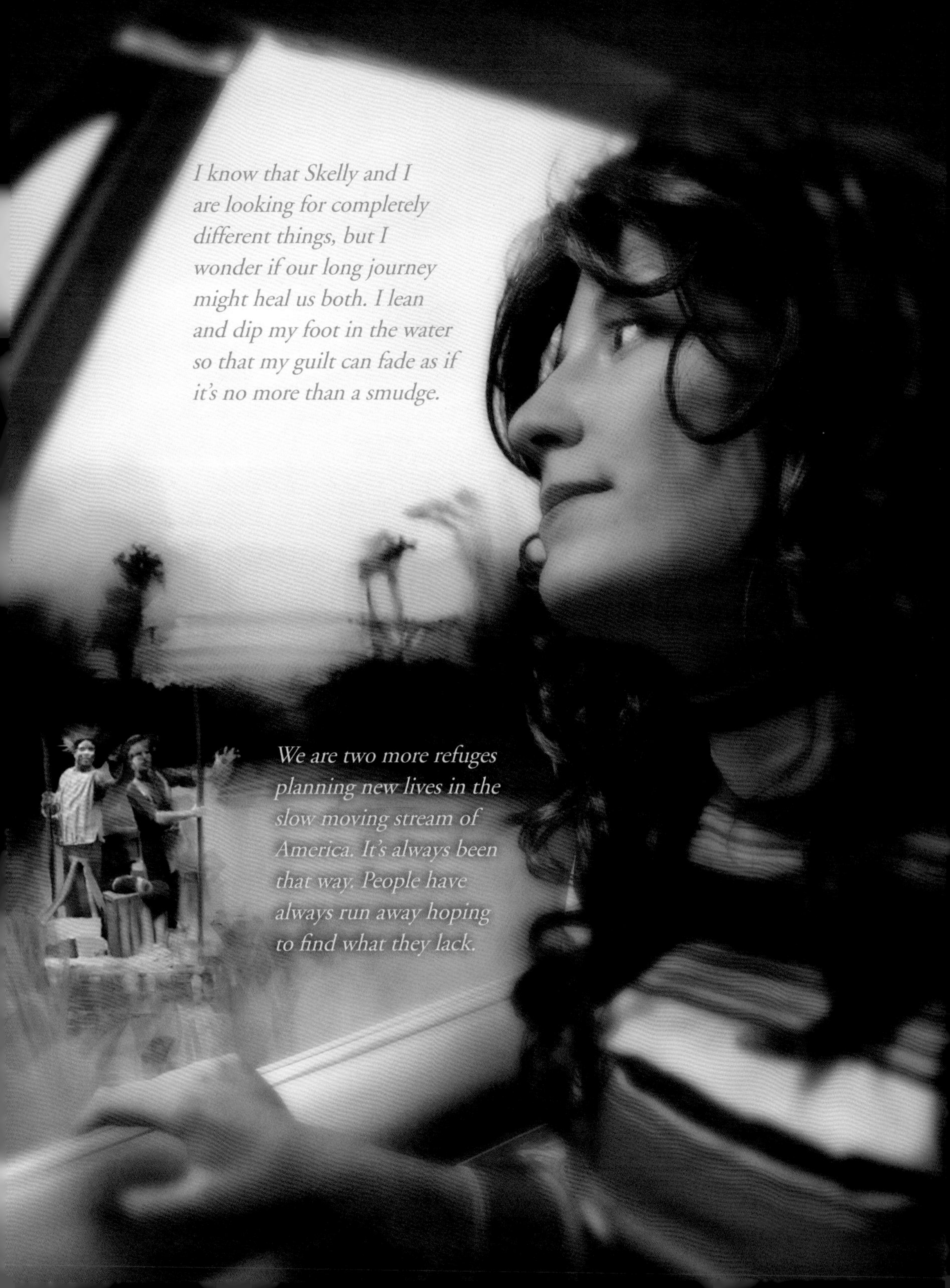

I know that Skelly and I are looking for completely different things, but I wonder if our long journey might heal us both. I lean and dip my foot in the water so that my guilt can fade as if it's no more than a smudge.

We are two more refuges planning new lives in the slow moving stream of America. It's always been that way. People have always run away hoping to find what they lack.

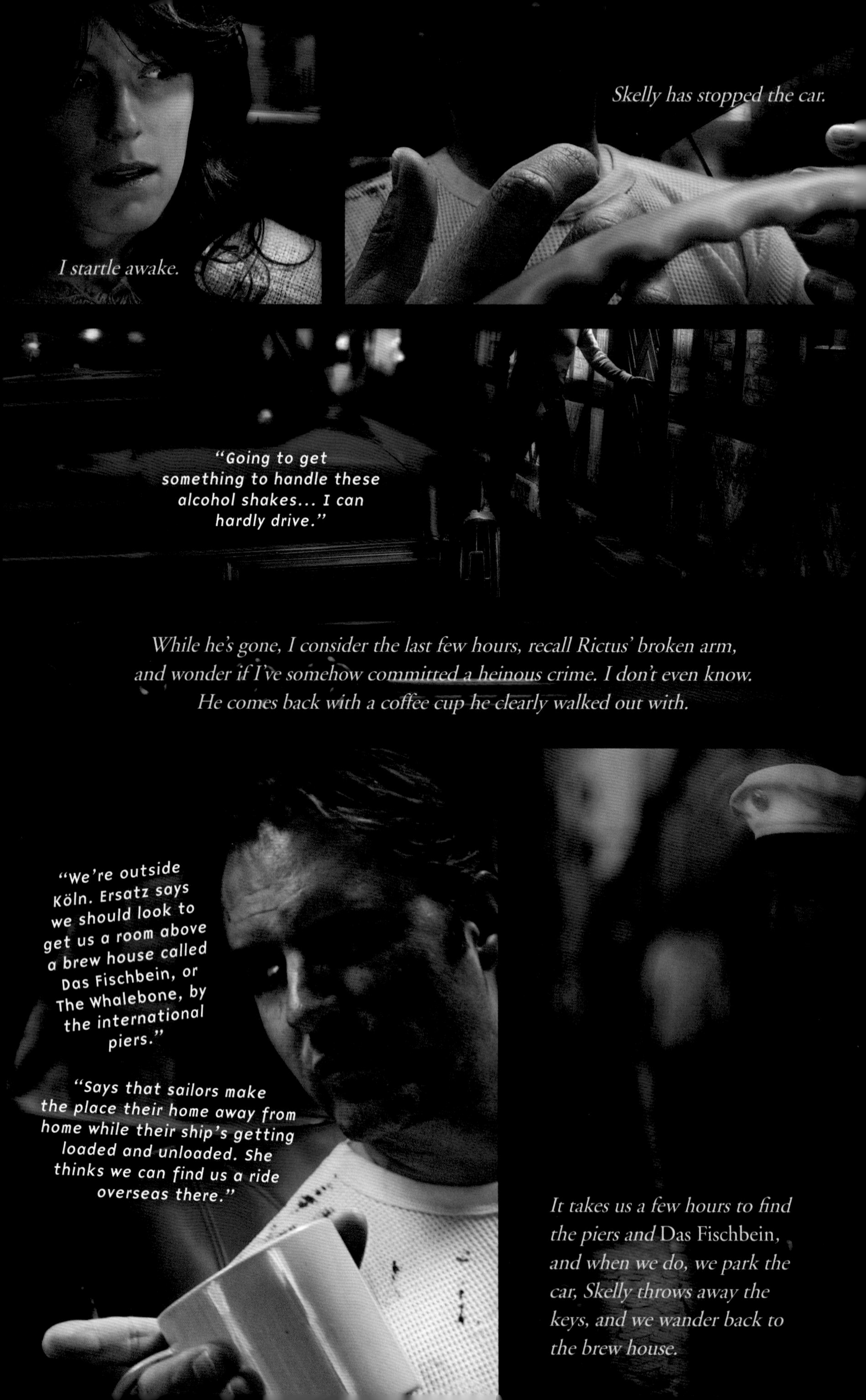
I startle awake.
Skelly has stopped the car.
"Going to get something to handle these alcohol shakes... I can hardly drive."
While he's gone, I consider the last few hours, recall Rictus' broken arm, and wonder if I've somehow committed a heinous crime. I don't even know. He comes back with a coffee cup he clearly walked out with.
"We're outside Köln. Ersatz says we should look to get us a room above a brew house called Das Fischbein, or The Whalebone, by the international piers."
"Says that sailors make the place their home away from home while their ship's getting loaded and unloaded. She thinks we can find us a ride overseas there."
It takes us a few hours to find the piers and Das Fischbein, and when we do, we park the car, Skelly throws away the keys, and we wander back to the brew house.

In the morning, Skelly gets up and says he's going to buy us travel clothes. The thing is, he's back within an hour.

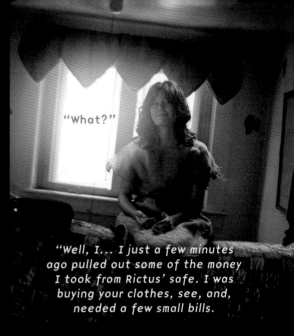

"What?"

"Well, I... I just a few minutes ago pulled out some of the money I took from Rictus' safe. I was buying your clothes, see, and, needed a few small bills.

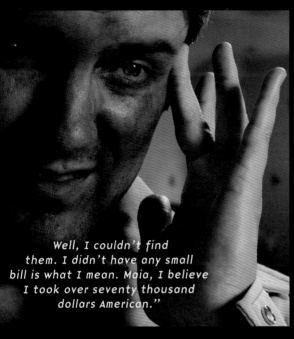

Well, I couldn't find them. I didn't have any small bill is what I mean. Maia, I believe I took over seventy thousand dollars American."

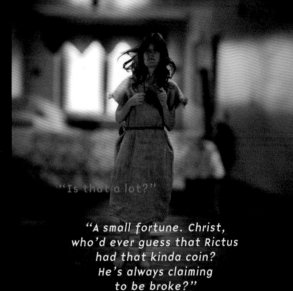

"Is that a lot?"

"A small fortune. Christ, who'd ever guess that Rictus had that kinda coin? He's always claiming to be broke?"

"Honey, ya carry this with ya when ya arrive in the States, and ya can buy a good life for yourself and family."

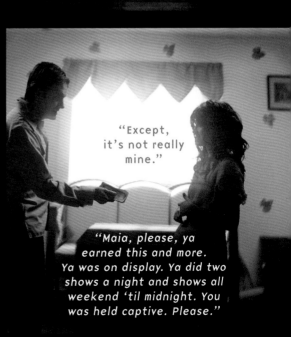

"Except, it's not really mine."

"Maia, please, ya earned this and more. Ya was on display. Ya did two shows a night and shows all weekend 'til midnight. You was held captive. Please."

Skelly goes down to drink alongside captains and first mates. He intends to ask them about my passage to America. Bored, I go out looking for a book to read.

My eyes are drawn to a title about the ocean called The Old Man in the Sea.

When I return, Skelly is out in front of Das Fischbein *wandering in circles.*

"Maia, got ya passage on a boat, but we gotta hurry."

"It leaves in about twenty minutes, so ya gotta get a move on."

"So... soon?"

"Sooner the better."

"Are you coming with me?"

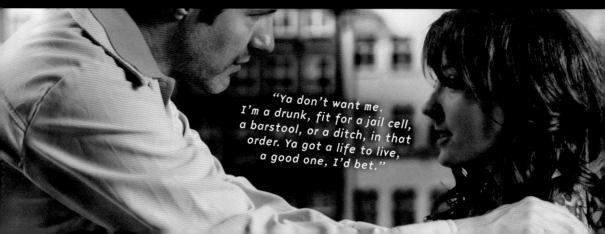

"Ya don't want me. I'm a drunk, fit for a jail cell, a barstool, or a ditch, in that order. Ya got a life to live, a good one, I'd bet."

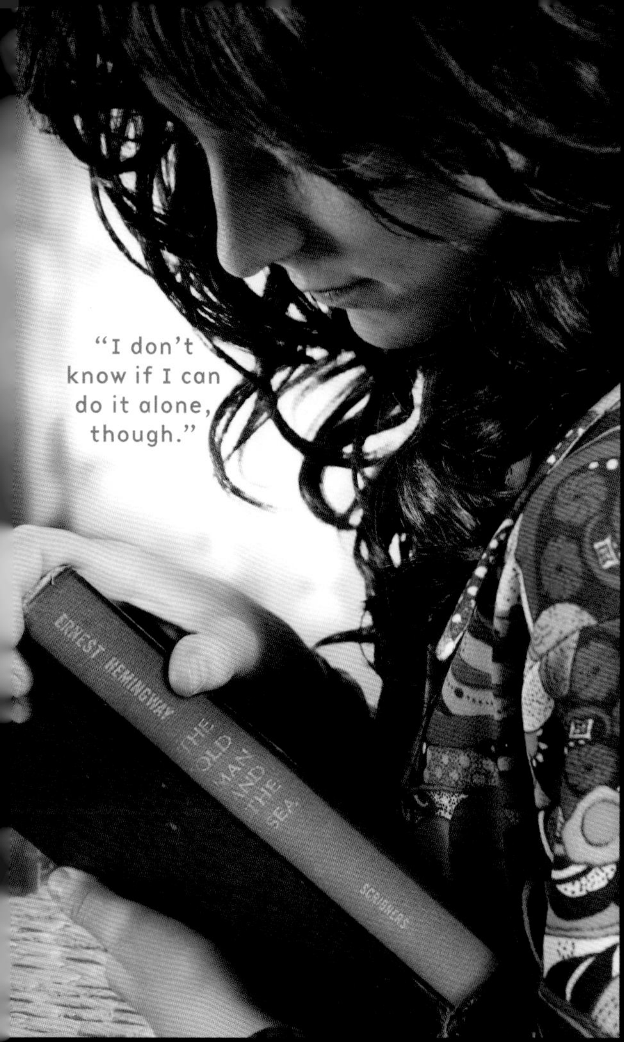
"I don't know if I can do it alone, though."
ERNEST HEMINGWAY
THE OLD MAN AND THE SEA
SCRIBNERS

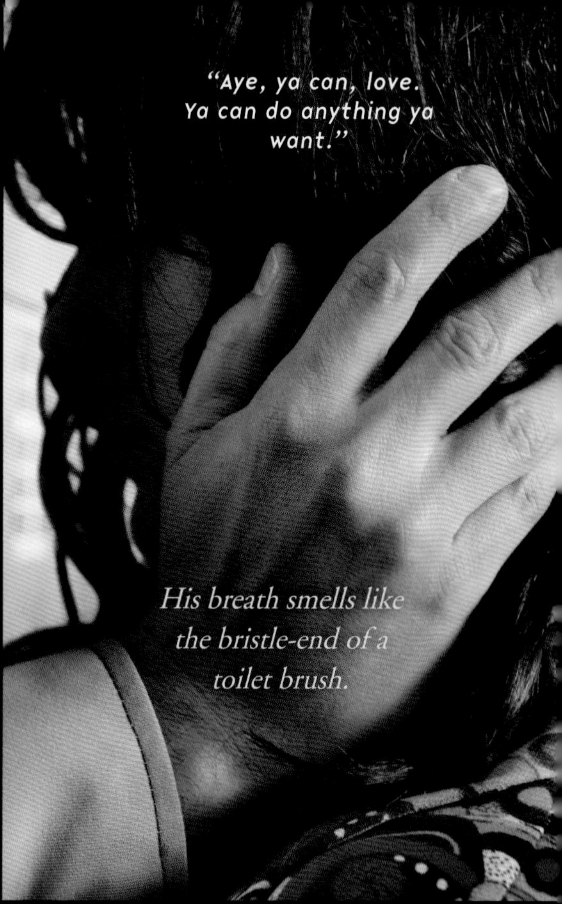
"Aye, ya can, love. Ya can do anything ya want."
His breath smells like the bristle-end of a toilet brush.

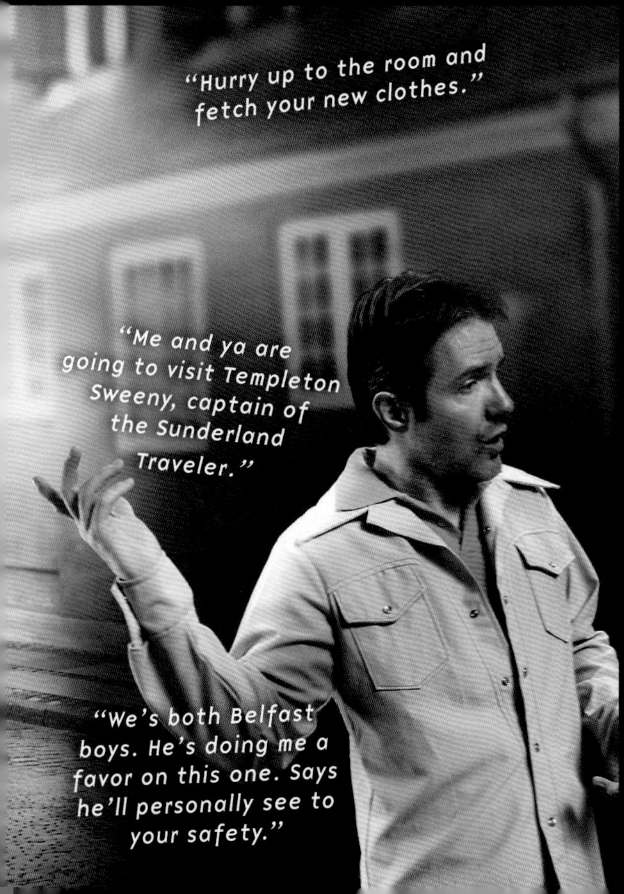
"Hurry up to the room and fetch your new clothes."
"Me and ya are going to visit Templeton Sweeny, captain of the Sunderland Traveler."
"We's both Belfast boys. He's doing me a favor on this one. Says he'll personally see to your safety."

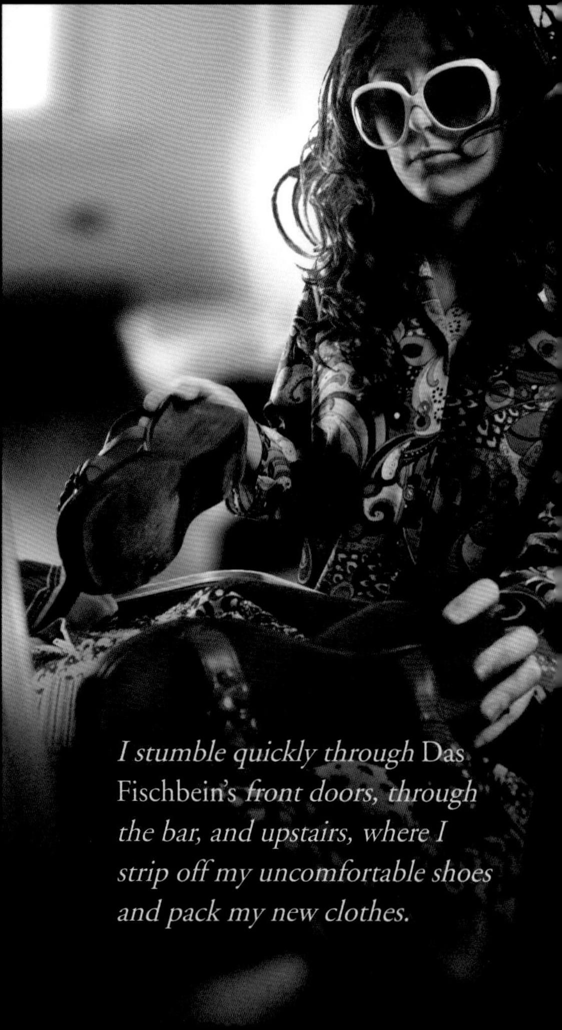
I stumble quickly through Das Fischbein's front doors, through the bar, and upstairs, where I strip off my uncomfortable shoes and pack my new clothes.

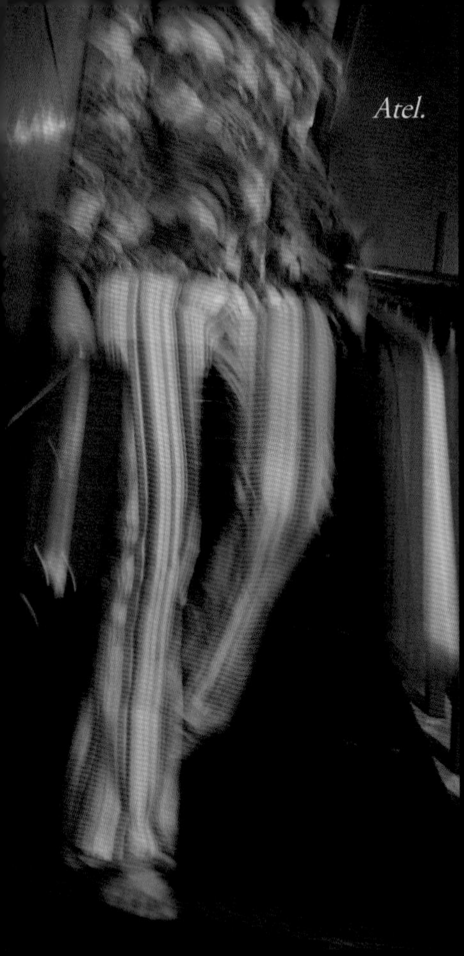
Atel.

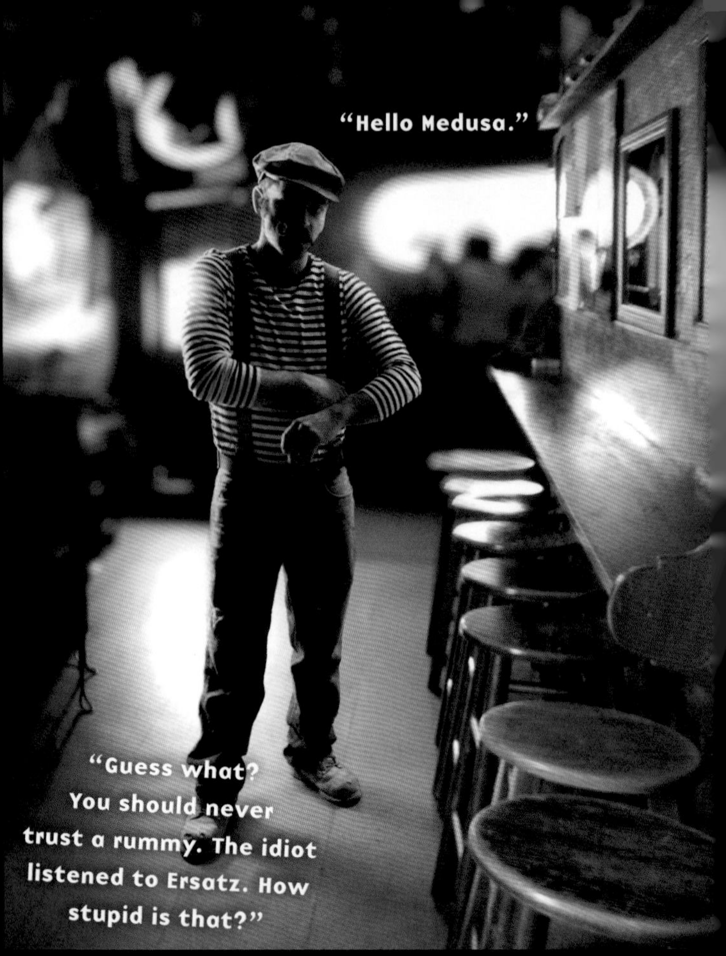
"Hello Medusa."
"Guess what? You should never trust a rummy. The idiot listened to Ersatz. How stupid is that?"

I am not the least bit surprised Ersatz gave us up.

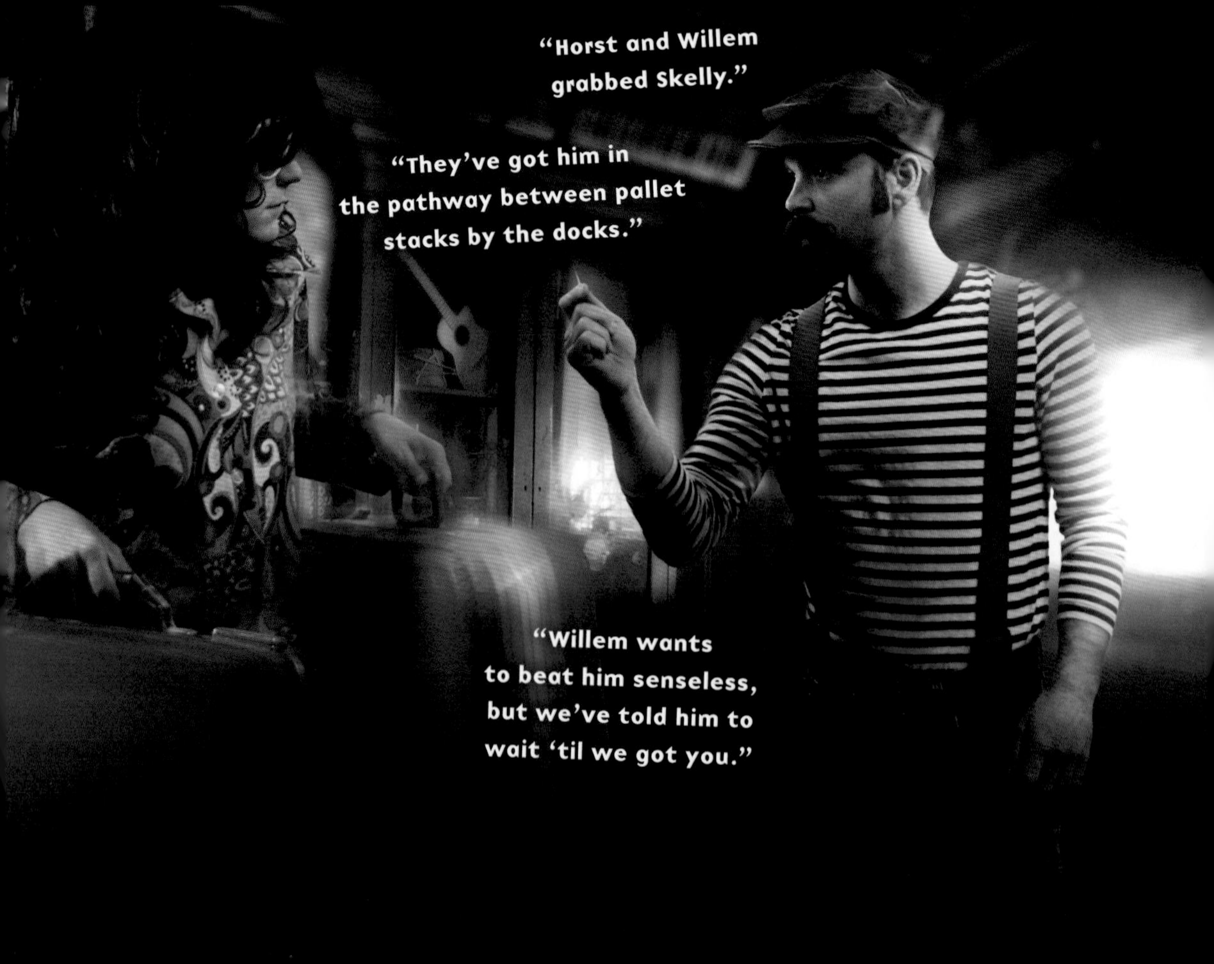
"Horst and Willem grabbed Skelly."
"They've got him in the pathway between pallet stacks by the docks."
"Willem wants to beat him senseless, but we've told him to wait 'til we got you."

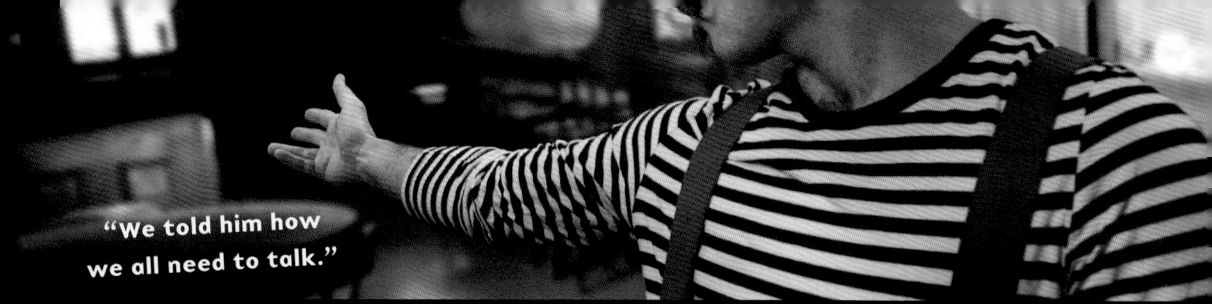
"We told him how we all need to talk."
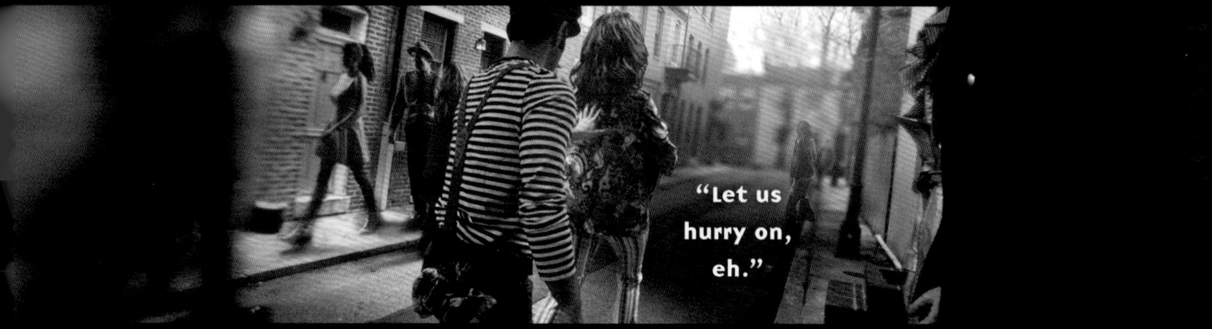
"Let us hurry on, eh."
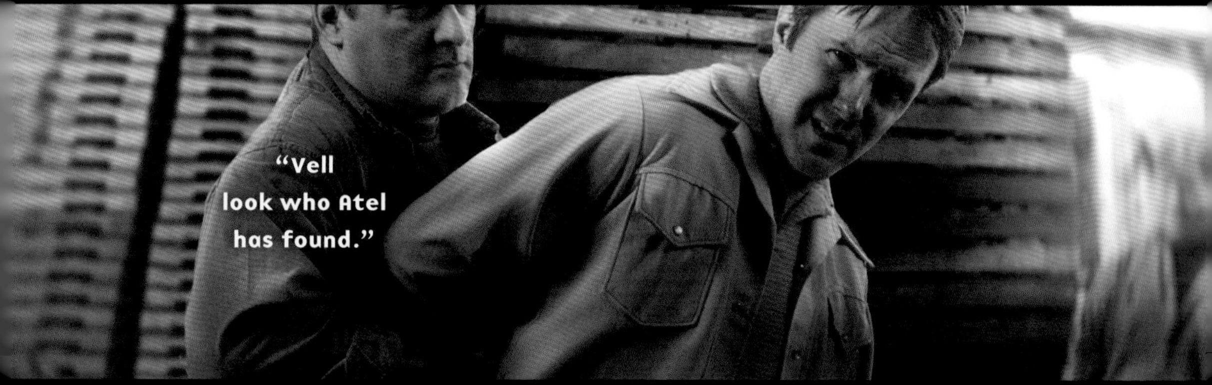
"Vell look who Atel has found."
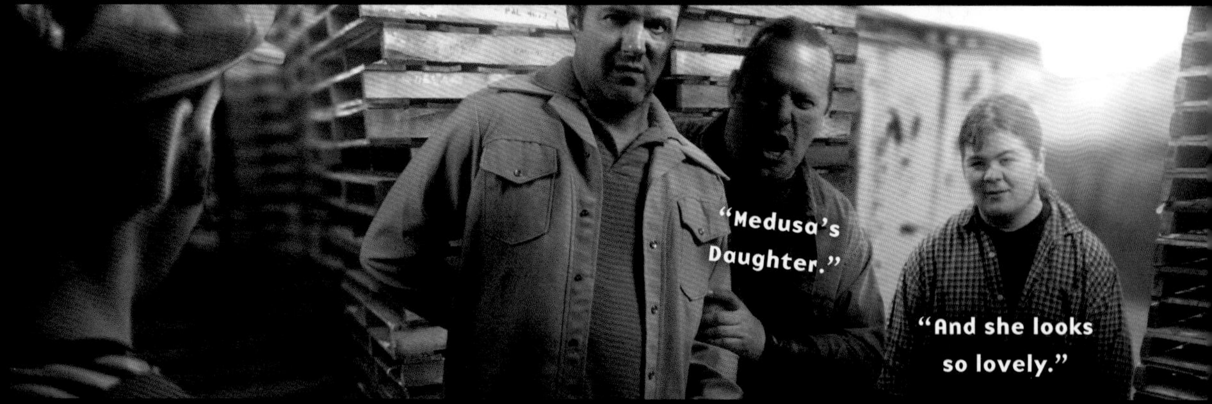
"Medusa's Daughter."
"And she looks so lovely."
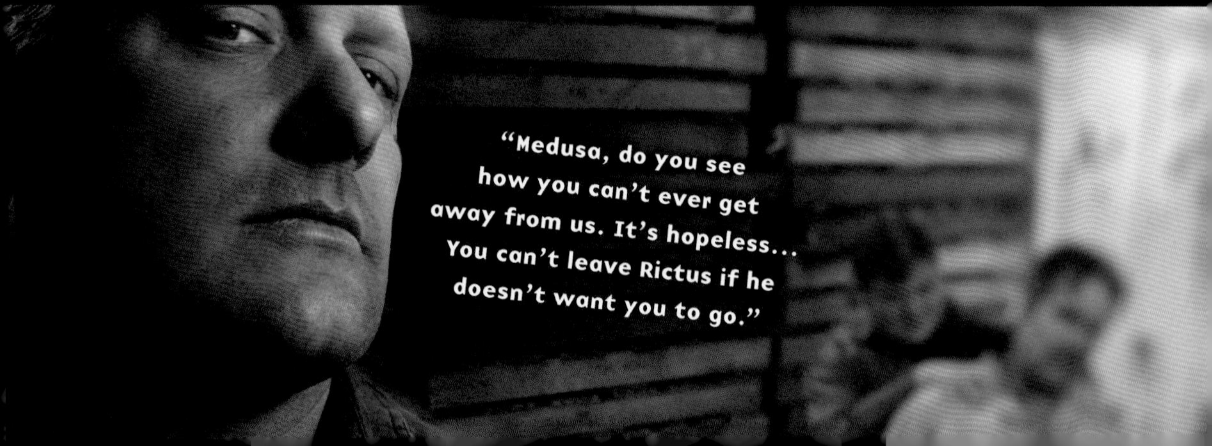
"Medusa, do you see how you can't ever get away from us. It's hopeless... You can't leave Rictus if he doesn't want you to go."

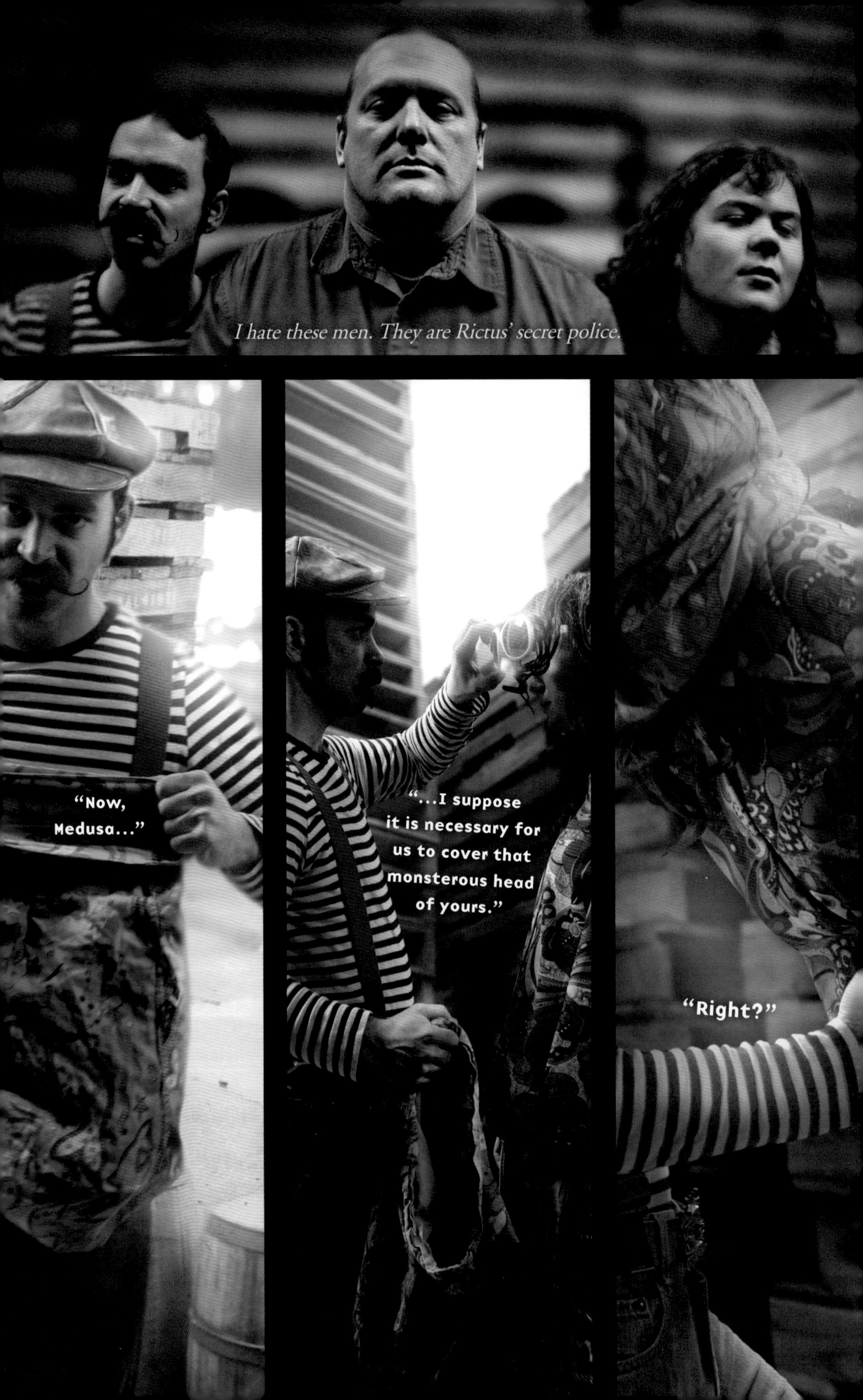
I hate these men. They are Rictus' secret police.
"Now, Medusa..."
"...I suppose it is necessary for us to cover that monsterous head of yours."
"Right?"

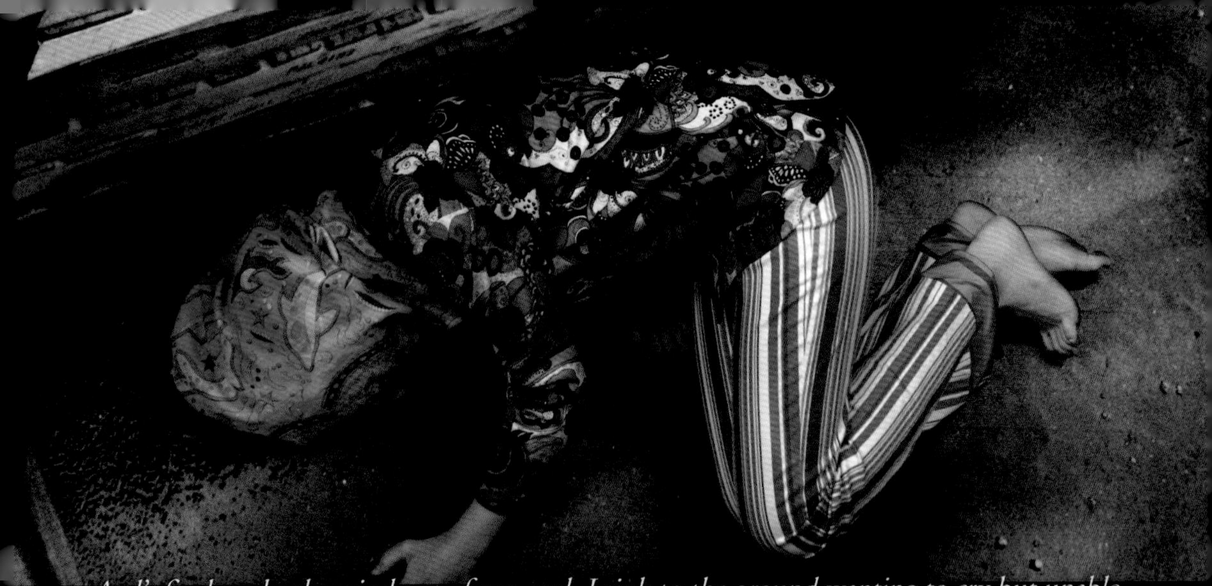

Atel's fist knocks the wind out of me, and, I sink to the ground wanting to cry but unable.

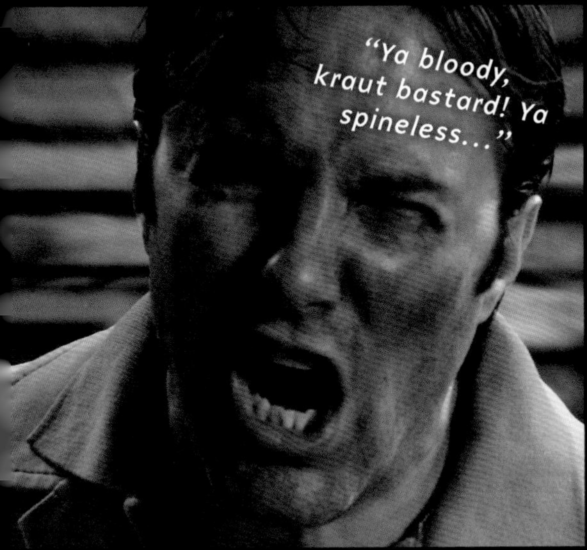
"Ya bloody, kraut bastard! Ya spineless..."

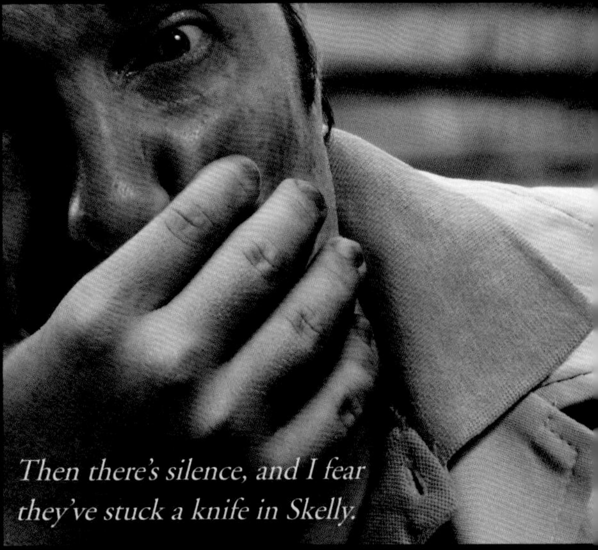
Then there's silence, and I fear they've stuck a knife in Skelly.

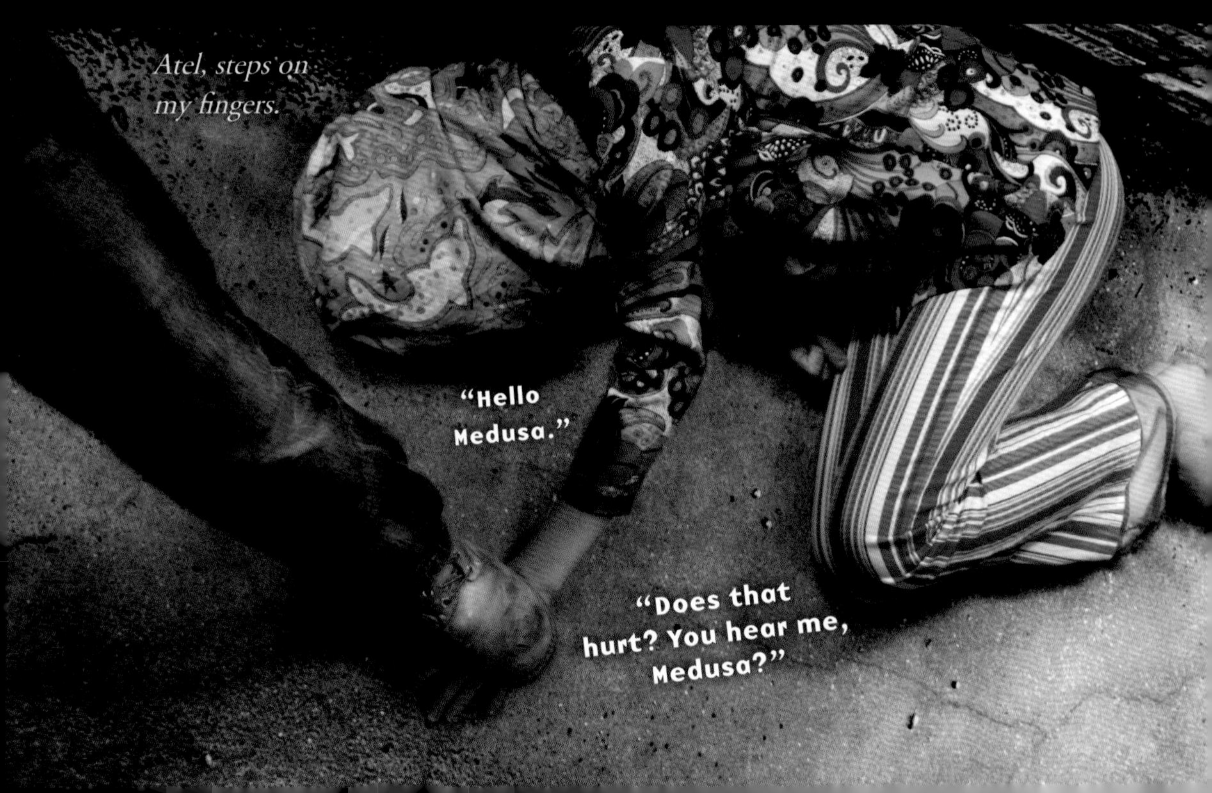
Atel, steps on my fingers.
"Hello Medusa."
"Does that hurt? You hear me, Medusa?"

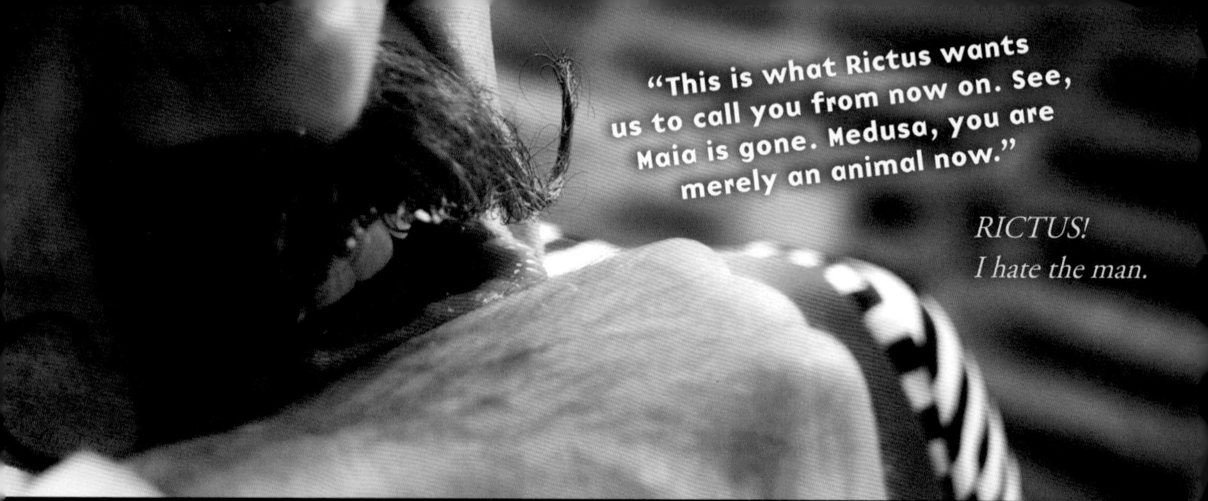
"This is what Rictus wants us to call you from now on. See, Maia is gone. Medusa, you are merely an animal now."
RICTUS!
I hate the man.

Bloodlust and rage seem to drown the crevices of my brain and I lash back.

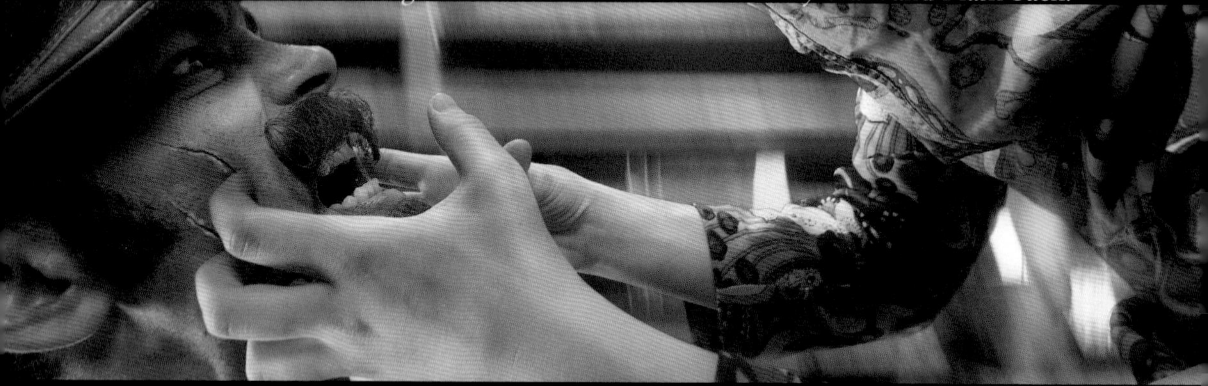

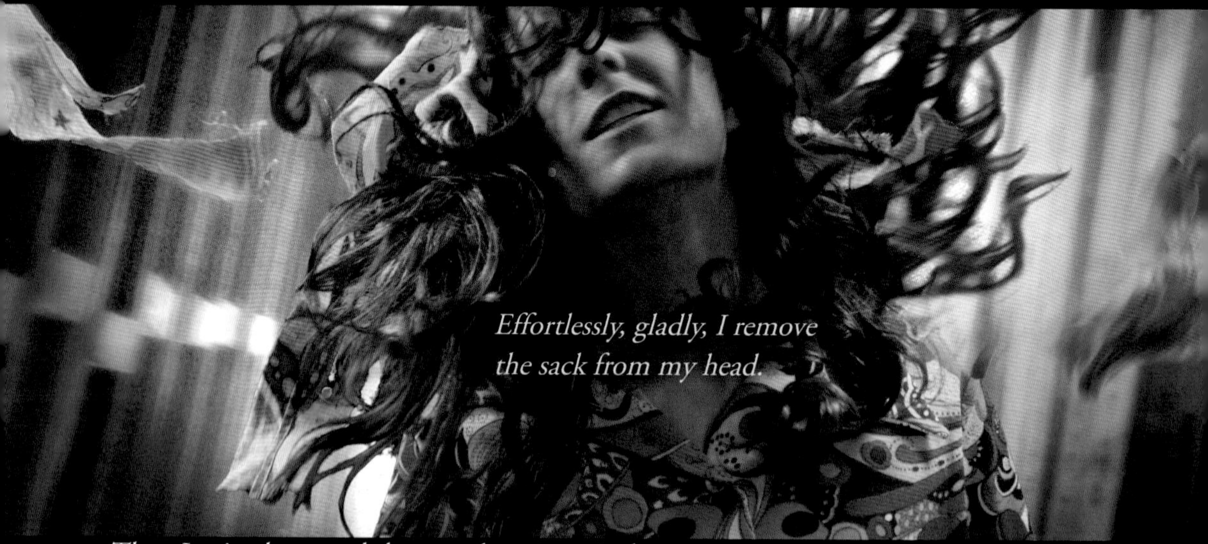
Effortlessly, gladly, I remove the sack from my head.

Then I spin about and slam a palette into Atel.

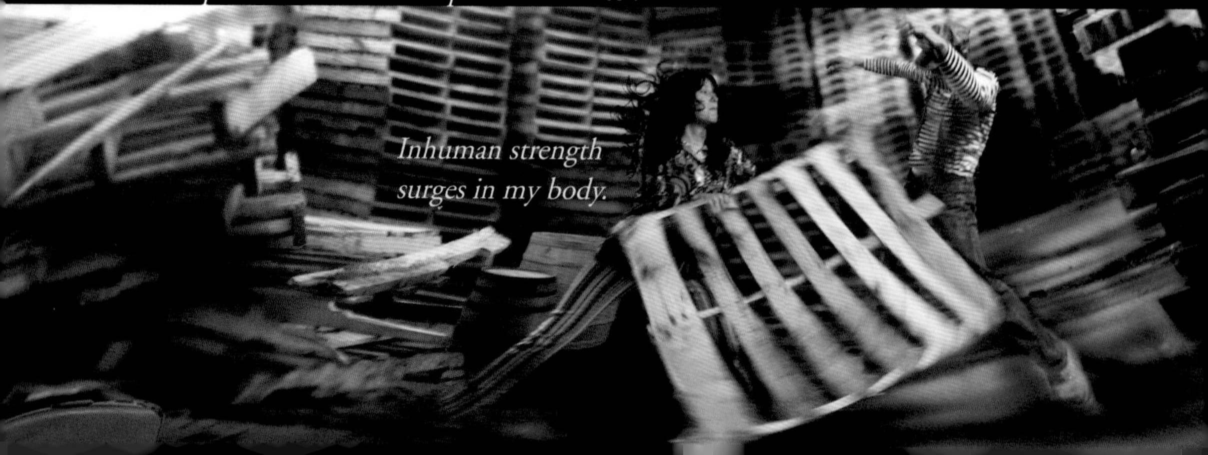
Inhuman strength surges in my body.

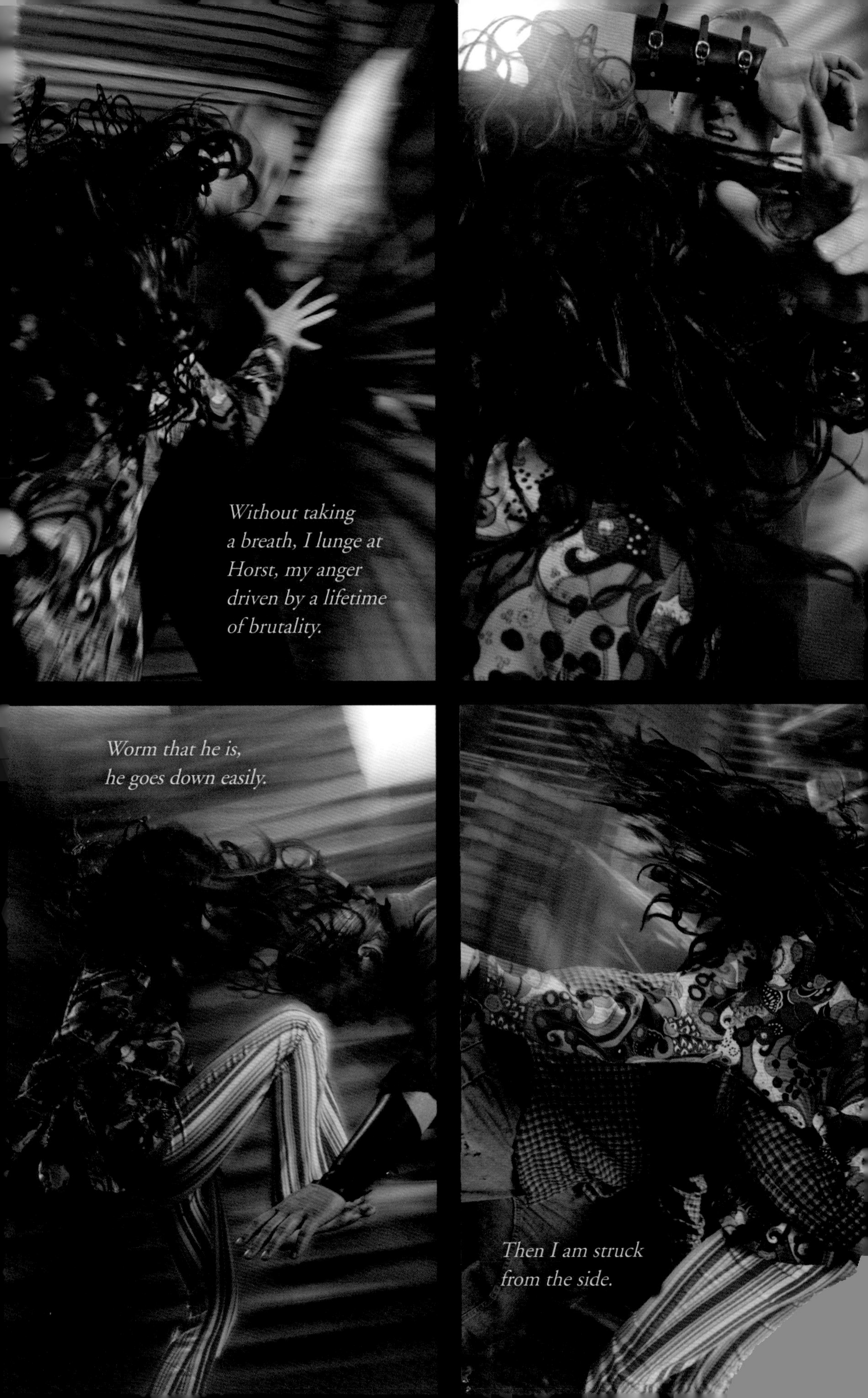
Without taking a breath, I lunge at Horst, my anger driven by a lifetime of brutality.
Worm that he is, he goes down easily.
Then I am struck from the side.

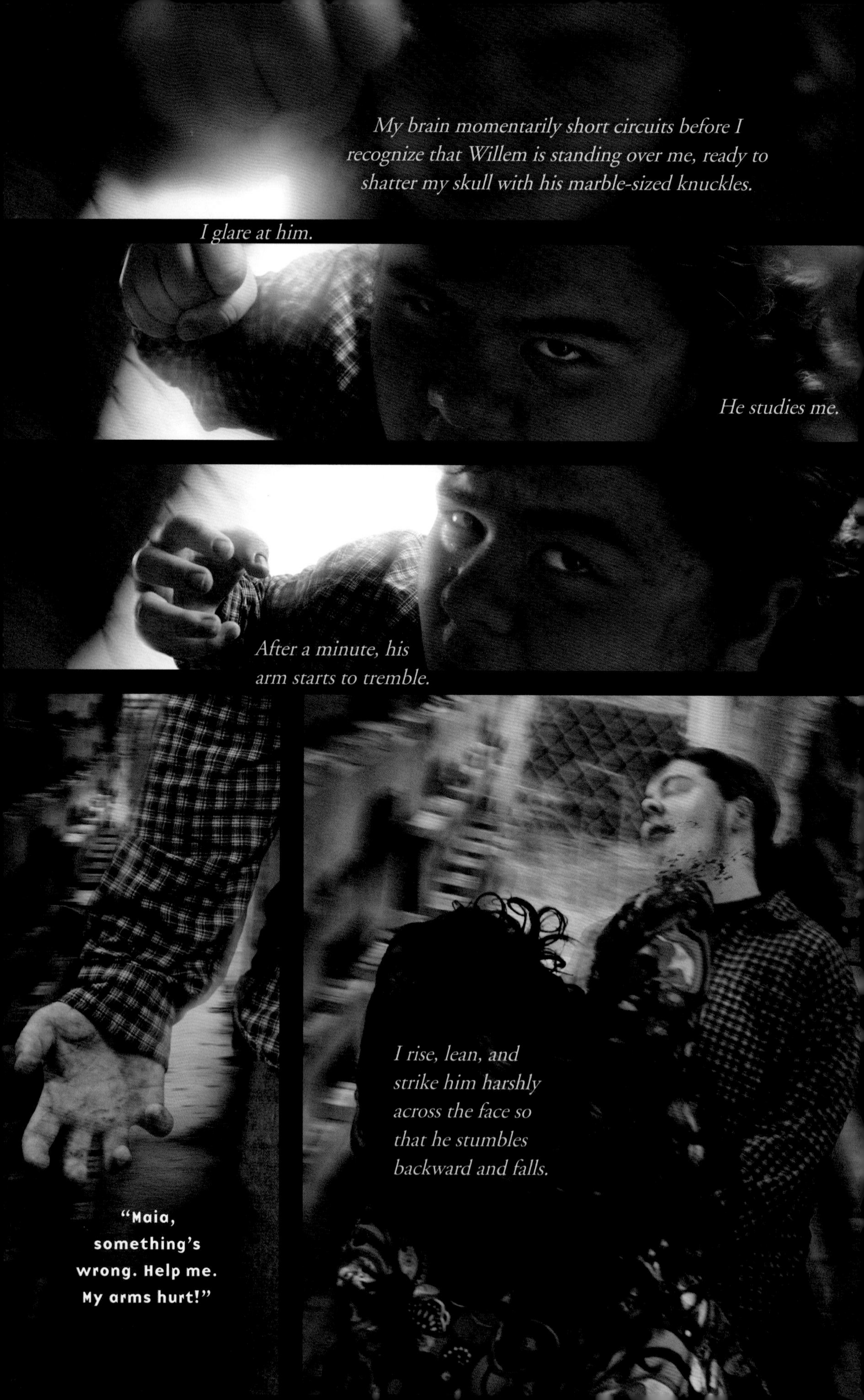
My brain momentarily short circuits before I recognize that Willem is standing over me, ready to shatter my skull with his marble-sized knuckles.
I glare at him.
He studies me.
After a minute, his arm starts to tremble.
"Maia, something's wrong. Help me. My arms hurt!"
I rise, lean, and strike him harshly across the face so that he stumbles backward and falls.

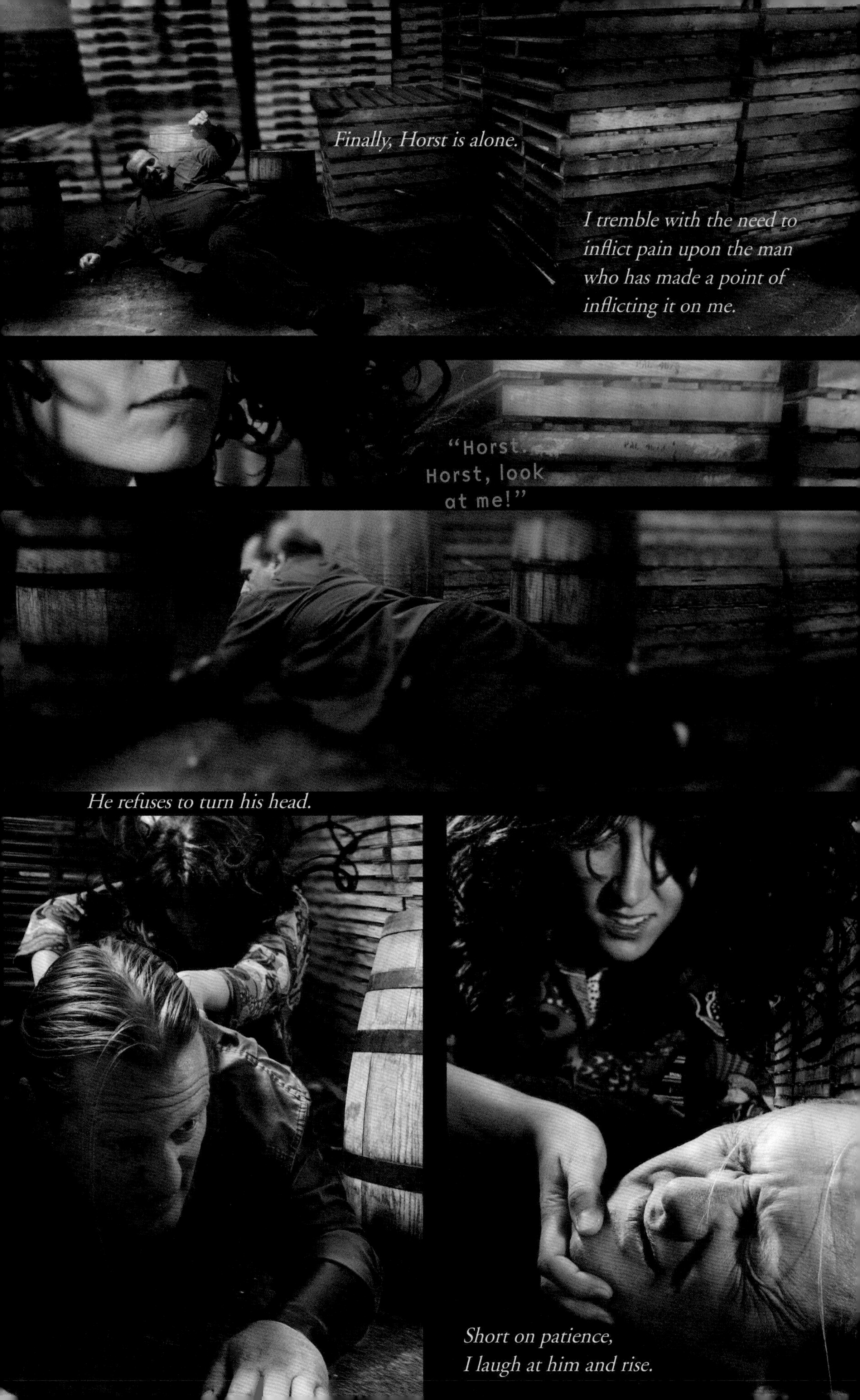
Finally, Horst is alone.
I tremble with the need to inflict pain upon the man who has made a point of inflicting it on me.
"Horst. Horst, look at me!"
He refuses to turn his head.
Short on patience, I laugh at him and rise.

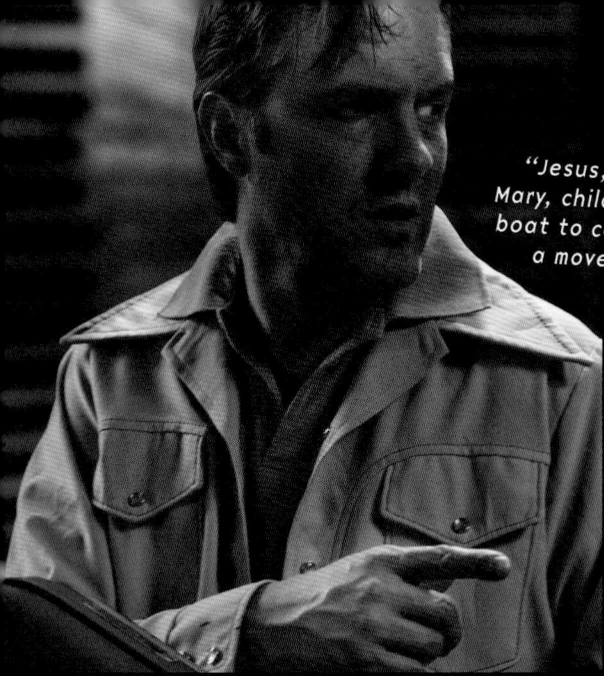
"Jesus, Joseph, and Mary, child. We got you a boat to catch. Let's get a move on, huh?"

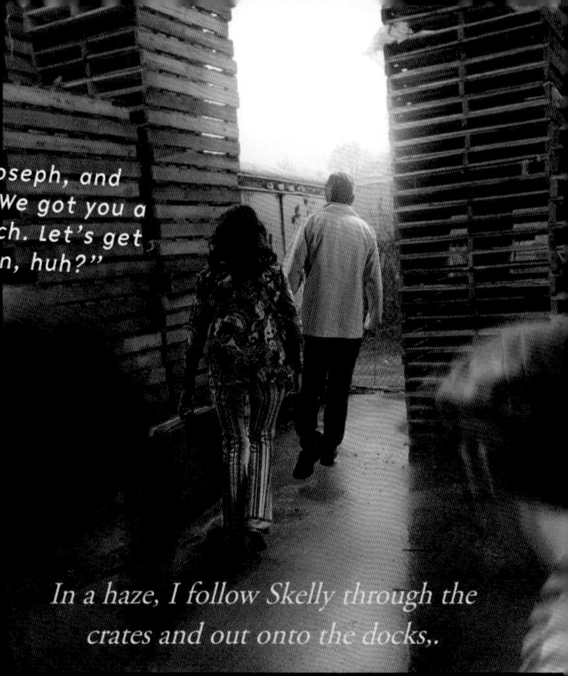
In a haze, I follow Skelly through the crates and out onto the docks,.

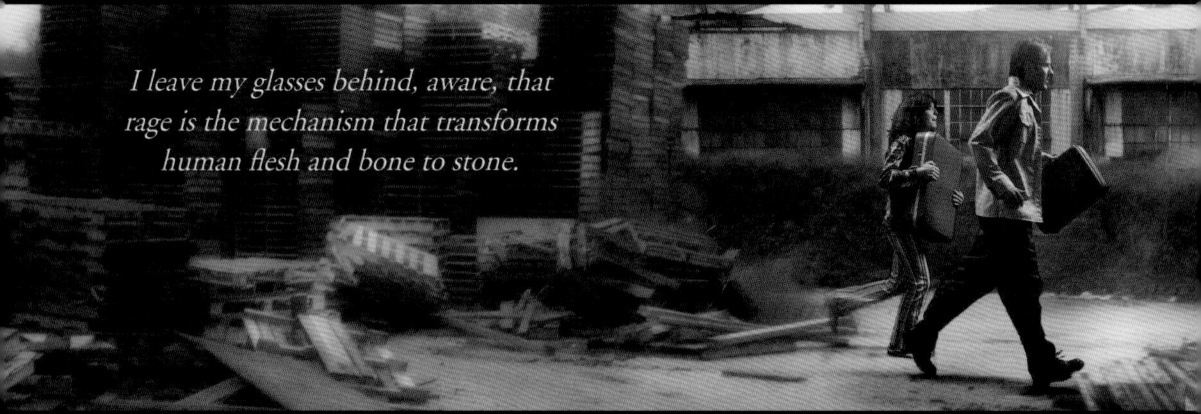
I leave my glasses behind, aware, that rage is the mechanism that transforms human flesh and bone to stone.

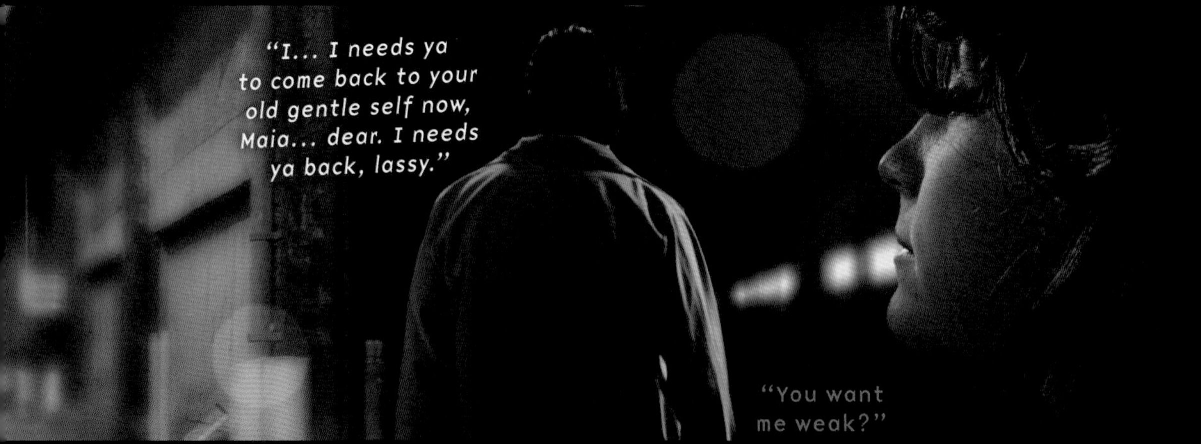
"I... I needs ya to come back to your old gentle self now, Maia... dear. I needs ya back, lassy."
"You want me weak?"

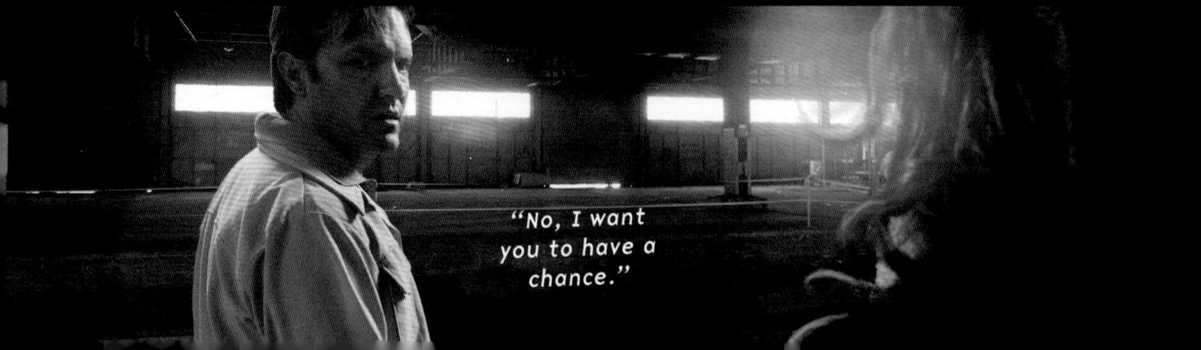
"No, I want you to have a chance."

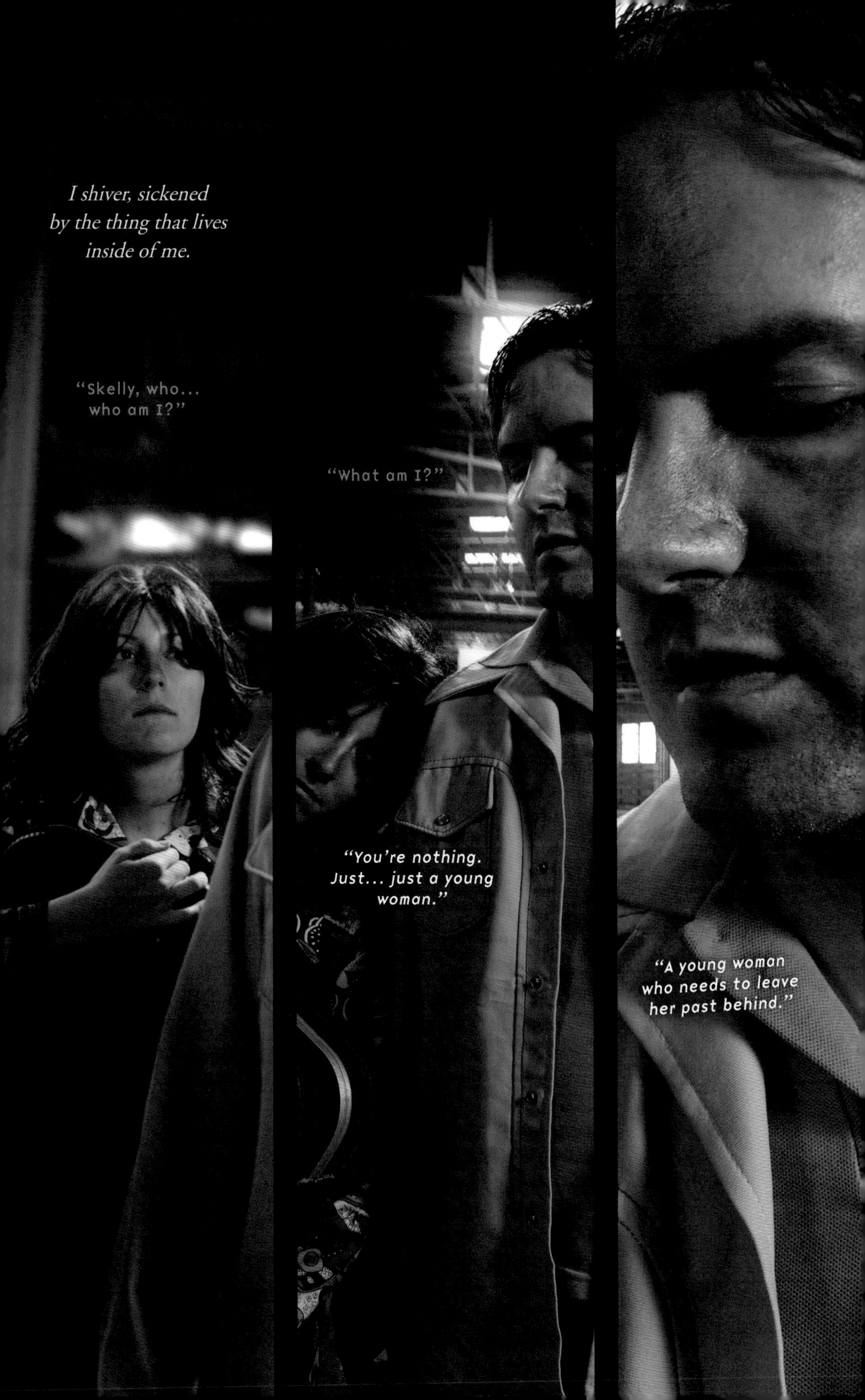
I shiver, sickened by the thing that lives inside of me.
"Skelly, who... who am I?"
"What am I?"
"You're nothing. Just... just a young woman."
"A young woman who needs to leave her past behind."

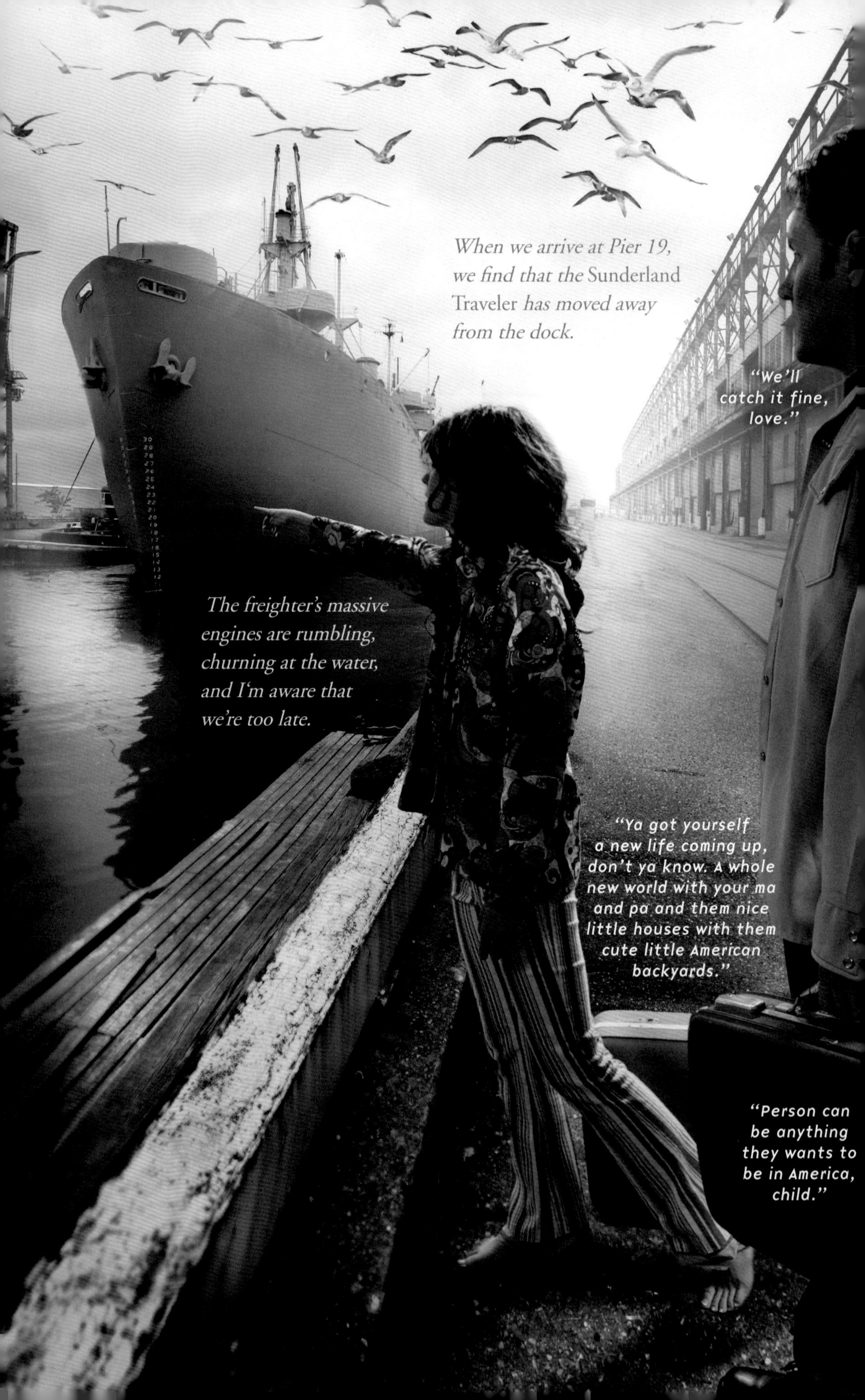

When we arrive at Pier 19, we find that the Sunderland Traveler *has moved away from the dock.*

"We'll catch it fine, love."

The freighter's massive engines are rumbling, churning at the water, and I'm aware that we're too late.

"Ya got yourself a new life coming up, don't ya know. A whole new world with your ma and pa and them nice little houses with them cute little American backyards."

"Person can be anything they wants to be in America, child."

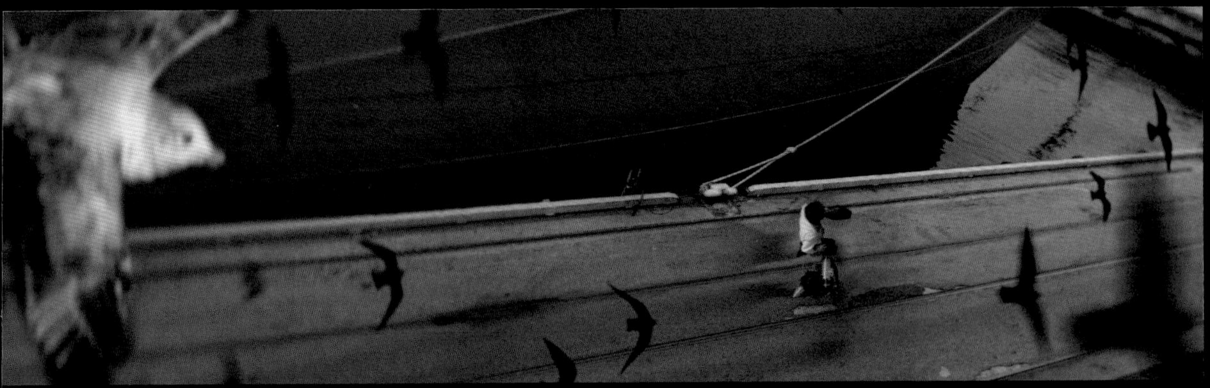

We rush down the long cement pier to a ladder. Skelly awkwardly clambers down to a floating paint platform below. I follow him, and he unties the platform from a cleat and grabs a rope that loops from the dock to the ship's stairway.

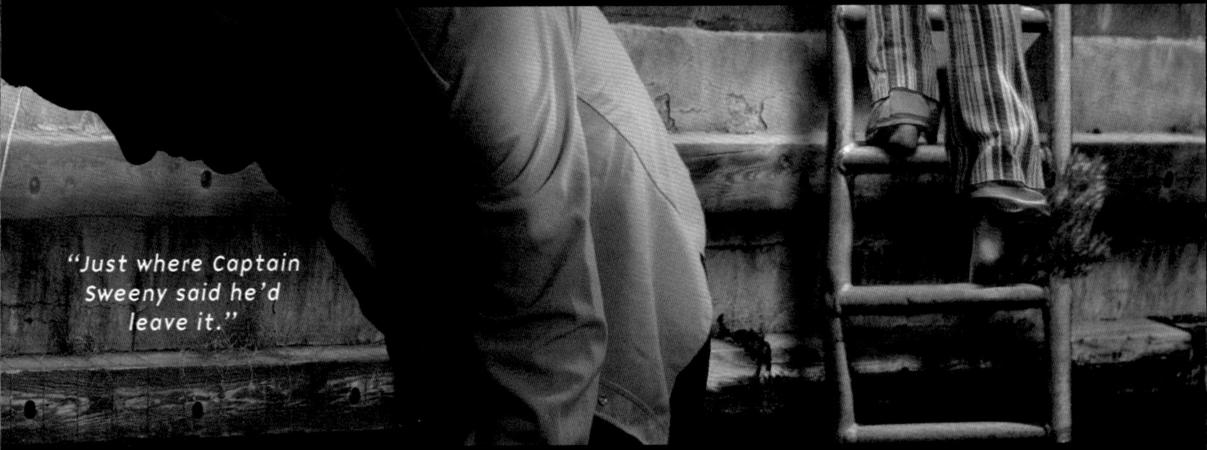
"Just where Captain Sweeny said he'd leave it."

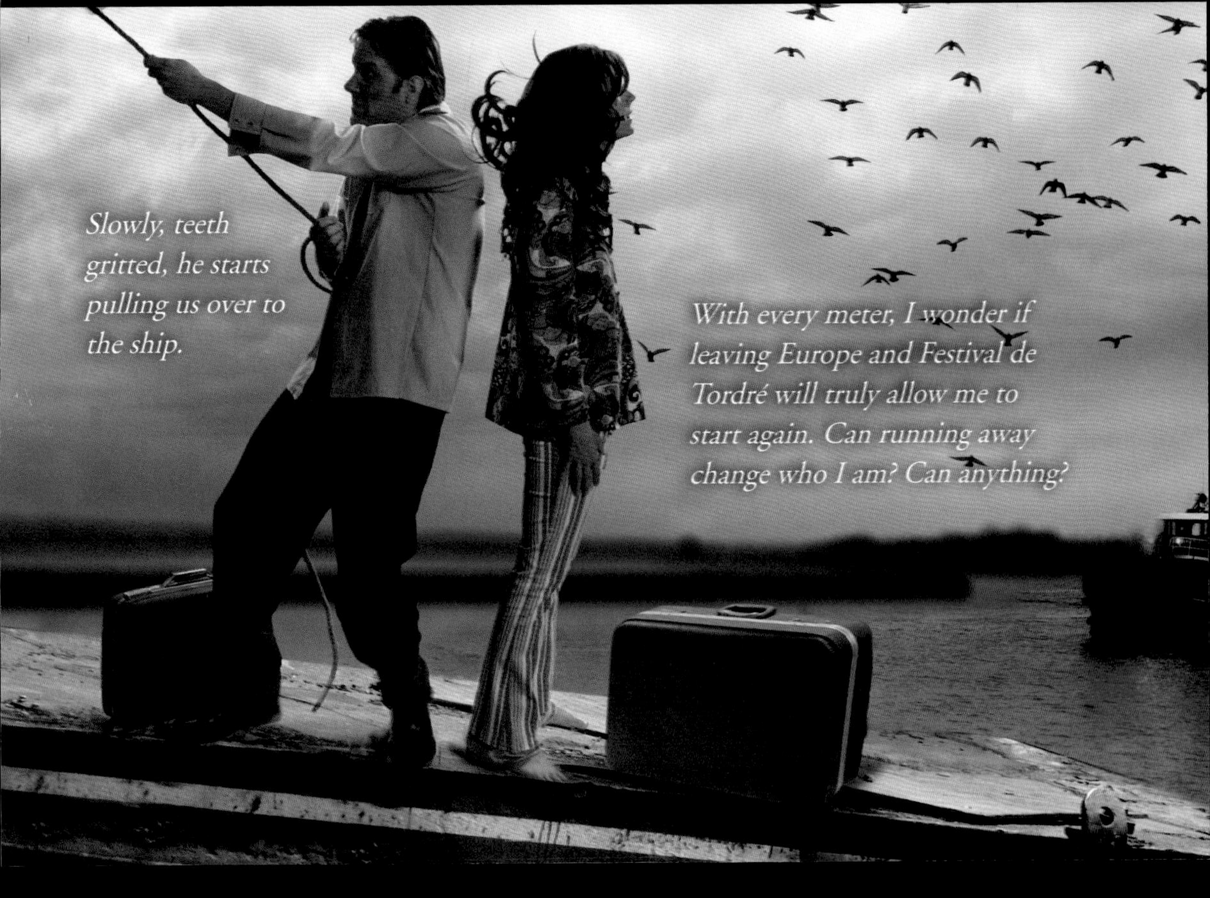
Slowly, teeth gritted, he starts pulling us over to the ship.
With every meter, I wonder if leaving Europe and Festival de Tordré will truly allow me to start again. Can running away change who I am? Can anything?

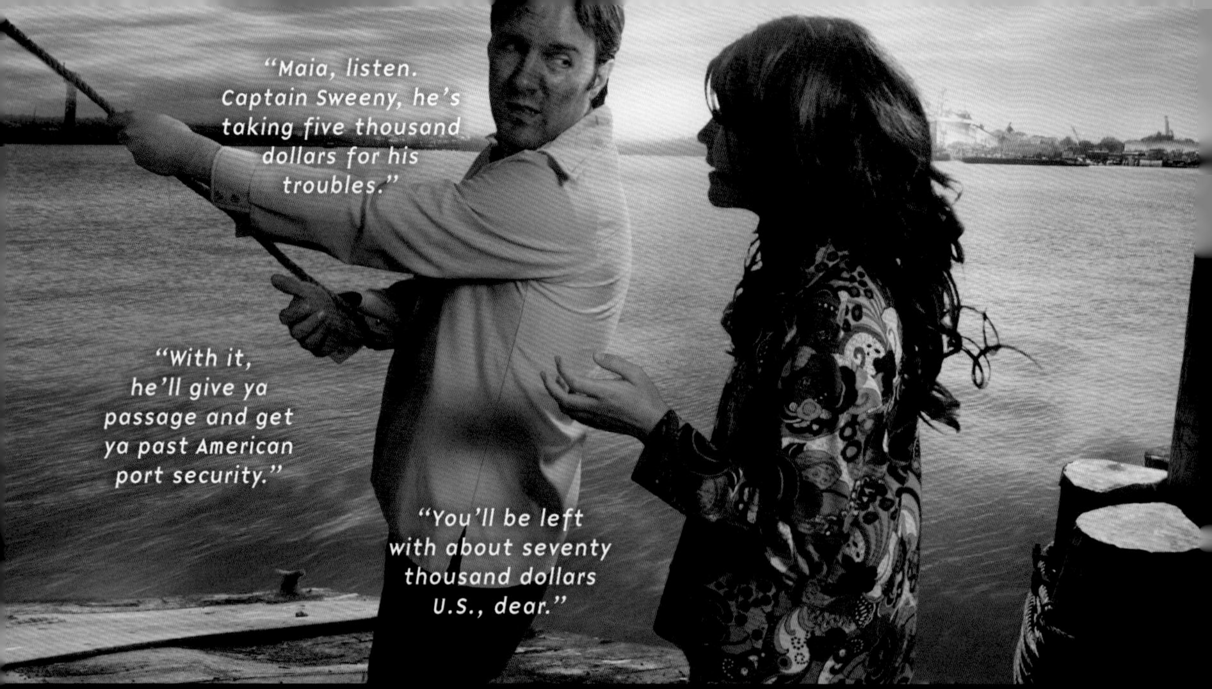
“Maia, listen. Captain Sweeny, he’s taking five thousand dollars for his troubles.”
“With it, he’ll give ya passage and get ya past American port security.”
“You’ll be left with about seventy thousand dollars U.S., dear.”

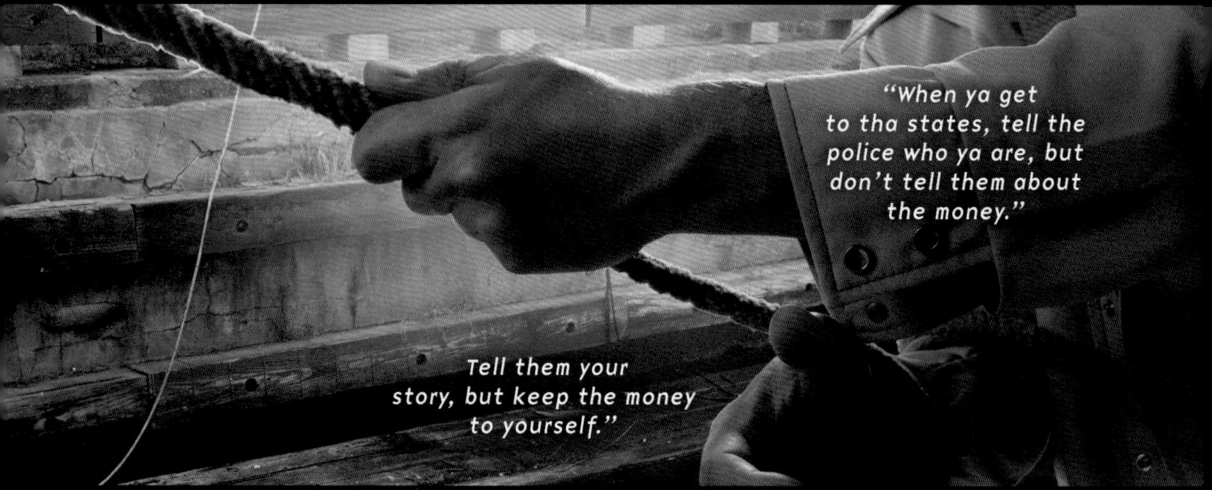
“When ya get to tha states, tell the police who ya are, but don’t tell them about the money.”
Tell them your story, but keep the money to yourself.”

“But what —”

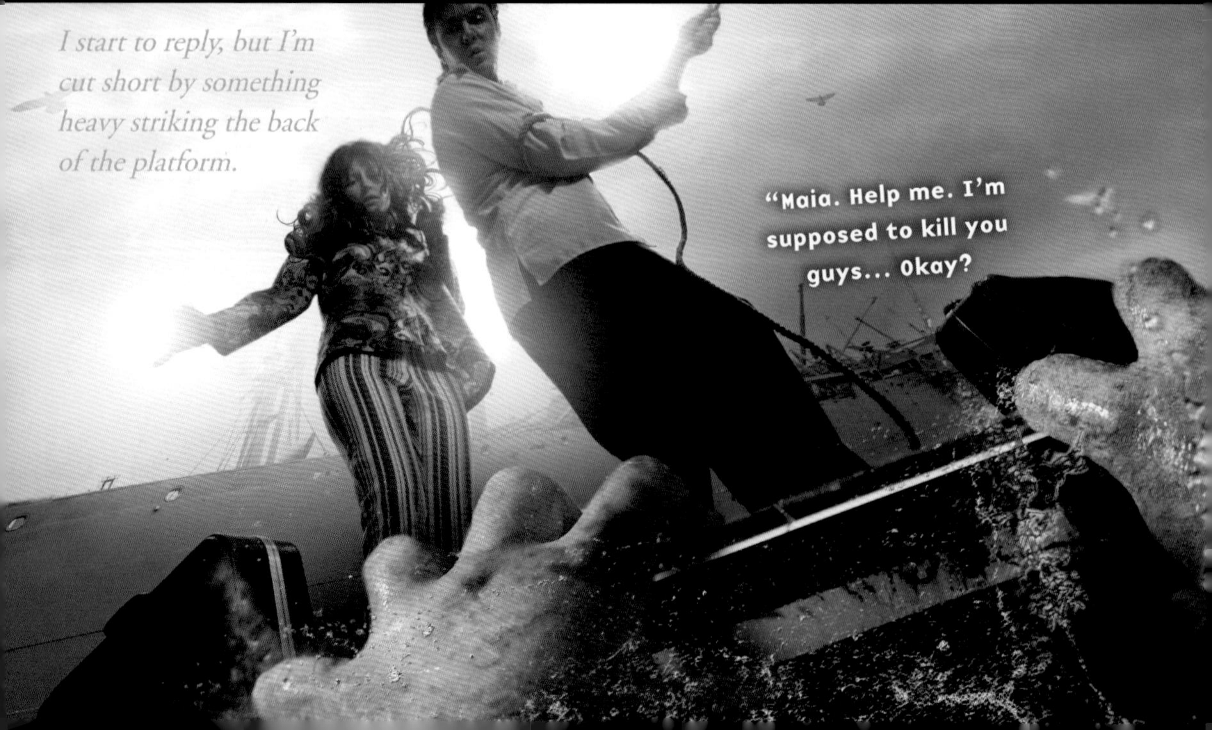
I start to reply, but I’m cut short by something heavy striking the back of the platform.
“Maia. Help me. I’m supposed to kill you guys... Okay?

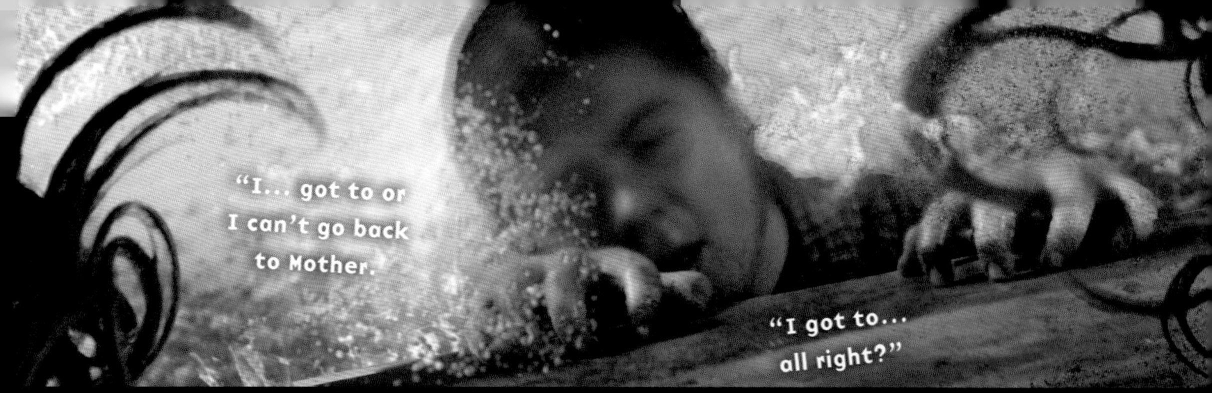
"I... got to or
I can't go back
to Mother.
"I got to...
all right?"

Throughout his life, Willem has been told who he is and what to do and he simply doesn't have the intellect to know better.

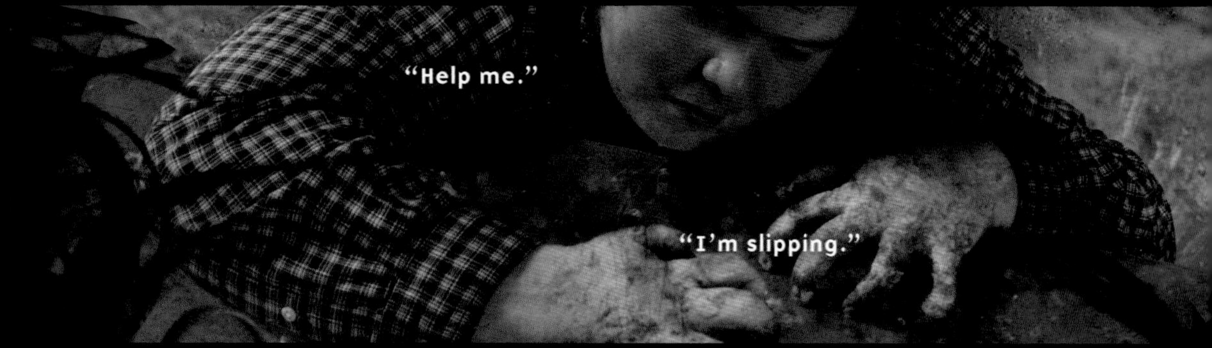
"Help me."
"I'm slipping."

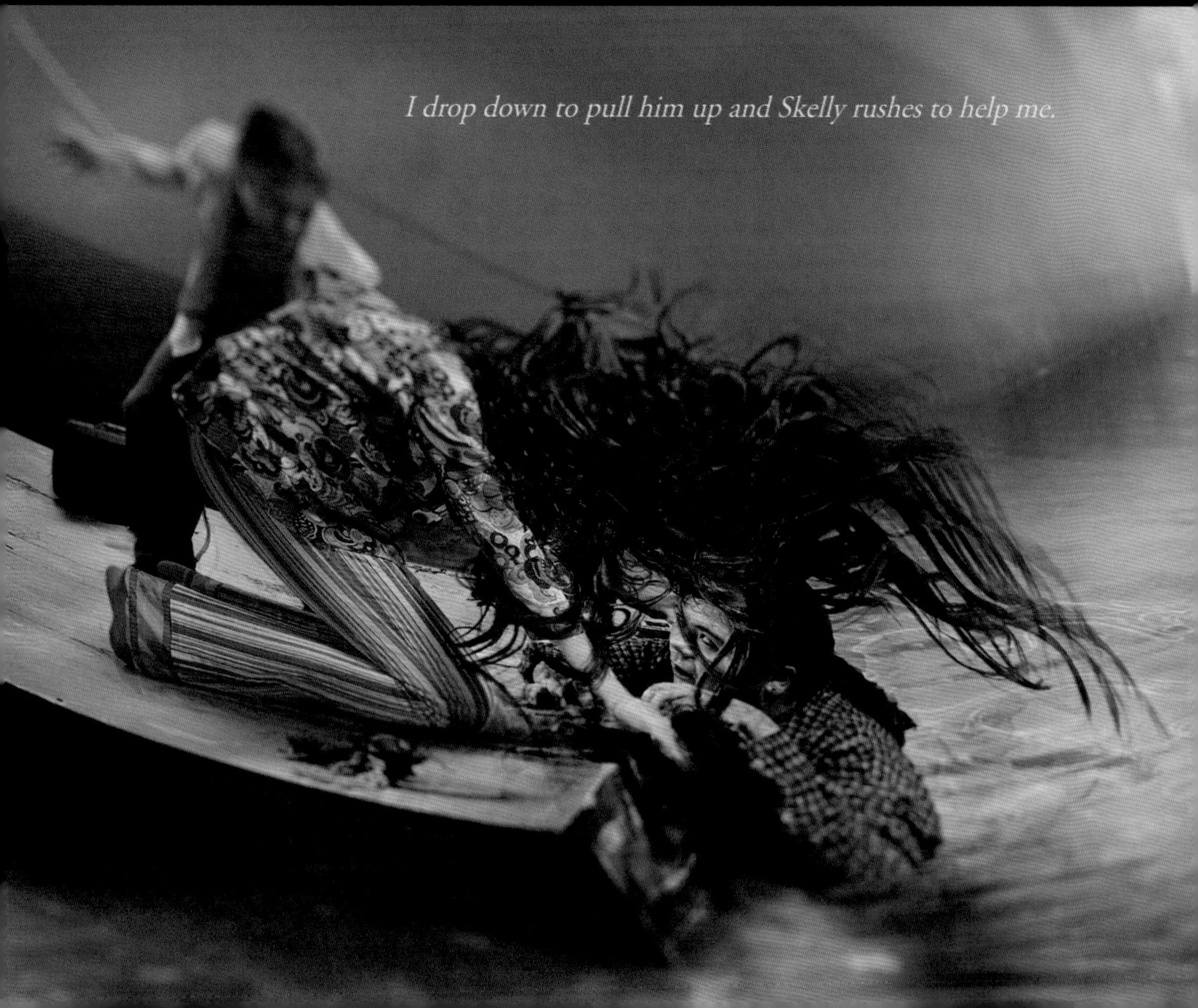
I drop down to pull him up and Skelly rushes to help me.

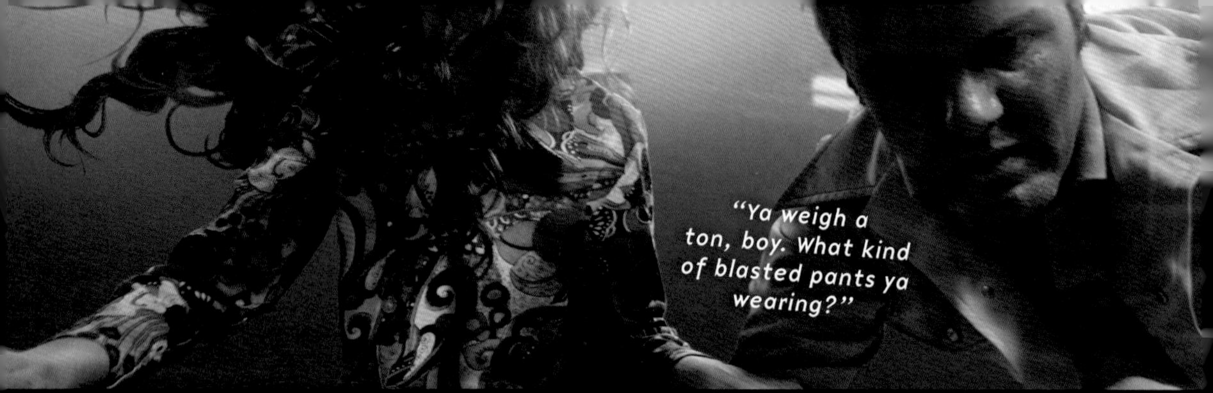
"Ya weigh a ton, boy. What kind of blasted pants ya wearing?"

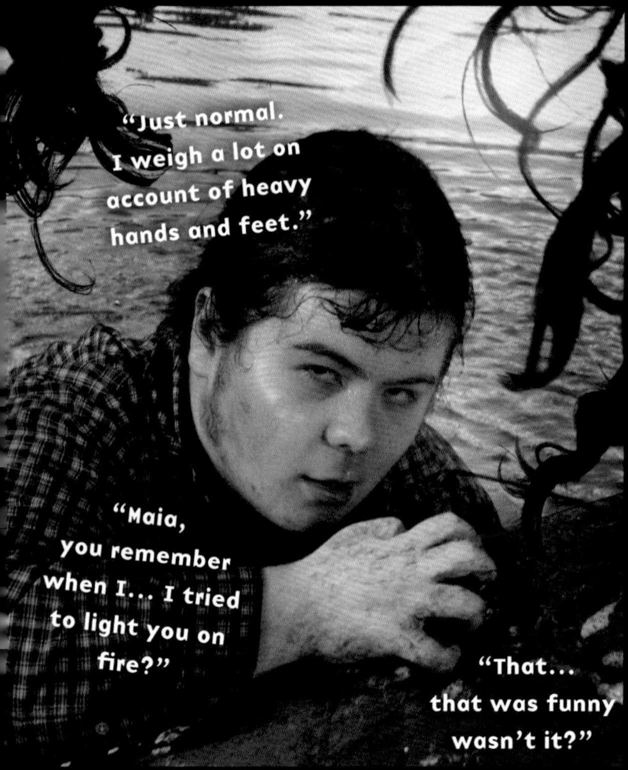
"Just normal. I weigh a lot on account of heavy hands and feet."
"Maia, you remember when I... I tried to light you on fire?"
"That... that was funny wasn't it?"

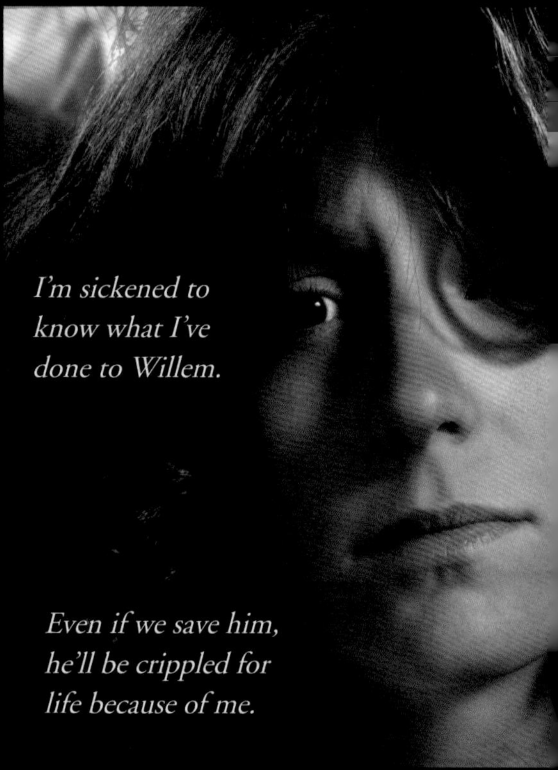
I'm sickened to know what I've done to Willem.
Even if we save him, he'll be crippled for life because of me.

Then his words sink in and memories from the past come back to me. I had been defending myself. I had hurt him in self-defense.

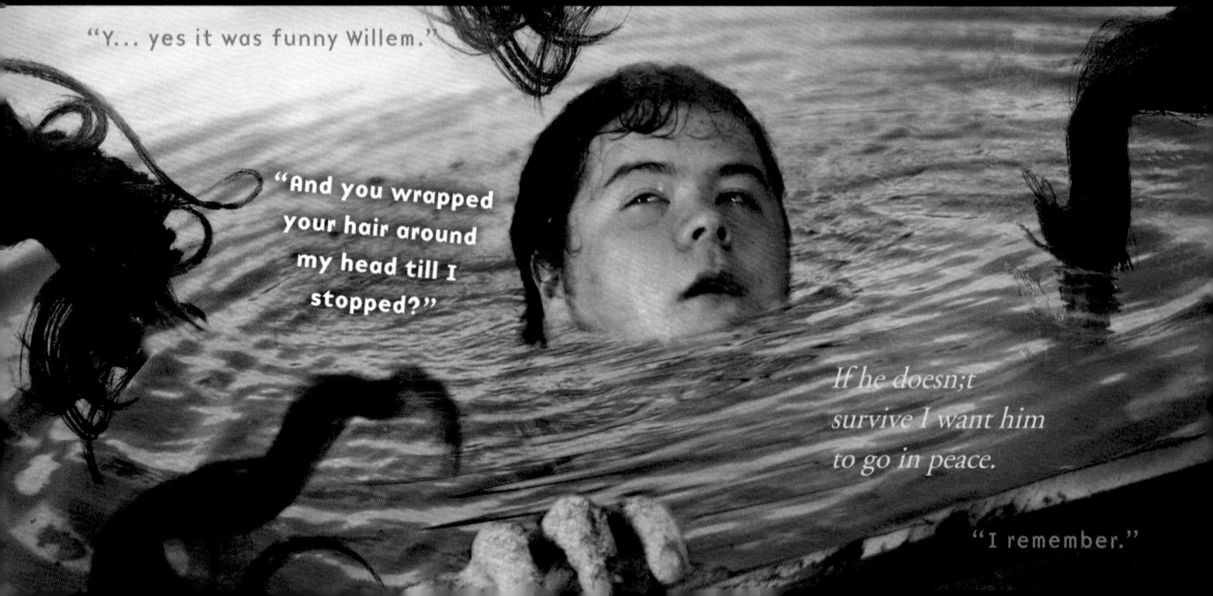
"Y... yes it was funny Willem."
"And you wrapped your hair around my head till I stopped?"
If he doesn;t survive I want him to go in peace.
"I remember."

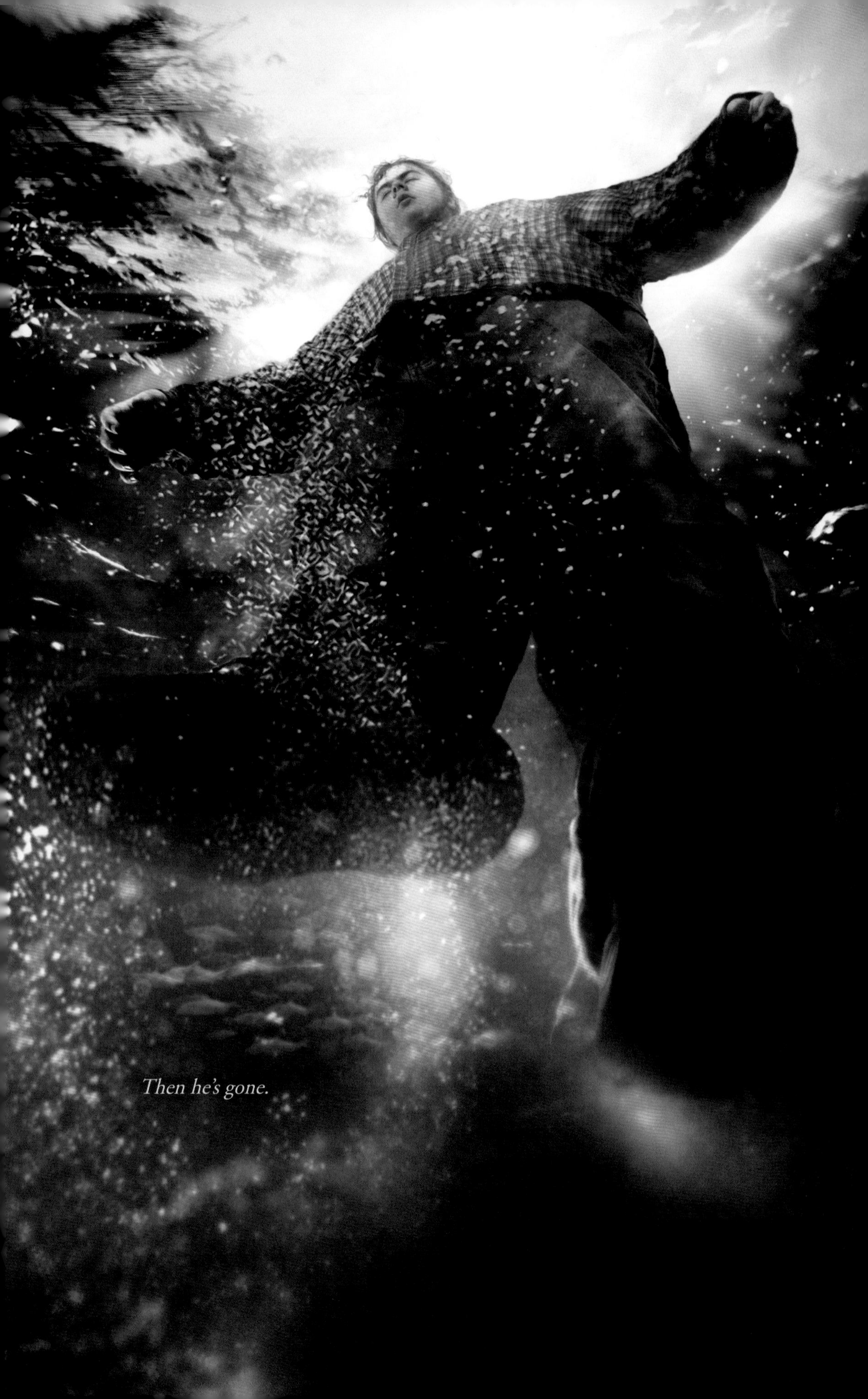
Then he's gone.

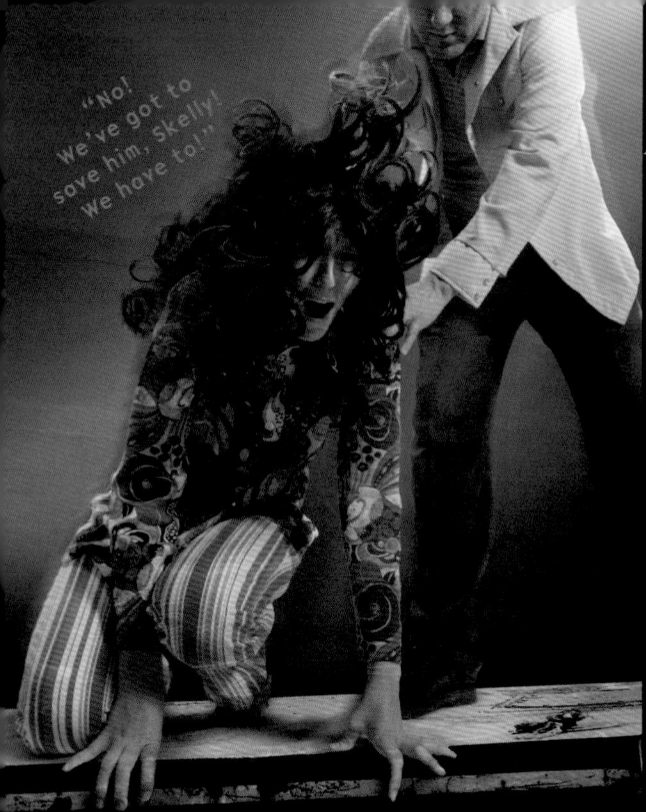
"No! We've got to save him, Skelly! We have to!"

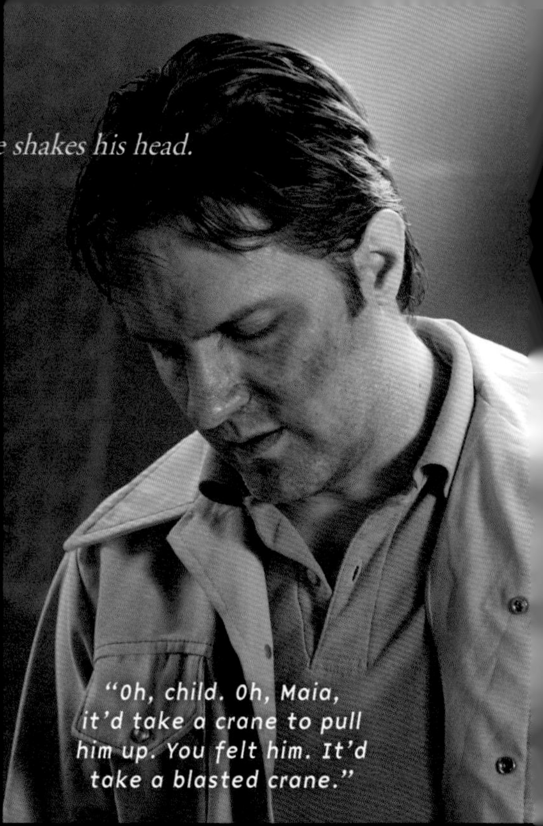
He shakes his head.
"Oh, child. Oh, Maia, it'd take a crane to pull him up. You felt him. It'd take a blasted crane."

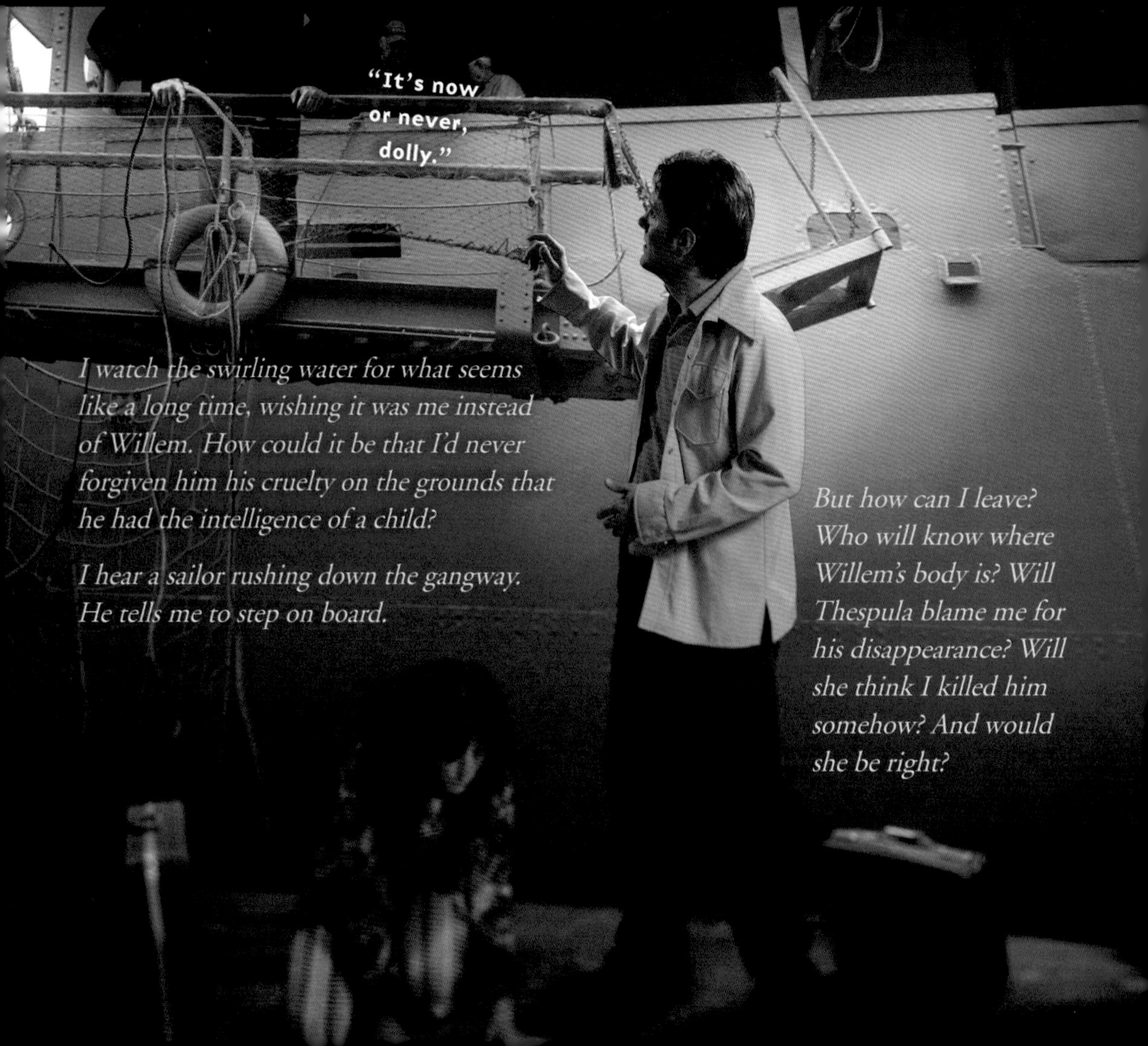
"It's now or never, dolly."
I watch the swirling water for what seems like a long time, wishing it was me instead of Willem. How could it be that I'd never forgiven him his cruelty on the grounds that he had the intelligence of a child?
I hear a sailor rushing down the gangway. He tells me to step on board.
But how can I leave? Who will know where Willem's body is? Will Thespula blame me for his disappearance? Will she think I killed him somehow? And would she be right?

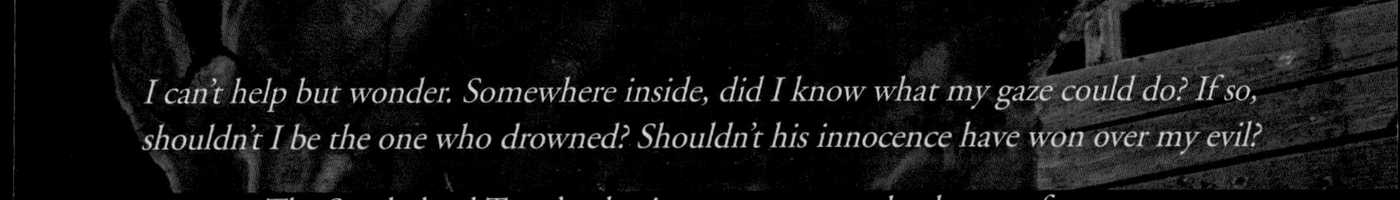
I can't help but wonder. Somewhere inside, did I know what my gaze could do? If so, shouldn't I be the one who drowned? Shouldn't his innocence have won over my evil?

The Sunderland Traveler *begins to move very slowly away from us.*

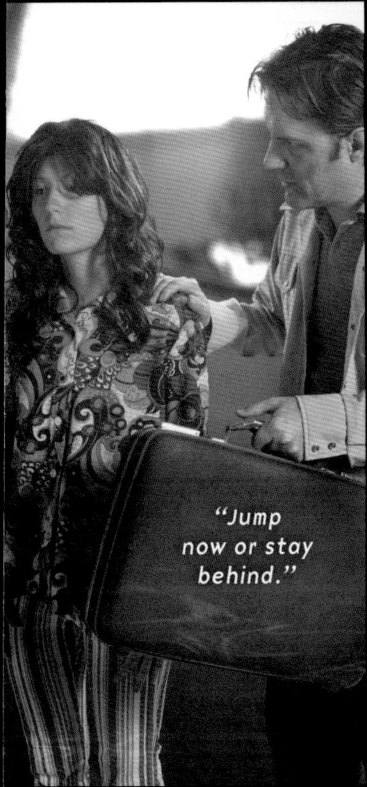
"Jump now or stay behind."

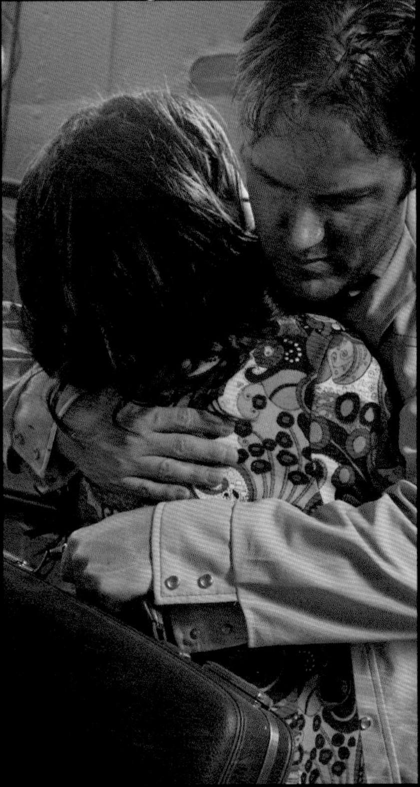

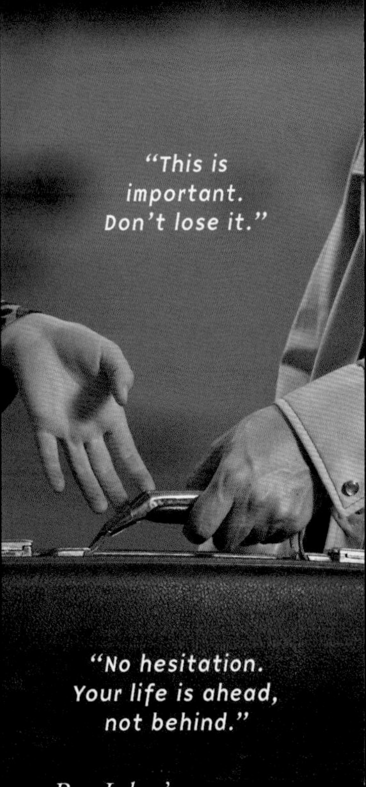
"This is important. Don't lose it."
"No hesitation. Your life is ahead, not behind."

But I don't move.

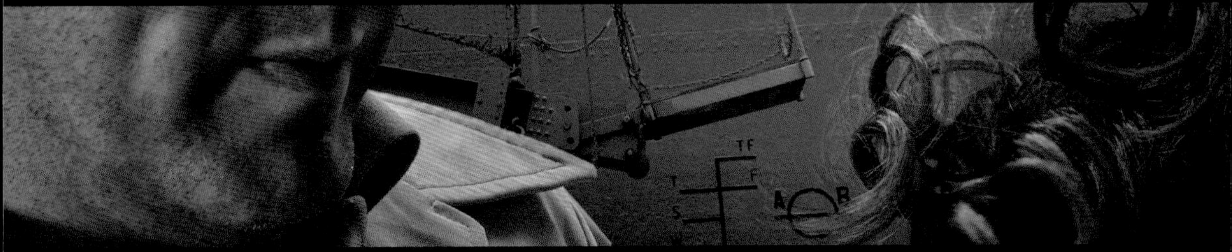

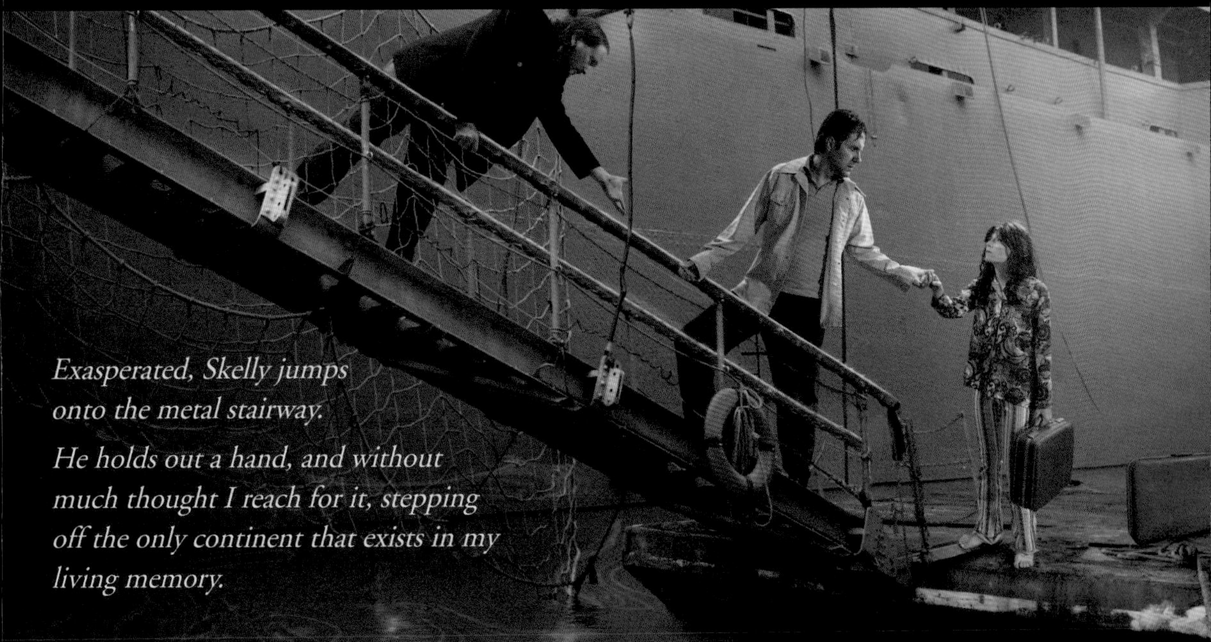
Exasperated, Skelly jumps onto the metal stairway.
He holds out a hand, and without much thought I reach for it, stepping off the only continent that exists in my living memory.

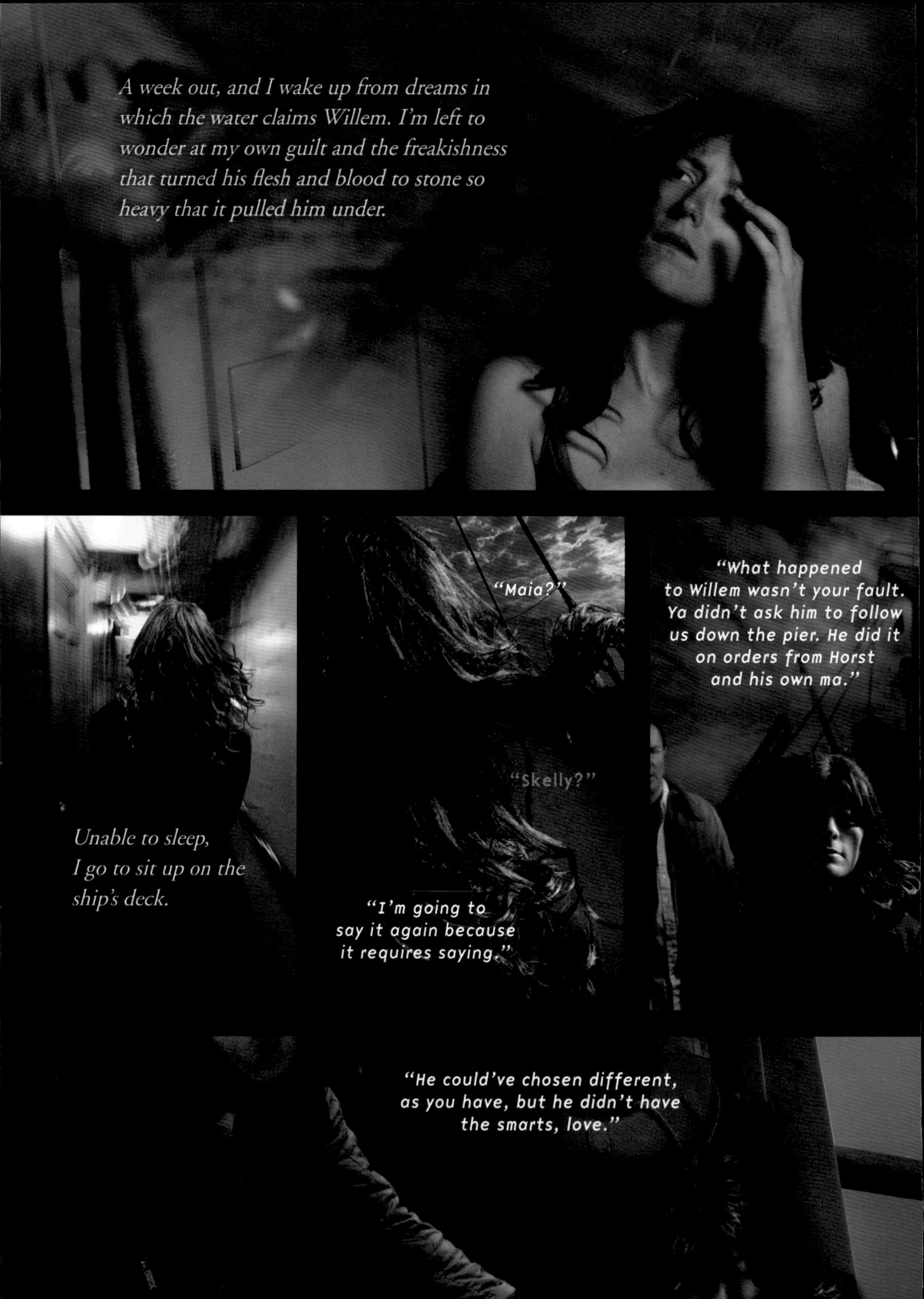
A week out, and I wake up from dreams in which the water claims Willem. I'm left to wonder at my own guilt and the freakishness that turned his flesh and blood to stone so heavy that it pulled him under.
Unable to sleep, I go to sit up on the ship's deck.
"Maia?"
"Skelly?"
"I'm going to say it again because it requires saying."
"What happened to Willem wasn't your fault. Ya didn't ask him to follow us down the pier. He did it on orders from Horst and his own ma."
"He could've chosen different, as you have, but he didn't have the smarts, love."

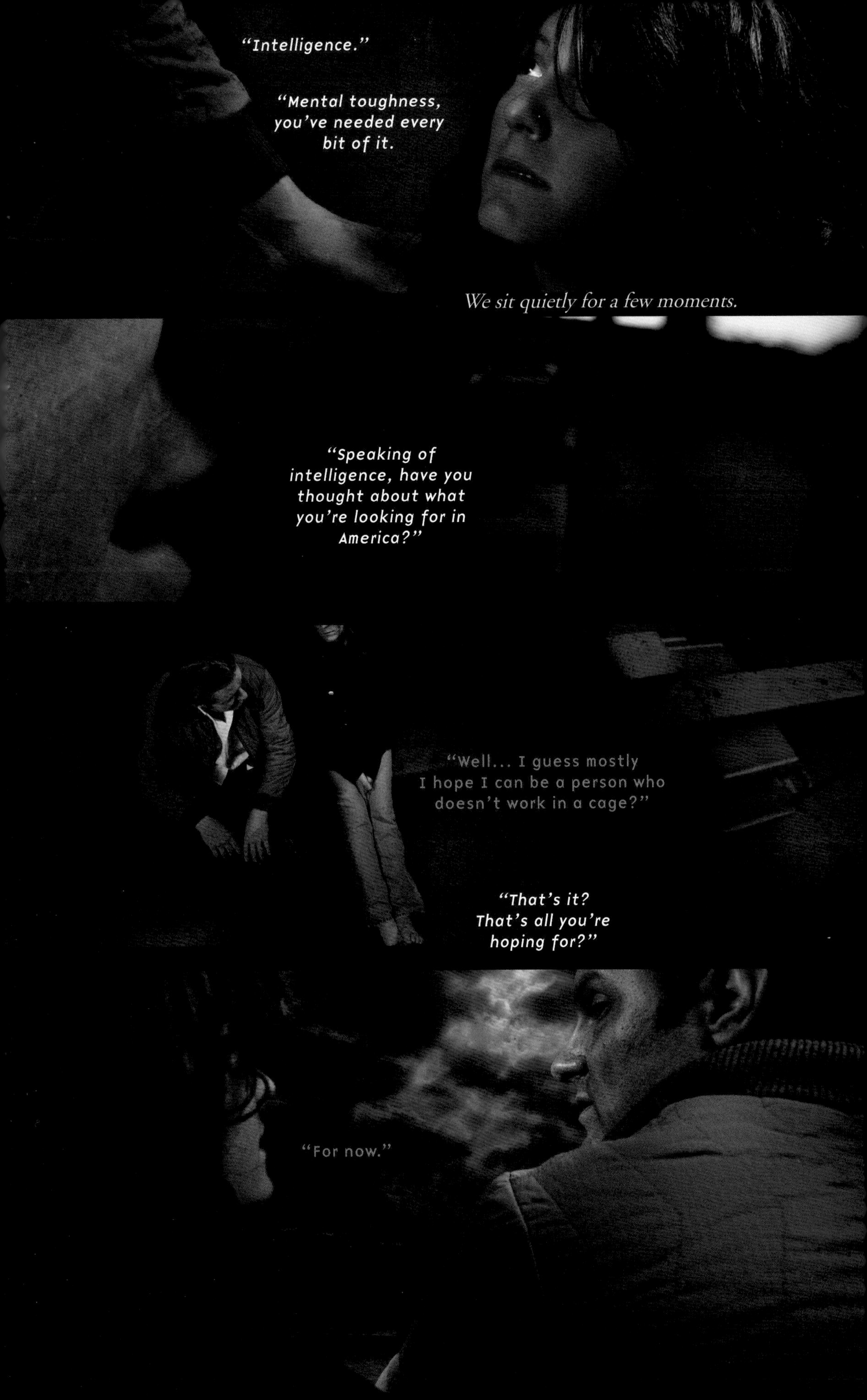
"Intelligence."
"Mental toughness, you've needed every bit of it.
We sit quietly for a few moments.
"Speaking of intelligence, have you thought about what you're looking for in America?"
"Well... I guess mostly I hope I can be a person who doesn't work in a cage?"
"That's it? That's all you're hoping for?"
"For now."

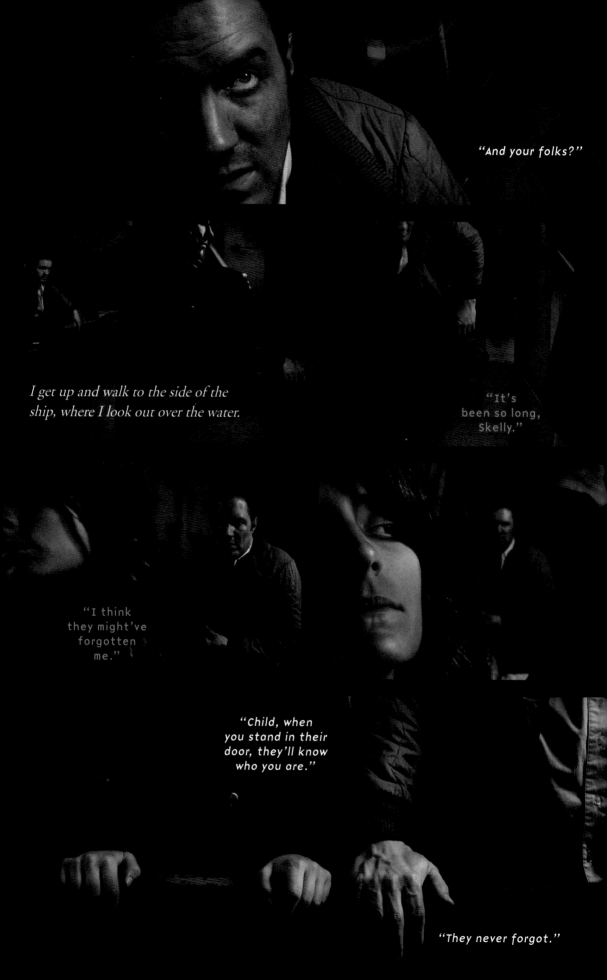

"And your folks?"

I get up and walk to the side of the
ship, where I look out over the water.

"It's
been so long,
Skelly."

"I think
they might've
forgotten
me."

"Child, when
you stand in their
door, they'll know
who you are."

"They never forgot."

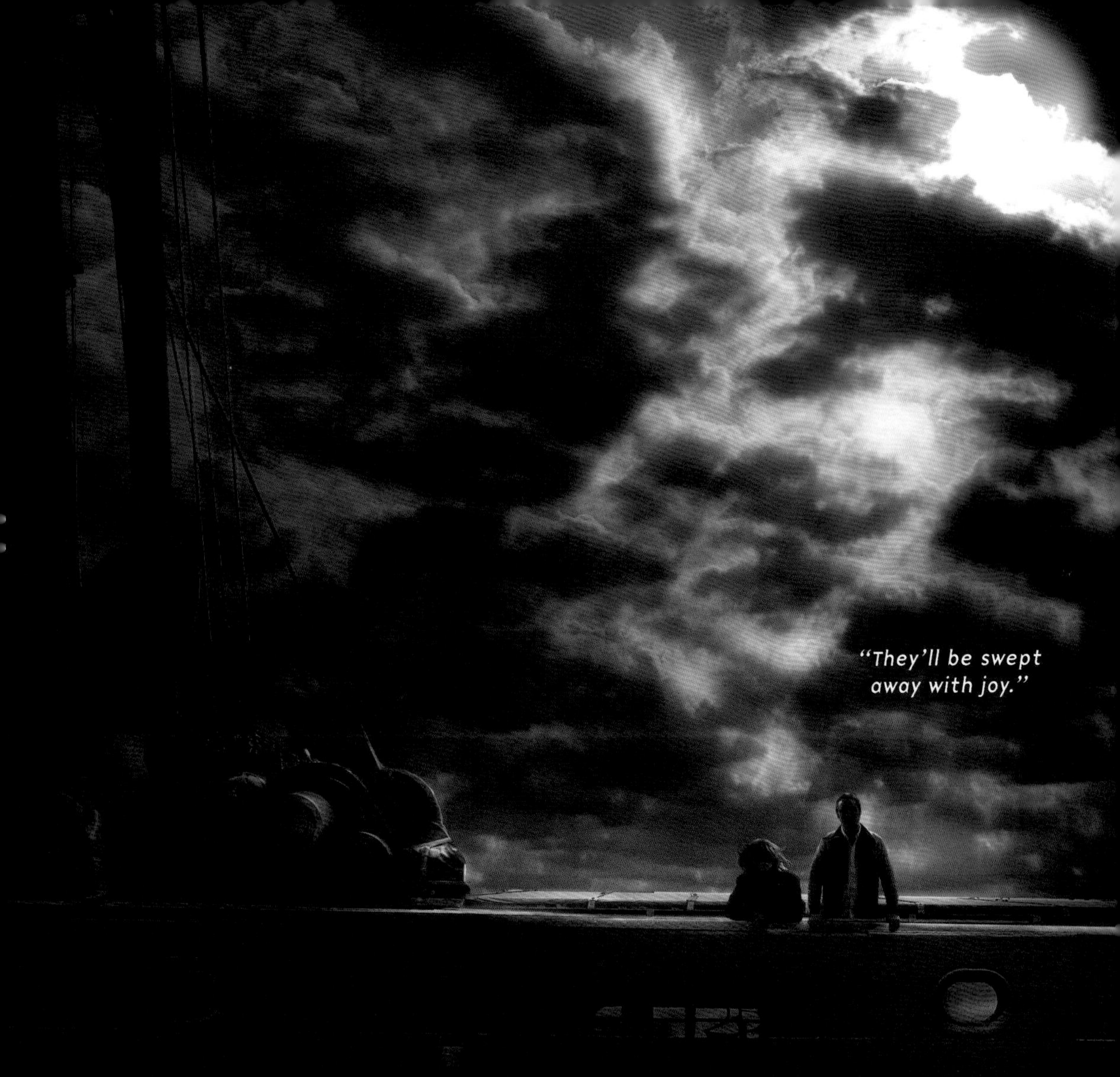
"They'll be swept away with joy."

"Swept away with joy?" It sounds like magic.

I hear the sound of gulls overhead, the conversations of sailors somewhere mid-ship, and the sound of my living hair adjusting in the breeze.

Softly, I say–

"Goodbye past."

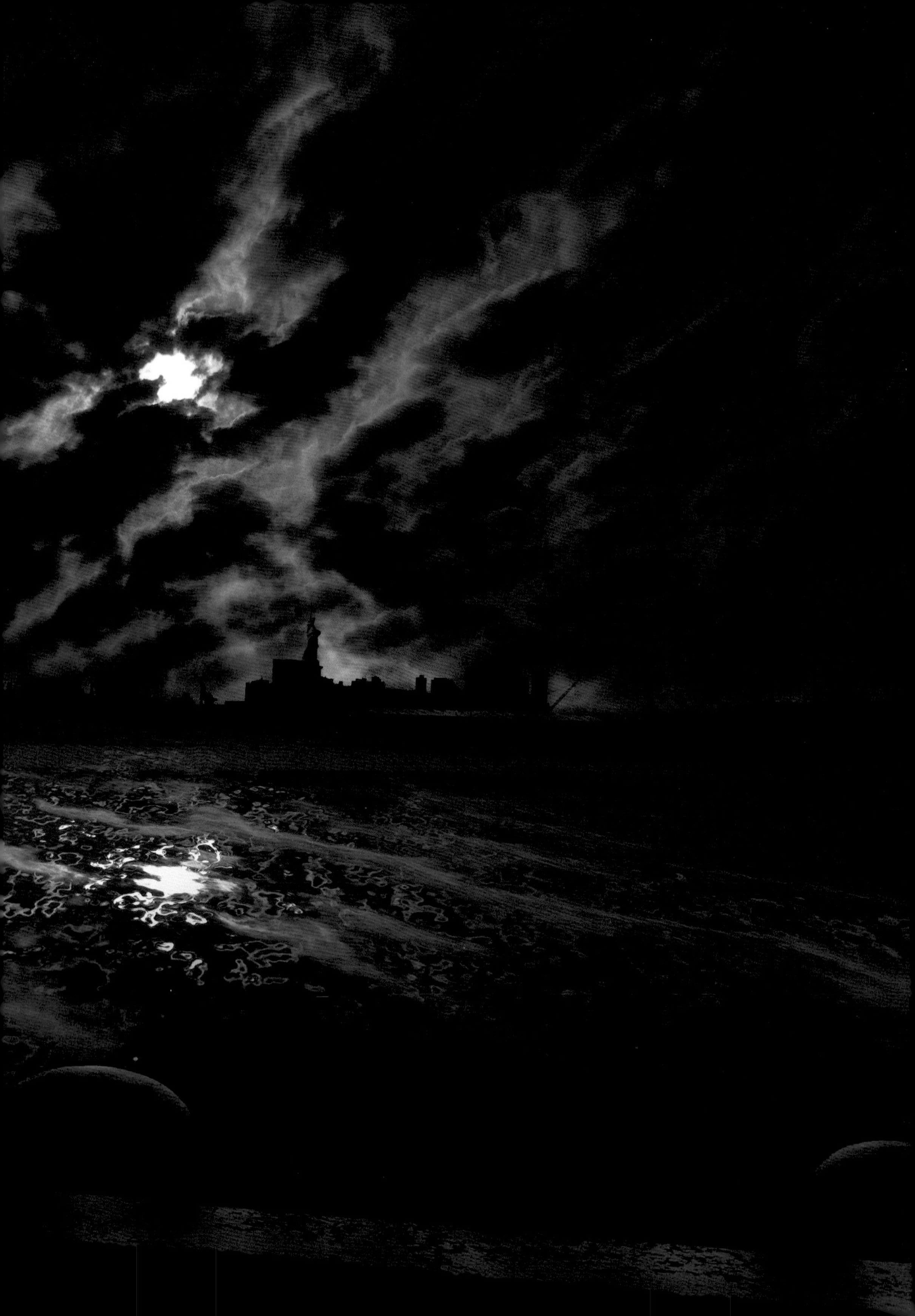

Dear Thespula:

Even though you don't like me - and I don't think you're nice - I am writing so that you will know what happened to Willem . He drowned in Köln. I saw it happen and tried to save him , but I couldn't. Before he went under he talked about you. He said nice things. I wanted you to know.

Also, can you make sure someone that likes books gets mine? They're in my trailer if they aren't already thrown out . All of them are good stories except for The Captain's Soul Mate. They shouldn't be ruined just because everyone thought I was strange.

I sent you a picture of me and Skell y. Show it to Rictus if you want. He can't touch me now because I'm safe in America. By the way, it's the bicentennnial celebration here. We got here on America's 200th birthday.

In closing, I'm really sorry about Willem. I'm still sad about it. What I realize is that he only did what he was told. If he could've learned how to unlearn what he knew,maybe he could've changed.I guess it's thesame for all of us.

Sorry.

With condolen ces,

Maia Gasol

Maia Gasol

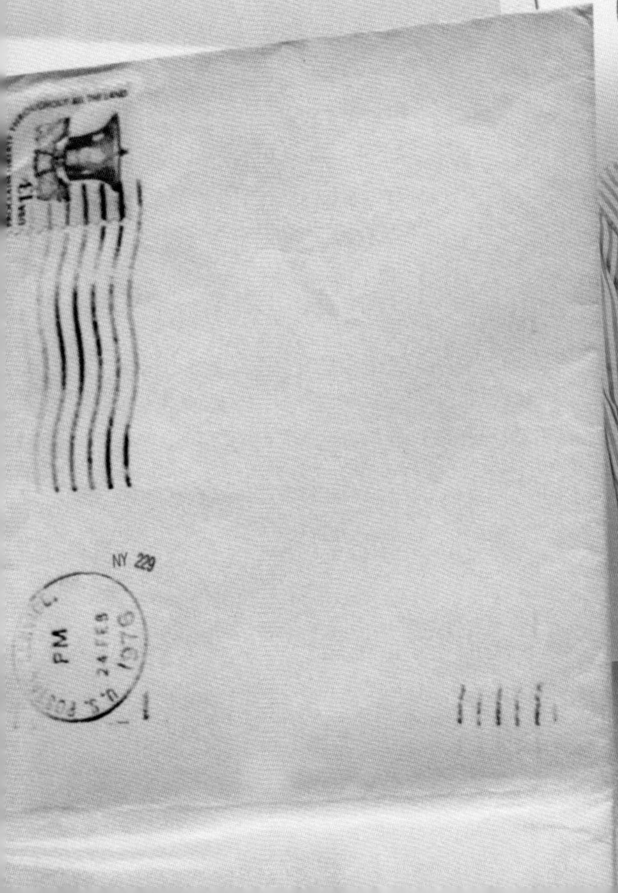
NY 229
PM
24 FEB
1976

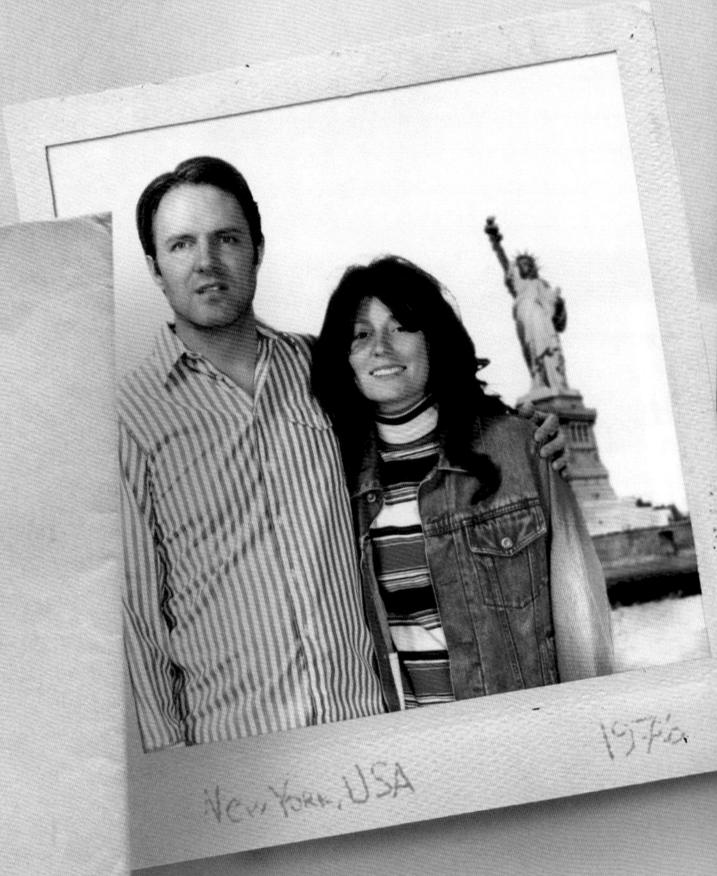
NEW YORK, USA
1976

cast
in order of appearance

Maia .... Lauren Marks
Rictus Fitch .... Mike Vogel
Skelly .... Douglas C. Price
Boy at Cage .... Duncan Parke
Young Maia .... Calla Fuqua
Store Owner .... Robert Parke
Cat Lady .... Joyce Parke
Horst .... Chris Brown
Photgrapher .... Mike Northrup
Atel .... Adam Krandle
Willem .... Nicholas Etheridge
Housekeeper .... Betsy Gordon
Thespula Dalton .... Kathleen Adrian
German Officer .... Dan Buccino
Ersatz Errata .... Kathryn Parke
Air Base Doc .... Paul Voos

Carnies: Ted Alsedek, Keri Burneston, Paul Galbraith, Charon Henning (sword swallower), Mick Kipp, Trixie Little, Uli Loskot, The Evil Hate Monkey, Christie Otvos, Spoon Popkin, S. Noelle Powers, Kris Roth, Ric Royer, Rick Wilson, Lily Stark White. *Crowds:* Miles Anderson, Jesse Anderson, Claire Bailey, Quinn Bailey, Andy Beiderman, Jerry Buettner, Maurine Buettner, Aaron Campbell, Andra Dixon, Dorothy Dobbyn, Addison Dowd, Loughran Dowd, Richard Dowd, Laura Dulski, Emily Etheridge, Mark Etheridge, Rebecca Ford, Gabriel Fuqua, Max Glick, Shawn Jones, Victoria Kaak, Fred Kaak, Austin Kaak, Julie Lauffenburger, Bridgette Lawrence, Lisa Matthews, Margot Milburn, Leslie F. Miller, Serena Miller, Kirk Osborn, Anya Price, Benjamin Price, Harry Shock, Jane Shock-Osborn, Kerri Shulze, Arnee Simmons, Eliot Smith , Lizzie Smith, Maggie Smith, Holly Taminack, MacKane Vogel, Cassidy Vogel, Halle Voos, Amelia Voos, Kim Webster.

Special thanks: Robert and Joyce Parke, Hank Young and Ann Boulton, Charley Levine and family, Lisa Coleman for her amazing soundtrack, Michael Van Huffel for book trailer, Jeff Springer and Custom Model Railroads for miniatures, Kim Lawler, Bob Cicero—Globe Poster, Debbie Rich at Digital Anarchy, Alan Greenberg, Cathy Evans—Shoot the Moon for Rictus' coat, Ninth Life in Hampden for retro clothing, Jerry Dadds & Brook Yeaton for vintage trailers, German deli place, Ozzie the cat, Frank and Gayle Murray for their amazing tent, Kait Ciuchta, Johnny Fox, Jules Smith, Bertha's on Broadway, Captain Mike Schneider and the John Brown Liberty ship, Jack Gerbis and the Maryland Film Office, Kevin Perkins, Leslie F. Miller for bird photos, Joe Giordano

Thank you to our Kickstarter Supporters: Toné Compito Wellington, Ben & Valerie Margolin, St Paul Peterson, Cassandre Mills, Dan, Terri, John and Carly Hobson, Michael and Eileen Crocetti, The Souper Freak Food Truck, Kemil, Yanis and Mohamed Gaouaoui, Dawn Runion, tiag® (The Informatics Applications Group), Stephen Cordova (NewPhidias), ValleyTone, Square One Entertainment

Jonathon, aka Scott, Fuqua wants to profoundly and humbly thank the same vital and caring people as Steve Parke as well as a few special individuals who showed faith, patience, and the ability to see when he couldn't, know when he couldn't, and without question, envision, when his vision failed. First, he thanks the crushingly talented Steve Parke for his at times exhausted and at times tireless work to find a way to make our work work. He thanks Steve's kindly wife for being tolerant beyond measure. He thanks his own beautiful, loving, funny, and very time-consuming family, Elegant Julie, Charming Calla, and Effervescent Gabriel, for consuming his time with things that brought happiness, contentment and pride in the midst of the odyssey that eventually saw this concept to completion. What would he do without them? Well, not much of anything worth mentioning. He'd like to thank his calm and caring mother, unintentionally humorous step-father, his very best siblings, brother Clay and sister Kate, and their generous and eccentric families. He'd like to extend thanks to his special (in a good way) in-laws, Jim and Sue and their massive extended family, all of whom continued to talk to him during visits, vacations, and holidays as he tried to explain what the hell he was attempting to do but hardly could. He'd like to thank his longtime, cynical, and faithful friend Hank Young for being Hank, and his wife Ann for being who she is and not Hank, though Hank is not such a bad thing to be. Hank is Hank, and Scott would have it no other way. He'd like to thank Steve's parents, specifically for grinning in the face of what seemed like disaster and never spitting on him, though he would've if he'd been them. He'd like to thank his close friends, Glenn and Marian, Michael and Beth, Paul and Lauren, Anita and Josh, Paul and Cissy, Lanny and Teddy, Dennis and Carol, Babs and… well, everyone, and I mean everyone, he leaned on, moaned to, and cried in front of to get this thing out the door. He wants to thank Lauren Marks for lending her modelesque beauty and great air of mystery to the task of being Maia, and his own daughter, a mind-bogglingly powerful little actress who isn't so little anymore for being the young Maia. He thanks Doug for just about being as cool as a person can be and stitching, with his chiseled features and good humor, the scenes together. He gives a shout out to the psychologist who kept him together through a nanometer of thick and a thousand miles of thin. He wants to thank Susan for being a brilliant book designer and also dealing with two lunatics so well. And, of course, he thanks anyone and everyone who participated in the process of making these varied stories, contributing their likenesses, their time, their life, their money, and a lot of goodwill to this work. Scott is tired and bent, somewhat broken, but always assisted back to a standing position by so many infinitely generous people. It is beyond his meager ability to express his appreciation.

Shot entirely with a Nikon D200 and assembled in Photoshop on a Mac Pro. Propping, storyboards, costumes, makeup and art by Steven Parke unless otherwise noted.

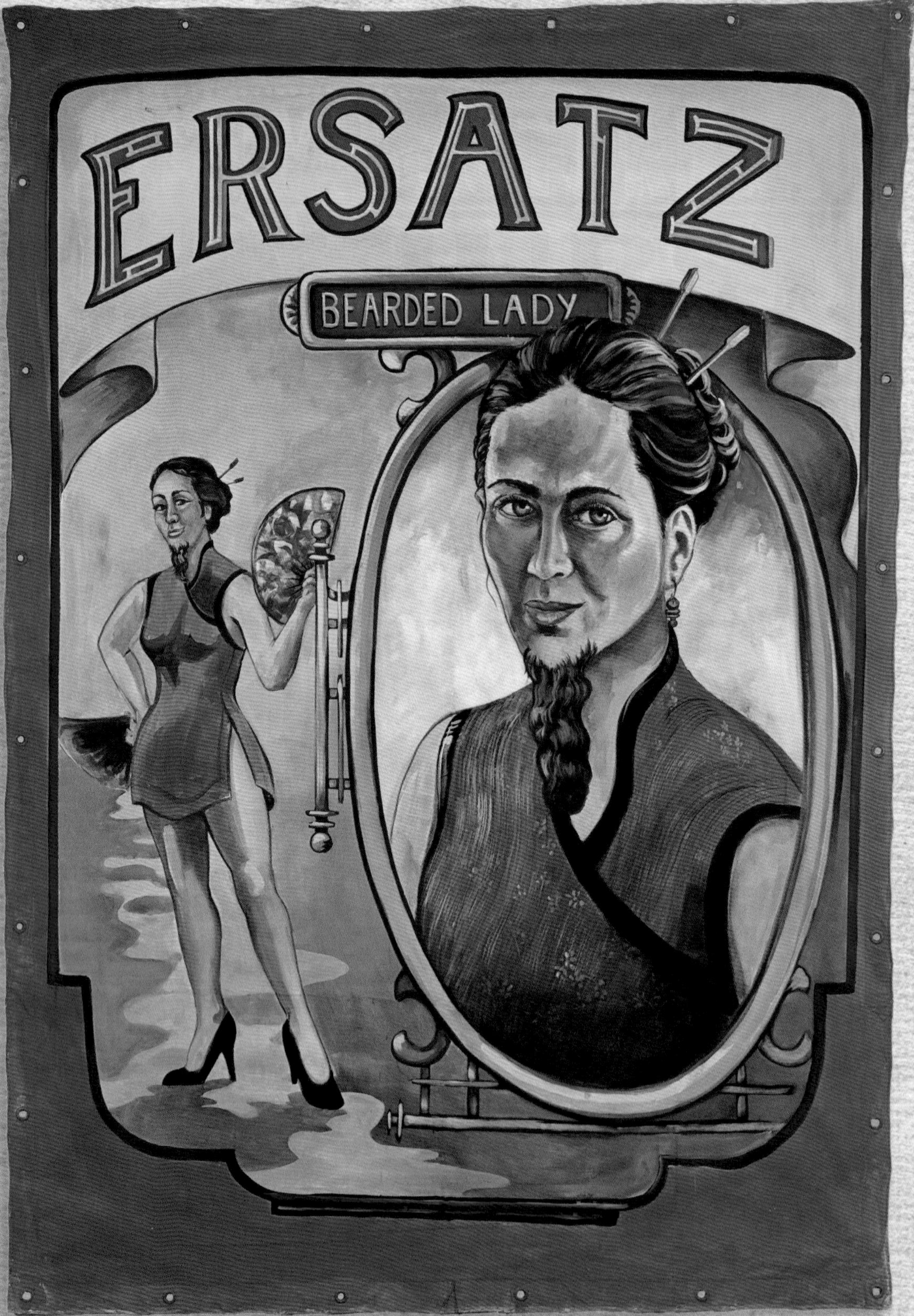
ERSATZ
BEARDED LADY

Kim Lawler, paint on canvas

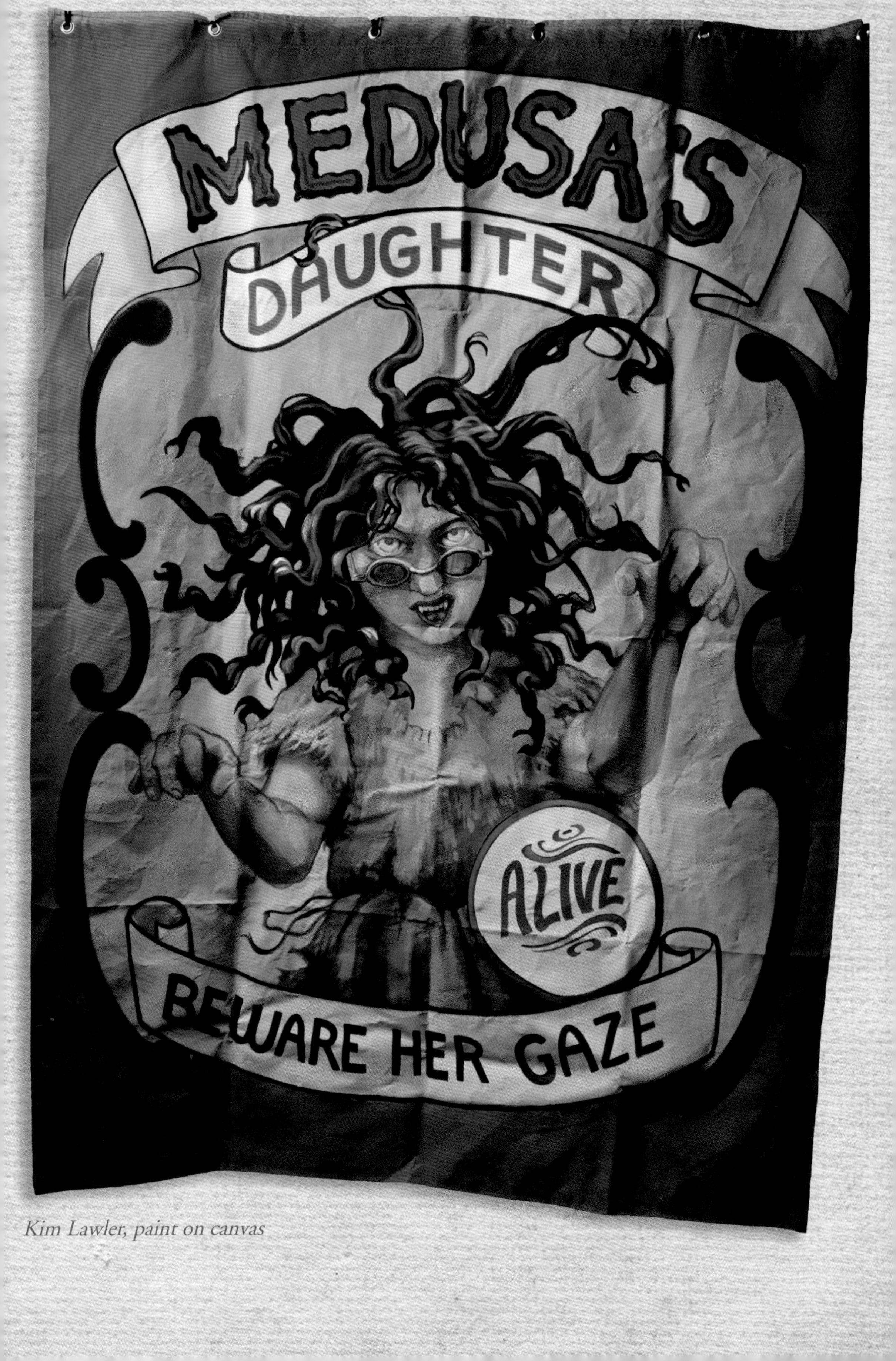
MEDUSA'S
DAUGHTER
ALIVE
BEWARE HER GAZE
Kim Lawler, paint on canvas

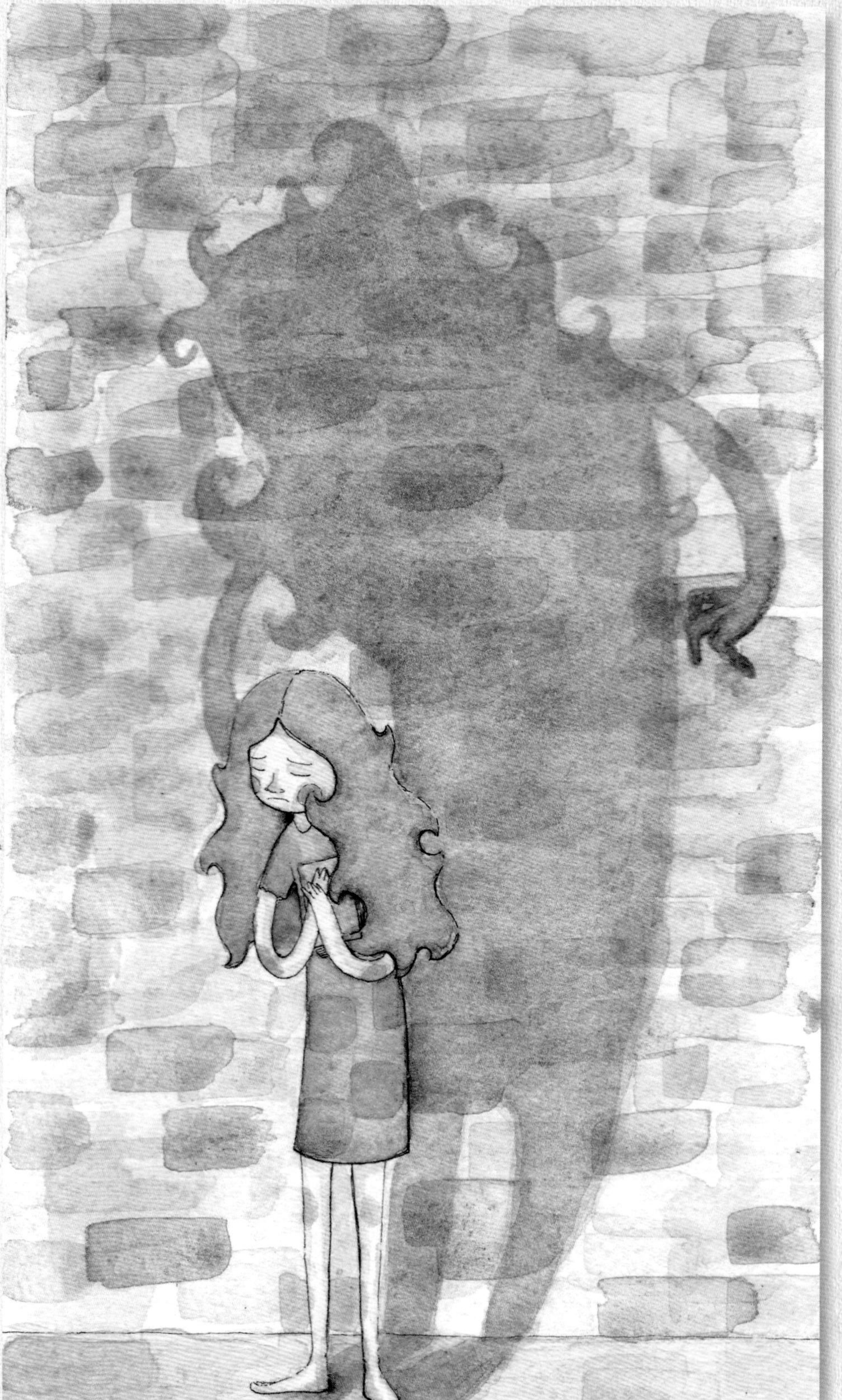

Ashley "Ace" Price, watercolor

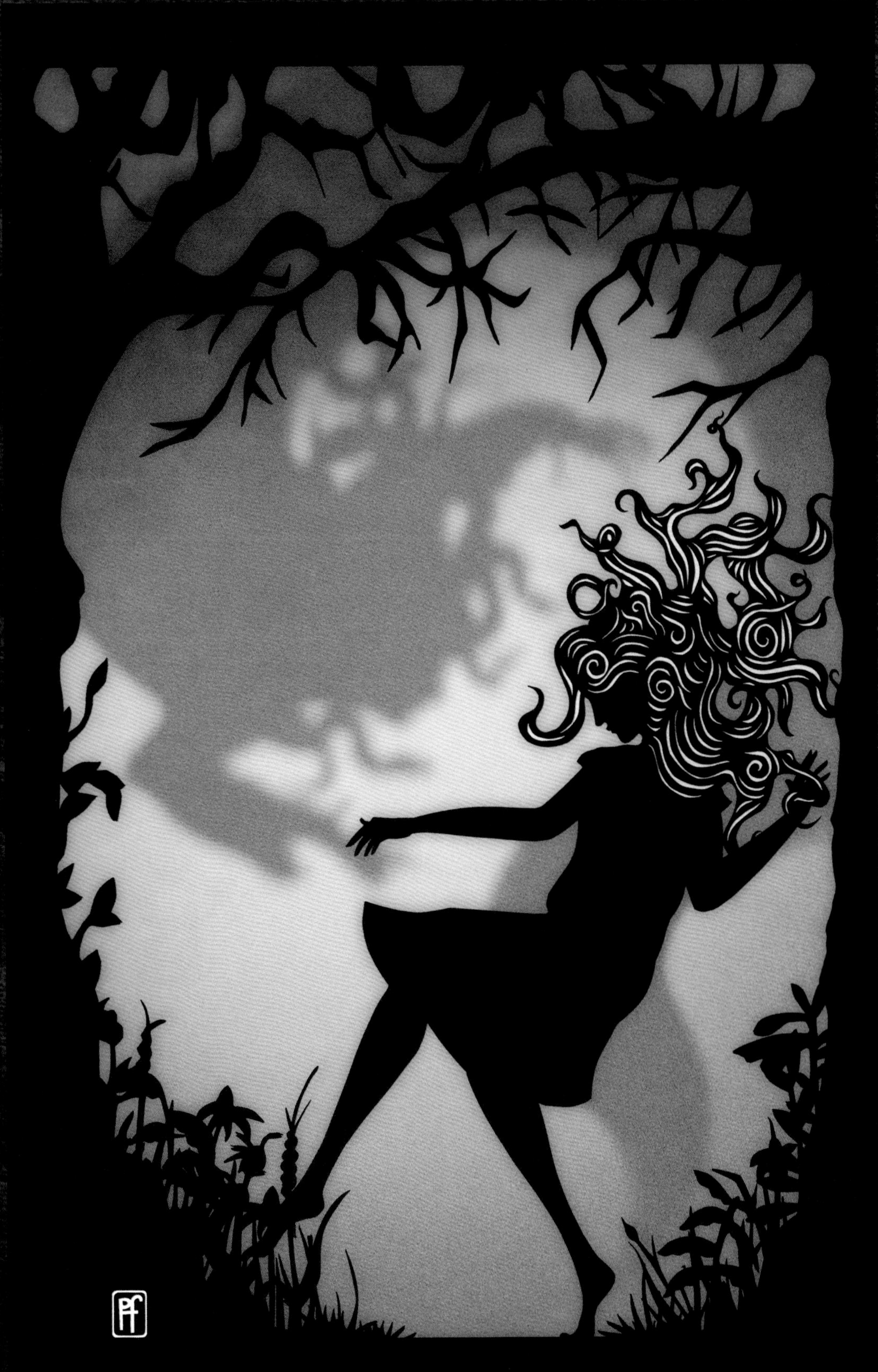

Penny Forester, cut paper

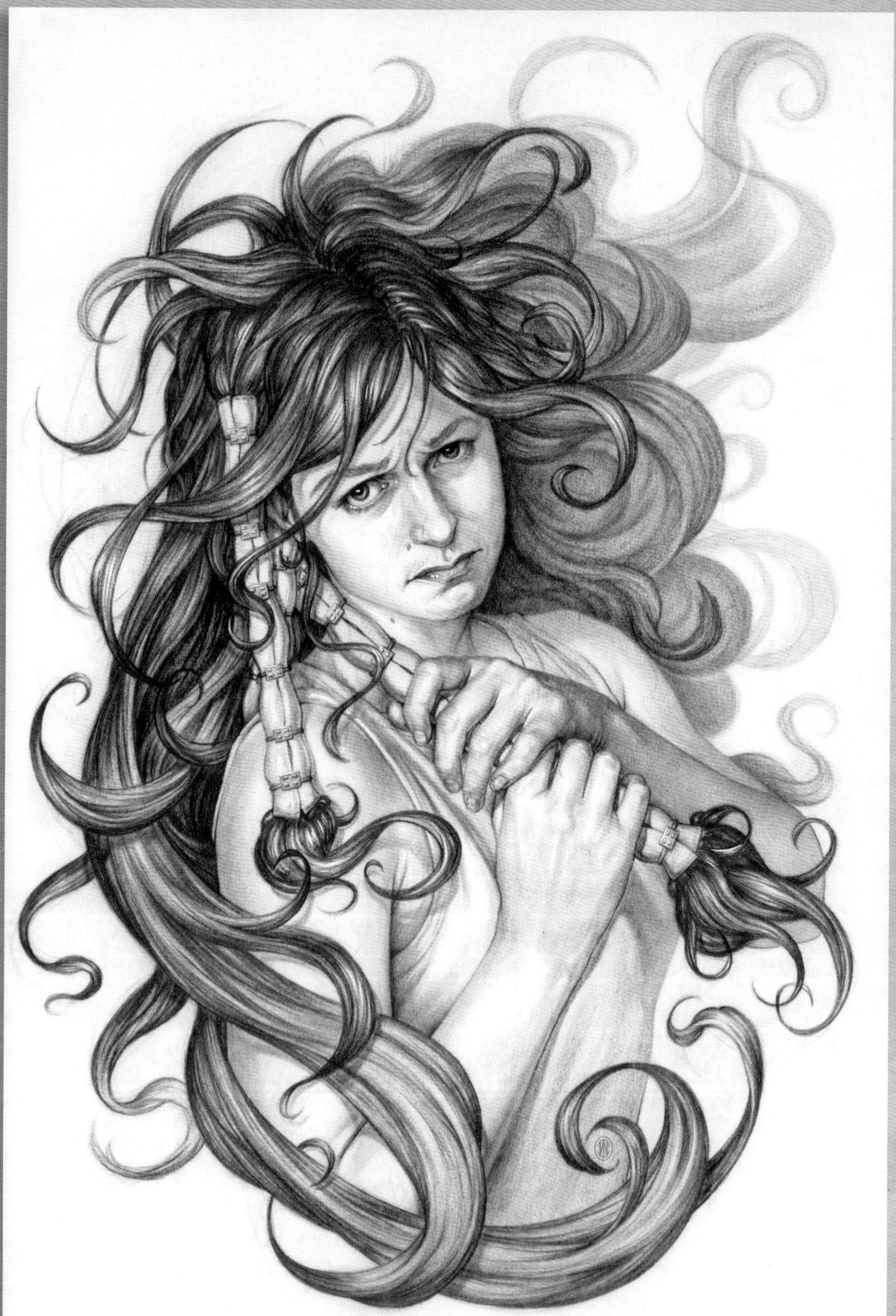

Walter O'Neal, pencil on board

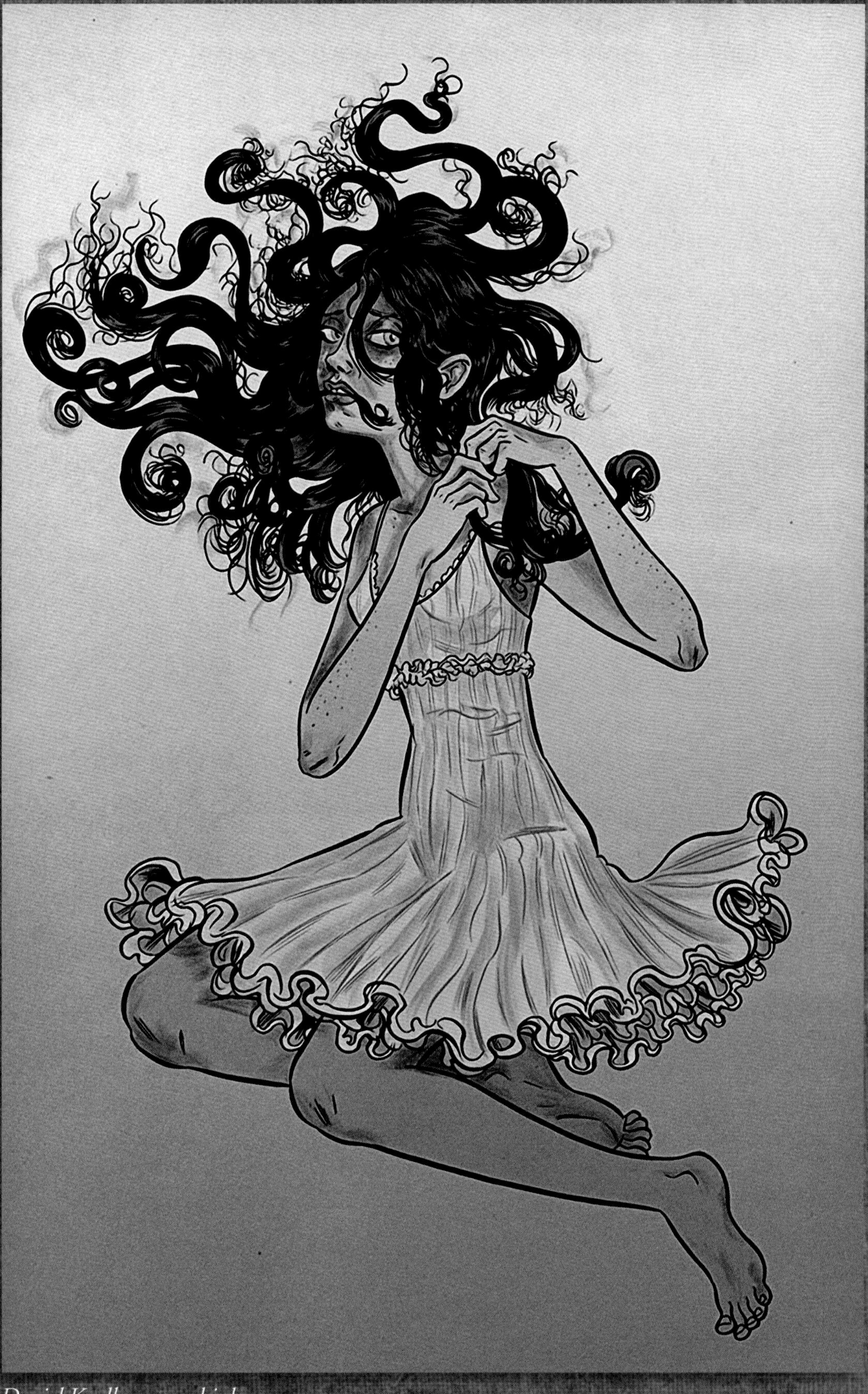
Daniel Krull, pen and ink

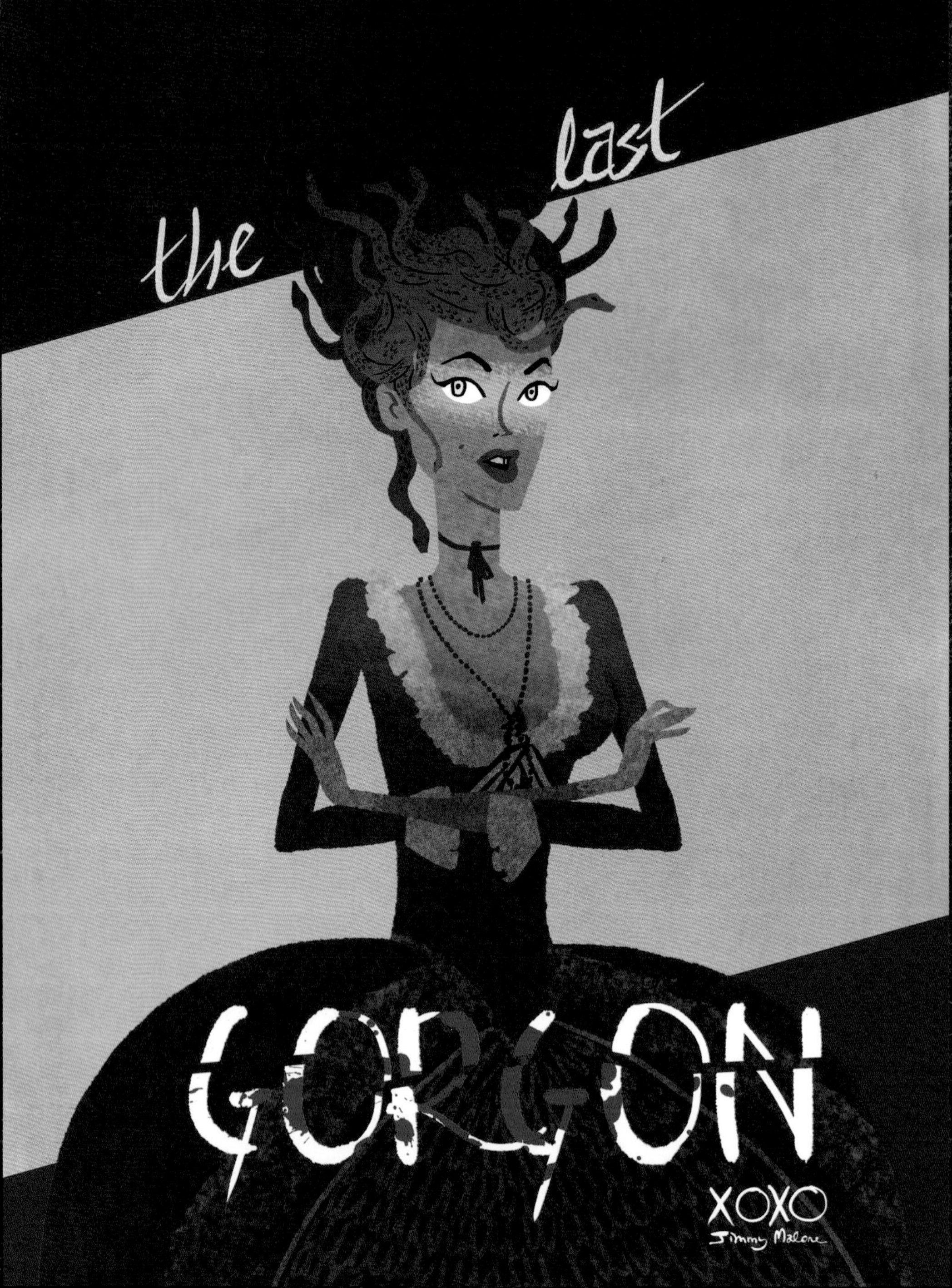

the last
GORGON
XOXO
Jimmy Malone

Jimmy Malone, digital art

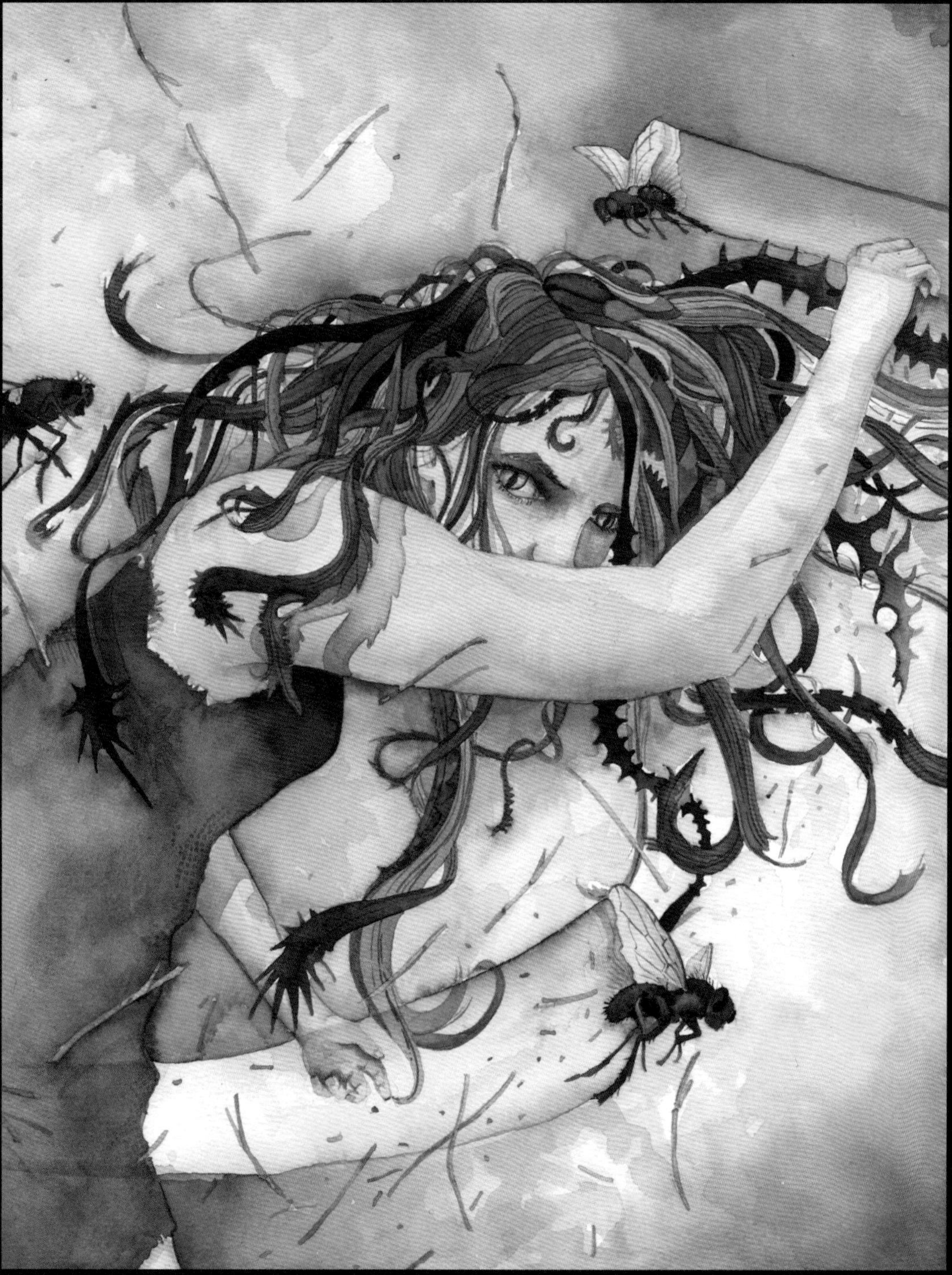

Jonathon Scott Fuqua, watercolor

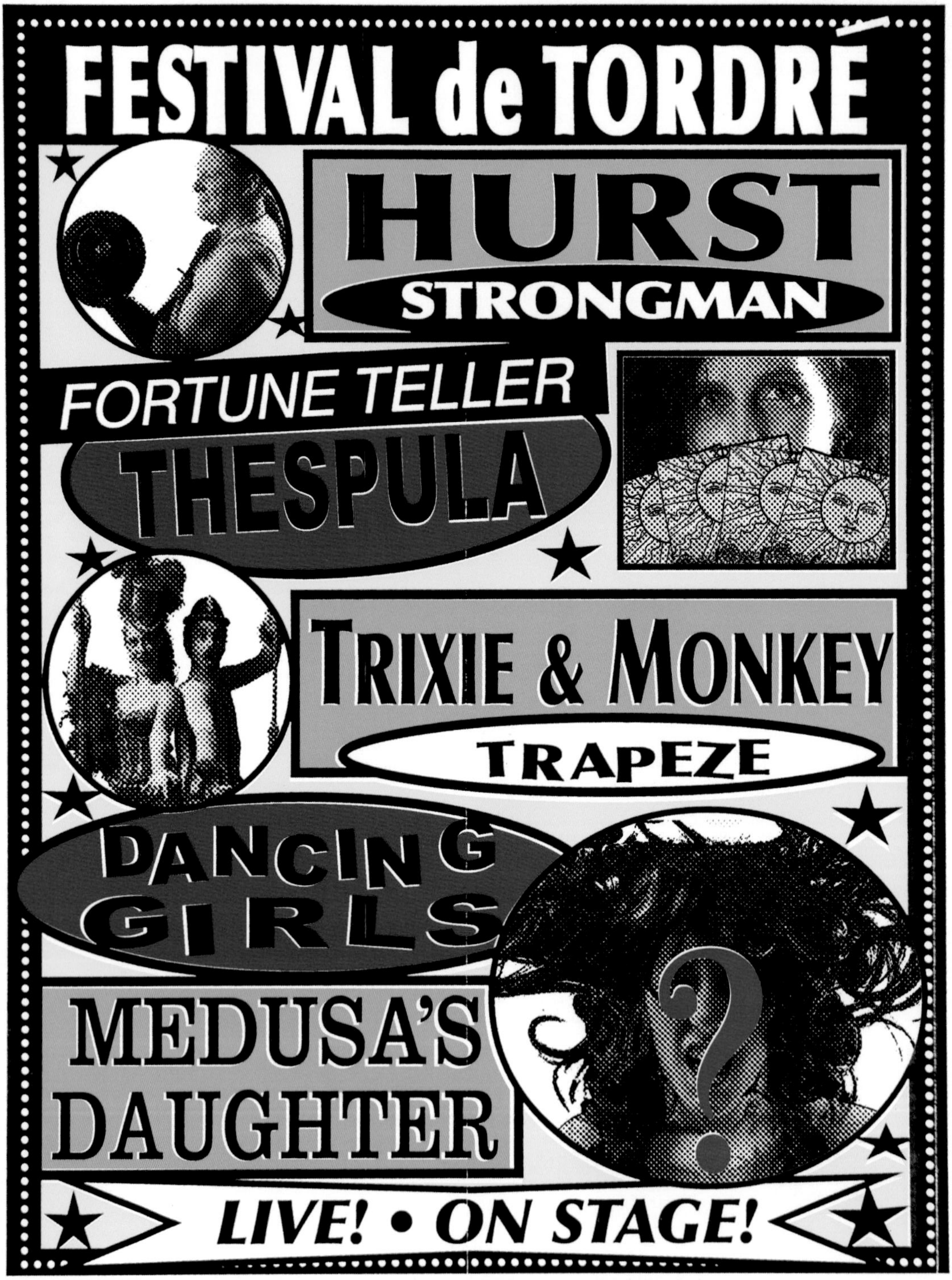
FESTIVAL de TORDRÉ
HURST
STRONGMAN
FORTUNE TELLER
THESPULA
TRIXIE & MONKEY
TRAPEZE
DANCING GIRLS
MEDUSA'S DAUGHTER
?
LIVE! • ON STAGE!

GLOBE POSTER PRINTING CORP • BALTIMORE, MD